A Tangled Summer

Caroline Kington

First published in Great Britain in 2006
by Orion,
an imprint of the Orion Publishing Group Ltd,
Orion House, 5 Upper Saint Martin's Lane,
London, WC2H 9EA.

1 3 5 7 9 10 8 6 4 2

A CIP catalogue record for this book
is available from the British Library.

ISBN-13: (hardback) 978 0 7528 7370 1
(trade paperback) 978 0 7528 7371 8
ISBN-10: (hardback) 0 7528 7370 9
(trade paperback) 0 7528 7371 7

Typeset by Deltatype Ltd, Birkenhead, Merseyside

Set in Monotype Fournier

Printed in Great Britain by Clays Ltd, St Ives plc

The Orion Publishing Group's policy is to use papers that
are natural, renewable and recyclable products and made
from wood grown in sustainable forests. The logging and
manufacturing processes are expected to conform to the
environmental regulations of the country of origin.

www.orionbooks.co.uk

For my mother.

Acknowledgements

I have had an enormous amount of support and encouragement in the writing of this book, from my friends, neighbours and the village book club.

Particular thanks are due to Richard Curry for the time we spent together on his dairy farm and his endless patience in responding to yet another farming question, and, similarly, Cate Mack, who runs a rare breed farm; to my sister, Belinda who faithfully read each draft; my daughter, Isabel, whose feedback was always invaluable and constructive; Alan and Liz Booty for a million different things; Ben Wolstenholme for coming to my rescue over Christmas with a piece of tracing paper; David Webster for being there when the computer needed him; Hannah Joss and my son, Adam, for keeping me on track with Alison and her mates; Gill Coleridge for her support and advice; Broo Doherty for being the best thing that happened to the book; Kate Mills for being so enthusiastic and Genevieve Pegg for her support; and most of all, to my husband, Miles, who gave me everything I needed to sit down and write.

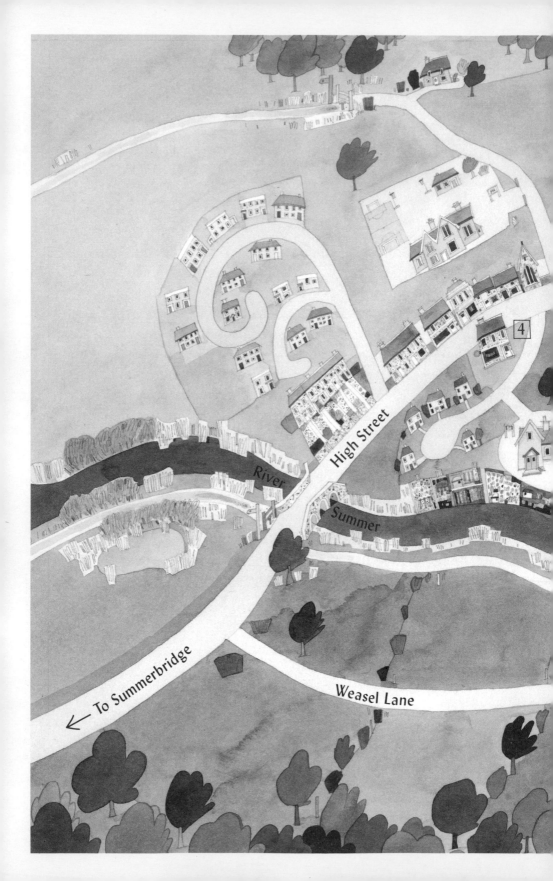

Summerwoods

3

To Bath

1. Marsh Farm
2. The Manor House
3. Summerstoke House
4. Shop and Post Office
5. Forester's Arms

5

2

1

Summerstoke Ridge

I

Although it was still an hour to daybreak, the night sky was shifting colour and lightening in the east. It was too early for the full dawn chorus, but one or two birds had already started limbering up with a fragmented twittering; a nightingale, at full throttle, was singing in the small copse of trees by the farm gate, and, far off, Alison Tucker could hear the shriek of a screech owl. She peered at her watch. It was nearly 4.30 a.m.

The track down to the farm was nearly half a mile long and, confident that no one would spot her, Alison wove her way home, savouring the sounds and smells of the night and, at one point, taking off her shoes so that she could walk barefoot on the dew-laden grass verge.

She'd had a great night and it had all started out so unpromisingly. She'd spent the day studying for her A-levels and her mother had suggested that, come the evening, she should relax with a bit of telly; Alison had thought she'd scream with the tedium of it all.

Then Hannah, her best mate, had phoned. She'd just got back from holiday, somewhere hot; her parents were out for the night and she'd thought she'd have a bit of a party. If Ali was up for it, Nick, Hannah's boyfriend, would pick Ali up from the end of her drive at 11.15 p.m., after he'd finished work at the pub. Alison had been definitely up for it.

Knowing there was very little point in asking her mother if she could go out at such an hour, she had said goodnight, gone up to her room, changed, then slipped out of her bedroom window to meet Nick. Alison lived on a farm, way out of town, which was why Hannah had arranged the pick-up. In this way, Alison had been able to participate in more late-night parties than her mother had ever dreamed of.

It was a warm night and to avoid any incriminating smell of tobacco a small group of her friends had gathered at the bottom of Hannah's garden, next to the vegetable patch where the scent of Hannah's dad's prize sweet peas mingled with the fusty, cloying smell of the compost heap. Here they had lolled about on chintzy cushions taken from the house and scattered on the sun-baked lawn. Hannah had lit a motley collection of candles in saucers and empty wine bottles, raided her parents' cupboards for crisps and peanuts, and found some frozen garlic baguettes, which she'd re-heated in the microwave. Nick had bought a large bottle of vodka from duty-free, and six of them had gathered to drink the vodka, share duty-free fags, compare tans and swap photos and stories: stories of assignations with a Pedro or Carlos or Juan; of drinking until legless; of dancing till dawn; and of skinny dipping in a blue-black sea by the light of a huge strawberry moon ...

As she walked down the track, on her left Alison could make out the black stripe of the river and, beyond, the occasional twinkling light from the village of Summerstoke. Narrowing her eyes, she let her imagination drift: the river she saw as the edge of a limitless, dark ocean; Summerstoke became some tiny, exotic fishing village where, waiting for her in a bar, was a tall, dark, handsome boy, with mocking eyes and—

She tripped over a large stone on the uneven track and ended up flat on her face on the grassy bank. Unhurt, she rolled onto her back, gazed up at the stars and wondered what it would be like to swim naked in the sea at night. She would never admit to her friends that she was envious, but she was. Her family never had enough money to go on a daytrip to Bournemouth, let alone the sun-kissed shores of the Med.

She stretched her arms out, crossed her ankles, and propping her head on her hands she lay for a moment, on the dew-damp ground, letting her thoughts drift over her situation.

Sometimes, she thought, she would burst with frustration.

Marsh Farm, the safe, loving world of her childhood, she now found confining and claustrophobic; it held nothing for her. The world was beckoning and she so wanted to explore it; there was so much she wanted to do, but she couldn't see how to escape. She didn't particularly care about the sorts of places her friends went to on holiday – no, it was the fact that they were able to go at all, whilst she was stuck at home, that made her restless.

She sighed deeply. It was made worse this summer because she hadn't got a holiday job, which meant no money and no independence. The whole family had agreed that she should concentrate on her studies and on getting the best possible grades for the coursework that had to be completed next term. She knew that her grandmother, particularly, had set great store by her getting a university place and was as enthusiastic as Alison, if not more so, about Alison's declared intention of becoming a vet. But that enthusiasm, plus her mother's obvious pride in her daughter's brains, didn't allow Alison any room for manoeuvre; it didn't give her the privilege of doubt, or allow her to change her mind, and she felt as trapped by her future plans as she did by her current situation.

Momentarily she thought of her father. He'd died when she was seven and her memories of him were hazy impressions of a tall, smiling man who would scoop her up onto his shoulders, and from those dizzying heights she had looked down on the world. With him, she had believed all things were possible. If only she could feel the same way about her life now. If only she could say no to the people she loved most in the world; if only she could turn her back on the farm and find ... oh, she didn't know what, precisely, but certainly adventure, and certainly a lover ...

The screaming bark of a dog-fox startled her, breaking her reverie. She scrambled to her feet. The sky was getting lighter by the minute and she realised she could not afford to linger much longer.

Alison was, she had admitted to Hannah, a bit tipsy, not being used to vodka, but she was not that drunk and when she rounded a bend and the dark silhouettes of the farm buildings loomed

3

out in front of her, she checked her watch again. Nearly 5 a.m. Good. Stephen wouldn't be up to fetch the herd in for milking for another half-hour. She would be able to reach her room without being seen.

The gate to the farmyard was ajar; she slipped into the yard and stood, for a moment, in the deep shadow cast by a barn. The farmhouse, its front illuminated silver in the moonlight, looked down over the farm buildings. Her two brothers, Charlie and Stephen, had rooms at the back of the house and Alison was confident they'd be snoring their heads off at this hour. Her mother, however, was a light sleeper and had a room at the front, next to Alison's own. Alison stared up at it. The curtains were firmly drawn.

The only other person she had to reckon with was Gran, but since her room was right at the top of the house and Alison had no reason to think she would be staring out across the farmyard at this time in the morning, she felt it was safe to step into the moonlight and cross the yard. She headed for a water butt standing next to the porch of the front door, and climbing up onto that, she shinned her way over the canopy of the porch and up in through her open bedroom window.

Elsie Tucker, Alison's grandmother, had been unable to sleep. It was hot at the top of the house and because she had all the windows open, the sounds of the night disturbed her fitful slumbers. But it wasn't the heat, or the screech owls, or the shrieking fox, or the screams of a dying rabbit, or the nightjar, or the nightingale that kept her awake so much as her thoughts, wrestling with the problem that increasingly troubled her: what, if anything, she should do to rescue the parlous state of the farm's fortunes. For years she had told them that what they did with the farm was their own affair – she wasn't interested. But although she might maintain that line in front of her family, she knew it wasn't true and she cared – cared very much.

Elsie tutted, threw back the wool blanket – she had dismissed the idea of duvets as a modern fad – and climbed out of the old-fashioned bed, with its elaborate mahogany headboard and horsehair mattress, slipped on a pair of old carpet slippers and padded across to the window where she leaned on the sill, sighing and feeling her years.

An antique dress mirror that she had brought with her to the farm when she married stood by her wardrobe and caught her reflection in the moonlight. A trick of the silvery light smoothed out the wrinkles of her face, caused the long, thick plait of grey hair hanging loosely over one shoulder to shine with life, and flattered the diminutive body in the high-necked flannelette night-dress. If Thomas, her husband, had still been alive and lying in their matrimonial bed, he would have seen Elsie, his bride, at the window and not the seventy-nine-year-old widow who leaned on the sill, gazing sadly out on Marsh Farm, which had been her home for sixty years.

The sky was full of stars, but streaked with a faint yellow in the east. Dawn was not far off.

'Oh, Thomas,' she whispered, 'look at it ...' The farm sat in the darkling light like a marooned hulk, shabby and getting shab-bier, on a slight rise in the middle of a picture-book valley. But it wasn't a picture-book farm, not any more.

Elsie had kept hens that had clucked and scratched in the yard; Jenny, her daughter-in-law, couldn't cope with birds and so they had been eaten and not replaced. The duck pond, which once had been alive with ducks flapping, whistling and quacking, had become a muddy indentation, its banks mashed to a gluppy pulp by the cows that pushed into the yard at milking time, a clump of reeds all that was left to mark its whereabouts.

In the orchard, where Elsie had grown sufficient apples to pro-vide the farm with its own cider, the trees were gnarled, covered with fluorescent grey lichen, and producing a diminishing crop of small, bitter, canker-ridden apples in the autumn, which were allowed to lie where they fell.

In the garden at the back of the house, where Elsie had grown most of the family's vegetables, Jenny had beds given over to strawberries, which she loved, but which were always denuded by slugs, against which she fought a losing battle. There was a small, crooked greenhouse in which she grew tomatoes and a sorry-looking vegetable patch where straggling clumps of spinach, slug-infested cabbages or lettuce could be found, according to the time of year. Elsie snorted with contempt at Jenny's efforts, but made no attempt to help or advise her.

And then there was the house. It was an attractive building, but, apart from Elsie's own rooms, it was showing the same wear and tear as the rest of the farm. Tiles had slipped, paint was peeling, broken windows were patched, not replaced, and both the house and yard were surrounded by a growing bank of discarded machinery and broken vehicles, the flotsam and jetsam of farm life.

The whole place was a shabby shadow of the farm she and Thomas had been so proud of. And things were getting worse.

Stephen, her grandson, had not been able to conceal his anxiety when he received the call from the dairy telling him his last batch of milk had been rejected. Unfortunately for him, Elsie had been present when the call came. He had muttered some excuse about a water-heating unit not working properly, but for Elsie it was symptomatic of the whole decline she could see about her. She blamed her grandsons for their general attitude and lack of commitment to the farm, and told Stephen as much. He didn't fight back; he never did. He was just like his mother, Jenny, in that respect, Elsie thought scornfully. At least Charlie, his brother, had a bit more spunk about him.

She was just about to move back to her bed when a movement in the yard below caught her eye. It was her granddaughter, Alison, fully dressed, moving out of the shadows and across the yard. Elsie, who had been present when Alison had told her mother she was going to bed, watched in amazement as she slipped towards the house and out of sight.

Elsie was shocked. Alison was her favourite, the one most like her, and in Elsie's opinion the only one with any brains. She had set her heart on Alison going to university, the first Tucker to do so. When Alison had first confided in her that she dreamed of becoming a vet one day, she had been absolutely thrilled and had given Alison every encouragement. But Elsie knew that if Alison were to succeed, she would have to work hard; really hard. And now, here she was, jeopardising all that, gallivanting off in the night when everyone thought she was asleep.

Simmering with anger, Elsie climbed back into bed. How often had Alison done this before? When she said she was studying in her room, what proof did they have that she hadn't gone out? She always played her darned music so loudly and insisted on not being disturbed – a perfect cover for slipping out of the house whenever the fancy took her!

Early sunbeams were playing over the white plastered walls and thick oak beams of her attic room when Elsie finally fell into an uneasy doze, her sleep a jumble of images of herself, her fingers stiff and clumsy, trying hopelessly to attach a set of clusters to a cow's udder; Thomas, by her side, telling her in his soft, patient voice that she wasn't to fret; and a small child, whom she identified as Alison, running away from her, laughing and calling to her, dangerously close to the edge of the riverbank.

It was well after eight o'clock when she woke, much later than she liked. As she splashed her face with cold water, she thought about how best to deal with this fresh problem. Young Miss Alison couldn't get away with it, that's for sure, but unlike Stephen, she would fight back and so a direct confrontation wasn't necessarily the best approach. But Elsie was feeling tired and scratchy after her disturbed night and she was ready for a good fight.

Fortunately for them both, perhaps, there was no sign of Alison in the farmhouse kitchen when Elsie arrived down for breakfast. Both the boys were absent, too. Jenny was at the stove, burning toast under the grill. 'Hello, Elsie,' she said brightly. 'You're late down. Did you sleep well?'

When her son, Jim, her only and much cherished child, had first brought Jenny home, Elsie had conceded that she was indeed a very pretty girl without an ounce of malice in her, but she had quickly decided that in every other respect the girl was a fool, and she had not changed her mind, even when Jenny married Jim, bore him three children and grew plump and tired, running the farmhouse without complaint. She knew she was being unfair: Jenny had always tried hard to please her, and was loved by everyone else; but she blamed her daughter-in-law for the weakness of her grandsons, the decline of the farm's fortunes, and generally everything else that she didn't like – even, though she rarely acknowledged it, for the premature death of her son – so she took a perverse pleasure in putting her down whenever she could. Unfortunately for them both, Jenny made it easy for her.

'Would you like some toast, Elsie?'

'Toast, yes – not charcoal. I'll make it myself, thank you. Where's Alison?'

'Still asleep. I'm going to take her up a cup of tea in a minute. She's working so hard, poor lamb.'

Elsie snorted and ungraciously took the cup of tea Jenny had poured for her. She sat herself down at the kitchen table and scowled at the sight of the kitchen. It was the living heart of the farm and under Elsie's rule it had reflected her personality, her energy and her orderliness. Now ... in her opinion, it was a testament to just how bad things had become under Jenny's incompetent reign.

It was a long room, illuminated only by the sunlight filtering through a rather grubby square sash window behind the sink, and a light, which was permanently on, hanging over the kitchen table. The ceiling was low, a tracery of broken plaster visible under the paint that had yellowed with age and years of grease. In a fit of energy one year, Jenny had started to wash the ceiling, but had got distracted and never resumed her labours, so one patch was lighter than the rest, but not much.

The kitchen table, a long oak rectangle, was a battleground of things that needed a home, including a large bag of dog biscuits, empty jam jars, a roll of cheap wrapping paper, a couple of jumpers Jenny had bought from the jumble sale intending to unpick and re-knit, and a basket of dusty nuts left over from Christmas.

The wallpaper, its floral pattern so faded it was a distant memory, was peeling with damp and covered with pictures the children had drawn in various stages of their childhoods: Alison's first picture of a horse when she was two, Stephen's portraits of his mum and dad, done on his first day at school, Charlie's rocket, drawn when he was seven; Jenny wouldn't throw them away, even those that had been stained by tomato ketchup the time Charlie had shaken the bottle so violently that the top had flown off and the wall had been liberally spattered.

Next to the stove, Gip, the farm's dog, had her basket, a large broken wicker affair lined with an old blanket. The floor was covered with linoleum, peeled and cracked, and so stained with years of muddy footprints, dog hairs and dirt that any washing and sweeping of it made very little difference to its general appearance.

All of this Elsie viewed anew and felt keenly as a reproach to herself for not having intervened sooner to stop the decay.

The telephone rang, interrupting her gloomy reverie. Jenny answered. 'Marsh Farm ... Jenny Tucker ... yes ... yes, she's right here. Elsie, it's for you. It's a Mr Ian Webster. He says he's an old friend; he needs to have a word with you, urgently.'

With some surprise, it being barely nine o'clock, Elsie took the call.

The magistrates' court had been built next to a school and on this hot Thursday morning the sound of childish laughter and shouts from the playground mingled with the noise of traffic and, unfettered, drifted in on shafts of sunlight through the bars of the open windows.

Charlie Tucker licked his lips. He had never been in a court before. He had been in a police cell before, had been ticked off by a senior policeman a couple of times for drunken behaviour, and had collected a number of speeding fines, but he had never before been in a magistrates' court and he was not enjoying the experience, not one little bit. What made it worse was the presence of his grandmother in the public gallery. She had entered just as he took his place in the dock, and at the sight of her his knees had given way and he had sat down.

The old lady had not looked at him, but stared ahead; her face, which betrayed no expression, was thin and weathered, devoid of make-up. The other occupants of the public gallery lolled about in various combinations of T-shirts, tracksuit bottoms and trainers, their flabby bodies and pale, pudgy faces liberally tattooed, pierced and bejewelled. She, however, looked as if she had stepped across a timewarp. Her iron-grey hair was pinned up under a small straw hat and she was dressed in a long-sleeved, cream blouse and a tweed skirt, over which, in spite of the warmth of the day, she wore a khaki-green loden waistcoat. She looked what she was: every inch a countrywoman.

Charlie had groaned inwardly as he got back to his feet. He had thought he had been successful in keeping his appearance before the beaks well away from his family's notice. Of them all, the last person he wanted to witness his humiliation was his grandmother. Throughout the proceedings he avoided looking at her, but as he stuttered through his explanations and apologies, he was aware of her gimlet eyes and pursed lips. It was her presence, rather than the faintly bored-looking trio on the bench, which caused him to perspire freely and to lose the cocky insouciance that he normally adopted in times of difficulty and which, on this occasion, would not have done him any favours.

The magistrates left the courtroom to mull over their decision. They were gone only a few minutes, but already it seemed like an eternity to the young man in the dock. He was unused to wearing a suit and it showed. He was tall and muscular and his jacket barely fitted. He had given up trying to button up his shirt at the collar and tried to disguise the fact with the only tie he'd been able to find, a joke Christmas present from his sister, decorated with bright yellow 'Smiley' faces. He was a good-looking man with a thick head of hair, shiny with Brylcreem, and a pair of carefully cultivated mutton-chop whiskers that framed his lean, weatherbeaten face. He had thought about shaving them off that morning, to improve the impression he would make, but he loved his whiskers, and the realisation that if he removed them he would have two ridiculously large, white shadows in their place, saved them. Under normal circumstances his brown eyes were merry, his appearance cocky and life, for him, was a good laugh. Today, however, he sat dejectedly, shoulders drooping, listening to the sounds of the children playing outside.

'It's torture, that's what it is,' the defendant thought bitterly. 'I bet it's done deliberately. The beaks go out, give the teacher a ring – "Oh, is that the teacher? We've got a nice one in the dock at the moment; we're just off to have a cup of coffee so send the little kiddies out please, lots of noise and laughing, that's the ticket! That should make him feel a whole lot worse." Well too bloody right it does! And what's Gran doing here? How did *she* find out? Bloomin' 'eck, I'm really going to be for it!' And Charlie Tucker, thirty-two, a farmer rather more by birth than inclination, sat on the edge of his seat in the dock and fixed his eyes steadfastly on the floor in an effort to avoid any chance contact with the basilisk glare from 'her' in the public gallery.

The door to the retiring room opened and he jumped in spite of himself.

The clerk – young, blond and bored – scarcely glanced up from sorting through a large pile of case notes. 'Stand please.'

A plump young woman in a tight blue dress, with mousy hair, not much older than Charlie himself, was followed by the chairman, stout, middle-aged and balding, in a pinstripe suit with a florid yellow handkerchief drooping from his breast pocket, and by the third magistrate, a West Indian, in his late thirties, dressed in a sober dark suit and dark shirt. Charlie had thought he looked pretty cool, a kindred spirit, and during the hearing had addressed his comments chiefly to him, hoping to engage his sympathy. He searched his face now for some sign of comfort, as the magistrates took their seats. There was none. His face impassive, the magistrate glanced at him with complete indifference before turning to listen to the chairman.

'Well, Mr Tucker, you've told the court you'd had a "bit to drink" and you climbed up onto the bear for a "bit of fun".' With obvious disdain, the magistrate viewed Charlie over his half-moon specs. 'It wasn't much fun though, was it, when you couldn't get down? And it wasn't much fun for the police or the fire brigade when they had to rescue you. These services are stretched enough as it is, without having to rescue a drunk from the consequences of his folly.'

The clerk stretched out a finger, pressed a button and the windows whined shut, cutting off the jubilant sounds of the playground that were threatening to drown out the chairman's homily.

'You were fortunate that the bear you chose to mount above the lintel of the pub was sufficiently robust to withstand your weight and that neither you, nor it, nor any member of the public suffered any injury as the result of your absurd prank. Had that been the case, you would have appeared before us on a much more serious charge. Don't you think, Mr Tucker, that at the age of thirty-two, it is time you grew up?'

The magistrate paused to emphasise his point, allowing the old lady's harrumphed agreement to add to Charlie's discomfiture, before dismissing him with, 'We note your evident remorse and your embarrassment; we have given credit for your early guilty plea and for your apology. We are going to dispose of this by way of a fine. You will pay the court seventy pounds and, taking account of your lack of means, you will make a contribution of twenty pounds towards costs.'

'Ninety quid! Blimey, Charlie. Where you gonna find ninety quid?' Lenny Spinks, Ken's partner in crime, stared up at Charlie. His hands and face were smeared with grease, and he was dressed in filthy blue overalls, the sleeves rolled up above his elbows, arms liberally tattooed, and long, streaky-blond hair tied back in a ponytail

Lenny was the only employee of Marsh Farm and part-time at that. He had been fixing a tractor engine on the cracked and weedy concrete forecourt of an old barn that flanked the central yard of Marsh Farm, when the battered white van had screeched to a dusty halt and a disconsolate Charlie had climbed out.

'They let you pay it off weekly. But Lenny, that weren't the worst of it. You'll never guess who turned up in court.'

Lenny, whose imagination was not the strongest in the world, looked blank. 'Steve? Yer mum? Ali?'

Charlie gloomily shook his head, 'Nah, if it'd been any of them, even Alison, it wouldn't be so bad. Stephen would bellyache about the fine; Mum'd just be glad I didn't fall off the flaming bear; and Ali'd just make lots of clever-clever, sarky comments about how her big brother can't hold his drink and that riding a stone bear is the closest I'd ever get to mounting anything on four legs. No, it was Gran, Lenny.'

'Elsie? How did she find out?'

'God knows. Probably looked into her crystal ball or consulted her tea leaves, or whatever them witches do. Her nose is into every blooming pie; she knows everything that goes on, no matter what I do to stop her finding out stuff. God, she makes me feel about six inches tall!' And he relapsed into a depressed silence.

'Did she say anything, after?'

'No.' Charlie sighed. 'This magistrate said ... what a pompous old git ... he said ... well, it don't matter what he said, but then I heard Gran suck in her breath and I knew I was for it. She left the courtroom before I'd even left the dock.'

Lenny was curious. 'What did he say then?'

'Doesn't matter. Thing is, though, Gran is mad at me and she'll be plotting something. Courts don't take that into consideration, do they?'

'What?'

'Mad old grandmothers who can make your life hell if they choose to.'

'I don't know why you don't tell her where to get off. After all, you run Marsh Farm, you and Steve. It's the sweat of your labours what puts the jam on her bread.'

Charlie gloomily pulled at one of his sideburns. 'True enough, me old sparkplug, but you're forgetting one tiny little detail: she owns half the farm. If I don't jump to her tune, she'd probably cut me out and leave her share to Ali – they're as thick as two thieves – and where would that leave me?'

'Working for your sister?'

'Over my dead body, mate!'

Stephen Tucker, emerging from the milking parlour where he had been struggling with repairs to a pump that should have been replaced years ago, looked across the yard and saw his older brother by the tractor, in conversation with Lenny Spinks. Nothing unusual in that; Lenny worked mainly for Charlie. No, what caught his attention was the sight of his brother in a suit. The last time he could remember Charlie in a suit was when he was best man at Lenny's marriage to Paula, some six years ago. Before that, it was at their dad's funeral, ten years ago now.

He crossed the yard to join them. It was nearly midday and the continuing heat had succeeded in turning the usually muddy yard into a dustbowl. Dust had settled on everything and it felt as if it had taken him twice as long to clean up after milking. He felt fractious, and an ill-tempered frown marred his usually amiable face.

Two years younger than Charlie, Stephen, compliant, docile and cautious, was the antithesis of his brother. Physically he was not quite as tall, although neither had reached the six-foot height of their father, something both boys had aspired to when younger. Their colouring was similar, but Stephen's mop of chestnut-brown hair was cut short and he was completely clean-shaven. His complexion was more ruddy than his brother's and he was well-covered, if not chubby, where Charlie was lean.

'Hey, Charlie, what's with the cloth? You off to a funeral or summat?'

Lenny, who was considerably shorter than either brother, smirked up at him, 'His own, by his reckoning.'

Stephen didn't much like Lenny Spinks.

As a child, Stephen had trotted admiringly in Charlie's wake, a willing partner in his charismatic brother's madcap schemes, often unfairly taking the lion's share of the blame when things went wrong. Then, in his teens, Charlie discovered motocross and Lenny Spinks, and Stephen was no longer needed. The two boys drifted apart. Then, when Stephen was twenty, Jim Tucker, his father, was found face down on the silage clamp, dead from a massive heart attack.

Gran owned half the farm, and her son had left his share equally between his three children. Alison was only seven at the time of his death, so it fell to Charlie and Stephen to shoulder the responsibility for running the business, which they did, reflecting their inclinations and dispositions. Charlie took over all the arable cultivation; Stephen took care of the dairy herd and the milk production, and Lenny, who was a few years older than Charlie and therefore more versed in the ways of the world, was drafted in by Charlie as a hired hand, 'him bein' a whiz with machinery an' all.'

Marsh Farm was not a large or profitable enterprise and Charlie and Stephen were not particularly efficient farmers, but they muddled along, bumping into debt and out again, more by chance than design. But Charlie had ambitions. Full of unchannelled energy, he was always coming up with some moneymaking enterprise to which Lenny was usually privy. These schemes were designed to pluck the farm out of the red but somehow they always seemed to leave them no better off or, more usually, the poorer.

Seeing Charlie in a suit and in close conversation with Lenny, therefore, immediately roused Stephen's suspicions.

'What are you two up to, then?' he demanded, grumpily. 'I thought you were starting on the barley today. You're leaving it a bit late, ain't yer? There's no way I'm going to help you out, so let's get that clear for a start. We've started rehearsals this week and I've promised Mrs Pagett I'll be there.'

In the same year Jim Tucker died, Stephen had discovered amateur dramatics. Or rather, it had discovered him, and ever since then every spare moment was spent in its service.

'Don't worry, I wouldn't dream of depriving your little society of its star turn.' Charlie started to walk towards the house. 'I'll just get into my overalls, Lenny, an' I'll be with you. With any luck, we can work on till dusk; weather's looking good.'

'Okay, boss. Hey, I can see your gran's car comin' down the track!'

To the surprise of his brother, Charlie fled into the house. Stephen did not linger to question Lenny – he had his own reasons for not wanting to come face to face with his gran that morning – and disappeared off the scene almost as quickly as Charlie.

2

Alison sat in the window of her bedroom, nursing a headache and watching the scene in the yard with a scowl. It's bad enough being stuck here all summer, she thought bitterly, but not to be able to go to the movies, or bowling, or clubbing ... It's so humiliating.

The problem, as always, was lack of money and for that, Alison blamed her brothers.

'Ali, it's gonna be wicked — we've got the rest of the summer sorted.' Hannah had phoned her that morning to continue the conversation of the night before. 'And with any luck there'll be a massive disco to finish it off. Nick's been given a card by some guy who might employ him — he says he heard of these events. Think of it, Ali ... beating your brains out to the music. They line up really good DJs. It'll be so cool — boogying the whole night away, swigging bottles of Ice ... Ali, if Nick's right, we can't miss it!'

'Of course not,' she said. 'No probs,' she said. 'Can't wait.' And when Hannah had rung off, Alison had gone in search of her mother and her monthly allowance.

'I'm sorry, dear,' Jenny had said helplessly, her eyes streaming from the pile of onions she was chopping. 'There just isn't any spare cash this month. Stephen says the milk cheque is right down because of the batch that got contaminated when the pump broke, so he can't spare anything; and Charlie says, what with harvesting this month, he's going to need all the spare cash he's got to pay for Lenny's extra hours.'

Her two brothers were meant to take it in turns to fund her

monthly allowance, and, in fact, what Charlie had said to his mother was, 'It's Steve's turn to find her allowance. No way am I going to give the kid money she ain't earned when it's not my turn. Nose permanently in a book … What good is that? Bloomin' hell, she should get herself a job. I did when I was her age.'

Jenny had remonstrated feebly. 'Now, Charlie, you know it's her exam year. It's important she works at her books and does well. You want her to go to the university, don't you?'

'It won't stop her from comin' to me for cash I ain't got,' came the morose reply and Jenny had left, empty handed.

When Alison learned from her mother that she would not be able to have her allowance for August, she had stared at Jenny in disbelief, then exploded, stormed out of the kitchen, and had gone back up to her bedroom, where she glowered down on her unsuspecting brothers in the yard.

'They're useless, absolutely useless! God knows how I'm going to afford to go to university at this rate!'

Engulfed by self-pity, she went back to her desk and the biology project she had been trying to finish when Jen had phoned.

She angled the magnified glass of the make-up mirror. Stephen had given it to her last Christmas and she had placed it on the corner of her desk so that she could monitor the progress of any eruptions. She always did this when she felt gloomy; it made her feel satisfyingly worse. As it happened, her skin was relatively clear so there was no satisfaction to be had from squeezing black-heads.

Morosely, she stared at her distorted reflection. Unlike Charlie and Stephen, who had inherited their father's brown hair and brown eyes, she shared her mother's fair colouring. She wore her hair long, and she had a small, pointed chin, high cheekbones and intense green eyes. Her eyes were greener than her mother's and her features altogether sharper and more restless. She resembled Elsie in stature, but she was still sufficiently like her mother for it to be remarked upon far too often for Alison's liking. She loved her mother; she just didn't want to *be* like her; no way!

'She always does their dirty work for them; she's putty in their hands!' Alison spat at her reflection. 'She should stand up to them; she's such a bloody doormat. Gran's right.'

In fact, Alison was always defending Jenny against accusations of a similar sort from Elsie Tucker, but on this occasion she felt Jenny had let her down.

'It's not fair!' Alison said to her reflection for the umpteenth time. 'If I haven't any money, then I can't go out; and if I can't go out, I'll *never* meet anybody. I'll die a virgin!'

At seventeen, Alison had got through a number of boyfriends, none of them particularly serious, and none of them had given rise to the level of passion that, in her dreams, she felt should be the precursor to her first sexual experience. By the end of the previous term she was aware of being one of a rapidly decreasing number who had not had sex. Whilst this did not particularly worry her, she did not want to be identified as a saddo, or a reject. Her place in her group of friends was unassailable when it came to talking about music, or films, or politics, or even fads of fashion, but when it came to discussing what it was like, she felt less than fully integrated and had to fall silent.

So she had decided that this summer she would find someone and *do* it. So far, absolutely no one had materialised, and the way she saw it, she had only three weeks left to meet anyone before the term started, and her intacta state became an embarrassment.

'Oh, bugger it!' She slammed her book shut. 'I'm not giving up. There's got to be a way.' And because she always thought more clearly about her family and how to best deal with them when she got away from them, she decided to take her elderly and rather fat pony, Bumble, out for a ride.

The downstairs cloakroom was full of old wellies, battered waterproofs, broken umbrellas, unwanted walking sticks, hats, scarves and gloves of every description, the Tuckers never ever throwing anything away on the grounds that you never knew when they might come in useful. Being the only member of the family to have a tidy disposition, apart from Gran, by the time Alison had retrieved her hat and boots, she had managed to work her ill-humour into a satisfying state of fury against her whole family.

In the kitchen, chopping pounds of unwanted green tomatoes, Jenny sighed when she heard Alison thrashing and banging about in the cloakroom. Her youngest child reminded her of the nursery rhyme that went: 'When she was good, she was very, very, good, and when she was bad, she was horrid.'

Alison in a mood she found very difficult to deal with, and tended to tiptoe round her in a placatory manner that made Alison worse and infuriated her sons. 'If only she could have been a bit more like Stephen,' Jenny thought to herself wistfully. 'He was always such a sweet-tempered child.' Jenny adored her two boys, but when she had become unexpectedly pregnant again, she had longed for a girl – a girl she could dress in pretty clothes, with long fair curls and big blue eyes, a dainty little dancer who would enchant everybody who saw her, and who would radiate sunshine and happiness wherever she went.

The door crashed open and a hissing, spitting, black-browed ball of fury erupted from the hall, scarcely stopping in its tracks to flash a look of contempt at Jenny's mild enquiry – 'Oh, are you off out, dear?' – before it disappeared into the yard, slamming the kitchen door behind it with such force that the drawing-pin fastening a bunch of dust-encrusted invoices to a noticeboard gave way, sending the bills skeetering all over the floor.

Jenny picked them up, sighed again, and resumed her chopping. 'Poor Ali,' she thought to herself. 'Life can't be much fun for her at the moment. Having to do all that schoolwork; I don't know where she gets her brains from, but I don't see as it's much of a blessing. She should be out with her mates, having a laugh, flirting with boys … that's what she *should* be doing.' And Jenny dreamed on, remembering when she was seventeen, living with her sister, Lizzie, and her parents, in Weston-super-Mare.

By seventeen, she had already left school and had found work as an assistant in a wool shop in the centre of the town. She loved her job: she loved knitting, had always loved knitting; she loved stroking the different wools, loved the colours, and loved discussing patterns with her customers. When she finished work on Saturday afternoon, she and Lizzie would swallow down their tea and then get ready for a night on the pier with their girlfriends. Lizzie was two years younger, but they shared a bedroom, shared their lipsticks, shared their clothes and shared their friends. All that had come to an end when she met Jim Tucker.

'Jim.' Jenny smiled to herself and, climbing a wobbly chair, went to lift down a heavy, large, pickling pan from a shelf above the Rayburn. The whole shelf and everything on it had acquired a thick patina of black, rather oily-looking dust. Jenny drew her finger through it with dismay. 'Bugger that filthy old stove,' she muttered. 'Luckily Elsie can't reach up here; I haven't got time to clean it now. Never mind, what the eye don't see ...' and she climbed down with the pan, gave it a cursory rinse, and pouring into it the chopped onions, green tomatoes and a large quantity of malt vinegar, her mind drifted back over the well-worn memories of the time she had first met Jim.

It was an outing of his local Young Farmers Club. There were about fifteen of them, identically dressed in cords and checked shirts. With nudges and giggles, she and her mates had watched them approach down the pier. They were less cocky and less lippy than the usual gangs of boys the girls traded comments with, sticking together in a tight formation and gazing around like a group of foreign tourists. They were a bit older than the types who usually looked for entertainment on the pier on a Saturday night. Jenny and her friends, accomplished man-trackers that they were, had kept them in their sights, grouping and regrouping in the Wimpy, the arcade, the funfair and on the promenade, until finally, back at the dodgems, the tall, dark, curly-haired one she had picked out for herself climbed into the seat next to her, before Lizzie had time to take her place, and said softly, 'Are you followin' I?'

'Are you followin' I?' she softly repeated aloud, carrying the heavy pan and its contents over to the stove. She had loved the sound of his voice and missed it, even now. Stephen sounded most like him. Until he had grown his whiskers, Charlie had been the one who most looked like him, but Stephen had his father's temperament, which Jenny, quite irrationally, attributed to the fact that he was the only one of her children to have been planned.

A blissful year had followed that first meeting, courting on the sands when the weather permitted, or huddled in the coffee bar at the end of the pier when it didn't. Then she had turned eighteen and heavy petting gave way to the real thing, which, in Jenny's private opinion, was less enjoyable.

Their time together was limited, as she only had Sundays free and he had to get back for the milking by teatime. A couple of times he had persuaded her to visit his father's farm and then had run her back home after supper. She had found the formality of these occasions unnerving; she was terrified of Jim's mother, who had a lacerating tongue and X-ray vision; and although his father seemed kindly enough, he rarely spoke. The farm she found alien and uncomfortable, not at all as she had imagined. It was at the end of one of these visits he had asked her to marry him. She had hung back, loving him, but loving her own home, her life in Weston, and her job in the wool shop. In the event, becoming pregnant with Charlie had settled the matter and she had moved in, barely nineteen, to live with her new husband on the top floor of the farmhouse.

Her daydreams of past times ended abruptly with the sound of screeching brakes and a car door being opened and slammed. Jenny didn't need to look out of the window; she knew who it was, and braced herself to deal with whatever prickles her mother-in-law would throw at her when she came into the kitchen. Seconds later the front door of the farmhouse was opened and shut with such force that the whole wall shook. A calendar of West Country scenes, courtesy of Express Dairy, detached itself from its nail on the wall and slid down behind a chest of drawers. Retrieving the calendar (she liked the pictures, but more importantly, it had been marked with deadlines by which certain bills had to be paid) and pinning it back onto the wall, she wondered what could have put Elsie in such a mood. Normally she would use the back door from the farmyard into the kitchen, like everyone else. Her use of the old front door was significant and ominous.

The hall door suddenly opened and her mother-in-law poked her head round, clearly irritated. 'What is that awful smell, Jenny? It's everywhere! I hope that's not our supper you're cooking?'

'No, no, Elsie, of course not. I'm making tomato chutney, that's all. I'm sorry about the smell; I expect it's the malt vinegar. Perhaps it shouldn't boil like that—'

'My God, woman, are you ever going to learn to cook? One day you'll end up poisoning the lot of us!' And the door slammed shut, sending the calendar on its downward path again. Jenny pulled a face at the closed door. 'Poison – what a good idea!' she muttered and went to retrieve the calendar once more.

Jenny's relationship with her mother-in-law had not improved over the years. She knew Elsie regarded her with contempt and Jenny, in spite of the fact that she was now fifty-one, still felt awkward and stupid in Elsie's presence. If Alison hadn't been just seven when Jim died, and the boys still so immature and needing her, she would have left Marsh Farm as soon as it was decently possible after the funeral, and gone back to Weston-super-Mare. 'But now, more's the pity,' she reflected mournfully, 'that seems even less likely than ever.'

The money they had collected from Jim's insurance had all been spent, and even the money she had been saving for a rainy day had gone. 'Every day seems to be a rainy day,' she sighed, taking off her flowery pinafore, mopping her hot sticky face with it, and smoothing back the wisps of hair that had escaped from her bun (Jim had loved her long blonde hair and she had never had it cut short, but the colour was fading now and years of cheap shampoo had destroyed its silky texture). She looked around the kitchen with another rueful sigh.

Every year Jenny had vowed to clear and clean the kitchen, but there was always something else to do. She was not an efficient housewife, she knew that, and there were moments, as now, when she felt the extreme untidiness of the kitchen. But Jenny was not introspective and her gloomy state did not last for long. Anyway, she comforted herself, it was too hot for housework. She turned, instead, to a pile of knitting on the kitchen table. The soothing click of the needles and the feel of the wool through her fingers worked its magic and for a while she knitted and dreamed of her escape to Weston-super-Mare, in the company of Jeff Babbington, the local vet and Jim's best friend.

In the gloomy hall, lined with oak-stained wainscoting, Elsie mounted the staircase. It was wide and wooden, and creaked even under her slight weight. The stair runner was so worn that only faint traces of the original pattern could be detected clinging to the bare thread. Each step of the staircase contained its own pile of discarded clothing, shoes, or magazines, either on the way up or on the way down. A faded blue blind was pulled down against the sunlight on a large landing window at the back of the house, giving a faintly luminous glow to the gloom.

Elsie, still grumbling about the smell, paused for a moment outside her granddaughter's room. Having witnessed her grandson's humiliation in court, her blood was up, and she was ready to challenge Alison about her late-night activities. But the door was firmly shut, there was no answer to her knock and the absence of the discordant music that Alison loved suggested that she was out, so Elsie went on up the stairs to her own quarters on the top floor, a comfortable haven in the shabby, old farmhouse.

She had been about the same age as Jenny, in her early fifties, when Thomas, her husband, had died. Immediately, she had announced that Jenny was now the farmer's wife and should run the house and domestic livestock. She had abdicated all responsibility for any further cooking and cleaning, and in return for giving them the house, Elsie expected her son and his wife to provide her with board and lodging. Her son was delighted with the arrangement and thought it entirely reasonable, but Elsie knew that the life of a farmer's wife could be thankless, certainly was hard, and that she had handed Jenny a maggoty apple.

The smell of the boiling malt vinegar followed Elsie into her bathroom. 'It's not enough that Jenny is a useless cook,' she thought savagely, 'but her incompetence is catching – look at Charlie, look at Stephen: feeble, the pair of them! Wretched woman – she doesn't belong here; she should go back to Weston-super-Mare.'

Elsie didn't care that she was being unfair to Jenny, or that she herself, having a totally independent income of her own, had the wherewithal to help her family if she was so inclined. Her father had left her, his only child, a number of substantial properties in Bath, but she had never told any of them quite how well off she was. It concerned her that if they knew just how much she was worth, they would be constantly applying to her for help, not standing on their own two feet, and that the nest egg she felt she needed for her old age would be gobbled up. Her favourite maxim was 'Do not ask, as a refusal often offends', and this had been so dinned into her family that they didn't ask, although when times got really tight there was a lot of muttered resentment.

She turned on the fan to try and disperse the smell of the vinegar and glared into the mirror. There was nothing cosy, soft, or grannyish about the face that glared back, with glinting eyes and a challenging set to the chin.

She didn't see herself as mean; on occasion she could be generous, although her gifts were often hedged with cautious thrift, just in case they got the wrong idea. Jenny had longed for an Aga to replace the old kitchen stove, and Elsie bought her a second-hand Rayburn; at ten, Alison had longed for a pony and Elsie had bought her Bumble, retired from the local riding stables, small, fat and elderly; at seventeen, Charlie had longed for his first motorbike and, through the small ads page in the local paper, Elsie bought him a moped; and when Stephen passed his driving test and longed for a neat little saloon to take his mum out on days off, his gran bought him an elderly Reliant at a bargain price, from a friend who could no longer see to drive.

She went into her bedroom. The smell had even permeated

here. Exasperated, Elsie drew back the bright floral curtains and threw open her window. Carefully she drew out the long hatpin that held her straw boater firmly in place and removed her hat, patting the iron-grey bun of hair back in place. She then took from her bag a slim, dark green box, embossed with 'The Dressing Room' in fine gold writing.

Elsie's attire was unexceptional. She always wore the same sort of clothes, with a waistcoat for warmth, whatever the weather. She eschewed all ornamentation, apart from a silk scarf worn loosely knotted around her scrawny neck. What nobody knew, or could guess, was that Elsie had a passion for silk underwear.

If the girl in the lingerie shop felt any surprise at Elsie's quarterly visits and self-indulgent purchases, she was too well bred to show it and she had guided Elsie, over the years, through the changing fashions in corsetry. Today she had persuaded Elsie to try her first underwired bra. Although her breasts were withered and small, Elsie had always been proud of her trim figure and she was secretly pleased when Jenny lost her slim shape and had become round and plump.

'*She* wouldn't be able to get into this bra, 32A, certainly not!' Elsie thought triumphantly as she lovingly touched the delicate lace trim. She pulled off her jumper and blouse, unhooked the creamy silk garment that had been her favoured choice that morning, and slipped on the new bra, critically examining in the mirror the effect of the underwiring, and stroking the pale blue silk and lace concoction. She loved it – it made her feel good; slowly, the black mood that had descended upon her in the magistrates' court lifted.

'But it's time to act,' she said aloud, decisively. 'I've let them muddle along for too long. The magistrate was right: it's time Charlie grew up, and Stephen too, for that matter. And as for Alison – she's not going to mess about any longer, if I've got anything to do with it!'

It was time for some clear thinking, and the best way to achieve this, in her opinion, was to occupy her hands doing something else. On her way home she had noticed the first flush of black-berries in the hedgerow. She would go out and pick berries, not for jam or jelly, pies or crumbles, but for the highly potent fruit cordials she conferred on a favoured few at Christmas.

3

'Blimey – I wouldn't mind that little bugger myself. I wonder what her top speed would be; ain't she a beaut, Lenny?'

It was late afternoon and very hot; the air seemed to shimmer with dust and the hedgerows drooped, dusty and silent, dark sanctuaries for the small mammals and birds that had survived the combine's blades. A good two thirds of the barley field was now stubble and Charlie and Lenny were taking a quick break from harvesting when a sleek black Lamborghini drove slowly past.

Lenny was not so impressed; 'I'd rather have her worth in bikes, meself. Never been one for those fancy Italian jobs. Now if I'd that sort of money to blow I'd get a Yamaha; a YZ one fifty. Yer wouldn't see me fer dust …'

'Nice, I grant you, but me, I'd go the whole hog, get a two fifty …' It was their favourite topic of conversation – what motocross bikes they would buy if money were no object and they didn't have farms and families to hold them back.

'Hey, look: there she goes again.'

The car had turned and was driving back down the lane, more slowly this time. Its smoked-glass windows made it impossible for the two men to see who was driving.

Charlie scratched his head. 'I wonder what they're after. Weasel Lane's a dead end.'

'Mebbe they're lost.'

'Mebbe …' But Charlie, answering his mobile, quickly lost interest in the cruising car. 'Oh, hi, Sarah, how are … sorry, love, I meant to call but … no it was okay – got off with a small fine, nothing much to worry about … No, I'm sorry I didn't … you were? Well you shouldn't have been – you know me … water off a duck's back … What? … Tonight? … I dunno, me and Lenny are really busy … we've started the harvest and I've no idea what time we'll finish … Okay, I'll try. I'll give you a call.' He switched his mobile off with a sigh.

Lenny grinned. 'Trouble?'

'She's upset 'cause I didn't phone her up after my starring appearance in court today.'

'Well, she did dare you to climb up onto that thing – perhaps she was feelin' guilty?'

'Perhaps. But she's starting to cluck, Lenny. I can't bear it when they get serious. I think it's time to move on.'

'Well there's a surprise.' Lenny was laconic. 'The way you carry on, you're gonna work your way through every available skirt in Somerset. Don't tell me you've got a new bird in yer sights?'

Charlie tapped the side of his nose and grinned. 'As a matter of fact, Lenny, me old sparkplug, I have. Come on, we'd better get a move on or there'll be no drinking time for us this evening.'

As he climbed into the tractor, Charlie looked back up the lane and whistled. 'There it is again.' The Lamborghini was making its way down the lane past the field yet again. 'They're not lost, Lenny, whatever else they're up to.' And as they watched, the car pulled over to the field entrance and stopped. 'Well, well,' said Charlie softly. 'It's my guess we're about to find out what it is they're after.'

Stephen hurried across the yard. His cows out to graze on the fresh grass and the sluicing of the milking parlour finished, he had just time to change and swallow a bite of supper before he was due at the rehearsal.

Jenny was at the kitchen table, knitting a sweater of the most glorious hue, tears slipping unheeded down her cheeks.

'Mum, what's up? What's wrong?' Stephen went to her in alarm; he seldom saw Jenny cry.

She looked up in surprise. 'Wrong, dear? Nothing's wrong. Why?'

Stephen's eyes started to sting and water. An acrid smell assailed his nostrils. 'Aw, Mum, what is that awful smell?'

Jenny placidly resumed her knitting, 'Green tomato chutney, dear.'

Every year, Jenny seemed to produce more green tomatoes than she ever did ripe ones, and every year, all their friends and neighbours, and the WI, received more jars of green tomato chutney than they could ever want.

'Angela phoned and asked if you could pick her up on your way in. She's got lots of things she needs to take to your rehearsal.'

'Oh, right. She's been collecting props, I expect. It's early days, but she likes to get ahead. She's good like that.'

Angela Upton was the Merlin Players' assistant stage manager and the producer's general factotum. Stephen liked Angela; she didn't alarm him, unlike the majority of the Players, and in her company he felt comfortable with himself. She worked in the town's library and it had been meeting Angela there when he was on a mission for his mother and grandmother that had led to his introduction to the Merlin Players.

He had been looking at a poster advertising a play, and a young girl who, with her frizzy brown hair, timid expression and huge spectacles, reminded him of the numerous mice regularly caught by Samson, the farm's cat, stopped and asked him shyly if he was interested in theatre. He had replied, equally shyly, that he didn't know the first thing about it, and she explained that she was meant to be doing the backstage work on the production in question, but was finding it impossible to find anyone to help her with the set construction.

'I hope those Merlin people appreciate you and Angela.' Jenny put her knitting to one side and started to busy herself getting Stephen's supper ready, while he made himself a cup of tea. 'You both work so hard. I hope they don't take you for granted!' She put a pan of water on the hot plate for frozen peas and peered into the oven to check on the state of the dish baking there. The faintest whiff of burnt potato reached Stephen's nostrils.

'I enjoy it, Mum, otherwise I wouldn't do it.' It was true: he had been the stage manager for the Merlin Players for ten years now and the thrill had not yet worn off. He loved the rehearsals; he loved the sounds of words he often could not understand; he loved the stomach-clenching adrenalin-kick as he gave the calls to curtain up; he loved the vulnerability of the actors when, lost for words, they turned to him in a mute appeal; he loved the smell of the paint, the smell of the grease, the smell of dust burning in hot lanterns. He loved everything, everything, except being on stage himself.

When Angela had first persuaded him to go along, the producer, desperate for male performers, and presented with a tall, well-built young man, had tried to persuade Stephen to try for a part. So great was his fright, he nearly passed out, and even now, when he had to read in for a missing actor, his face would redden and his voice squeak with terror. He had once confided to Angela that his enjoyment of the whole experience was blighted by the producer's insistence that he took the stage for a vote of thanks on the last night. 'It's getting so as I start thinking about it from curtain up on Wednesday. By Saturday teatime I'm in such a funk I can't eat a thing.'

His family, unaware of any of this, regarded his continuing enthusiasm with considerable bemusement.

'Here's your food, dear: shepherd's pie. Eat it while it's nice and hot, then you can get changed after.' As he sat himself at the table, Jenny, glancing across at him, picked up her knitting and tried to adopt a casual-but-interested tone. 'Is it all the same people, or have you got any new members joined up for this play?'

Jenny nurtured hopes that belonging to the Merlin Players would provide Stephen with opportunities to meet 'the right girl' as she put it, but in the years he had been devoting his spare time to production after production, not a single girl had come to the farm, apart from Angela that is, who helped him paint the scenery and make the props.

31

Stephen, wolfing down his pie, was familiar with the unspoken enquiry, and sighed. 'We're a bit short, so Mrs P is bringing along her au pair. I haven't met her yet. She's from Romania.'

'That's nice.' There was silence for a moment, then a hopeful, 'Perhaps she would like to come and visit the farm.'

Stephen was dismissive. 'Perhaps, Mum, perhaps.' He shovelled a mouthful of minced meat into his mouth, then grimaced. 'I hate to say it, but even this food tastes of vinegar!' He looked up. 'I know I'm having my supper early, but where is everyone? Seems awful quiet.'

'Your gran's having her supper in her room, on account of the smell; Charlie says he and Lenny are working late; Alison came back from riding Bumble, went to her room and I haven't seen her since. If you're going into Summerbridge, dear, you might offer her a lift. I think it'd do her good to spend some time away from her books and she could go and see some friends while you're doing your theatrics.'

'Aw, do I have to, Mum? She'll just give me an earful about her allowance.'

'Yes, well, I don't think it would do no harm for *you* to explain just how things are.'

A tap on the kitchen door interrupted them. The cheerful countenance of Jeff Babbington, the vet, peered round the door. His two favourite Tuckers greeted him warmly and he came into the room. He was a tall man of ample proportions, in his mid fifties, with a ruddy colour, shrewd blue eyes under bushy brows, and deep laughter lines that etched his face. His hair was still thick and wavy and brown, liberally flecked with grey, and he had a habit of ruffling it with both hands when he threw back his head and laughed, which he did often.

As Jenny fussed over the kettle, Stephen pushed his plate away and stood up, belching apologetically. 'Thanks for the food, Mum. Sorry I can't stop, Jeff, I've got to dash. Got a rehearsal this evening.'

'Oh, what is it this time? Nice bit of light comedy? A whodunit? I could bring your mum.'

'I'm not sure she'd understand it. I'm not sure I do, come to that. Mrs P says it was written three hundred years ago and it's a romantic comedy, for what that's worth. It's called, um ... Bow something ...'

'*The Beaux Stratagem*,' said Alison in the Land Rover, a short while later, 'by George Farquhar; he was Irish.'

'Well, it's all Irish to me, ha ha!' said Stephen, the weak joke an attempt to lighten the atmosphere between them. She had accepted his offer of a lift, but as he had predicted, she had given him a hard time. It had been somewhat tempered by Jenny pressing a five-pound note into her hand as they left, with an apologetic whisper. 'Don't be too cross with Stephen, dear. He really is struggling. Here, take this. I was saving it for a rainy day.'

Alison was not inclined to let her brother off the hook, but in the face of a humble apology she had relented and had changed the subject, choosing instead to lash out at that which, next to his cows, she knew was dearest to his heart.

'Why on earth does your producer choose such archaic rubbish? I suppose it's because they all like poncing around in long dresses and wigs, fiddling with their fans and swordsticks ... lah, zounds, me lud, and stap me vitals! How you can persuade people to part with good money to watch that lot making prats of themselves, beats me!'

'You don't know what you're talkin' about ... they're really good. At least some of them are. We nearly won the Rose Bowl a couple of years ago and now Nicola is back, we reckon we stand a good chance with ... with ... Bow Strategy.'

'Who's Nicola?'

'Oh,' said Stephen, keeping his eyes fixed on the road, hoping that Alison would think the creeping blush warming his face was due to the evening sun, 'she's just a girl who used to belong to the Players when I first joined. She left and went to a drama school in London. She's, um, in between acting jobs, for the moment, and Mrs P has persuaded her to take part in the ... the ...'

'*The Beaux Stratagem*. You're going to have to remember

what it's called, Stephen, if you're to have any street cred. What's she like?'

'Who?'

'Nicola, the actress. What's she like? Do you fancy her?'

To Stephen's intense relief, before he had time to reply they passed the war memorial in the centre of the town and Alison caught sight of a bunch of her friends gathered around a small cluster of motorbikes. She shrieked at him to let her off and, having made a hasty arrangement for the return journey, slipped out of the car, the subject of Stephen and Nicola temporarily forgotten. Nicola – who had been the object of Stephen's secret passion ever since he had first met her ten years ago, then a precocious seventeen-year-old with glossy dark curls and blue eyes set firmly on starry horizons. He had fallen desperately, hopelessly in love with her and although her visits to Summerbridge over the years were infrequent, his passion had not abated.

'Pepperoni, ham and pineapple, or a meat feast?' Paula Spinks shouted, her head inside an old chest freezer that Lenny had rescued from a tip and got working again.

'Pepperoni, please, love. Charlie?'

'Pepperoni'll do me too, darling, thanks.'

Charlie stretched out on the battered old sofa, removing a plastic sten gun from the small of his back as he did so. For a moment he reflected on the curious conversation he'd had with the man who had climbed out of the Lamborghini.

He was a flash bugger; not much older than Charlie, in a dark suit, dripping in gold and wearing dark glasses. He'd walked over to them, asked who owned the land and then had drawn Charlie out of Lenny's earshot and asked him if he would consider renting him the field for a short time. Charlie had said if there was money in it, he would, and started to ask him what he'd want it for, but Dark Glasses had forestalled any further questioning, taken Charlie's number, and said he'd be in touch and that Charlie was not to say anything to anybody, not even to Lenny, who was looking on, full of curiosity. And that was that. Charlie shrugged – something and nothing.

He and Lenny had worked on until quite late and he was starving, but the thought of Elsie waiting to cross swords with him at home had led to him abandoning all thoughts of going back to Marsh Farm to eat and throwing himself on the mercy of Paula, Lenny's wife.

She appeared at the door of the little sitting room, two large pizza boxes in her arms, and said cheerfully, 'These won't take two ticks in the microwave. I've put some more beer in the fridge, Lenny. When you've got a mo', darlin', can you go and turn the kids' telly off? Time they was asleep.'

From the noises, thumps and yells upstairs, which were sufficiently loud at times to drown out the sound of the TV permanently on in the corner of the room, it seemed Paula and Lenny's numerous progeny were anything but ready for sleep. In fact, Charlie had noticed, both Paula and Lenny seemed completely immune to any noise their children could make.

The Spinks family lived in cheerful chaos in a small cottage that was tied to Marsh Farm. This meant that Charlie was able to claim a proportion of Lenny's services in lieu of rent. Lenny seemed to have a number of ingenious, not always legal sources of potential income that, with the money Paula made from cleaning, seemed to keep them just above the poverty line.

Despite having produced four children in six years, Paula was still quite pretty. She had once been told that she looked like Joan Collins and she was so proud of this fact she had gone out of her way to cultivate the look with liberal quantities of mascara, eyeliner and lipstick. She was slim, taller than Lenny, a fact emphasised by a shaky, back-combed tower of black hair and the stiletto shoes she wore at all times. She was not bright, but very affable, and, not for the first time, Charlie found himself envying his friend.

Lenny, it seemed to Charlie, had got life sorted. Not that it was the sort of life that Charlie himself would want – he didn't want to live in a small cottage with four children at everybody's beck and call. But Lenny was content; he and Paula were a comfortable item, and neither of them had any greater ambition than to make enough money to pay their bills, indulge their kids, and go on holiday to Torremolinos, or somewhere equally exotic. If only he could be so contented. But he wasn't like them. He knew he didn't want to settle down with the sort of women who were attracted to him, but equally he wasn't sure how he could break out of that circle and find someone more challenging; or, he privately admitted to himself, find a way of life that would excite him more than farming ever would.

He found himself thinking about Lenny's set up again later, at the pub, sitting at the corner of the bar and watching Linda, the landlady, pulling pints, chatting to the customers and ordering her little fiefdom as she liked.

Linda had been at school with him. At fifteen he had fancied her something rotten. In those days she'd had long bleached hair and huge black-lashed eyes that glared out from under a fearsome fringe. They had snogged in the bike sheds but had fallen out because she told everyone he was 'green' and he had retaliated by saying she smelled. When they left school behind, she had disappeared off the scene for a while and then had reappeared, minus the bleach and fringe, with a husband, Stan, who was a publican, quite a bit older than Linda. Charlie and Linda's friendship had been renewed when, four years ago, shortly after Linda had given birth to a little girl, Stan and Linda had bought The Bunch of Grapes, a free house and Charlie's regular haunt.

Charlie admired Linda – he thought she was lively and courageous. She was tall and slim, her brown hair cropped stylishly short, and she had a generous mouth and laughing hazel eyes. Not pretty, but handsome, and she controlled the antics of her regulars with great good humour, unlike Stan, who was generally a lot more taciturn.

They have a good life, too, thought Charlie to himself, draining his glass, although they work bloody hard for it. And where's

Stan tonight? Poor old Linda is always holding the fort these days. And where's Beth? Why isn't she here? Beth was the new, regular barmaid and Charlie, as Lenny had rightly suspected, had her in his sights.

For a moment Charlie sat dreaming into his beer, imagining what it would be like to own his own pub, be able to drink unlimited quantities of beer and at the end of the day, tumble into bed with ... with ... His daydream came to an end. He had done plenty of tumbling in his time, but for the life of him he couldn't think of anyone he'd like to share a bed with permanently.

'Penny for them, Charlie?' Linda smiled at him. 'Another pint? Not like you to be here in your overalls this time of the evening. Not been home yet?'

'Nah, me and Lenny finished late, so I grabbed a pizza up at his, then thought I'd have a couple before I go and face the old battleaxe.'

Linda had been privy to countless moans from Les about Elsie Tucker, since they had been kids together.

'What's eating her this time?'

So Charlie, reviving slightly with a fresh pint in one hand and a sympathetic ear on the other, told Linda about his experiences in court that morning and the unwelcome appearance of his grandmother.

Stephen asked Alison the same question as he drove her home. 'Mum says there's trouble brewing. Have you done anything to rile her, Ali? Did you tell her I couldn't find the money for your allowance this month?'

Alison was riding high on an unexpectedly good evening with her mates, who had fallen in with a small gang of bikers. One in particular had caught her attention and she was busy trying to work out how she could meet up with him again without giving her interest away. However, she had decided on a way to get Elsie to lend her some money, so any intimation that her gran's mood was less than sweet was critically important.

'No of course not. I wouldn't stoop that low. I haven't done anything that I know of. Damn and blast. I bet it's Charlie. It usually is!'

Stephen was about to leap to his brother's defence, as he inevitably did whenever Charlie was blamed for something, when the image of Charlie that morning in a suit, running into the house at the mention of Elsie, flashed through his mind.

'Well,' he said ruefully, turning off the main road into the village of Summerstoke, 'I reckon we'll find out soon enough, and whatever it is, she'll make us suffer, you can be sure of that.'

But on one point Stephen was wrong – Elsie had decided that until she could see a way through, she would say nothing to any of them, so that when Alison and Stephen arrived home, there was no sign of her.

Jenny, when asked by Alison what was 'eating Gran', shook her head. 'I've no idea. She hardly exchanged a word with me, not even when I went to collect her supper things, and she refused to come down and watch telly.'

'Sounds like there's a storm brewing,' Stephen said gloomily, 'and I hope it's not my head it's gonna break over!' In spite of his mother's protestations that he was, in all things, completely blameless, he went to bed with a heavy heart, his thoughts alternating between broken water pumps, no milk cheques, and the lovely, elusive Nicola, who had smiled so sweetly at him when she had arrived at the start of the rehearsal, and then had said nothing to him for the rest of the evening.

4

According to the vicar, whose passion was for local history rather than for his flock, the village of Summerstoke had grown up on the side of a valley where, in the early middle ages, the river was shallow enough to cross for a few months in the year. The high street had once been part of an old drover's road that ran down from the Mendip Hills to the river, crossed the valley, and made its way up onto the outlying fingers of the Cotswolds, where it connected with the Fosse Way and other routes across the heartland of old England.

The ancient track had long since been replaced by a metalled road; the old flood plains had been drained and the river banks built up to prevent any meandering, which meant that a bridge had to be built to cross the deeper, swifter water, and Summerstoke Bridge now marked the lower boundary of the present-day village. The vicar had proudly produced a pamphlet explaining all this; a modest pile had been placed in the church of St Stephens, and visitors were invited to take a copy in return for a modest donation in the 'honesty box'. The box had remained steadfastly empty, but the vicar was gratified to see the pile dwindle.

Summerstoke was generally perceived to be a pretty place to live. Its proximity to Bath and Bristol, the motorways and the commuter lines to London, meant that house prices were high. On their first visit to Summerstoke, house-hunters would proclaim ecstatically about the church bells, the daily procession of cows along the high street and the presence of the village shop. Inevitably, once they moved in, those cries became ones of complaint:

'Sunday is meant to be a day of rest ... Do those bells have to ring so loud, so often?'

'Those bloody cows – doing their doings all over the road; it must be a health hazard. Why does he have to bring them along the high street?'

'The shop is useless; if I have to go to Sainsbury's for my smoked oysters, I might as well do the rest of my shopping there! And it's so expensive – do you know how much they charge for butter?'

The village shop and post office, struggling for survival, was owned and run by Rita Godwin, Jenny Tucker's best friend. It was situated right in the middle of the village, near St Stephen's, the parish church, and the manor house, and the pub.

The Forester's Arms looked hospitable, but it was not a friendly local. It had been turned into a 'gastro' pub, employing a chef with a name and with an eye to inclusion in good food guides. Consequently, it actively discouraged certain of the locals, Lenny Spinks and Charlie Tucker amongst them, from dropping in for a pint.

The houses, mostly pre-Victorian, were all stone-roofed and built of honey-coloured sandstone, the front doors opening directly onto the pavement with large, hidden gardens behind. In more prosperous days, quite a number of the houses had been shops, but these were long gone and were now all private dwellings known as The Old Bank or The Forge or The Old Bakery, and so on. There were few original villagers left and they lived mainly in the meaner cottages, or on the small council housing estate tucked out of sight at the bottom end of the village, or in the odd sixties housing development that had sprung up before anyone had shouted 'planning permission'.

Locally, the half of the village that stretched from St Stephen's down to the river was known as Lower Summerstoke, and in the opposite direction, Upper Summerstoke. The larger houses, the bigger gardens and the greater egos were all in Upper Summerstoke.

The two farms in the parish, at either end of the village,

mirrored this social division: Marsh Farm, occupying the rather boggy land on the other side of Summerstoke Bridge, at the bottom end, and Summerstoke House Farm, looking down over the village and the valley, at the upper end. They couldn't have been more different.

'I don't bloody believe this!'

Hugh Lester, of Summerstoke House, had just driven over Summerstoke Bridge and was looking down on the world from the driver's seat of his brand new, gleaming Land Rover Sport, expecting to be home in a matter of minutes, when he was confronted by the swaying hindquarters of a herd of cows ambling up Summerstoke's main street.

Stephen had finished the afternoon milking and with the aid of the family dog, Gip, was taking the herd on its daily perambulation through the village, back to graze on the lush meadows beyond.

Fuming, Hugh Lester was forced to grind down to second gear and trail in their wake. He was already in a bad mood and since the cause of it was the Tucker family, this delay compounded his fury. Stephen, glancing over his shoulder, registered who it was being held up and nodded an acknowledgement.

Hugh Lester ignored him.

'The whole sodding afternoon wasted, and now this!' He muttered under his breath, banging the steering wheel in frustration. It was a hot, airless day and Hugh's immaculate khaki shirt was beginning to wilt and stick to his back, dark patches appearing under his armpits. He tapped a button, the windows slid shut and the air-conditioning sprang into icy action. He longed to get home, have a shower and down a large gin and tonic, but he was trapped. There was no way past. The village had just the one main street. There was nothing he could do – a position that always brought out the worst in Hugh Lester – and he was forced to trail in the wake of Stephen Tucker's herd until he reached the entrance to his drive.

Summerstoke House was Victorian. It had been built by a successful merchant who had wanted to marry off his daughters

41

to local gentry. Its tall windows and lofty gables proclaimed its superiority as a residence, and it was sufficiently set back from the road to allow itself a gravel courtyard with an ornamental fountain in the middle. A high stone wall and elaborate iron gates operated by an electronic device kept the world out.

Summerstoke House farmyard, which had been in existence long before the present house was built, was tucked out of sight and approached by a separate entrance on the outskirts of the village. It bore no resemblance to the farm that had been there originally, the merchant having demolished the old farmhouse, and subsequent owners having modernised and invested in new buildings so that now state-of-the-art barns housed state-of-the-art farm machinery, with ultra-modern grain stores and all the associated equipment that a skilful manipulation of EU subsidies had made possible. The only livestock visible on this farm were horses — lots of them.

Closer to the house, a smart quadrangle of stables had been built to house the very expensive nags that were kept in livery here and a menage completed the farm buildings. That had caused some consternation in the village, as its roof was visible from the road. But it had got planning permission anyway. Hugh Lester and his wife, Veronica, were used to getting their way. Except, that is, when it came to the Tuckers.

'An excrescence on the landscape' was how Hugh Lester described Marsh Farm and there were many who thought like him. It divided the village of Summerstoke into two camps: those who joined the Lesters, loudly denouncing the state of Marsh farm as a disgrace, expressing opinions like 'the sooner they sell up and move on, the better'; and those who resented the newcomers, townies, rich buggers, and fat cats, of whom the Lesters were regarded as the worst example, even though the family had lived in the village nigh on forty years.

Hugh Lester had moved to Summerstoke with his parents and older brother when he was seven. His father had been a successful industrialist who had bought the house and farm so that his family could live in the style his wife expected, and so that he could play at farming, whenever he could make the time. He was passionate about cattle breeding, and at different times Belted Galloways, South Devons, Longhorns and Highland cattle grazed the upland pastures of Summerstoke Farm, together with his pedigree herd of Herefords.

The day he triumphantly negotiated the takeover of a rival company, Hugh's father suffered a massive heart attack. Unfortunately for him and his wife, it occurred whilst he was driving her home on the M4. His car had ended up under the wheels of a truck transporting veal calves to the continent, and Hugh became an orphan at the age of twenty-four.

Hugh's brother took over the firm, and Hugh took on the farm. He lost no time getting rid of all the cattle, and sacked his father's long-suffering manager. Apart from his horses, for which he had a passion, he had no interest in livestock of any sort. An intelligent reading of market forces led him to decide to turn the farm over to cash crop production.

Accordingly, whatever produced the subsidies, Hugh produced. Pastures were ploughed up, hedgerows grubbed out, field divisions removed, the soil fed and fed again with chemicals approved by the NFU and the Ministry of Agriculture to make the desired plants grow and the undesired to wither. The woodlands were spared and stocked with pheasants. His parents had entertained shooting parties; Hugh made a business out of it. Similarly, his father had extended the stables and stocked them with horses to entertain his wife and their friends; Hugh extended them still further and, putting a number of his richest pastures under the hoof, he turned Summerstoke Farm into a highly profitable livery stable.

The cows finally ambled past the gates of Summerstoke House and with a snarl at Stephen's impassive back, Hugh turned the wheel into his drive, narrowly missing his wife's car and almost hitting his son's bike.

He stomped into the cool, dark hall of the house, shouting as he went: 'Vee! Vee! Where the bloody hell are you?'

While the fortunes of many farmers around him had dwindled, Hugh Lester had become richer and richer. In the process, at the age of thirty he had met and married Veronica, five years his junior. Veronica, known to her friends as Vee, had been participating in a dressage event at Badminton. She had not been very impressed when he first introduced himself. Hugh was a good-looking man, with dark, almost black curly hair, cold blue eyes and a strong jaw, but he was barely five feet six and Veronica was a good two inches taller. But they met again at a point-to-point, and Hugh on horseback was a very much more desirable proposition, particularly when she discovered what else he had to offer.

In the course of time, they had two children: a boy, Anthony, now nineteen, and a girl, Cordelia, now fifteen; who, when they were both old enough, had been packed off to boarding school.

Veronica appeared at the top of the curved, highly polished wooden staircase, her slim figure silhouetted in the light that streamed from a long, elegantly draped window. She was dressed for tennis. 'I'm here, Hugh. There's no need to shout like that. You were a long time.'

'I would have been back a damn sight sooner if I hadn't got stuck behind Tucker's herd taking an afternoon stroll up the high street,' he growled.

Vee lightly descended the staircase and followed Hugh into his study.

'Something wrong, darling? You do sound put out.'

'George Ranwell hasn't delivered.' Hugh slumped into a leather swivel chair behind a huge mahogany desk that seemed to reduce him to the size of a Lilliputian. 'Bloody Tuckers are refusing to budge. He said they didn't even look twice at my last offer.'

'But it was a generous increase on the first one.'

'Not enough to interest them. Bloody morons – they're looking a gift-horse in the mouth. What a bunch to have to deal with!'

Ordinarily the Lesters would not have wasted any time or

energy on a family like the Tuckers. The Tuckers, however, had something that the Lesters wanted very badly. That was land. The livery stables were filled to capacity, and it was only by the judicious management of their fields that the grass survived. Veronica and Hugh wanted to expand their empire and run a stud, but for that they needed more land, and, to get round planning restrictions, land where buildings suitable for conversion were already in existence. Marsh Farm was the obvious solution. The Tuckers, however, had no intention of selling to anyone, let alone the Lesters, whom they saw as unpleasant, stuck-up snobs who would do the Tuckers down given half a chance. On this point, they were not wrong.

Veronica sighed and came into the room. She was expected on the tennis courts at the club in half an hour, but she knew better than to leave Hugh simmering. 'I thought they were teetering on the brink of ruin and would do anything for cash.'

'No, no – it's more complicated than that. The stumbling block is the old granny. She owns half the farm and George says she's as shrewd as they come.'

'Then offer them more – if she's that shrewd she must know you're offering way under the current market value.'

'Vee! Be reasonable. I'm going to have to invest a great deal in the building work. Bugger current market values. That farm's a mess and I've offered as much as I'm prepared to pay. We'll just have to wait until they go bankrupt. Then they'll be sorry they didn't accept my offer.'

Veronica smiled at the petulant expression on her husband's face. 'I can't see you being content to sit back waiting for that to happen. We'll have to give them a little help, won't we?'

Hugh stared at her for a moment. 'Well, there's a thought. What had you in mind?'

Vee took out a lipstick from her purse and peering into a little compact, caressed her lips with the creamy stick. 'You've told me often enough that Marsh Farm staggers from crisis to crisis. Why don't we do a little gentle squeezing? It shouldn't be difficult to nudge them over the edge.'

Hugh looked at her admiringly. For a forty-something woman, she was in very good shape. Her long brown legs were flatteringly topped and tailed by a short tennis skirt and white ankle socks; her waist was trim, her breasts firm and round under that tiny cotton top; admittedly her nose was a bit sharp and her eyes and teeth slightly protuberant, but her hair, held back in a wide white band, was still as thick and blonde as it was the day he met her. And she was bright – by God she was! Without her, he doubted the livery stables would have been half as successful. He licked his lips. He still found her very desirable, but he knew she disliked sex outside the bedroom, and outside bedtime hours.

'I don't mind doing a little squeezing, but I may not be very gentle.'

She smiled at him and flung her cosmetics back in her bag. 'I've got to go. I've got a tennis date. But I'll leave you to think about two courses of action you might take. One is Lenny Spinks.'

'Who's he?'

'Lenny Spinks is the husband of our cleaning lady, Paula.'

'Why should I be interested?'

'Local talk has it that without the help of Lenny Spinks, Marsh Farm would not be able to function.'

'You're right. I'm interested. Go on …'

'He keeps all their derelict machinery going. He's some sort of whiz at engineering or mechanics or whatever it is. Paula is forever droning on about how good he is with his hands and I don't think it's just pillow talk, although from the number of kids they've got—'

'I get your drift – take Lenny Spinks away from Marsh Farm …'

'And you will deal a very effective blow to their efficiency. So, offer him a job at a rate he can't refuse.'

'I'm sure I could find a use for a man with his talents.'

'Once Marsh Farm is ours, you let him go, of course.'

If only he could take her now, strip that top from her brown, smooth shoulders, cup her breasts in his hands and bury his face in her soft belly. It had always been like this: the more ruthless, the more Machiavellian, the more vicious she was about the people in their lives (himself excluded of course, for he wasn't any sort of masochist) the more he desired her.

He swallowed hard and said, somewhat thickly, 'I'll get on to that this afternoon. Lenny Spinks ... and what was the other thing you had in mind, Lady Macbeth?'

She laughed and ruffled his hair. 'The three weird sisters, the Misses Merfields.'

The puncturing of his libido was instantaneous. He stared up at her resentfully. 'You must be joking. Those witches. Why should I humiliate myself again?'

The Merfield family, who had lived in the Manor house since time immemorial, owned the water meadows on the village side of the river. Hugh had longed to get his hands on them for years, but the Merfields had rented the land to the Tuckers ever since Elsie and Thomas, with the help of Elsie's father (then the Mayor of Bath and appalled at the thought of his only child marrying a tenant farmer), had bought Marsh Farm from them. The fields were adjacent to Summerstoke Farm; lush, rich meadows, and Stephen's cows flourished on them.

Vee picked up her bag and slung it over her shoulder. 'Because, Hugh, if you can get those meadows off them, the life of Marsh Farm as a viable dairy unit will be at an end.'

'But there's no way those bitches would agree.'

Vee smiled coldly at him. 'I have it on good authority the Merfields thought you were an arrogant little shit when you tried before, but that was some years ago. Go and eat humble pie for a change; exercise your charm, darling. It shouldn't be too difficult for you to twist three old ladies round your fingertips.'

'For once, Vee, I don't share your optimism. Why should the Merfields change their minds?'

'Because the Tuckers are in even more of a mess now, and that must be as apparent to the Misses Merfields as it is to the rest of the village. I can't imagine they feel any particular loyalty to people like the Tuckers, particularly Charlie Tucker. He's hardly a pillar of our community, and now he's made such a fool of himself—'

'What are you talking about?'

'I was magistrating today. I got it from Guy. He was chairing Court One; said he'd had a chap in yesterday by the name of Tucker, charged with being drunk and disorderly. You know that pub in Bath, The Bear, the one with the big white bear over the porch? Charlie Tucker was so drunk he climbed up onto the porch and tried to mount it.'

Hugh let out a crack of laughter.

Vee smiled maliciously. 'Then he couldn't get down again and had to be rescued by the fire service. What a fool! Anyway, darling, I put a call into Richard G and asked him if he'd be running the story. "Too good to miss," he said, particularly as an onlooker had provided them with a splendidly compromising pic of our Charlie. Go and see the ladies, and take a copy of the paper with you. You know how straitlaced they are; I'm sure they would be most interested!'

If only Anthony and Cordelia weren't home for the holidays. Vee, sobbing and screaming, always guaranteed his climax, which had become more elusive of late. Still . . .

'What a little schemer you are,' he said admiringly. 'Clever girl!'

'I must go,' she said crisply, 'or I'll be awfully late. We'll talk more this evening. Cordelia is having an overnight with friends and I don't expect Anthony will join us for dinner.'

'Who *are* you playing tennis with?' Hugh asked curiously, getting up and following her out.

'Gordon White.'

'That little turd. Why on earth are you playing him?'

Veronica was impatient. 'Really, Hugh, I don't see how you can shout at Anthony for swearing when you use such words yourself. He's a creep, I grant you, but he could be very useful to us.'

'How?'

They walked across the gravelled courtyard to Veronica's

bright red Porsche. Veronica slung her racquet and bag into the back of her car and turned to Hugh, looking ever so smug and rather like a picture he had once seen of a shrew consuming a worm. 'I'll tell you later, darling. It's a long shot and he might not play ball, but if he does ...' She let out the clutch and as the car moved slowly off, called out, 'Paula's in the kitchen. Go and speak to her about Lenny. This time next year, I promise you, Marsh Farm will be ours.'

Hugh did speak to Paula, and Paula, much, much later, remembered that Mr Lester wanted Lenny to give him a ring about possible employment. But Lenny, tired out from the day's labours and having consumed a six-pack as well as two meat feast pizzas, let out a loud snore and would not be woken.

5

Elsie Tucker brooded through Thursday and Friday. Her displeasure hung over the house, more insidious than the smell of the green tomato chutney. Charlie made himself as scarce as his work allowed, whilst the others speculated about who, or what, could have provoked Gran in such a way and did their best not to aggravate the situation.

Jenny finally finished the sweater she had been knitting and proudly showed it to Alison.

'Oh Mum, it's beautiful! You're so clever!' Alison was genuinely impressed and Jenny glowed. Alison rarely paid her any compliments. 'Why don't you sell your jumpers yourself? You'd make a fortune. I bet Mrs Whatsername will sell it for a couple of hundred at least.'

'At least,' Jenny agreed, burying her face in the soft wool garment in a fond farewell before wrapping it carefully in white tissue and placing it in a flat cardboard box. 'But you have to remember, dear, Mrs Moorhead is a very successful designer. Someone will buy this for that price because it's designed by her, not because Jenny Tucker knitted it.'

'But she pays you peanuts and makes a fortune out of your work. It's exploitation, Mum.'

'No, it's not. I enjoy doing it, and I'm very grateful for what she pays me.' Jenny had been working for Mrs Moorhead for some years and she meant what she said. The wool and the designs were sent to her, and it gave her the opportunity to work, not only on interesting patterns, but also with the most wonderful wools, the colours and textures of which far surpassed anything she could ever afford. She was forever pointing this out to anyone who might listen, usually Stephen, who was the only one happy to help her wind the skeins into more manageable balls.

Jenny finished wrapping the parcel and glanced at the kitchen clock. 'Good, if I hurry I'll be just in time to catch the post. Ali, love, would you mind starting on those potatoes, or lunch'll be late again and with your gran in such a funny mood ...'

'I'll take the parcel. I could do with some air and I'm a faster walker than you.'

Jenny counted out some change and, encouraged by the pleasant half-hour they had spent together, took the risk of asking her moody daughter if she was planning to go out with her friends that evening, it being Saturday.

'What with?' Alison snapped. 'I can't spend the whole evening sponging off them.'

'Well, now the jumper's finished, love, I'll soon have some cash. Mrs Moorhead's always so good with her payments. I could let you have a little.'

Alison, looking at her mother's tired face, softened. 'Thanks, Mum. I don't know what my plans are yet, but if I do go out I might borrow a bit. I wish Gran wasn't in such a mood. Normally I'd ask her. Hey, I'd better dash if I'm going to get to the shop in time.'

Jenny moved to the sink to watch, through the kitchen window, the slight figure of Alison in tight-fitting jeans and sun top, her hair scraped into a bobbing pony tail, as she walked quickly across the yard and out of sight along the track to the road, the parcel under her arm.

'Poor Ali,' said Jenny softly to herself. 'It's not easy for her. Not for any of us,' she added gloomily, looking down into the sink at the muddy water with scum and little bits of debris floating on the surface. Stephen had dug the potatoes earlier. He was very proud of the crop he grew for her and Jenny hadn't the heart to tell him she'd rather buy them ready-washed from the supermarket. She hated scraping potatoes; she would rather have gone to the post office and had a quick chat with her mate, Rita, who as village post-mistress was a good source of all village gossip. But Alison was right. Jenny had never learned to drive so she would have had to walk, and being overweight and slow she would probably have missed the post. The sweater was already overdue and she had been anxious to see it off by the weekend.

'You would think,' she thought crossly, 'that not driving and having to walk everywhere would give me enough bonus points to eat a Mars a day, or at least guarantee I lose an extra pound a week.'

Encouraged by Rita, Jenny had secretly been going to Weight Watchers. It had not been an unmitigated success. She had hoped the family would notice the pounds falling off her, but they hadn't noticed anything, and truthfully, the pounds hadn't fallen off that easily. Rita had given her the enrolment fee as a birthday present. Only she knew of Jenny's secret dreams concerning the local vet.

Jeff Babbington had been Jim Tucker's oldest friend; he had been best man at his wedding to Jenny, and was godfather to Alison. Jenny had gone unexpectedly into labour at a time when Jeff was on the farm, helping a temperamental cow give birth to twin calves. He had then helped in the delivery of Jenny's baby, Alison. His wife had died of cancer some thirteen years ago, and with no children to worry about him, he led a comfortable bachelor life, which he appeared to be in no hurry to alter. Jenny knew he was fond of her, and he spent a lot of time in the Marsh farm kitchen, very much part of their family.

She had fancied Jeff Babbington for a long time, as Rita knew. 'But he doesn't see me as a woman, Rita, not as, you know, any-thing he might fancy. Plump and comfortable, that's me.'

Once the first flush of lust had given way to childbirth and routine, sex was not the first thing that Jenny missed when Jim died. There had been times over the last ten years when she had been physically disturbed by strange feelings: tinglings in her groin, strong desires to fondle her breasts and rub her hand over her belly and touch herself in places that she was so ashamed to mention she had no name for them. But she tended to dismiss these feelings as hormones, time of the month, or menopausal. However, as she confided to Rita, 'It seems a shame that I might live another forty years and never, you know, have IT ever again.' Ruefully, she had added, 'But Rita, I'd die of embarrassment if I ever took my clothes off ... all that flab!'

So the drive to lose weight had an added urgency. But at least, she consoled herself, he had seen her naked, when she was at her most vulnerable. Not that he ever referred to that occasion without laughing and making jokes about those two stupid calves.

Jenny sighed and plunged her hands into the muddy spume. Perhaps she should give up potatoes.

Alison walked rapidly down the track towards the road. It was a warm day. The sun was high in the sky. The track was dusty, the hedgerow was dusty, the fields were brown, and the trees were dressed in a dull green crepe, uniform and lustreless, the vibrant colours of early summer long gone. The horse chestnuts were showing signs of an autumnal shift, and ripening blackberries had appeared, as if overnight, on the straggling bramble bushes.

'God, this summer's gone quickly!' Alison reflected. 'I can't believe Gran isn't out here after those berries for her cordial. Maybe I'll pick some for her this afternoon and find out what's bugging her.'

As she walked, her thoughts drifted from her grandmother's bad mood to the conversation she'd had with Hannah on the phone that morning.

Alison had been keen to find out from Hannah what she knew of the biker who had joined their group on Thursday evening. There had been too many in the group for Alison to exchange more than a couple of words with him, but she was interested and wanted to know more.

Hannah's boyfriend, Nick, worked part time in a motorbike shop in Summerbridge and Hannah told Alison that the boy, whom they knew as Al, had bought bits for his bike there. He had an old reconditioned BMW that Nick particularly admired, so the two had fallen into conversation; Nick liked him, and had invited him to join them that evening. That was all Hannah knew about him. Then it was her turn to be curious.

'Why the interest, Ali? Don't tell me you fancy him. Didn't think you liked bikers. Wouldn't it be fantastic if you and he became an item? We could go off on the bikes somewhere and I could tell my mum I was going out with you, and it'd be the truth. Brilliant! She gives me such stick if she thinks I've been on Nick's bike. Shall I tell Nick to get him to join us? Are you coming out tonight, by the way? He did seem cool. A bit posh for a biker, maybe, but I could see you and him together . . .'

Alison laughed. 'I only wanted to know who he was, Hannah. Yeah, I thought he seemed pretty cool. But that's as far as it goes.' But just the possibility of seeing him again excited her and had put her in the good mood that had taken her down to the kitchen to chat to her mother.

Hannah's rosy vision was easier thought of than done, though, Alison reasoned. From what she had told Alison, Nick had no idea where he lived, or how he was to be contacted. *If* – and it was a big if – he came into the shop when Nick was working there, then Hannah would make sure that Nick invited him. And *if* that happened, it could be excruciating, with both Hannah and Nick watching their every move. That was supposing he did fancy her, and if he didn't come, or didn't make any move towards her, then how would she feel?

'Oh bugger it! Bugger, bugger, bug—' She broke off in amazement and stood for a moment, staring, not able to believe what she saw in front of her.

Outside the village post office was a distinctive, rather battered motorbike.

As she stood there staring, trying to unscramble her brain, the boy about whom she had been fantasising, walked out of the shop unwrapping a packet of cigarettes.

For a moment he looked as startled as she felt, then smiled and walked up to her.

'Hi. This is a surprise. Didn't expect to see you here. Alison, isn't it?'

Her brain desperately trying to instruct her to behave in one way and her body determined to act in another, Alison smiled at him, trying to appear cool and unconcerned, hoping he'd put the redness of her cheeks down to the warmth of the day. 'Oh, hi,' she laughed. (God, how stupid her laugh sounded! Don't laugh, don't simper, he'll think you're a moron ...) 'Yes, I'm Ali; and you're Al, aren't you? A friend of Nick's, mad on bikes.' (Talk about stating the obvious. Now he'll be convinced you're a moron. Got to do better than this or he'll be off in a flash.) 'I noticed it last night. A nineteen sixty-five BMW, isn't it?'

If he thought she was a moron, he didn't let it show. 'Yep, my pride and joy. I bought it last year. It was a real wreck, but I've been rebuilding it. D'yer know about bikes, then?'

'Me? No, not really. Why?'

'Well, not many girls I know would know either the make or the year, or be interested.'

Alison, having spent the greater part of her childhood listening to Charlie enthuse about bikes of every description, tried to look interested. 'My brother's keen. He was always tinkering with an old BMW when I was little – he's older than me – and he used to give me the odd ride.' The last time, when she was eight, had been the last one *ever* as far as she was concerned, for careering round an impromptu obstacle course he'd created in the farmyard, the bike had hit a rusty piece of concealed machinery and she had sailed over his head to land in the muddy remains of the duck pond.

Al unwrapped his cigarettes and offered her one. Regretfully she shook her head – she'd tried smoking and hated it, but it would have been so cool to take one ... to have him bend over her and light it. He was quite a bit taller than her, lean rather than thin, with a longish, pointed nose, short dark spiky hair and an earring in one ear. She liked that. She watched him light his cigarette. He was not exactly good-looking, but he had strong features and she liked what she saw.

He exhaled some smoke and looked at her curiously. 'So what are you doing here? You're the last person I expected to bump into. I thought you lived in Summerbridge.'

'I could ask you the same question. As a matter of fact, I live near here, but my mates are all in Summerbridge, so that's where I tend to hang out. So what are *you* doing here?'

'Just passing. I was testing the bike and needed some fags. Luckily the shop was still open.'

An alarm went off in Alison's brain. She wheeled round in time to see the blue blind in the shop door, with its 'closed' sign, firmly pulled down. Simultaneously, the post office van pulled out from the side of the shop and sped off.

'Oh no! Oh shit!'

'What's the matter?'

'I've gone and missed the post, that's what. Bloody hell, and I knew I didn't have much time. Shit, shit, shit!'

'Can't it wait till Monday?'

Alison was really fed up and all self-consciousness evaporated. 'No, it can't. Or rather it shouldn't. It's late enough already and I said I'd post it. Bumping into you put it right out of my mind. How bloody stupid! Oh bugger!'

'Is there somewhere else still open?'

'Not round here. I'd have to take it to the main post office, in Summerbridge.'

'Well, let's do that, then.'

'What?'

'I'll give you a lift on my bike. Can you borrow a helmet from your brother?'

Her vow never to have anything more to do with bikes forgotten, Alison's excitement at his offer was immediately tempered by the thought of what he might make of Marsh Farm, and worse still, that they might run into either one of her brothers. For a moment she stood, an indecisive bundle of conflicting emotion. Then inspiration struck.

'Wait here, that is if you really don't mind. Here, hold my parcel. I'll be right back. It would take too long to get to mine. I've got a better idea.' And she tore off down the road, leaving Al gazing after her.

By the time she returned, he had stubbed out the cigarette and was sitting astride his bike. Alison, somewhat apologetically, showed him the helmet she'd borrowed. It was pale blue, covered with silver stars and on the back, a huge, decorative pair of black-lashed, lustrous eyes.

Al gave a crack of laughter. 'That'll set BMW fans goggling. Jump on. Wedge your parcel between us – I haven't got any panniers – and hold on tight. You know to lean with me, don't you, but not too much or we'll be over, and keep your knees tucked in.'

With a kick and a roar they were off, and Alison, her arms round Al's waist, was the most excited she could ever remember being. Fleetingly, she thought of her mother expecting her back for lunch, and of the anxiety her non-appearance might engender; but, she thought, she would only be late, at the outside, by an hour; the flak would be worth it and anyway, the parcel had to be posted, didn't it?

In the event it was nearly two hours later that Al dropped her off outside the village shop.

The spin through the leafy back lanes to Summerbridge was all too quick and she got there in plenty of time to post the parcel. But then he had persuaded her to go and have coffee with him in a little Italian café that she didn't know existed. Alison's family didn't drink coffee and her experience of this particular beverage had never extended beyond instant, which she endured with a shudder when she couldn't get tea. But having turned down the cigarette, she wasn't going to jeopardise the opportunity of prolonging this adventure by being so wet she wasn't prepared to drink coffee, or because she had to be home for her dinner.

The café, at the end of a little pedestrian street, was buzzing, but they managed to grab a table that had just been vacated on the pavement outside.

'What'd you like? Cappuccino?'

She hesitated for only a second and then said, as nonchalantly as if she'd been drinking cappuccinos all her life, 'Yeah, great. That'd be nice. Thanks.'

The coffee he bought her was like nothing she had ever tasted.

Almost intoxicated, she drank this dark, slightly bitter brew through a layer of creamy foam, her tastebuds fooled into thinking sweetness by a thick sprinkling of chocolate.

The conversation was hesitant and somewhat awkward to begin with, the usual boy-meets-girl opener; it was a ritual, she observed, that seemed to be the tedious prerequisite of any new relationship.

'How old are you?'

'I'm seventeen, eighteen in October. And you?'

'Nineteen ... so you go to college in Summerbridge?'

'Yes, I'm going into my second year. You?'

'I'm at uni. At Durham, reading Zoology, also going into my second year. What A-levels are you doing?'

'Biology, maths and science. I want to go on to Bristol and study veterinary science.'

'That's ambitious. Do you want to become a vet?'

'Yep. Why not? Or are you like my brothers and think girls should only aspire to be nurses – animal or human, doesn't matter which?'

That acerbic reply made him laugh and the awkwardness eased. He bought her another coffee and neither noticed the time slipping by, so absorbed were they by their conversation and each other. In repose his face was stern and his dark eyes glittered. The black T-shirt and biker's leathers he wore reinforced this slightly forbidding image. But when he relaxed and laughed, his eyes crinkled and softened, and when he talked, his features became animated.

He told Alison that his first love was his BMW; she made him laugh with a description of her experiences on the back of Charlie's bike. They talked with great animation about their respective tastes in music, and she learned that he was into heavy metal, though that didn't prevent him from liking other music as well. They swapped favourite authors and favourite films and favourite actors ...

When Alison realised that a considerable period of time had elapsed since she had set out to post the parcel, her bravado suddenly deserted her and she leapt to her feet – a little like Cinderella rushing from the ball, she thought later – and told Al she had to get back, right away. He made no attempt to keep her any longer and gave her a lift back to Summerstoke. At her insistence, he dropped her off outside the village shop.

As casually as she could, climbing off the bike, she asked if he was going into Summerbridge that night.

He hesitated then answered, ruefully, 'No. I can't. I've got to work this evening. Are you?'

Alison was desperately disappointed, but did her level best to hide the fact and replied lightly, 'No. I'd no plans to.'

There was a slight, uncomfortable pause, then, stuttering her thanks once again, she started to undo her helmet.

He suddenly grinned. 'Those stars suit you. Pity about the jeepers-creepers on the back. Think you can borrow it again to-morrow?' Alison gaped at him. 'We could go for a proper spin; if you'd like to, that is. I could pick you up about two, if you're free?'

'Two would be fine.' She tried not to sound too enthusiastic. 'I'm sure I can borrow the helmet again – that's if you don't think it upsets the BMW's image too much.'

'Oh, I think we're big enough to take it. Where shall I pick you up?'

'Here. That would be great. Thanks, Al.' And she turned and ran down the street. Al watched her until she stopped at the end of the village, by the bridge, and hurried up the path of a shabby cottage garden. Then, with the engine chugging noisily, he turned the bike and headed off in the opposite direction.

'She'd been gone for two hours. Two hours! I don't have to tell you how upset her mother was. Jenny's always had a vivid imagination, too much for her own good, if you ask me, so that by the time young Alison finally turned up, the foolish woman had lived through her daughter's abduction, murder, inquest and funeral. When she walked through the door, Jenny was one step away from expiring herself. Silly woman! Never had any control over those children. If it had been me, I'd have put Alison over my knee and given her a sound spanking.'

'Can't do that these days, Elsie, love. They'd do you for assault.' Ronald was an old friend of Elsie's and very used to these long diatribes against her family.

'That's half the problem: too much interference from the Nanny State. 'Spare the rod and spoil the child' – that's what I've always said and now Jenny is reaping the consequences. Soft she is; I've always said so. Soft! Pah!'

Elsie almost spat with disgust. Ron patted her hand. 'Don't upset yourself, love. You've done what you can. Here, have a drop more of this Muscat.' He topped up the slender wine glass by her side. He and Elsie always ate cake and drank dessert wine on Saturday afternoons. They took it in turns to provide the cake or wine, and part of the pleasure was the challenge to find something different each time.

'I must say, this is jolly nice.' He topped up his own glass. 'You found a good 'un here, Elsie.' He sipped it appreciatively and Elsie watched him with pleasure. He might be eighty, bald and rather stout, but he always twinkled at her, was immensely patient and had a fine palate. She did enjoy his company. He patted her hand again. 'So, did Alison say where she'd been?'

Elsie snorted. 'Oh, some garbled tale about meeting a friend and missing the post, so she went to Summerbridge, to the post office there.'

'Why didn't she phone Jenny? You gave her one of those mobile things for her birthday, didn't you?'

Elsie snorted again. 'Waste of money that was. Hardly ever uses it. Says she can't afford the top-up cards, whatever that means. The more they have these days, the more they want and they're no happier for it, nor do they behave any better.'

'Another slice of Panettone Limone?' Ronald knew of old that Elsie, out of sorts with her family, if not discouraged, would go on to find fault with every one of them, and the world in general, before grumbling herself back into good humour.

'That would be very nice, Ronald, thank you. Those Italians

certainly know a thing or two about cakes.' She bit into the large slice and a spurt of lemon syrup trickled down her chin.

'So, have you decided what to do about your Charlie? He must be on tenterhooks, you not having said anything.'

'I've hardly seen the chump!' said Elsie with satisfaction, dabbing at her sticky chin with a tissue. 'He's doing a very successful job of avoiding me, but I've been in no hurry. It's Sunday tomorrow. He won't miss Sunday lunch. They none of them do, no matter how inedible it is. Good time for family business and I shall give them a piece of my mind, Stephen as well as Charlie. And as for Alison ... What does she think she's doing? It's time they bucked their ideas up. They can't carry on like this, and they can't expect me to bail them out by dying conveniently and leaving them all my money to squander and fritter away.'

Putting her plate down and swiftly finishing off the rest of her wine, she pulled back the bedclothes and climbed stiffly out of the bed. 'Ooh, my old limbs are getting stiff!' She stretched out her skinny arms as far as she was able, her thin, sagging body, corrugated with age. Ronald looked on admiringly from the bed.

'You're still a fine figure of a woman, Elsie.'

She looked at him with some asperity and reached for her silk underwear.

'You must be getting short-sighted, Ron. I'm a wrinkled old crone, a sour old woman, a bad-tempered old bag, and many other things besides!' Then she softened. 'But Ronald dear, you always make me feel like a fine figure of a woman.'

6

Charlie drove his battered van slowly down the farm track, whistling softly to himself. The night was warm, the sky full of stars, and for the first time in days he felt really cheerful. His appearance in court, like a bad dream, was beginning to recede, and apart from the fine, which would be a struggle to pay, there seemed to be no further fallout from it. Much to his relief, it did not seem as if his grandmother had said anything about it to the rest of the family, nor had she made any attempt to give him an earful. Admittedly, he had gone out of his way to avoid her, but he did not underestimate her determination and knew that if she had wanted to pin him down before now, she would have done. He briefly toyed with skipping lunch the following day, but Sunday dinner was an occasion that his mother had always insisted none of them should ever miss, even at harvest time, unless they were ill, and he could think of no other excuse strong enough.

He and Lenny had worked until nearly dark. Lenny had not hung around for his customary pint as he was babysitting; Paula was working for the Lesters that evening. Charlie had had two dates lined up. He grinned in the dark. He'd managed the evening all right, he thought, and the prospects were looking good.

His current girlfriend, Sarah, was a pretty blonde girl in her late twenties who he'd been attracted to because she was not only sexy, but also full of high spirits and lots of fun. They had been going out for three months, almost a record for Charlie, but, as he'd described to Lenny, she'd become more serious, possessive even, and for Charlie, that was a death knell. 'It's always the way with birds,' he thought, as the van, like a boat in a choppy sea, lurched from pothole to pothole along the track. 'Soon as they get a partner, they want to tie the knot. I like being free, I like having fun … why should I want to get married and change all that?' Sarah had recently started dropping hints, lingering outside jewellers' windows, and making him spend more time with their married friends; Charlie was more than ready to cut loose. There was part of him that was regretful. He'd had a really good time with Sarah, but he was ready to move on and meeting Beth had helped that decision.

Beth had recently come to work at The Bunch of Grapes, and from the first, Charlie had been attracted. She was, he thought, the model of an ideal barmaid: about twenty-five, of medium height, shoulder-length blonde hair, great, dancing blue eyes and, best of all, large shapely breasts and a tiny waist. From the moment she started work she was a hit with all the customers and from the way she chatted, joked and flirted with them all, Charlie had no expectations that she might view him any differently. But then, yesterday evening, he and Lenny had gone to the pub for a few pints after work.

The pub was crowded and Charlie, pushing his way through to be served, caught sight of Linda in the lounge bar looking, unusually for her, rather out of sorts. In the public bar, however, where Beth and Stan were serving, the atmosphere was lively with plenty of good-humoured back-chat between themselves and the drinkers. Beth served Charlie, and counting out his money, he made a play at persuading her to make a date. Beth was, Charlie could have sworn, about to refuse, when Linda appeared behind her and asked her, rather coldly, Charlie observed, to go and bring up some bottles of juice from the cellar.

'Okay, Linda, I'll just sort Charlie out with his change. Oh, and Charlie – I'd love to. That is, if Linda doesn't mind me dating a customer!'

Linda flushed and smiled at Charlie, relaxing a little. 'Don't be daft – why should I mind? Hello, Charlie. Your gran shown her hand, yet?'

Charlie grinned. 'No and I don't think she's going to now, fingers crossed.'

Beth was working Saturday night, but as he had already promised to take Sarah to the cinema that evening, Charlie arranged to pick her up at closing time and take her, at her suggestion, clubbing.

The evening had worked like a dream. True, Sarah was very put out when Charlie dropped her back home immediately after the film had ended, but she couldn't deny that he had been yawning all the way through the film and needed to get some sleep, as he had to be out early to cut barley the following morning. He had resisted her attempts to tie him down to their next date, saying he would phone her, and closed his eyes to the look of misery that had settled on her face when he left.

He made it to The Grapes just in time for last orders. It was Stan's turn to be in a sour mood this evening, and he was barely civil to Charlie when he served him his pint, but Charlie, his head full of the prospect of having Beth to himself for the next few hours and wondering if he would make it with her that night, was unconcerned.

The clubbing scene was one that Charlie was not used to. He was amazed at the youthfulness of the average clubber; he disliked the intense heat, the volume of the music, and the crowds of giggling, drunken clubbers four deep at the bars, queuing for the toilets and occupying every available table in every nook and cranny in the subterranean premises. He'd hoped that, in semi-darkness, he and Beth would snog the night away. No such luck. There was no room for snogging couples on the crowded dance floor and Beth resisted sitting out on the black leather couches for more than one number. Charlie was also aware of being stared at, which made him uncomfortable. A drunken youth shouted out something that made a couple of girls turn, stare, and then start giggling.

'What are they staring at?' he asked Beth, plaintively. 'What did he say?'

She looked amused. 'He called you Fred West.'

Charlie threw back his head and laughed. 'Why on earth should he call me that? Do I look like a mass murderer?' He was wearing a white cotton shirt tucked into a pair of jeans, with the sleeves rolled up above his elbows. With his clear, tanned skin, even, white teeth, strong chin and long, muscular body, Beth readily conceded that he did not, but she said, pointedly, 'It's probably your whiskers, Charlie. They're real mutton chops, aren't they?'

Charlie fingered them with pride. 'Yep, but I don't see as they are anything to laugh at.'

'But they make you look like Fred West – or worse, the Wurzels,' came the reply. And thereafter, when he had tried to kiss her, she had complained about his whiskers tickling her.

In spite of all that, they'd had a good time. Beth was an energetic dancer and in a short fitted red dress, shaking her bosom and her bum every which way to the rhythm of the music, she attracted a lot of admiring glances. In the end, however, Charlie was caught out by a genuine, not-to-be-ignored fatigue. The time it had taken to get to Bath, his long day in the field, the oppressive heat and the general crush in the clubs finally led to huge, irresistible yawns, and at three o'clock in the morning he had driven Beth back to her home and accepted, without much fuss, her refusal to allow him to share her bed.

But it was a promising start, he said to himself, as he drove into the farmyard. She was not going to make it easy for him, and he liked that. But she had promised that she would go out with him on her next day off, although she was not sure when that would be.

Charlie let himself into the kitchen. A faint moonbeam was shining through the kitchen window, its shaft dimly illuminating the dead cactus and the dying Busy Lizzie on the window sill, touching the edge of the sink, the back of a chair; the silvery, grey pathway losing itself in shadows across the kitchen table. The silence of the room was interrupted only by the busy tick of the electric clock and the rumbling snores from Gip, in her basket, who knew her master and so did not wake from a well-earned sleep, even when he snapped on the electric light.

'I won't take her clubbing though, that's for certain,' Charlie thought, rummaging in the bread bin for a couple of slices. 'Blimey, it cost a bomb, and for what? Jigging around to rotten music and drinking fizzy water.' He found some margarine and a pot of strawberry jam and made himself a sandwich, collected a bottle of beer, and took his snack up to his bedroom.

He didn't bother to put his light on, but stepped over the piles of clothes, boots, CDs, motorbike brochures and motocross magazines, his old guitar, and the odd beer bottle that formed a permanent obstacle course between his door and his bed, and lay on his duvet fully clothed, munching his sandwich in the dark. His last thought, before he fell into a deep sleep, was of Sarah. He'd have to give her the old heave-ho. A pity – he liked her and he hated the thought of giving pain to anyone he liked. Beth wouldn't expect him to go down on one knee, he was pretty sure of that. She'd be fun, without strings.

'Bloomin' 'eck, what's this doin' 'ere?' A bleary-eyed Lenny, in crumpled T-shirt and pyjama bottoms liberally decorated with the unshaven yellow features of his favourite cartoon character, stared with astonishment at the huge black eyes staring up at him from the chair on which he'd just been about to sit. He held up the pale blue crash helmet. 'Paula? You bin goin' out with someone I don't know about?'

'Don't be daft,' said Paula amiably, patting into place the back-combed tower of hair that was teetering off-centre through lack of attention. 'Alison borrowed it off me yesterday and wants it again this afternoon, so it didn't get put away. Here's yer break-fast.' She placed a large plate of fried eggs, bacon, sausage and beans in front of him, poured out two mugs of tea and joined him at the wobbly, Formica-covered kitchen table Lenny had rescued from a rubbish skip. She lit a cigarette, glancing, as she did so, out of the open door at her children charging around the long, untidy garden, which was littered with a myriad of bright plastic toys.

'I don't know how they keeps on goin' like that in this heat. I reckon it's hotter today than it was yesterday. Will you fill the paddlin' pool up for 'em, later?'

'I filled it yesterday – what do they do, drink it?'

'Wouldn't be surprised.' She chuckled and puffed at her cigarette. 'They sit on the edge and let the water run out. The way they're goin', there's gonna be no grass left by the end of the summer.'

''Taint much of a lawn, anyway. Fact the whole garden's bit of a tip. We oughta grow some vegetables—'

'You say that every year! You'd never eat 'em and nor would the kiddies.'

'S'pose you're right.' Lenny folded a slice of bread and dipped it into the egg. He looked at her fondly. She was still a bit of all right. She might not have had time to do her hair, but her foundation was on, her eyelashes liberally mascara'd and her mouth was a generous crimson bow. The little pink boob tube and brief denim skirt left nothing to Lenny's imagination and he felt a faint stirring in the depths of his pyjamas, but looking at her more closely, he could see traces of natural shadow under her eyes. 'You came back late last night. I don't remember yer comin' to bed.'

'That's 'cause you was snorin' like a pig. I'd tried to wake yer, 'cos I wanted to pass on Mister Lester's message before I forgot again. Give me some stick, he did, for not doin' it before. Bloody cheek!' Paula snorted and took a consoling drag.

Lenny, about to bite into his sausage, which he had smeared with a large blob of tomato sauce, looked up, interested, the sausage suspended halfway into his mouth. 'Message, for me, from old man Lester? What's he want with me?'

'I dunno. Just said for to tell you to give him a ring. Something about work, he said. He told me Friday, but you was out with Charlie till all hours and I forgot.' She gloomily inspected her fingernails. 'My nails are in a terrible state. It's all that bloomin' washin' up. She won't let me put her poncey stuff in the dishwasher, case it breaks. Don't matter about my nails breakin'!'

'Why don't ya sue her?'

Paula ignored his suggestion and carried on, enjoying her grumble. 'God, did that dinner party go on and on – what on earth do they find to talk about? That's what I'd like to know. And *she* wanted me to stay and serve coffee. Then, just as I'm finishin', absolutely knackered, in *he* comes, not a word of thanks but starts moanin' 'cos he hadn't heard from you.'

'And he didn't say what for?'

'No, I told you, just said he had some work for you and you was to ring him. Mind you, I wouldn't wanna work for him, he's 'orrible. Not as bad as her, though. I hate her; she's such a sarky old cow. If we didn't need the money, I'd tell them where they could stuff their job. You finished?'

'Yes thanks, love. I could do with another cuppa, though. Can I nick one of your fags? I'm clean out.'

'You're always saying you don't like menthol, but it don't stop you bumming my ciggies.'

'Needs must. I wonder what old Hughie wants, then. He's never asked for me before. Didn't think he knew I existed.'

'He's probably heard how good you are.' Paula looked at Lenny proudly. She was ten years younger than he was and though he was a couple of inches shorter than she was, with a broken nose and missing two front teeth from a motocross accident, she adored him as much as she had when, as a fifteen-year-old, he had taken her out on her very first date. 'What you don't know about engines ...'

Lenny yawned. 'Yeah, well ... me and Charlie's got a lot on at the moment.'

'This'll be paid work, Lenny.' There was a slight edge to Paula's voice as she put a fresh mug of tea in front of him.

'Yeah, yeah. I'll give him a ring and see what's what.'

'Don't you forget.'

'Like you, you mean. No, don't worry, I won't. I'll do it this afternoon.'

*

But, of course, he did not. He met Charlie, as planned, for an afternoon at a local motocross rally. They were not racing; their bike was still missing an essential part, so they had planned to spend the afternoon sizing up the opposition for the next big rally, cracking a few cans with other bikers, and exchanging news and views.

It was an ideal afternoon for a meeting. The sun was hot, the sky forget-me-not blue; the red dirt, churned up by the twisting, snarling bikes, hung in the air before slowly drifting across to dust bush, grass, tree and punter alike. Knots of bikers and their families picnicked on the grass around their vans, or in the shade of the hedgerow at the edge of the field. In the still air, the smell of hot dogs and burgers mingled with fumes from a hundred exhausts; the relentless, hysterical commentary crackling from the loudspeakers was drowned only by the ear-splitting cacophony of the engines when the bikes, as one, tore out of the starting gates and threw themselves, spluttering and screaming, over the hillocks, round precipitous bends, up through the woods, then down the final straight to the flag and the cheering crowd.

It was not a big meeting, and most of the participants were known to Charlie and Lenny. It should have been a good afternoon, but Charlie was not in the mood. Lenny realised that soon after they had met up. The twinkle had gone from his eyes and they were dark and dull; his countenance, usually open and cheerful, was unsmiling and shut. Normally garrulous and sociable, Charlie said hardly a word, acknowledged soulmates with barely a grunt, made no attempt to flirt with any of the girls who greeted his presence with encouraging smiles and waves, accepted a beer without enthusiasm, and watched the sport with no sign of pleasure. Finally Lenny, not given to expecting or encouraging personal confidences, was driven to ask Charlie what was bugging him.

'Only you've been a right old misery since we got here, Charlie, and it ain't like you. If you wanna go, just say the word. You can take the van and I'll get a lift back with Pete or someone.'

Charlie groaned. 'Sorry, mate. I shouldn't have come. I should have stayed behind and murdered the old bat. Put us all out of our misery.'

'Elsie? What's she been up to?'

'She's issued an ultimatum,' said Charlie heavily. 'We had the works this lunchtime. She produced a newspaper with ... with a picture of me on the front page. Where the hell did they get that from, eh? Some clever dick Flash Harry with nothing better to do than go round taking photographs without asking.'

'What was it of?'

'Me. On that bear.'

'Gawd!'

'Yep. You should've seen the smirk on Gran's face when she showed it. Pretending she was so shocked; she was enjoying every moment, the old bitch.'

Lenny, who had been present when Charlie had mounted the bear in question, did his best not to smirk and looked sympathetic. 'What did the family say?'

'As I predicted – Mum was upset but glad I hadn't hurt myself; Ali made some clever-clever not-very-funny remark; Steve bitched about the fine and then sniggered over the photograph ...'

But Stephen hadn't sniggered for long. Elsie was ready for a fight, and she was going to take them all on.

'I've been thinking about what that magistrate said: "It's time you grew up, Mr Tucker." He was right. It is time. What do you think you were playing at, eh? Climbing on a bear – a grown man! Kids' games! And it applies to you, too, Stephen. Look at you both. Into your thirties and no sign of wife or kiddies. Where's the next generation of Tuckers coming from to run this farm – the farm that my money and your grandfather's hard work secured for you? And is it in profit? Is it flourishing? No, it's not. And why not?' She glared at them, challenging them. All averted their gaze, unable to answer her, or too circumspect to want to.

The Tuckers were sitting round the kitchen table, where all their meals were taken, for Sunday lunch. Elsie, at the head, sat in a large old wooden carver that had been part of the kitchen since time immemorial; the others, either side of her, occupied a motley collection of chairs of various ages and different degrees of instability. They always sat in the same places, on the same chairs: Jenny and Alison sat on Elsie's left, their backs to the window and closest to the sink and the stove, Charlie and Stephen on her right. Jenny had just cleared away the remnants of a shoulder of lamb (traditionally re-served the following day, bulked out with baked beans – her version of shepherd's pie. Stephen loved it; the rest of the family didn't) and had just placed a large dish of apple crumble on the table when Elsie launched her attack. She had served out the crumble, but overcome with the evidence of Charlie's humiliation, had lost all appetite for pudding and sat there, staring at Elsie, wishing, not for the first time in her life, that something would remove her mother-in-law – painlessly of course – from their lives, once and for all.

Elsie slammed the newspaper down on the table and continued her harangue.

'Because you none of you take this farm seriously, that's what. You've had your living handed to you on a plate and unless you start working for it, you'll lose it; working hard, mind, not this faffing around: a bit here, a bit there, then off to motocross or amateur dramatics!'

Unwisely, Jenny attempted to defend her boys. 'But they've got to have some fun.'

With contempt, Elsie cut her off. 'Why? Until they've earned it, they're having fun at the expense of the farm. You've brought them up soft, Jenny; they don't know the meaning of graft.'

Stephen, who got up every morning at five to see to his cows, thought this was a bit rich and started to protest.

Elsie took no notice. 'No, Stephen, I mean what I say: you don't understand hard work, commitment, teamwork. Your grandfather and I worked as a team; we put this farm on its feet and made it profitable. Our milk and cream, my butter and cheese, were the best in the county. The prizes we won, the reputation we had! Where's it all gone, eh?'

Stephen went red in the face and blurted out, 'That's not fair,

Gran. Our milk—' But he got no further; Elsie interrupted him with a shake of her head. 'You think you work hard, Stephen, but why was that batch of milk rejected? Has it happened before? I never thought the day would come when Marsh Farm milk would not be thought good enough ... and have you wondered,' she glared round at them all, 'why Hugh Lester is making such derisory offers for our farm, eh?'

'Because he's the type who will always try and get something for nothing, that's why,' Charlie growled resentfully. 'He's an unscrupulous, land-grabbing toad who respects nothing and no-body.'

'That's as maybe. But if he looks round this farm and sees what I see – decay and dereliction everywhere, then I'm not surprised he sets so little value on it. He'll be back, you can be sure of that. I hope I'm not alive the day you're forced to sell to the likes of him, and if I've got anything to do with it, that day will never come. I've not interfered; I've given you your chances, like I gave Jenny and your dad theirs, but it's got to a point when I can't sit back any longer and watch my hard work, and your grandfather's, go to the wall.'

'So what do you want us to do, Gran?' asked Alison, who was watching the clock with increasing agitation. She had arranged to meet Al at two and it was now nearly one thirty. Normally lunch would have been well over by one o'clock. Gran's unforeseen attack threatened disaster. She couldn't see how she could slip away inconspicuously, and if she didn't turn up at the appointed time, would Al wait?

'I'm going to give you an ultimatum. Do you know what an ultimatum is, Charlie?' she said sharply to her grandson, who sat sulkily toying with his plate of apple crumble.

Resentful, he looked up. 'Yeah, it's a posh word for black-mail.'

His mother gave a slight moan. Experience had taught her that it was no use standing up to Elsie in this sort of mood.

'Don't be absurd, young man. If you do as I tell you then one day you'll thank me for it; if you don't, then you'll only have yourself to blame for the consequences.' She paused, allowing her words their full dramatic effect. Four pairs of eyes, two green, two brown, stared at her, waiting.

She drew in her breath and sat back in the wooden armchair looking at them all. 'I'm giving you,' she said, fixing her gaze on Charlie and Stephen, ' – one year. If at the end of that year you've not found yourselves wives, or turned the fortunes of the farm around in a very material way, you will forfeit your share of my estate. I'll change my will and cut you out.'

Charlie let out a shout of disbelief; Stephen's jaw dropped; Jenny put her head in her hands, moaning gently; and Alison, staring at her grandmother, gave a short laugh. 'You're joking, Gran?'

'Oh no, I'm not,' Elsie replied grimly. 'I was never more serious; and don't think you're getting away with it, Miss Alison. I'm disappointed in you – you're as rackety as Charlie here.'

'What?' Alison stared at her grandmother.

'Suffice it to say, I know all about your night-time excursions, my girl. You're meant to be studying this summer, working for good grades. The way you're carrying on, there's no way you'll get them.'

Jenny looked up, puzzled. 'But she's working really hard, Elsie – they all are. You're being too hard –'

'I've always said you were a fool, Jenny. You don't see what's going on under your nose. They're all doing exactly as they please and they'll reap the consequences. But it's not too late.'

'How am I gonna find someone to marry me?' Stephen blurted, agonised.

'I don't want a wife; no way!' Charlie shouted, getting to his feet. 'This is mad, Gran … you can't make us marry.'

'No, I can't, but I can offer a little incentive. If you find a wife, then your share of my estate is secure, and I shall make your share over to you on your wedding day; if you don't, then your share will be divided equally between Stephen and Alison, assuming that is, that Stephen and Alison also comply.'

'So what's your plan for me, Gran?' asked Alison sarcastically.

'I know in your day there were child brides, but I'm not eighteen yet. Are you expecting *me* to find a husband? What must *I* do to make sure I'm not cut out of your will?'

'So what did she say she wants Ali to do?'

Charlie and Lenny sat in the sunshine, leaning against Lenny's van, the noise of motorbikes roaring unheeded in the background, as they mulled over Charlie's predicament.

'She's got to get to university before she's twenty-one or she loses her share.'

Lenny whistled. 'Bloomin' 'eck, bit of a tall order, ain't it? The old lady's barkin'. So if you don't marry, what happens then?'

'She'll leave my share to Stephen and Ali; and if *they* don't jump to it and I do, then I get their share, and if none of us do, then she says she's gonna sell. She'd got it all worked out.' He surveyed the motocross crowds without enthusiasm, then turned to Lenny. 'I haven't got the heart for this today, Lenny. She's fucked me up good and proper.'

'Aw, come on, mate! Here, I'll get some beer.' Lenny jumped up and headed off in the direction of the beer tent, returning in a short space of time with a couple of cans. He urged one on his friend. 'Come on, get that down you. And cheer up, it's not that bad.'

'Oh yes it is,' replied Charlie grimly, chugging the beer. He ran his fingers through his hair and distractedly scratched the nape of his neck. 'Look, I've only told you this because you're my mate, but you've got to swear you won't tell anyone, not even Paula. I don't want anyone knowing until I've decided what to do. Swear?'

'Of course, I swear. I'll drink on it.' Lenny took a long swig of his beer, then, still trying to get his brain round Charlie's news, shook his head in disbelief. 'What's she *on*? You don't want to get married. These things don't just happen!'

'Tell me about it. I tell you, she's living in another century. She should be certified.'

'No chance of that?'

'On today's performance, she should be. But this is no joke; she's deadly serious. My life's never going to be the same again. Once word gets out, I'll be a laughing stock amongst my mates and as for any crumpet I do fancy, they'll run a mile.'

'Or get their claws into you when you don't want 'em to. I fancy your Sarah will be champin' at the bit.'

'Exactly,' said Charlie heavily, and they both relapsed into a gloomy silence and finished the beer.

'You could always marry someone,' ventured Lenny, cracking his can and tossing it in the direction of an overflowing rubbish bin, 'then divorce her after Elsie died.'

'Elsie will live for ever!' Charlie replied bitterly. 'Besides, divorce someone these days and they take you to the cleaners. I'd be no better off.'

'It's a pity you can't find someone like Paula.'

'Too right. You've got it made there, Lenny. C'mon, I'll get some more cans.'

'Look on the bright side, mate. You might meet someone you fancy, good and proper. You've never had no trouble pulling the birds, not like poor old Stevie. What's that poor bugger gonna do?'

7

Once Elsie had stalked out of the kitchen, cutting short all their protestations with, 'It's no use you all moaning and sulking. My mind's made up!' Alison had leapt to her feet, muttered a swift apology to her mother – who was in such a state of shock she hardly registered Alison's departure – grabbed her bag and ran out of the kitchen. The clock showed five to two. She had five minutes to go before she was late. In the yard she careered into Jeff Babbington.

'Steady there, young Alison – almost had me over. Where are you off to in such a hurry then, eh?'

Alison was fond of Jeff, but she was not going to be delayed by anything and, shouting over her shoulder, she rushed on. 'Sorry, Uncle Jeff, I'm meeting some friends and I'm late. Mum's in the kitchen. Tell her I'll make up for not doing the washing up later. Bye.'

Her thoughts raced. Damn, damn, bloody Gran! What a bombshell; and why choose today of all days? I'm never going to make it on time. Will he wait? He'd bloody better! I'll never forgive her if I miss him ... And what was all that about, all that stupid stuff? How's poor old Stephen going to find a wife? It's archaic! Where's she at? She's showing her age. Maybe she's going senile ... she didn't sound ga-ga, but how do y'know? Oh Al, please, please be there ... please wait.

At the farm gate she checked her watch. It was a good ten minutes' walk to the village shop from the house and even though she had run all the way up the track, it was now two o'clock. She could have cried with vexation. She was hot and dusty, and the last thing she wanted was to turn up looking eager and over-heated. She had spent ages in front of the mirror, peering at her face for signs of any blemish that might need covering up, then trying to decide what to wear with her jeans. Finally she had settled on a sleeveless blue T-shirt with a matching jacket. Hannah had given it to her ages ago, on the grounds that it didn't fit and the colour didn't suit her. The blue certainly suited Alison, but she wasn't sure about the jacket because it had a beaded hem – it was fussier than she normally liked, but as she needed something for the bike and she didn't have another jacket she would be seen dead in, it would have to do.

The whole evening before, and that morning, she had run and re-run the trip into Summerbridge in her mind: the coffee bar; what he'd said and hadn't said; how he looked; how he felt on the bike with her arms around his waist; how she felt; how she would look when they met up again; how she would play it cool and disinterested; how he would find her fascinating and mysterious; how the right moment would be found for their first kiss, and then, maybe, after that . . .

Never had the distance from the farm to the village seemed so long. Alison groaned out loud and slowed to a walking pace, trying to cool down. She was nearly at the bridge and once over that she would have a clear view of the high street and he would be able to see her coming. She could go and collect Paula's helmet after they'd met.

Her heart thudding, her mouth dry, she walked over the bridge, her eyes scouring the road in front of her. She stopped, overwhelmed with the disappointment. The street was empty. Of all the possible scenarios, it had never occurred to her that he might not turn up. She looked at her watch again; it showed nearly five past. She wasn't *that* late; surely he would've waited five minutes. And if he didn't, then he wasn't the sort of person she wanted to go out with anyway! He was probably late, too . . . probably had difficulties extracting himself, like she did. If she didn't walk too fast, then they would probably arrive at the shop at the same time. Probably.

Slowly she walked up the street, straining to catch the growl of a motorbike. A warm wind sent a plastic bag whispering across the road; a few golden brown leaves, discarded by a gigantic chestnut, drifted past; the open gate to the Spinks' garden creaked gently on its hinges and in the back garden she could hear the children shrieking with laughter; a dog barked; through an open window came the sound of a cricket commentary; a group of starlings shrieked and chattered, invisible in the heart of a holly tree; and overhead, in the blue, blue sky, she heard the faint disembodied rumble of a jet plane. But no motorbike. No sodding motorbike.

She reached the shop.

'Now what?' she said aloud, bitterly. 'How long am I supposed to wait? It's not fair! What have I done to deserve this?' She had really liked Al, and because her sense of anticipation had been so great, her disappointment was the greater. As she stood in the shade of the shop's porch, all recent injustices were summoned to compound her mood, Elsie's ultimatum included, and she started to rage.

'Bloody hell, why should I go to sodding university just because *she* wants me to? Charlie's right. It's blackmail. Well, it won't work with me. She can give my share to them. What would I want with the bloody farm? It's a stinking albatross, that's what it is, and she can stick it up her backside!'

So deep was she in her dark ruminations that she didn't hear the sound she so longed for until the motorbike was at a standstill. Startled, in a spiky, angry mood, she whirled round and confronted Al as he switched off the bike and removed his helmet.

'You're late!'

This was a different Alison from the girl Al had taken to Summerbridge the day before, the one with whom he thought he might have an idle fling before he had to go away. Her green eyes sparked at him and challenged him.

'Yes, I'm really sorry. I couldn't get away. Have you been waiting long?'

'Long enough. I thought you weren't coming and I'd wasted my time. I was about to go.'

'I'm glad you didn't.'

At that, Alison relented a little. He really was quite cool: long legs in black leather astride his machine, thin black baggy T-shirt, his skin tanned, hair spiky and dishevelled, eyes dark and glinting. But she wasn't going to be taken for granted and raised her eyebrows, unsmiling. 'Really?'

'Really.' He smiled back.

Jenny was sitting alone amid the debris of Sunday lunch when Jeff walked in. Sensitive to the suffering and distress of animals, he was more immune to the emotional needs of human beings. But as soon as he walked into the kitchen of Marsh Farm he sensed that all was not well. The kitchen table reminded him of the three bears returning to their bowls of porridge; only in this case, it was apple crumble – five bowls of it, only one of which had been eaten. The Tuckers never having had the wherewithal to buy a dishwasher, greasy crockery and cutlery were piled on the draining board, in the sink and on the food-spattered stove. Unwashed saucepans and baking dishes sat encrusted with residual traces of potato, boiled cabbage, carrots, gravy and flakes of meat.

Gip immediately sat up in her basket, her tail thumping enthusiastically, but Jenny didn't even raise her head and he had never, in his recollection, arrived at Marsh Farm without Jenny jumping up to offer him something to eat or drink, apart from that time when she was in labour with young Alison. Truth to tell, he found Jenny's cakes rather heavy going and avoided eating Tucker family meals, as far as he could, without giving Jenny offence. But he relished Jenny's attentions all the same, and the lack of them now alarmed him.

'Jenny, are you all right? Where is everybody? I met Alison in the yard just now, dashing off to meet some friends. Is something wrong? Shall I make us a cup of tea?'

The kindness in his voice touched Jenny and she dissolved into tears. In between sobs and hiccups and Jeff patting her hand and making her tea, she told him about Charlie's misadventures, the terrible mood Elsie had been in, Ali's unexplained absence the day before, which had made everything worse, all leading up to Elsie's ultimatum over lunch.

At first Jeff was too amazed to say anything, then ruffling his hair, he threw back his head and laughed and laughed.

Jenny stopped crying and stared at him peevishly. 'I don't see what there is to laugh at in all this, Jeff Babbington. Elsie has told the boys if they don't get married they don't get their share of the farm from her. Where are they going to find wives from, just like that? And if they do, what if they don't like me? What's going to happen to me? To all of us? Supposing Ali doesn't get into university and the boys don't find anyone? Elsie would get rid of the farm.'

Jeff wiped the tears of laughter from his eyes. 'Eh, but Elsie's got a sense of humour. Charlie to get a wife – that's a good one. Sounds like she's been reading too much romantic fiction. Don't worry, love, when she calms down she'll appreciate she can't order people's lives like that. You shouldn't let her get to you the way she does. Where are Stephen and Charlie, by the way? What did they think of Elsie's idea? I can't imagine Alison taking too well to it, either!'

'No,' she replied mournfully, 'but I don't think she was really listening. I could see she had one eye on the clock all the while, and as soon as Elsie left, she jumped up and shot off. She didn't even stay to do the washing up.'

'Perhaps she's got a date. She was in a tearing hurry – she said to say she was sorry about the washing up. Said she'd make it up to you later. But I'm surprised Stephen isn't here to give you a hand.'

'He had a rehearsal. He was furious though, I could tell, Jeff. It takes a lot to get him mad, but I could tell he was as angry with Charlie as with Elsie. It's not fair! *You* know how hard he works. Elsie just won't see that, because the farm isn't doing as well as she thinks it should. It doesn't make him a bad farmer, and Charlie does his bit. We all know it's a bad time for farmers and they've been unlucky—'

'Jenny, you know what I think of your two boys. Stephen's

80

a fine stockman. Given half a chance and a fair wind, he could make something of this farm. Charlie is certainly full of ideas, but he's not as steady. So maybe Elsie's right; maybe having a wife might calm him down; maybe he might become a bit more responsible. But I don't see as this is the right way to go about it. Maybe if instead of chasing after a wife he threw his energies into turning the farm around and bringing it out of the doldrums, Elsie would relent.'

'Yes, well, actually she did say something of the sort. But I think no one was listening to her by then; they were so cross and upset.'

'Well, there you are, then. The solution lies in their hands. It's a ruse to spur them on to do something instead of just drifting along. It's not that bad, love. Come on, drink up your tea.'

Jenny did as she was told, but sat there looking so dispirited, her hair spraying out of the plastic slide on the back of her head, a grubby, flowery pinafore over her short-sleeved white blouse and printed cotton skirt, that Jeff racked his brains for something that would restore her to a more cheerful state.

After dropping in on the Tuckers he had been planning to take himself off on a friendly visit to a rare breeds farm that had recently opened some miles away. He had occasionally gone out with the Tucker family on trips before, particularly after Jim had died and Alison was still little, but he had never thought of taking Jenny by herself.

He looked at her drooping over her mug of tea. She was no longer the slender little thing Jim had brought home, but, Jeff thought, she was comfortably chubby and very feminine. Without ever thinking much about it, he liked the fact that she never wore trousers and that her hair, unfashionably long, was scooped up in that bun thing on the back of her head. She was usually so cheerful, and it distressed him to see her look so low.

He got to his feet. 'Come on, Jenny, leave the clearing up. A bit of sunshine will cheer you up. I'm going to visit Northwood Farm. Do you fancy coming with me?'

Jenny thought she might faint.

Stephen had indeed been in a state of shock when he left the house and drove off in the battered old Land Rover. If it weren't for the fact that he had promised to pick up Angela with her props, he probably would have made his excuses and for the first time since joining the Merlin Players, missed that afternoon's rehearsal. Until Gran dropped her bombshell he had been more worried about being late for his rehearsal, assuming that whatever she produced in the way of ordnance, it wouldn't be directed at him.

It's all Charlie's fault, he thought bitterly to himself. If he hadn't made such a pillock of himself, this would never have crossed Gran's mind. And why bring me into it? What have I ever done, except work my fingers to the bone? If I was allowed to farm the way I want, we wouldn't be in this mess. Bloody hell, where on earth does Gran expect *me* to get a wife? I've never even had a girlfriend; not really. Chance would be a fine thing! She's off her head. Perhaps when she's calmed down a bit, Mum can persuade her to change her mind, leastways, where I'm concerned. No one's gonna marry me.

But he didn't feel very optimistic about Jenny's chances with Elsie; she'd never been successful before.

Driving from Summerstoke to the outskirts of Summerbridge, his mind desperately cast over all the girls he knew. He lingered longest on the image of Nicola Scudamore with her dark, soft curls and sparkling blue eyes, her straight little nose and cupid's bow mouth, her dainty hands and slender waist, her voice, so low, so soft, so sweet, so ... so ...

If only ... oh, if only ... but he'd never have the courage to ask her out, let alone marry her. But he had to – *had* to do something if he wasn't to lose his share of Gran's inheritance.

In something of a state, he drew up outside the little stone terraced house where Angela had a bedsit. He turned off the engine and sat for a while trying to regain his composure. He decided to say nothing about his problems, not to Angela, not to anyone, for he reasoned if the world knew he was looking for a wife, they would either laugh at him or turn tail and run in the opposite direction.

'It's like some bloody play!' he said out loud, bitterly.

'What is?' asked a voice at his elbow. Angela had been watching out for him and now stood by the open window of his Land Rover, her arms round a large box. She was looking up at him, her large eyes blinking in concern behind her outsize spectacles, her lightly freckled face pale from days spent in artificial light, surrounded by books.

Stephen blushed in confusion. He would like to have confided in her, but deep down he felt ashamed. Elsie had touched a nerve, a private concern that he had shared with no one; so, denying himself the comfort of sharing his troubles with Angela, he hastily reassured her he had not meant anything in particular, and busied himself loading the vehicle with the props she had been gathering, tirelessly, over the last week.

When they were in rehearsal, the Merlin Players met twice a week and every Sunday afternoon in an old school hall that belonged to Summerbridge College's Adult Education Department, one normally used as an overflow room for public examinations. It was here they also put on their performances, although they had aspirations to perform in the College Theatre and to rub shoulders with professionals. But that was an experience as yet denied them and they had to make do with the humbler surroundings of the old hall.

The room was long and rectangular, the windows too high to see out of – they could only be opened by a long pole operated by the caretaker. Heavy, old-fashioned, pale-green-gloss radiators lined the walls, belting out a stuffy heat in the winter and ice cold in the summer. The scuffed parquet floor was littered with black plastic stacking chairs, and at the end by the entrance were stacks of wooden tables with thin steel legs. At the other end was the stage. Having originally been designed to impress rather than engage its audience, it was slightly too high for theatrical purposes. The heavy curtains that framed the proscenium were patched and faded and likewise the black drapes that hung round the stage, forming the wing space, were scarred with countless repairs. It was a shabby, oppressive space, where the smell of paint, old fabric and dust mixed with polish and cleaning fluids. It was womb-like, unreal, forgotten by time, and Stephen loved it. Like the milking shed, albeit in a different way, it was his kingdom.

'Good, no one's here yet,' Stephen grunted, carrying in Angela's box. He and Angela always aimed to arrive ahead of Mrs Pagett and the cast. 'Where do you want these, Ange?'

'I'll set up a props table on the floor for the moment, then Mrs P can check them out. Do you want a hand to mark up the stage?'

According to how far into rehearsals they'd got, they would set the stage with furniture or simply mark it with tape.

'No thanks, I can manage. I'll set up the command post first.'

Angela giggled.

June Pagett, the producer, ruthlessly drove her band of players from production to production. Of indeterminate age, but certainly somewhere in her late fifties, she would bark out her instructions in tones rich and husky from almost continuous smoking. She rarely smiled. She was rather short and stout with heavy features; her freckled skin was concealed under a mask of make-up, and her hair, once ginger, was now faded and white on the crown of her head, and a bright, nicotine-stained orange on her temples. Little was known of her background, but she would let drop the occasional reference to a time when she had been on the stage, or famous names she had worked with or with whom she had once been close friends. She was one of a doughty band of speech and drama adjudicators who terrorised local amateur festivals and ran their own Am Dram groups with a tyrannical grip, as she did The Merlin Players.

Stephen placed two of the tables in the centre of the hall to form June's operational base. From here she would bark out her instructions, moving restlessly from table to stage, cardigan draped over her shoulders whatever the weather. He set a chair for himself. At this stage of the rehearsal, she needed him there to annotate the script.

In fact, apart from when they wanted something from him, it

was the only time in the whole process anyone paid any real attention to Stephen. As they fretted and argued over choreographing the play, it was his job to note down all their movements, which he did with great patience, endlessly rubbing out and recharting. The actors were meant to notate their scripts as they went along, but most didn't do that and appealed to him to 'refresh their memories' or to arbitrate over a disputed movement. Stephen was always relieved when this process was over and he could retire to the anonymity of the stage manager's corner.

Stephen didn't really like actors very much – a view he shared, he had discovered when comparing notes at festivals, with other stage managers, simply because the attributes that drove people onto the stage and the SMs into their little corners, were antipathetic. Most of the actors or actresses he encountered were loud, emotional, and entirely self-centred. June Pagett, he sometimes thought guiltily, was the worst of them all; but having to boss that lot around, he reasoned, she had to out-do them. There were exceptions of course, and happily Nicola Scudamore was one of them.

Sagely, Stephen put it down to talent. 'The more talent they have,' he had once observed to Angela, 'the more human they are. It's as if they don't have to pretend they're something they're not, 'cos they are.'

Angela had understood what he meant, and with guilty pleasure they had drawn up a list of the Merlin Players, allocating marks for talent as far as they could tell, and marks for ... well, for 'being nice', as Angela put it. These marks were constantly revised, and after rehearsals, when they all retired to the local pub and the actors shrieked and performed for their own amusement, Angela and Stephen would whisper together, marking them up or down.

Of course they had their favourites, but were sensitive to the other's preferences. Angela, perhaps inevitably, didn't like Nicola; Stephen didn't much like Gerald O'Donovan, a solicitor in his early thirties who had once helped Angela over some tricky pronunciations when she'd had to prompt a Molière production.

85

Gerald was a bachelor, tall and thin with a mocking self-confidence. His forehead was high and bony, framed by elegantly groomed, dark hair, parted in the middle; he had a long aquiline nose and an overactive left eyebrow which would arch at the slightest provocation. Stephen felt nervous in his company, sensing that he, Stephen, was the subject of some private joke. In the current production he was cast as Aimwell; Nicola was Dorinda.

Both Stephen and Angela agreed that Robin Roberts, an estate agent playing Archer, was an oily creep and not at all right for the part. He was forty, barely five foot six, plump, with thinning reddish hair that he smeared over his balding crown.

And then there was Mrs Brownsword, who was Lady Bountiful but far too old and far too fat for her role, as usual, and they doubted she would ever learn her lines. They liked her, though; she was very good-natured and had a deep-rooted chuckle that made her unnaturally brown curls bob and bounce, her eyes narrow into slits and disappear in the folds of her face and her little round body rock backwards and forwards. She was an old friend of June Pagett and the only one of the company who remained completely unperturbed by June's barbed comments, even when they were directed at her, as they often were when she couldn't remember her lines. In truth, Mrs Brownsword could not have managed to get through a performance without Angela or Stephen feeding her the script and she, in turn, fed them chocolates from a box of Quality Street that permanently resided in the bottom of her bag.

Maybe because it was a hot summer's day and the actors wanted to be elsewhere, or because June Pagett had a hangover from a dinner the night before, or because Stephen was unable to put Elsie's melodramatic ultimatum out of his mind, but that afternoon's rehearsal was bad-tempered and prolonged. As June drove the actors through the scenes, Stephen's level of concentration wavered and he missed a number of moves. This became evident when there was a dispute over what had been agreed in a particular scene, and Nicola was involved, which made it worse. He had blushed redder than usual when she had greeted him upon her arrival and the whole afternoon he had been unable to look her in the eye. When the disagreement over the moves arose, she turned to him, appealing for his support, but all he could do was grow red and look foolish. She gave a disappointed shake of her head and turned away. Mrs Pagett was less restrained.

'Really, Stephen, what's got into you this afternoon? I rely on you to faithfully record what we decide. The stage manager's book is the only record we have, the only documentation of our artistic process. It's the transcript of my thoughts, my creativity … I need it. We all need it. We don't want to have to start from scratch again because no one can agree on what was decided. If you can't concentrate, hand the book over to Angela and go and do something useful. Have a look at those props of hers. The majority of them just will not do, will not do at all – quite the wrong period.' She turned to the actors. 'Now then, darlings, we'll have a quick tea break and then on to Act Two, Scene One, with Dorinda and Mrs Sullen. Angela, have you put the kettle on?'

The afternoon dragged on. June was having difficulty with a scene involving the oily Robin Roberts and Mrs Pagett's au pair, who had been forced by her indomitable employer to take the part of Cherry, the Landlord's daughter, as a means of improving her English. She was a student from Romania, in her early twenties, tall, plain and lumpy. No shrinking violet, Roxanne seemed to view the proceedings with ill-concealed contempt and stalked the stage with an arrogant toss of her head.

'Lof ess I kernow not what eet coms I kernow not ow an goes I kernow not wayne.'

'Very well, an apt scholar.' And following the stage direction, Robin Roberts put out his hand and tickled Roxanne under her chin. She immediately slapped his hand away and boxed his ear.

'Why you do that? You keep you feelthy hands to yourself!'

Nursing his sore ear, Robin Roberts protested, 'But I was chucking you underneath the chin – look, you stupid girl, it says here, "Chucks her under the chin"!'

'Well, I don't like this chucks. Chuck me, I go. Right?'

'For goodness' sake, let's get on with it. Roxanne, I'll explain this scene to you later, but for the moment, can we just concentrate on blocking the movement?' June's patience was wearing thin but she was determined to get to the end of the scene.

The lateness of the hour was ignored, much to the irritation of the other actors. One or two pointedly picked up their bags and hovered by the door, although none was quite brave enough to announce their departure. June had always made it clear that if anyone wanted to be a member of the Merlin Players, they had to abide by the rules of the society; one of the rules was that no one left rehearsal before the producer gave permission.

Stephen, in particular, was getting anxious. The cows had to be brought in for milking at five-thirty. Having incurred June's wrath already this afternoon, he didn't want to do so again, but the cows could not wait. His face went red, his stomach turned to water and his mouth went dry as he summoned up all his courage to speak.

'Excuse me, Missus. But your time is up. I'm waiting to close the hall. I thought you lot finished half an hour ago. Haven't you got homes to go to?'

Saved by the caretaker, standing at the back, jingling his keys, his eyes gleaming, teeth bared. Stephen had once whispered to Angela that he was like the crocodile in Peter Pan who had swallowed an alarm clock, and that he stalked June Pagett in much the same way as the reptile stalked Captain Hook.

June turned to do battle, and as if on cue, the actors chorused their farewells. Stephen, sighing with relief, hurried to put things away.

He became aware that Nicola had detached herself from the main group making their farewells, and was coming over to him. He kept his head down, rearranging the contents of a box he had just filled.

'Stephen.' Her voice was slightly husky and so sweet. Like a ripe apricot, he thought to himself, although he didn't think he'd ever tasted one. The thought sent his senses swimming.

'Stephen, are you all right?' She sounded concerned and

Stephen was so overcome he could scarcely bring himself to stammer, 'Y-yes ... I'm fine ... thanks.'

'Only you seemed preoccupied this afternoon. I'm not used to you looking so miserable.'

'Was I? Sorry.'

'You're not fed up with us, are you?'

'With you?' Stephen was amazed.

'Only it would be awful if you were. Mind you, with an afternoon like this one, I wouldn't blame you. Honestly, I don't know how you put up with us.'

'No, no, really, it's not you, I love ...' Confused, Stephen became increasingly overheated. Little beads of perspiration broke out on his top lip and his hands became damp and sticky. He stuck them nervously into the pockets of his jeans and hunched his shoulders. 'I love it, really. Just had some ... it's nothing. Really.'

'Good. I'm so relieved.' She touched him lightly on the arm. 'We rely on you, Stephen; remember that.'

Stephen, in a daze, watched her rejoin the others, link arms with Gerald O'Donovan, and say something to the group that made them burst out laughing. He longed to be part of that group, laughing with her, so easy. He could still feel her touch on his arm, hear her voice in his ears, see her sweet, concerned expression.

'Are you all right, Stephen?' Angela was at his elbow. She looked hot; her face was moist with perspiration and her wispy hair curled, damp and drab, against her pale, freckly skin. 'Only time is getting on and I know you was worried about the cows. Don't worry about dropping me off,' she added, as Stephen, groaning, almost ran around the hall stacking the chairs the actors had not put back. His actions were critically supervised by the caretaker, who slammed tight the windows, bearing his pole triumphantly aloft, having won this round in the ongoing war between him and June Pagett. She, a wan Roxanne in her wake, left them to it with an imperious farewell and an instruction not to be late on Tuesday.

'When are we ever?' Stephen growled.

Angela stared at him. She looked worried. 'I can finish off here, Stephen. If you could take the props in your Land Rover, then I can walk back. I really don't mind.'

But it was clear she was tired, and Stephen felt ashamed. 'No, no, ten more minutes won't make no odds. Cows will moan a bit, but they'll have to put up with it.'

'I've a better plan. Why don't I come back with you and give you a hand? We can sort out these wretched props afterwards, then you can drop me back, if you don't mind?'

The idea appealed to Stephen. He was exhausted by his own thoughts, and having company as sympathetic as Angela's would be a welcome relief from them. She had met the cows before and wasn't frightened of the beasts. He looked at her. Her big specs had slipped to the end of her nose; her mouth looked pinched and anxious, her skin blotched, and her chin, which she rubbed when she was nervous, was pink and prominent; her body shrank into the all-purpose dungarees she wore for rehearsals, and the little pink T-shirt emphasised the skinniness of her neck and arms.

'Poor Angela,' Stephen thought. 'What a pity she's not more attractive.' He instantly felt ashamed.

'Great idea. That is, if you've nothing better to do?'

Angela, the prospect of a long summer evening alone in her bedsit before her, hastily reassured him.

Her arms round Al's waist, Alison leant against his back, protecting herself from the turbulent air whipped up by the speed of the bike. Always aware of the proximity of the lean body in front of her, of her thighs pressed against his, of moving with him as they swooped and cornered, she found the ride exhilarating. Having eschewed bikes since that incident in the farmyard, she had forgotten, until Al had taken her to Summerbridge the day before, the sheer physical excitement of being on a bike: the deep growl of the exhaust, the rhythmic sway from side to side as they wove in and out of lines of cars crawling towards the coast, and the thrill of speed when Al opened up the throttle and everyone else was left behind.

He had suggested going down to the coast and she, not having the faintest idea of where they were going or how long it would take, had agreed; the bike ride could go on for ever, as far as she was concerned. By the time they turned off a narrow lane and bumped across a stony track to a car park, however, her bum was sore and her legs, even though protected by her jeans, were roasting from the exhaust pipes and she was glad to climb off.

She stood and looked around as Al settled and locked the bike. The car park was little more than a field and in every direction, cars sparkled in the afternoon sun. Here and there, grouped round open doors and hatchbacks, family groups were picnicking; one or two kites were flying high, almost motionless in the blue sky; nearby a group of youths were playing a noisy game of football; sitting in their cars, people dozed or were listening to the cricket on their car radios, the sound of the commentary floating across from different directions like a wraparound sound system; and dotted here and there, on the grass, in various stages of undress, people were sunbathing, snogging, or sleeping. Of the sea there was no sign.

Alison turned to Al. He had pulled off his helmet and was grinning. 'Not the first here, I see.'

She laughed. It was impossible to feel disappointed. 'Not exactly. But where's the sea? I thought you said we were going to the seaside.'

'And so we are. We have to walk the next bit. I hope you've got a good head for heights. Come on.' He started to walk away and for a moment she stared after him, feeling what? Let down? What had she been expecting? A kiss? They'd only just met, for Chrissake … but he might at least have taken her hand before he set off …

Al turned, the sunlight glinting off his earring. 'Ali?'

'Coming.' They had the whole afternoon ahead of them, she thought, and anything might happen.

*

91

The rays of the late afternoon sun were slanting low and gold over the farmyard when Charlie arrived home. There was nobody about. Gran's car was missing from the yard; the kitchen was empty; the dishes from lunch were still on the table and there was no sign of his mother, which was odd; there was no music coming from Alison's room; and there were no cows in the yard, which meant that Stephen hadn't arrived back to start the milking.

'It's like the bloomin' Marie Celeste!' he declared out loud, standing in the middle of the deserted yard, scratching his head. 'Perhaps they've all gone and left me to it – abducted by aliens, never to return. Fat chance!' He thought about bringing in the cows for the evening milking, but he wasn't feeling very charitable and was rather hungover from the afternoon's drinking. He toyed with going back to Lenny and Paula's, but decided an evening with the marrieds would depress him even further.

The sun was still quite warm and the air was full of the gentle musings of wood pigeons. He liked this time of day and rather than slump in front of the telly to watch *Red Dwarf*, as he had planned (it never failed to cheer him when he was particularly fed up), he thought he would walk across the fields to The Bunch of Grapes. The pub sat on a crossroads about two miles out of Summerstoke and so by the time he walked there Linda would have opened up. He fancied an evening propping up the bar, flirting with Beth and having a chat to Linda. Linda was bright, and she might even have a few ideas about how he could get round this stupid plan of Elsie's.

As it turned out, he didn't get much of a chance to have a quiet tête à tête with Linda. When he arrived, the door of the Grapes was shut. Having pushed it in vain, Charlie scratched his head, puzzled. It was after six, and in the summer Stan and Linda opened on the dot to catch potential customers returning home from a day out in the Mendips, or Wookey Hole, Wells, or Glastonbury, all of which were not far away. A main road to Bath and Bristol whizzed past the pub's front door; the little back lane to Summerstoke bordered one side, and thick, cool, green woods stretched around the back. The darkness of the trees created a natural frame for the old inn, which was built of local stone, aged over the centuries into a deep gold. It had mullioned windows, now winking brightly in the evening sunshine, and was covered with Virginia creeper already turning scarlet.

From an upstairs window Charlie could hear a child crying and then the sound of Linda's voice. He called up, and moments later she looked out. She seemed, he thought, a bit stressed.

'Oh, it's you, Charlie. I'm running late. Hang on a moment; I'll be down.'

The door's locks were scraped back and Linda, a little girl in her nightclothes dangling on her hip, let him in. Linda looked unwell, he thought. She had no make-up on; her cropped hair, normally spiked with gel, lay flat against her head; the large dangling earrings she usually sported were absent, and although she was dressed for work, she was not wearing any shoes and her lack of heels made her seem smaller and vulnerable.

'Charlie, do us a favour, love. Stan ain't here, the bar staff haven't turned up yet and Jessie here won't settle down. Can you open up and hold the fort for a bit? I don't expect we'll be busy for a while. I won't be long, honest. Give yourself a pint, on the house.'

Charlie was not used to being in the pub so completely alone at opening time and he enjoyed himself. A faint smell of polish mingled with the all-pervasive smell of beer and tobacco. The sunlight, glancing in through the windows, lit the motes of dust floating and sparkling in the air, emphasising the shadows in the room. The public bar had a flagstone floor and was dotted with assorted wooden tables and chairs with a number of high stools against the bar for favoured customers such as Charlie. There was a large inglenook fireplace where, except in the hottest weather, Stan usually kept a fire burning. It wasn't alight today and the fireplace was full of ash, cigarette butts and crisp papers. Unwashed glasses stood on the bar, along with a number of overflowing ashtrays. Evidently the clearing up from lunchtime had not been completed.

Charlie wandered through into the saloon. It told a similar

story. Piles of plates and dirty cutlery had been stacked on the counter. The tables were sprayed with spilt salt and splashes of food. The carpeted floor was littered with used paper napkins and the odd menu, and the chairs had not been pushed back into place. Here too, the fire was dead in the fireplace.

Charlie was puzzled. Linda took pride in having an immaculate pub and worked hard to keep it so. 'Odd,' he muttered. 'What's going on?'

Then Charlie, who never washed up or cleared away at home if he could help it, set to and cleared away the glasses and plates, wiped the tables with a tea towel and straightened the chairs, cleaned the bar and polished glasses. For the first time that day he felt almost happy. Overhead he could hear Linda moving about, then the warbling of a mobile phone and the low murmur of her voice. He was in no hurry for her to come and take over. A couple came in and he served them drinks. A few more drifted in and he served them. An old drinking companion, Skip, hailed him.

'Charlie, me ol' mate – what's this? Taken up a new job, eh? Farmin' don't pay?'

Charlie filled him in and Skip gave him a broad wink. 'Couldn't be nicer: me ol' mate behind the bar, how about one – two, even – on the house, before she comes down?'

Charlie, who had quite forgotten to pour himself the pint that Linda had offered, felt uncomfortable and was about to jeopardise a friendship when Linda hurried into the bar.

'Oh Charlie, I'm really sorry to leave you so long. Jess just wouldn't settle. And I've had a call from Beth; seems she can't make it tonight so I'm all on my tod. Just my luck! I'm really sorry.'

Charlie was sorry about Beth and wondered, briefly, why she hadn't turned up – she'd said nothing to him about not working that evening – but he responded to the note of desperation in Linda's voice. He put an arm round her shoulder and gave her a squeeze. 'No wuz, I've enjoyed myself, really. Look, Lin, if you're on your own tonight, shall I stay this side of the bar, give you a hand? I don't mind, honest.'

She smiled at him gratefully, and looking across the bar at Charlie's crony, took him up on his offer. 'Charlie, I'd be really grateful. You could cover the lounge – it shouldn't be too busy in there – and I'll stay in here. Skip, a pint of your usual?'

Charlie waited for the opportunity to ask about Stan's absence and seek Linda's advice about Elsie. But the opportunity was a long time coming, for shortly after Linda joined him in the bar a coach party arrived and she and Charlie were kept busy for the rest of the evening.

When all but the last reluctant locals had gone, they drew breath.

'Blimey, Linda,' said Charlie ruefully, 'I came here for a quiet pint and a chat, and I've not had either! And my stomach's rumbling a storm. I've not eaten since lunchtime.'

Lunchtime. The memory of it all rose in his gut like undigested grub, lurking to give him bellyache all night. He sighed heavily.

'I'm sorry, Charlie, I should've thought. Look, pull yourself a pint and I'll go and put some of the Chicken Kiev from lunch in the microwave.'

Working behind the bar had driven all thoughts of Elsie out of Charlie's mind, but now he could think of nothing else. The beer tasted dull and when Linda returned with a plateful of chicken and chips, he found his appetite had gone. He pushed both plate and glass away with a sigh. The whole evening he had been lively and good fun, charming even the most awkward of Linda's customers, but now, slumped back in his chair, he looked dull and miserable.

Linda was concerned. 'Something up, Charlie? Not like you to be off your beer. You look as if someone's turned the light off.'

'No, I'm not all right. Far from it, Lin. The old witch has got me by the short and curlies ...' Groaning, he told Linda about Elsie's ultimatum.

Linda was gratifyingly shocked. 'It sounds like something out of Georgette Heyer! People just don't behave like that any more. What is Elsie thinking of?'

'Screwing me up right and proper, that's what. Thing is, Lin, you're my mate, and you know Gran: what'll I do?'

Lin looked at him thoughtfully. 'Do you want to get married, Charlie?'

Charlie shrugged his shoulders and stretched out in his chair. 'Who to? All the decent ones are hitched already.'

'What about Sarah? The few times you've brought her in here, you seemed quite keen on her.'

'I was, to begin with, but just because I fancy someone, don't mean I want to spend the rest of my natural with them.'

'But don't you think you might want to settle down someday? If you carry on the way you have been, Charlie Tucker, there won't be anyone available left. Or, more to the point, you'll decide you want to get married and discover no one will have you.'

Charlie sat up and looked at her in surprise. 'What do you mean? Aren't most girls dying to tie the knot?'

Linda laughed at him. 'That's terribly old-fashioned, Charlie. Women, thank God, are driven by a lot more these days than finding a man to cook and clean for. And if I was looking for someone to settle down with, I wouldn't choose a bloke with the sort of reputation you've got.'

'Lin!' Charlie protested, hurt.

She patted his hand. 'You're a great friend, Charlie, but you have to admit, you're a terrible flirt, and nobody wants the angst of being hitched to a roving eye.' For a moment, a shadow passed over her face. Then she smiled and said lightly, 'But you haven't answered my question. Do you want to get married?'

Charlie ran his fingers through his hair thoughtfully. 'Yeah, I s'pose so ... but not just at the moment, and not just because Gran says I've got to.'

'Then you're goin' to have to find a way round her. I'll have a think about it. But don't despair; it's early days yet, Charlie. She might see how stupid this whole thing is and change her mind.'

'And pigs might fly. But you're right – that's what I've got to do – somehow make her see how daft it is. But Lin, don't say

96

anything to nobody, will you? If this gets out I'll be a laughing stock, and any bird I might fancy won't be seen for dust.'

'Like Beth, you mean? No, of course I won't. You can trust me.' She got up and started to gather the plates. 'I don't know about you, Charlie, but I'm ready for my bed. If you could collect the rest of the glasses while I put these in the dishwasher, I'll let you out and lock up.'

On her way to the kitchen she turned and said lightly, 'Oh, Charlie, I haven't said how grateful I am you were here tonight. I didn't explain, but Stan's mum is ill and he had to go ... I really don't know how I'd have managed without you. You were great.'

'S'all right,' said Charlie, grinning. 'I enjoyed myself. Really. First time for ages.'

And he meant it.

8

A narrow gravel drive bordered by a high yew hedge skirted the churchyard and led to Summerstoke Manor. The gateway was made even narrower by a pair of stone pillars, on the top of which, balanced precariously, were large, ornamental stone balls, eaten by frost and decorated with ancient grey and gold lichen.

'Oh, bollocks!' As Hugh drove into the courtyard, his state-of-the-art, glistening, sporty Range Rover scraped against one of the pillars, causing one of the great stone balls to wobble precariously.

'Pity,' murmured one of the Misses Merfields, watching his arrival from a sitting-room window.

'What is, dear?' enquired another.

'That the ball didn't fall on Mr Lester's car. When he hit the pillar it looked promising for a moment.'

There was no doubt that the manor house had beauty and character where Summerstoke House had not. A long, low building, two stories high, with mullioned windows and creeper-clad stone walls, it stretched out either side of a great carved porch. At the back, the wings of the house faced into a courtyard bordered by a rose garden, with a wide green lawn stretching beyond that in a slope down to the river.

Hugh had always craved the house. Not because he had fallen for its beauty, or its history, but because he knew that it was regarded as by far and away the best house in the village. It was this secret craving that had put its mark on any dealings he had with the Misses Merfields. They were never going to give him what he wanted and viewed his want with a polite contempt that characterised their infrequent encounters with the Lesters.

Hugh surveyed the scraped and dented paintwork of his car and swore again. He cursed the Merfields for the gate posts, Vee for having made him come, and Cordelia for demanding to be picked up from a friend's house, which was the reason he had driven and not walked to the manor. He grabbed his mobile and the newspaper, slammed the car door and walked morosely across to the house. He sighed as he stood at the great carved portal and looked round for an alternative to the gnarled iron knocker, which clearly hadn't been used for years.

Vee had been furious when she discovered that he had let the weekend drift past without doing anything. He had been playing, that morning, with a newly installed computer when she had come into his study, fresh from putting a young, feisty horse through its paces. She had got the better of the horse and was in a good humour. That had instantly evaporated when she had asked him when he was planning to see the Misses Merfields.

'Really, Hugh. What are you playing at?' Impatiently, she slapped her crop in her hand and tossed her netted head. 'You had two simple things to do and you've not done either of them. Why haven't you phoned the manor? And why haven't you spoken to Lenny Spinks yet? It's pathetic! Are you serious about the stud? Because if we don't get this land then we might as well forget it!'

Hugh looked up from his computer screen and flushed resentfully. He withered when her anger was directed at him. 'I played my part,' she continued, 'even though I found it distasteful enough. But if you're not even going to try ...'

Hugh ground his teeth and found a bell concealed in the ivy. He pressed it, but could hear no responding sound. He waited a few moments, his irritation with the whole situation growing by the second, then he pressed it again, more viciously, holding onto it longer.

'All right, all right, all right! I heard you the first time.' An elderly woman with cropped grey hair and a neat, unassuming appearance glared at him from the door she had just opened. 'We're not deaf, you know. One ring is quite sufficient.'

Hugh, mumbling an apology, put on his most ingratiating manner and attempted to retrieve the situation. 'Thank you so much for agreeing to see me, Mrs Merfield. I won't take up much of your time, but I am sure—'

Before he could get any further he was abruptly interrupted. 'Good heavens, I'm not a Merfield. I'd have thought you'd know that by now; you've lived in the village long enough. I'm Nanny.'

There were three Misses Merfields resident in the Manor House: Mrs Merfield and her sisters-in-law, Miss Merfield the older, and Miss Merfield the younger. Very few people in the village knew their Christian names and could only hazard a guess at their ages, but it was believed that the youngest Miss Merfield was probably in her late seventies, and the oldest, Mrs Merfield, was in her mid-eighties. Nanny had joined the household as a young girl to care for Mrs Merfield's son, and when he left home, she had remained to look after the senior members of the family as they, in turn, sickened and died. She had always been known as Nanny by everyone, and speculation had it that she was older than the young Miss Merfield, but not as old as Mrs Merfield. They were all strong women, but appeared to live together in complete harmony, deferring to the senior Mrs Merfield in the event of any disagreement. They were reputed to be staunch Christians and to hold strong views about the 'moral decline of contemporary society'. Which was why Hugh was hopeful that the newspaper he clutched would prove useful in undermining whatever opinion they had of the Tuckers.

He followed Nanny across the hall and was shown into a long, rectangular sitting room with a low, decoratively plastered ceiling, and wainscoting painted silver-grey. A large fireplace occupied the far end of the room in which, Hugh was amazed to see – because the summer was one of the hottest he could remember – a small fire glowed. Around this were grouped a selection of huge sofas and elegant button-back chairs, where the ladies were sat, sipping tea.

Mrs Merfield, upright and elegant like a Queen Cobra, surveyed him from under hooded eyes. 'Ah, Mr Lester. Come in and sit down.'

Hugh sank into a deep, squashy settee, which immediately engulfed him. He had to struggle, his legs being rather short, to put his feet back on the ground and regain some semblance of dignity.

Mrs Merfield continued, graciously but without any warmth. 'We are having tea, as you see. Nanny, be so kind as to provide Mr Lester with a cup.'

Hugh, who hated tea, but lacked the courage to ask for coffee, weakly accepted the fragile cup and saucer handed to him. He declined the offer of milk or lemon, wondering how to broach the subject and get this ordeal over with as quickly as possible. He sipped his tea, to give himself a moment. It was horrible, scented and bitter.

'We get our Earl Grey direct from Gillards. Quite the most refreshing tea to drink in this hot weather, don't you think?' One of the Miss Merfields, equally elegant but with silver hair, boyishly cropped and streaked with pink, closely watched him. 'Have a biscuit. We've eaten all the chocolate ones, I'm afraid, but the arrowroot are very nice.'

He accepted her offer, hoping the sweetness of the biscuit would remove the horror of the tea. It was dry and cloying.

'Did you hit one of the pillars when you drove in?' asked the third Merfield, her eyes bright and wide, her smiling mouth vivid with lipstick. 'Only you should really be more careful. Those pillars are very old, you know. We don't want them damaged.'

'No, no, of course not.' Hugh, thoroughly discomfited, started to stutter out his apologies.

The Misses Merfields said nothing, just sat and watched him. His voice trailed away and there was silence. In desperation he took another gulp of tea. He decided to launch straight to the point. 'Er ...'

'Yes, Mr Lester?' said Mrs Merfield, cool, collected. 'What can we do for you?'

Alison took the call from the bank. She had been in her bedroom, at her desk in the window overlooking the yard, wrestling with a knotty equation. But her mind was not on her maths: her eyes kept wandering off the page to the distant view of the woods and her thoughts drifted into dreamy recollections of the previous afternoon.

Al had taken her down to the Dorset coast, near Durdle Dor, somewhere she had never been before. Once they had left the car park they had climbed a stile and clambered up a steep green slope. Then she saw it in the distance, sparkling to infinity – the sea. The smooth green folds of the downs broke off dramatically high above the water, and at the edge of the cliff she could only stand and stare, amazed and exhilarated. They had scrambled down a precipitous path to a tiny rocky cove; Al had taken her hand to help her down, and then hadn't let go ...

Then the phone rang. She knew her mother was outside wrestling with some weeds and wouldn't hear; Elsie, as a matter of principle, never answered the phone, and both her brothers were out on the farm, so she had jumped up and rushed down to the hall to answer it. As she sped down the stairs, an illogical voice at the back of her brain teased her with the fantasy that it might be Al, that he'd got her number somehow and was phoning to say ... But it was the bank manager, who wanted to speak to Charlie as a matter of urgency.

Alison tried Charlie's mobile without success, which didn't surprise her. He was in the middle of harvesting and would have turned his phone off. She sighed, and abandoning her maths and her daydreams, grabbed her old bike from a shed in the yard and cycled up the track in search of her eldest brother. The dust raised by the bike settled on her arms and legs and the afternoon sun was strong on her back. It was with some relief that she reached the road, shaded by its horse chestnuts. She thought that Charlie was probably harvesting in the fields at the far end of the valley, so she turned down Weasel Lane in search of him. The lane was very old and narrow with the occasional passing place, and with high banks on either side on which grew wild honeysuckle, white bryony, dusky pink foxgloves, bright yellow toadflax, straggling purple vetch and frothy, creamy white hedge parsley. At times the banks of flowers were replaced by an over-reaching arch of trees, of sycamore and rowan, oak and hazel, forming a cool green tunnel through which she sped. She passed a big bramble bush growing down the bank which made her think, with guilt, of the blackberries she still had not picked for Gran, and then she spotted the combine harvester in the middle of a half-cut field, a tractor and trailer trundling along by its side.

Charlie was not best pleased to get the bank's message. 'Don't they know I'm in the middle of harvest? What do they bloody want?'

'They wouldn't say. Just that you were to phone them, pronto.'

She lingered as Charlie made the call, and Lenny, never sorry to seize the opportunity of a break from work, climbed down from the cab of his tractor to greet her.

'Hi, Ali. Who's the boyfriend, then, eh? Didn't think bikers was your sort?'

Alison wasn't ready to share yesterday with anyone at the moment, least of all Lenny Spinks.

'They're not and he's not. I went out with a friend.'

Lenny was distracted from further teasing by a groan from Charlie as he finished his call, his face a picture of gloom.

'What's up, mate?'

'Never rains but it pours: first Gran, and now the bloody bank. Want to see me tomorrow, bugger the weather, bugger the harvest. They want to discuss the overdraft. "What's to discuss?" I say. "It's time to discuss how we might reduce it," he says, all prissy. Bloodsuckers! It's all very well you griping on about not having had fifty quid this month, Ali. Where am I going to find the necessary to get the bank off our back? Fancy tellin' Gran I'm gonna be up shit creek without a paddle and the last thing I want to do is saddle myself with a wife?'

As she cycled back to the farmhouse Alison thought long and hard. She had been so distracted by the afternoon with Al that she had not really given much attention to her Gran's pronouncement. Turning into the track down to the farm, she passed Stephen, Gip at his heels, on his way to collect the herd for the afternoon's milking. He barely nodded at her and walked on, shoulders hunched, miserable. 'Gran's done that,' thought Alison, 'and I've not often seen Charlie look so desperate. Even Mum has seemed elsewhere since yesterday. Gran can't get away with it. Trouble is, no one stands up to her. She's an old tyrant! Well, *I'm* not afraid of her!'

It had been a warm afternoon and Elsie was feeling dozy. She had settled in her favourite comfy armchair to read a book but had nodded off and been wakened by the sound of sticks falling into her fireplace. A pair of jackdaws were squabbling on the stack and their argument reverberated down the chimney. She disliked jackdaws and banged the chimney breast with vigour, dislodging a few clumps of soot as well as the birds. The physical action made her feel better; she hated snoozing in the afternoon; in fact she hated anything that reminded her of just how old she was getting. She looked at her watch: just after five o'clock. Goodness, she'd been asleep longer than she thought. Still, there was time for a cuppa and perhaps a short walk before supper. She had just plugged in her kettle in the tiny kitchenette created out of a cupboard at one end of her sitting room, when there was a tap at her door.

'Hi, Gran,' Alison poked her head round. 'May I come in?'

Elsie had been conscious of the fact that since her ultimatum yesterday, none of her family had been near her. She'd expected an appeal from Jenny at the very least, but unusually, Jenny had gone out in the afternoon and had barely spoken to her since. Charlie she hadn't seen at all, and the one time she saw Stephen, he gave her a look that reminded her of one of his cows. Alison had disappeared for the rest of the day and had not even visited in the evening to watch television with her, as was her custom on Sunday (their taste in viewing often being at odds with the rest of the Tuckers). Elsie enjoyed battles, and she'd been expecting this one to be a right royal one. She did *not*, however, enjoy a stand-off, so she was delighted to see her granddaughter; not that Alison had the slightest suspicion of that from the cool greeting her grandmother gave her.

'I'm just making myself some tea; would you like a cup?'

'Thanks, Gran.' Alison sat on the edge of a flowery chintz sofa, preparing for the right moment to launch her attack, and watched Elsie fiddle with kettle, pot, cups and saucers. They only ever drank out of mugs downstairs, but Elsie always insisted on using the bone china tea set that had belonged to her mother. Elsie's sitting room was neat and comfortable, in direct contrast with the family sitting room downstairs. The furniture was old-fashioned, the fabric of the furnishings reflecting the age and tastes of the occupant, but to Alison, particularly when she was a little girl, her Gran's set of rooms at the top of the house represented an almost luxurious haven from the poverty and chaos elsewhere.

When Elsie had settled in her armchair and was sipping her tea, Alison began, as mildly as she could. 'Gran, I've been thinking about what you said yesterday—'

'Well, I'm glad someone has.'

Alison suddenly felt cross. 'We all have, Gran. How could you think we haven't? What you proposed was ... is ... well ...' The words preposterous, unfair, stupid, ridiculous and unrealistic sprang to mind. 'Have you *really* thought about what you're asking us to do?'

'I don't usually open my mouth without my brain being engaged, Alison. Why should it be any different this time? I meant what I said. Your brothers are letting this farm slide towards bankruptcy and it's time they took stock. I'm not so foolish as to think there's a bride on every bush, although I've heard there are Filipino women ready and willing, who make good wives—'

'Gran!' Alison was shocked. 'That's little better than slavery. I don't believe what I'm hearing!'

Elsie ignored her. 'But I *did* say, and nobody seems to have taken notice of what I said, that if the fortunes of the farm are turned around this year, I will take back my ultimatum. It's up to the boys which way it's to be.'

'But you're not being fair. Maybe the farm *is* struggling compared to your day, but things have got a lot tougher for farmers – you know they have. You were farming after the war, when the government poured money into your pockets—'

Elsie snorted, but Alison pressed on. 'I admit I haven't taken as much interest in the farm as maybe I should've, but even I know that milk prices are much lower than they used to be and the cows just don't support the farm like they did. We could get rid of them and grow nothing but subsidised crops. Maybe you'd like that; I suspect Charlie would, but that would break Stephen's heart. Look how he was during the foot-and-mouth outbreak. He was so worried about his precious beasts and we all thought he was going to have a nervous breakdown. He couldn't work harder—'

'Other farms are flourishing. Perhaps if Stephen channelled his energies more effectively ... and Charlie is just a jitterbug.'

'I don't know what a jitterbug is, but I do know that you've just added another layer of worry and I really don't think that's fair, or necessary!'

Alison's exasperation stung her grandmother. 'Shouting at me won't change my mind, Alison. I want to see results and if I've put a little explosive into a stagnating situation, then all well and good.'

'Then what about me? What d'you expect *me* to do about the farm? I can't see that going to university is going to help in any way. In fact, it's going to cost a hell of a lot, more than we can afford, even assuming I get a place. I'd be much better off getting a job and earning some cash. Life would certainly be a bit more fun than it is at the moment.' Unknown to her family, Alison had explored this possibility before and had rejected it, but she was fed up with being taken for granted and was incensed by Elsie's attitude. 'In fact, Gran,' she continued, growing more heated, 'I don't *want* my bit of your share; I don't even want *my own* share. As far as a grant's concerned, I might be better off with absolutely nothing at all – at least then I'll know where I stand! And I won't be doing something I might not want to do, just because of threats!'

Grandmother and granddaughter glared at each other. Alison had gone off in a direction that Elsie hadn't foreseen. She was very proud of her granddaughter's brains and had set her heart on seeing a Tucker go to university. But she said, stubborn to the last, 'I'm not changing my mind. You've got to go to university; you know that's what you've always wanted. I don't know why you're risking it with all this gadding about—'

'What gadding about? What are you talking about?'

'Don't play the innocent with me, miss. How many times have you said goodnight and then slipped out of the house, returning at God knows what hour, eh?'

Alison scowled, but said nothing.

'You've got more brains than your brothers so why don't you use them? Get those exams of yours and while you're about it, why don't you come up with some ideas to help the farm, instead of thinking only of yourself?'

Alison was furious. 'Well, if I think only of myself, I've had a very good teacher!' She slammed out of Elsie's room.

'Six o'clock and don't be late!' No sooner had an exasperated Veronica Lester put the white and gold receiver down on Lenny Spinks and reached for her gin and tonic, when it rang again. She answered it curtly, but on hearing who the caller was, her manner changed. She sat forward on the edge of the red velvet Chesterfield and positively oozed honey. Coming into the sitting room of Summerstoke House, Hugh Lester, raw from his encounter with the Merfields, caught the tail end of her conversation.

'Dinner on Saturday ... and you'll stay the night? No ... No problem at all; we've plenty of room ... Good. I look forward to it ... No, thank *you*. We shall be delighted.' She put the phone down and threw herself back on the sofa, arms above her head, triumphant. 'Yee-es!'

'Oh no, not another bloody dinner party! Who's staying the night? Why can't they bugger off home?'

'Language, darling!' Vee was brimming with excitement. 'You'll never guess who that was.'

'I don't feel like playing guessing games at the moment: I've scraped the car against the Merfields' gatepost; I've been hung out to dry by those appalling women; and, in the middle of making my pitch to them, Cordelia called my mobile, wanting to stay another night with that ghastly friend of hers. Didn't do my cause with the old biddies much good – they seem to think the mobile phone is an invention of the devil from the way they went on about it. And Cordelia wouldn't take no for an answer. Bloody embarrassing it was. I could do with a stiff drink.'

'I'll fix you one in a mo, and then you can tell me all about it. But first I want to tell you who's coming to dinner on Saturday night: Harriet Flood!'

Hugh stared at her blankly. 'Who's she?'

'Oh honestly, Hugh, I don't think you listen to half of what I tell you. She writes the main feature for *Country Homes and Gardens*. She's thinking of doing a feature on Summerstoke House, and Hugh, more importantly, of doing a whole series of picture articles on us setting up the stud. She thinks it's a really good story.'

'Does she now? She might have to wait a long time to write it.'

Vee sat up and looked at him sharply. 'The publicity this would bring is too good to miss, Hugh.' She took in the petulant droop of his mouth, a sure sign that he hadn't got something he wanted, and softened her voice. 'Tell me about the Merfields, did you get anywhere with them?'

Hugh went over to a tall glass cabinet and, selecting his favourite single malt, poured a large measure. He turned and shook his head, 'I don't know; I really don't know. They sit there, three old witches and Nanny, another old witch. It's bizarre – they're all made up, posh frocks, posh hair-do's – one even had pink streaks; piles of make-up – I mean, what for? And they sit there making these little sarcastic comments.' He slumped into a leather armchair and gazed moodily into his glass. 'Next time, if there is a next time, I think you should go; you'd know how to handle them. They just made me feel a complete oaf.'

'But did you tell them what we want?'

'Yes, yes, of course I did. I was very polite and straightforward. I explained our plans and our need for those meadows and I offered them a very generous price. They said they had a good relationship with the Tuckers and they saw no reason to break that, so I showed them the newspaper and said how the Tuckers were becoming increasingly notorious and unreliable, and that the word was out that they were going to go bankrupt. They went very quiet when they saw the paper and I thought I was in with a good chance.'

'Then what?'

'Then my mobile went off. The whole time Cordelia was rabbiting on, I could see them glancing at each other. Cordelia wouldn't get off the bloody phone. Why did she phone me and not you?'

'Because I would have said no. So what happened when you rang off?'

'You can imagine – comments about how intrusive phones are at the best of times; "Can't the thing be turned off?" asked one, all innocent; "Do you take it with you everywhere?" "Doesn't it burn your brain cells?" Little digs like that, and how anti-social it is when mobiles go off in public and how they'd heard that one had gone off at the beginning of a performance of "The Rites of Spring", or some such bloody thing, so the conductor stopped the soloist … I tell you, Vee, I didn't know who I wanted to strangle more: Cordelia or the old biddies.' He took a huge gulp of whisky. 'And then, as if on a signal, Nanny got up and indicated it was time I went. There was nothing more I could do. I asked them if they'd think it over and let me know, and the oldest one just said, "We'll certainly think it over, Mr Lester. Good day." And that was that.'

Vee got up and went over to ruffle his hair. 'Poor darling. But they haven't said no, and if the Tuckers did go bankrupt ...'

She perched on the arm of his chair, and her buttocks, taut in a pair of silky slacks, swelled, round and inviting. 'And on that score, darling, I've heard something that should please you: my Mr Gordon White has played ball and Charlie Tucker has been summoned to the bank.' She smiled, well pleased with herself. 'I did my research, Hugh, and I found out that Gordon is the manager of the Tuckers' bank. *That's* why I played tennis with the little toad.'

'But he would never discuss a customer with you – that would be unethical. He wouldn't risk his job like that, even for a game of tennis with you.'

'Maybe, but there are many ways to skin a cat, and he's so anxious to please. Anyway, I let drop that we knew the Tuckers, that we know they are in dire financial straits and suggested that he might find further promotion elusive if he didn't attempt to retrieve some of the money the Tuckers owed the bank before they went to the wall ...'

Hugh stared at her. 'My God, Vee, I'm glad you're on my side.'

Vee purred. 'And I've had a few other ideas that will add to the squeeze – I wonder when the Tuckers' milking parlour was last inspected? I thought I would phone the hygiene inspectors as a concerned citizen, and suggest that all is not as it should be. They'll have to act and knowing the Tuckers, I bet they find something wrong. And even if they don't, the inspection alone will increase the pressure on them. Oh, and by the way, Lenny Spinks is coming to see you tomorrow evening at six. So you see, little Hughie, we're getting there.'

He groaned and stroked her bottom, 'Where's Anthony?'

She read his mind. 'He went off this morning. So with neither Cordelia nor Anthony here tonight, we can make as much noise as we like ...'

*

In the sitting room at Summerstoke Manor, the Misses Merfields were each occupied with their own thoughts, and each waiting for the signal that the time was right to share them. Then the door opened and Nanny came in, carrying a tray. 'I took it upon myself to make some more tea.' She placed the tray, laden with fine bone china cups, matching teapot, a bowl of sugar lumps and a plate resplendent with biscuits, on the low lacquered table in front of Mrs Merfield.

'And you've opened another packet of chocolate digestives. Clever Nanny,' approved the youngest, Louisa, reaching out an elegant, vermilion-tipped claw for the plate.

Nanny passed the cups round and then sat down with her own in a comfortable armchair next to the fire. In spite of the heat of the day she was dressed in thick stockings, a heather tweed skirt, a green jumper and white blouse. The colour was the only element of her costume to vary according to the season and her sombre stolidity was in direct contrast to the butterfly qualities of the two youngest Merfields and the black elegance of the widow.

'So, girls, what do we think?' Mrs Merfield looked round at them all, indicating the time had come to talk. 'You first, Nanny.'

'What I think is, he's a nasty piece of work. He knows what he wants and he will stop at nothing to get it.'

'Yes, he's a slimeball all right,' said Louisa, cheerfully helping herself to a second biscuit.

'But that doesn't mean to say he might not have a point about the Tuckers,' chipped in the older sister, Charlotte. 'Charlie Tucker really is in danger of becoming a bit of a spiv.'

'So it's a choice between a spiv who might not be able to pay the next quarter's rent and a slimeball who might be prepared to pay us a considerable amount more.' Mrs Merfield smiled faintly.

'Put like that, there really is no choice, is there, dear?' The youngest Miss Merfield nibbled at her chocolate biscuit and then giggled. 'I must say I enjoy our encounters with him. Lottie, did you make up that story about the soloist in "The Rites of Spring"?'

Charlotte, stretching her long, thin legs out in front of her to admire a pair of slender feet encased in red leather sandals, the same colour as the streak in her hair, smiled. 'No I did not; I heard it on Radio Four. Serve him right. Fancy conducting a conversation on the phone with his daughter, in front of us!'

'No manners and no breeding,' said Nanny firmly. 'You say there's no choice, Miss Louisa, but I say better the beast you know than a snake in the grass. And, excuse me, ma'am,' she said, turning to Mrs Merfield, 'but it's not as if we need the extra money, is it?'

'That's true, Nanny, but we are not a charity.'

There was a thoughtful silence.

Still lithe for her age, Charlotte rose to her feet and drifted over to a window. She turned to her sister-in-law. 'We first let the land to Elsie and Thomas, didn't we?'

'Yes, Charlotte. Do you think we should consult Elsie before taking it away?'

'Yes,' said Charlotte Merfield thoughtfully. 'Yes, I do.'

'And I agree,' said Nanny stoutly, putting her cup firmly on the tray as if to seal the matter.

'Very well. I will write to Elsie and invite her to tea next Tuesday.'

'But no arrowroot biscuits, Nanny!'

'I wouldn't dream of it, Miss Louisa.'

Alison lay on her back on her bed, staring at the cracks in the ceiling, the mournful strains of David Gray swelling in her headphones. The evening breeze gently stirred a stray cobweb dangling from the lampshade; a fly buzzed lazily across her face, and dancing patterns of light from the setting sun reflected off the old-fashioned polished wardrobe that had been a present from Gran years ago. Her eye observed these things, but her mind was engaged elsewhere, switching between Sunday afternoon with Al and her row with Elsie.

It had been a brilliant afternoon. They had scrambled on the rocks, paddled in pools and walked along the edge of the sea, darting from the reaches of the bigger waves and splashing through the shallower ones. They had stood, holding hands, the shingle sucking away under their feet till they eventually lost their balance, then stared out to the horizon where the blue of the sea lost its colour and became indistinguishable from the sky. He'd taken her to a place called West Bay where he bought her the best fish and chips she'd ever tasted. She didn't remember having enjoyed herself so much before, ever.

And yet, and yet ...

She stirred. Her initial euphoria had been replaced by an unidentifiable sense of dissatisfaction. True, he'd held her hand; true, he'd kissed her and not horrible, slobbery, tongue-in-the mouth kisses, either; but he'd been quite restrained and she didn't know, to put it crudely, whether he fancied her or not. And he hadn't kissed her until they had decided it was time to return.

Why did he leave it so late? Why the bloody hell didn't he kiss me earlier? We had the whole afternoon, she thought, frustrated. And when am I going to see him again? I don't know – I don't know anything. Okay, so when we kissed goodbye, he said he'd be in touch. Big deal – how? By text? Great!

She groaned. She hadn't told Al that she had no means of replying to his messages. She had hoped that somehow enough money could be scraped together to top up her mobile by the time he contacted her, but this row with Gran made that seem unlikely. She still hadn't told him where she lived, nor her telephone number – she didn't want to run the risk of one of her family answering the phone and making some fool-ass comment. But then, he hadn't given her that information about himself, either. She'd no idea where he lived. All she had was his mobile number.

'I guess that's cool,' she muttered. 'What else do I need? I've just got to play it low-key and wait for him to make the next move. What a sod that he's had to go off for the next few days ...'

Her mind switched back to Gran. One of the reasons for her visit that afternoon had been to try and borrow against her next month's allowance. If Elsie had agreed, then she would have had enough money for her phone, *and* their next date. If she didn't cough up with her share, she couldn't see Al hanging around for long. As it turned out, she had been so incensed by what she saw as Elsie's intransigence that she had lost her cool, banged on about not going to university and all that, and any question of begging for money had been forgotten until it was too late.

Perhaps it's not too late. Perhaps if I can find some way round the hole Gran's dug for herself, and us … As she continued to lie on her bed, the shadows growing in her room, her thoughts turned inwards.

Jenny, in the kitchen, was equally preoccupied, though not with Elsie. Jeff hadn't held her hand; he hadn't kissed her; he hadn't said they should go out together another time; but since she hadn't been expecting any of these things, she wasn't disappointed and, for her, Sunday afternoon ended all too soon.

She had been shy to begin with, and slightly over-anxious to please, but all that had evaporated when, swivelling her bottom to get out of his car, she had firmly planted her sandalled feet in a fresh cowpat. Dismayed, they both stared at the brown-green ooze between her toes, then Jenny, struck by such a ridiculous beginning to her dream day out, started to laugh (if she hadn't laughed, she told Rita later, she would have wept). Taking his cue from her, Jeff laughed, too, then fussed around, cleaning her shoes while she wiped her feet on the grass.

She felt an unfamiliar physical pang when she rested a hand on his shoulder as he bent down to put her sandals on, and again when, in an easy way, he took her elbow to guide her through the crowds round the pig sty, to see the piglets.

'My favourite farm animals,' he said. 'Much underrated by us humans. Cleanest, most intelligent beasts in the farmyard.'

Jenny, slightly overcome by the smell and the intensity of the high-pitched squealing as food was placed in the troughs, said nothing, but tried to look interested as he talked to her about the different breeds, and resolved not to serve him roast pork when next he could be persuaded to join them for Sunday lunch.

It had never occurred to Jenny that there could be so many different breeds of the same animal. As far as she knew there were cows, pigs, sheep, goats etc., and that was all there was to it. Under Jeff's informed tutelage, she became aware of how little she did know and felt somewhat ashamed that in all her married life with Jim and subsequently, she had learned so little about farm animals.

Not liking to appear too stupid in Jeff's eyes, she kept her ignorance to herself, nodding as if she knew what he was talking about and pretending she was familiar with all the different species. They finished the afternoon in the farm's tea shop and Jenny tucked in happily to a plateful of warm crumbly scones, thick red strawberry jam (her absolute favourite), with spoonfuls of buttery yellow cream. Jeff spotted the farmer (a woman, much to Jenny's amazement), and went over to speak to her while Jenny browsed amongst the books and small gifts on display. She found a child's guide to rare breeds and seeing Jeff still deep in conversation, made a surreptitious purchase, resolving to teach herself about the animals in case, just in case, he should take her out again.

She had it open on the table now as she finished labelling the chutney, listened to *The Archers*, and assembled supper for the family. Elsie poked her head round the door. 'Whatever it is, Jenny, I'll have it on a tray in my room. I've no stomach for that smell, or my family, at the moment, thank you.'

Jenny sighed and pushed the fruits of her labours to join an array of kitchen paraphernalia that permanently occupied one end of the table. Stephen came in from the milking shed just as she had put a plate containing a portion of rather grey-looking cauliflower cheese on Elsie's tray.

'Take this up to your Gran, Stephen, and I'll dish up for the rest of us. And give Ali a shout, would you? I think she's in her room, though she's very quiet.'

'Why can't Gran eat down here with the rest of us, instead of making more work for you? Got a bad conscience, has she?'

'I don't know about that, love, and please don't be rude to her.

It's bad enough that Charlie won't go near her, but I heard Ali shouting earlier and she banged the door so hard the whole house shook.'

'Ali shouted at Gran?' Stephen was impressed, 'That's a first. I wonder what she said.'

But later when he pressed her over supper, Alison wasn't interested in going over the details of her argument.

'The thing is,' she said, waving a fork at Stephen and Jenny, 'It's up to us to find a way out of this mess. You know what Gran's like – stubborn as old boots; she won't back down, no matter how much she might want to – I don't think she's thought her ultimatum through. Is she *really* going to move over for two more women on this farm? No. The thing is, she's really worried about the state it's getting into, and you can't blame her.'

Stephen, in the process of scraping out the last encrusted bits of the cauliflower cheese onto his plate, looked resentful. 'I do more than my bit. I can't help it if—'

Alison hastily reassured him. 'I know you do, Stephen. But the thing is that straightforward farming, particularly on the scale that we're at, is not paying. Not only is it not paying, it's losing. Old Lester must be the only farmer we know who seems to make money without blinking, and though we might sneer at it, I think Gran was rattled when he came back with that second offer.'

'She must know we'd never sell.'

'The very idea!' chimed in Jenny, clearing away the plates to the sink. 'Ali, fetch the bowls from the dresser, love. There's rhubarb and custard for pudding.'

'But supposing we had to?' Alison persisted, fetching the bowls and placing them on the table. 'No rhubarb for me, thanks, Mum.' She sat down and looked across at Stephen. 'Did you know that the bank has asked to see Charlie tomorrow, to discuss our overdraft?'

Stephen froze and then whistled with dismay.

Jenny dropped the spoon with which she was ladling out some bright yellow custard onto a browny-pink slush. 'Oh no, it's not fair – what more can we do? I struggle with my budget as it is.'

'How come he told you and not me? I'm meant to be his partner.'

'I took the call. Anyway, the bank and Gran between them set me thinking. Gran's idea that getting you two married will solve our problems is stupid, as is the idea that by threatening me she will get me to university. No, but what she also said was "if we managed to turn the farm around", and that's gonna be what the bank wants, too. The crazy thing is that if we got the farm on its feet, I think she'd put money into it. Same way a bank will lend if they think you're onto a good thing.'

'That's all well and good,' said Stephen heavily, 'but how? We're stretched as it is.'

'I know. But something Gran said; maybe we should rethink what we're doing. Instead of flogging a dead horse, maybe we should think of doing something different, put energy into things that might pay. Diversify.'

'I'm not giving up my cows!'

'We could have some rare breeds,' said Jenny, unexpectedly. Alison and Stephen stared at her. 'Well, um ...' she added lamely, 'people like to see them, like in a zoo, but working.'

'That's a good idea, Mum.' Alison was surprised and encouraging. 'That's the sort of thing I mean. Listen, Stephen, I think we should have a meeting, the four of us – not Gran – and bash ideas around. It can't do any harm. You persuade Charlie; he won't listen to me. And we should think of everything, *anything* that might make money, including,' her eyes fell on the jars of chutney, ' – green tomato chutney.'

Charlie had not been at all enthusiastic about the idea of a meeting when tackled about it that night, but it was the first time the brothers had exchanged more than two words since Elsie's bombshell and Stephen, still holding Charlie responsible for the terrible position Elsie had put him in, was more abrasive, more assertive than usual in dealing with his brother.

Taken aback by Stephen's stance, tired after harvesting all day, disappointed at having failed in the pub that evening to pin

Beth down on when their next date would be, and dispirited at the thought of his visit to the bank, Charlie didn't put up much resistance, apart from the odd sarcastic comment about his sister's sudden interest in the farm, and his inability to see that anything constructive would be achieved, sneering, 'Diversifying – is that an alternative to marriage?'

9

'Two hundred and fifty grams: that's a little over half a pound of pear drops.' Rita Godwin turned from the sweets she was weighing and peered through her large, lightly tinted specs at the tall, thin man standing on the other side of the counter. He had a large head, with a high forehead and a shock of thick greying hair, and from the weary way his body moved and the head followed, his pronounced stoop came from carrying a cranium too weighty for the shoulders that bore it. That head was turned in the direction of the scales and appeared to be counting every sugary pink and yellow boiled sweet shaken out of the jar.

'Is that all right, vicar?'

'Yes, yes, Mrs Godwin. It's foolish of me, I know, but I will never get the measure of metric.' His voice was soft and anxious and he tugged at the hem of the short grey vestment that proclaimed his profession, as if willing it to be long enough to conceal the hanging thread of a missing button on the waistband of his trousers.

'You're not the only one,' chipped in Jenny. 'I was bad enough at sums at the best of times. It beats me where Alison gets her brains from. She's doin' maths at A-level. Can you believe it?'

'You must be very proud of her, er ...' The vicar, old before his time, had the polite, slightly embattled look of someone who was trying to remember not only whom they were talking about, but whom he was talking to.

'Don't forget your *Telegraph*.' Rita was dying to resume the conversation she had been having with Jenny when the vicar had come into the shop. 'That'll be one pound fifty, please.'

With painstaking slowness, the vicar took out a battered leather purse and counted out the change.

'Thank you, Mrs Godwin. Good day.' With a nod and a vague smile that embraced both ladies, he left the shop.

'I swear he gets slower every time he comes in!' Rita chuckled. 'But I mustn't grumble – at least he comes into the shop, an' he's eatin' his way single-handed through that jar of pear drops.'

'Never liked 'em, myself. Give me a humbug any day.'

But Rita wasn't interested in comparing favourite sweets.

'Well now, Jenny Tucker, so what next? Did Jeff ask you out again? How did he leave it?'

The two women settled down to resume their tête à tête amidst the little stacks of West Country fudge, country craft biscuits, jars of locally produced honey, chutney and lemon curd that are found on the counter in most village shops and designed more for promoting an image of wholesome home cooking to passing trade than meeting the demands of the regular customer.

Rita was the same age as Jenny; she had moved into the village as a newlywed to run the village shop a couple of years before Jenny had arrived at Marsh Farm. She'd had no children and her husband, Rob, was a semi-permanent invalid with chronic back trouble. As a girl she had been quite plain, but middle age was kinder. She experimented with hair colour, curls, and make-up, and followed fashion slavishly, ordering what she could afford from her catalogue.

Life was not easy for Rita, but she was an ebullient woman with plenty of time for other people's troubles. She provided, together with the postman and the milkman, an unofficial, un-acknowledged, very essential support service to the elderly and infirm of the village and Jenny admired her deeply for it. The two women had quickly become close friends; Jenny envied Rita's strength and patience; Rita loved her friend's gentleness and humility, although at times the latter drove her mad, particularly where Elsie was concerned.

She had known about Jenny's secret interest in Jeff Babbington for a long time and had ceaselessly chivvied her friend to do something about it, without expecting anything, ever, to happen. Now that it had, she was almost more excited than her friend, who replied to Rita's frenzied questioning with a matter-of-fact, 'Well, he just dropped me back home. Didn't stop for a cup. Said he'd enjoyed himself. He was just, well, normal, Rita.'

'And he didn't say anythin' like "We must do this again some time"?'

'No.'

'So why did he ask you out in the first place? He's been comin' round to yours for years. Why did he suddenly take you out?'

Jenny hesitated. True, Rita was her very great friend, but she was a gossip – inevitable, perhaps, running the shop. But Jenny wasn't sure whether she could be trusted not to say anything about Elsie's little bombshell and could see it would be very difficult for her two sons if anything got out. 'He saw I was upset and thought it'd cheer me up. He's really thoughtful like that.'

'Why were you upset, Jenny? Not like you. I know Elsie's a pain in the bum, but you don't normally let her get to you. And the boys wouldn't do anything to upset you. Was it Ali? She can be a little madam, I know. I think you're a bit soft with her, I really do—'

Jenny interrupted her. 'No, no, it wasn't Ali, or the boys. If I tell you, Rita, you must swear not to tell anyone else. Promise me.'

Rita was intrigued. 'Of course I won't tell. I'm your mate. You can trust me.'

And so Jenny told Rita Godwin about Elsie's ultimatum. And of course, swearing them to secrecy, Rita subsequently told each and every other customer that came to the shop, and before the end of Tuesday, most of the village knew and were in stitches at the thought of Charlie Tucker being tied down at last, and at the idea of Stephen Tucker finding someone who might marry him.

As Stephen had a rehearsal in the evening, the family meeting was fixed for late morning, when Charlie got back from the bank and before Elsie appeared for lunch.

After Charlie had left to keep his appointment, Alison joined Stephen in the yard, where he was scraping down the slurry and, to his amazement, offered to give him a hand. The noise of the tractor and the sheer physical effort of the work made conversation difficult, but when they finished, she said, 'Stephen, I know I haven't made what happens on the farm my business, but it doesn't mean I don't care. And before you say anything, it's got nothing to do with the fact that I own a share.'

'A share that ain't worth much, as it happens.'

'So you and Charlie keep reminding me. Anyway, I want to know just how things are with the bank. Charlie looked awful when he went off this morning.'

'And well he might. The bank's got us locked in, in two ways. For one, we've a loan, which we have to pay interest on, and pay off a bit of the capital every month; for two, we've an overdraft which has a fixed limit and which, more than likely, we're way over.'

'More than likely – you don't know?'

Stephen and Jenny reacted in the same way to the appearance of any official-looking envelopes: they froze and then put them on one side to be opened later, possibly. If the financial management of the farm had been left to them, it would have collapsed long ago. Stephen, who was a careful manager in every other way, was ashamed of this weakness and therefore not as critical about Charlie's organisation of the finances as he probably should have been.

'No, not exactly. Charlie deals with all that side of the business and sorts the bills. But I do know he keeps on muttering about things being tight at the moment, which is why the money isn't forthcoming for my pump and why you didn't get your allowance.'

'How much is the overdraft?'

''Bout fifty K.'

Alison's jaw dropped. 'Fifty thousand? We owe the bank fifty thousand?'

Stephen felt hot and uncomfortable. 'More than that with the loan. That's about another sixty.'

'My God, it's worse than I ever dreamed of!' Alison fell silent, the schemes she had been thinking up suddenly looking paltry in the light of a debt of such magnitude.

'This way, Mr Tucker.' A bored young girl, bursting out of her regulation blouse and skirt, showed Charlie into a small, windowless room. 'Take a seat; Mr White will be with you shortly.' And she left, shutting the door firmly behind her.

It was hot in the room, and the large, silent fan, swishing round overhead, did little more than stir the warm air. There was nothing to interest or entertain or, more particularly, to distract attention from the nervous knot growing in his stomach. The room had been created by boxing off the corner of a much larger one and there was barely enough space for the desk with its computer, and the three wooden chairs. Light cream wallpaper with a silvery stripe lined the walls, on which were hung a series of pictures of palm trees. It was only the presence of those prints that prevented the place from being, in Charlie's opinion, rather like a police interview room.

The minutes ticked by and Charlie became increasingly uncomfortable. His mother had persuaded him to wear his suit and he could feel the perspiration trickling down his back. He had just decided to hell with it, he was going to take his jacket off and roll up his sleeves, when the door opened. A waft of aftershave preceded the entrance of Gordon White. He was not much older than Charlie, but the two men could not have been more different. Charlie was strong and upright – there was a freshness about him, a directness that some, like Gordon White, might find disconcerting. His eyes glinted with hidden laughter, his skin, not yet coarsened by the elements, glowed with health, and his ill-fitting suit accentuated the strength of his body. By contrast, Gordon White had already started sagging. His skin was pallid; he was slack-faced, and had eyes like boiled sweets; every hair on his head was a testimonial to an expensive hairdresser, and his handshake was flaccid and sticky.

Charlie disliked Gordon White on sight, and, smooth though

he was, the bank manager made little attempt to conceal his distaste for Charlie. He waved at Charlie to sit, and sat himself, turning straightaway to the computer as he talked.

'Thank you for coming in, Mr Tucker. I'm new to this branch, as you may be aware, and I've made it my business to go through all our customer accounts that are carrying large overdrafts. I have one or two little concerns that I need to air with you.'

As he continued and then invited Charlie to comment, it became clear they didn't talk the same language; Gordon White made no attempt to understand the problems Charlie presented to him, problems that were currently besetting any small-scale farmer. Sympathy, compassion and understanding were words simply not on the agenda. What made it worse was that when Charlie grew heated and loud, Gordon White remained completely detached, cool and quietly spoken.

They reached an impasse in their discussion; Gordon White stared at him for a moment, a half-smile on his face, then turned away to give the computer his complete attention. Charlie glared at the profile of the manager; he could swear that, right now, Gordon White was enjoying himself. The man was bad news. Charlie had met his type before and despised them. They were the school prefects of life; the head boys who became petty officers; the lizards of the business world; the petty sadists in control of small things, who regarded Charlie and his sort with ill-concealed contempt and who enjoyed humiliating them.

As if feeling Charlie's eyes on him, Gordon White looked up, his immaculately manicured fingernails gently playing over the keyboard as he spoke. 'Believe me, Mr Tucker, I hear what you are saying. Indeed, you are not the first farmer to be outfaced by circumstance and the bank has leaned over backwards to implement sympathetic packages for clients so impacted ...'

Charlie struggled to understand what Gordon White was driving at.

'But you will appreciate we are not a charity. You are not delivering, Mr ... er ... Tucker, so it's time for us to get a grip, to retrench, to safeguard our investments, you understand. When a business like yours is clearly not cost-effective—'

'It's not a business. It's a farm. We've just been through ten years of hell. It's not surprising—'

'No, it's not surprising, looking over the extent and nature of your enterprise. I would suggest to you it is just not viable. We've no wish to see you go bankrupt, Mr Tucker, but we are going to have to change gear, close the floodgates, as it were.'

Charlie looked at him, suddenly feeling very frightened. This was like being back in court. The magistrates had fined him ninety quid; this, he knew, was going to be worse, a lot worse. 'What do you mean?'

Gordon White smiled faintly and leaned back in his chair. 'What I mean, Mr Tucker, is that we need to implement certain measures to reduce the risk factor to our shareholders. And this is what we want you to do. I am sure you will see that we have bent over backwards to be reasonable ...'

But Charlie could see nothing reasonable in anything that Gordon White required of him. He argued, he shouted, he refused to agree, but at the end of the day, Gordon White had the upper hand and there was nothing Charlie could do about it.

Stephen and Alison had cleaned up and joined Jenny in the kitchen by the time Charlie returned. He went to his room to change out of his suit, without a word to anyone, and with foreboding, the other three awaited his news.

It was not good, and when he rejoined them in the kitchen, Charlie made no attempt to disguise the fact. Whilst the repayments were made regularly on the bank loan, it remained in place; the overdraft, however, had exceeded the agreed limit and not only did Gordon White insist it be brought down to that limit, he decreed that the limit itself should be reduced – those repayments to start at the beginning of the next month.

Unfortunately for the Tuckers, September was always the month when their outgoings were greatest, with farm insurance to be paid and the field rent to the Merfields due, quite apart from all the other bills that seemed to accumulate by the end of summer.

'How much?' Alison enquired, in a small, depressed voice.

'We're going to have to find an extra three thousand. Stupid bastard! Where does he think we're going to find that from? Anyone would think he wants to make us bankrupt!'

He looked grimly round the table. His mother was close to tears; Stephen had a dead, lumpen expression on his face and Alison looked as miserable as he'd ever seen her. In a small white T-shirt and her hair pulled back, she looked very young. It touched a chord, reminding him of times when his dad was still alive and his little sister thought that he, Charlie, had the answer to everything. His face softened.

'Well, come on. Let's start this meeting. Mum, I'm gasping for a cuppa. Ali, Stevie here says you think marriage might *not* be what Gran is after? It certainly wasn't one of shitty Mr White's suggestions.'

Jenny got up and fussed over the kettle and the teabags, while Alison went through her conversation with Elsie and the discussion she'd subsequently had with Jenny and Stephen about finding new ways of improving the farm's fortunes.

'Maybe you're right,' Charlie said thoughtfully. Alison nearly fell off her chair. Charlie generally gave her a hard time and never lost an opportunity to put her down. 'Maybe we *should* think of other things we could do. Okay, folks, so what grand ideas have you got up your sleeves then, eh?'

'I'll make notes.' Alison rummaged around the pile of papers at the end of the table and produced an old envelope and a pencil. 'Just in case we decide to follow something through. You go first, Mum.'

Jenny placed an assortment of mugs on the table and poured out the tea. Then, patting a stray wisp of hair back into place, she cleared her throat and shyly explained to Charlie her idea about rare breeds.

'There are so many different pigs, Charlie, you wouldn't believe it. I've been looking them up. If we didn't farm them for meat, we could have them as an attraction … open the farm to visitors.'

'That would fit in with what I had in mind,' chipped in Stephen, still in his blue work overalls and, ever hungry, eating a bowl of cornflakes. 'I was reading this article on ostriches. Apparently you can use every bit of the ostrich, except the eyes. We could farm them and turn them into an attraction. According to this article, there's a butcher in Bristol sells ostrich meat for an absolute bomb.'

'And then we could have a farm shop – we could sell ostrich feathers there, couldn't we, Stephen?' Jenny's state of near despair at Charlie's news was rapidly dissolving in the excitement of the moment. 'And we could sell other things, too – tomato chutney, jams, cakes, biscuits. I could make them. People like buying homemade things.'

Alison smiled at her mother's enthusiasm. 'You could sell some of your knitting as well, Mum, and we could sell Gran's liqueurs and cordials.'

'And if only I could free my strawberry beds of slugs and snails, we could sell strawberries, in season, and I could make strawberry jam.'

'Perhaps we should pick the snails and sell them as strawberry-flavoured snails, a local delicacy!' Alison quipped, adding, 'Actually, PYO is really popular – would our land be any good for soft fruit, Charlie?'

Charlie shrugged. 'Ask me another. We could find out, I guess, but don't underestimate the amount of graft that goes into that sort of farming. And if we took away the barley and grass, we'd have to buy in feed for Stephen's cows – unless, of course, all these schemes of yours are assuming we get rid of the herd.'

Stephen went pale. 'No way – you lay off my cows.'

Charlie became impatient. 'Look, Steve, we can't have it all ways—'

'We should think of other things,' Alison hastily interjected. 'And maybe stuff not directly connected with farming, but which uses the land.'

'Like motocross does, you mean – now you're talking my kind of talk, Ali!' At Alison's evident displeasure, Charlie threw back his head and laughed.

For the next half hour they battled on, racking their brains and throwing ideas about which seemed to get wilder and more unrealistic. After they finally lapsed into silence, Charlie'd had enough. 'Okay, folks, I've got work to do. Ali, what have we got so far?'

Alison read out the ideas that had made it to the back of the envelope. Charlie sighed, suddenly feeling raw again after his experience at the hands of Gordon White. 'Well, I don't think we're going to earn a fortune, even if we do get any of these ideas off the ground; certainly not enough to get the bank off our backs. There's only one way we can do that.'

'What's that, Charlie?' asked Stephen, looking hopefully at his brother.

'Bump the old lady off,' he said grimly. 'Get her off our case, and then maybe we could find out just how much she's really worth …'

'So what sort of ideas did y'all come up with, then?' asked Lenny, pouring tea from a Thermos. The weather had held, and he and Charlie had nearly finished cutting the field. 'Here. Fancy a biscuit?'

'Ta. Well, Mum was keen on rare breeds and selling stuff that she could make.'

'Like what?'

'Oh, you know: jams, pies, cakes, chutney, that sort of stuff.'

Lenny, who knew Jenny's cooking of old, goggled. 'You won't make much out of that, mate!'

'Maybe not, but she's keen to do her bit. Don't know where she got this rare breeds idea from. Could be worth looking into, but I reckon it'd cost too much to set up. Stephen's keen, but then he'd go along with anything that will allow him to keep his herd.'

'So where are you gonna find this extra three K the bank wants by the end of next month, Charlie?'

'I don't know, and I'm fed up with thinking about it.'

'Would you think of taking up old Lester on his offer?'

'Over my dead body. He's made two offers now, both silly money. What does he think I am – the village idiot? No, something will turn up, you'll see.' But he didn't feel as optimistic as he sounded and they finished their tea in a depressed silence.

'It's a pity,' Charlie observed as they stood up to resume work, 'that Marsh Farm is so bloomin' flat. If it weren't, we could have our own motocross circuit here. You should have seen Ali's face when I suggested it. I meant it as a joke, but I bet old Cruddy rakes in a fortune down at Farleigh.'

'You should do a deal with Hugh Lester. You know he wants your fields for his nags. Swap one of your meadows for Knoll Woods. We could build a cracker of a course in there.'

'Fat chance; he makes a mint out of them pheasants – ripping off hordes of bloody foreigners, firing in every which way ...'

'Lucky for us they seem to miss so many!' Lenny smirked and they both laughed.

'I bet shooting pays better than motocross.'

'Mebbe, but you can bet yer bottom dollar that motocross pays better than farmin'.'

'A lot more fun, too. Well, if you come up with any brilliant ideas, Lenny, bring 'em on in. Now let's finish this little lot off, then I'll stand you a beer at The Grapes, bank or no bank.'

'You're on, though it'll have to be a quick one. As it 'appens, I've got a date with old Lester this evening.'

Charlie turned and looked at Lenny, his eyebrows raised in surprise. Then he said lightly, 'Ooh, get you, hobnobbing with the enemy! What on earth are you going to see him for?'

Lenny was almost apologetic. 'He wants to offer me work, according to my missus. I don't mind taking a few bob off him.' Suddenly he clutched Charlie's arm. 'Look, Charlie, it's them – there they are again.'

Unnoticed, a sleek black car had parked in the lane by the gate and two men in dark glasses were walking across the stubble towards them.

Charlie climbed down from his cab, motioning Lenny to stay where he was, and walked across the field to meet them.

The two men looked incongruous, standing in the middle of a stubble field in dark designer suits, slick shiny shoes, and flashes of gold around their necks, fingers and wrists.

They greeted him without smiling.

One, slighter and younger than the other, got straight to the point. 'Hey, man, you said you was the farmer owned these fields?' His voice was flat, devoid of much expression, with an accent that Charlie identified as Estuary English from the television he watched.

'That's right.'

'We told you we was interested in mebbe renting 'em for a week?'

'Yeah?'

'Well, we are. As from now, for the next two weeks. This one, and the one next to it. We'll make it worth your while. You still up for it?'

'I might be.'

The second man growled warningly.

The first shook his head, wearily. 'Cut the crap, man. Either you are or you ain't. I haven't got the time to arse around.'

Charlie didn't hesitate any longer and the deal was spelt out to him. They wanted the fields left as they were, stubble and all, but he was to fix the gates so the fields could be secured, and when the time came, there would be more work for Charlie and his hired hand, if Charlie wanted it, for which they would pay extra.

The sum offered for the use of the fields had Charlie gasping, although he did his best to conceal the fact, and found his voice sufficiently to ask for a down payment. A bulging wallet was produced.

Much the same age as Charlie, they had obviously attained a level of prosperity that Charlie could only dream of, so it was with some considerable envy, the deal done, he watched them walk back across the field to the small layby where they had parked their car.

Seeing the men depart, Lenny came over to join Charlie. 'What's all that about, then?'

Charlie, fingering the large wad of notes that he had shoved into the pocket of his overalls, could barely speak with excitement. 'That, me old sparkplug, was something turning up.' His eyes shining, he punched the air. 'Yea-ah!'

His excitement was infectious. 'What? Come on, Charlie, what is it? You look as if you're gonna burst a blood vessel.'

'So would you if one minute you were staring ruin in the face and the next minute, enough lolly drops into your lap not only to pay the bloodsuckers at the bank, but to put up a fair whack for a reconditioned bike in time for the next Farleigh meeting!'

Lenny let out a whoop of joy. 'Bloody hell, Charlie. Why? What 'ave *you* got that they want so much?'

'These two fields, my boy, the ones we've just cut – they want to borrow them for a short while; but Lenny, before I tell you what it's all about, you've got to swear you won't say a word to anyone, mate, okay? Those guys were heavy about that; they don't want anyone to get wind, in case someone pokes their nose in. There's five thousand smackers riding on this, so forget you know anything!'

'Five thou—' Lenny could hardly speak. 'You're kidding me?'

'Nope. I've a little wad in my pocket as evidence of their good faith. I think this calls for a celebration.'

'You're on,' said Lenny.

'It'll take us another hour to finish the field, so let's crack on. I'll tell you what they want on our way to the pub.'

'What about Stevie?'

'What do you mean?'

'Are you gonna tell him about the deal?'

Charlie thoughtfully stroked a sideburn. He knew he should tell Stephen, but he knew his brother and realised that the strain of keeping anything like this a secret from the rest of the family would be too much for him. 'I'll tell him about it when it's all over.' He climbed up into his tractor and turned on the ignition.

'From next week, though, we keep him away from here – there's no reason for him to come up here, anyway.'

Alison sat at her desk, her head in her hands, her mobile next to her elbow, the text message winking insistently.

'Back Sat. Same place 7. Y/N. Have fun. Al.'

She felt bleak. No money, so no top-up, so no way of texting, and no other way of getting in touch.

'Oh, sod it!' she shouted at the top of her voice, but felt no better.

Elsie and Jenny, in the sitting room below, heard her.

'That girl needs to control her temper,' said Elsie grimly.

'I think she gets a bit fed up. Stuck in her room like that, with those books. Can't be healthy. She needs to get out more, poor Ali.' Jenny placidly clicked away at her knitting.

The memory of Alison slipping across the farmyard in the early hours of the morning flitted through Elsie's thoughts and for a moment she toyed with destroying Jenny's peace of mind, but she was feeling tired and the thought of the fuss and recriminations that would follow made her snap, instead, 'Then why doesn't she? Girl of her age should be out meeting people, doing things, having lots of friends. What's wrong with the girl?'

'She's got lots of friends but says if she starts sponging off them, they won't stay friends for long.'

'Quite right. But why should she sponge? She has her allowance, and a very generous one it is too, considering the state of the farm's finances.'

Jenny, suddenly alarmed, said nothing. They had tacitly agreed not to tell Elsie that Alison had not received her allowance. Elsie had a nasty habit of using facts like that to reinforce her never-ending diatribe about how useless they all were. She concentrated very hard on the knitting pattern.

Elsie, watching her, was not deceived. She could read Jenny so well.

'She *did* have her allowance this month, didn't she, Jenny?

Whose turn was it to pay her? Stephen's? Not like him to let her down. What is this farm coming to? I despair, I really do.'

'It wasn't Stephen's fault,' said Jenny defensively. 'He needed to buy something for the dairy. He had to have it, otherwise there'd be no milk for sale, and where would we be? And Charlie's got Lenny working on the harvest with him, so he didn't have any spare cash. It's just this month. Ali understands. It's a bit unfortunate that it's the holidays and she's promised to study and not get a job, which she did last year, of course. When the money for my jumper comes through, I'll be able to help her out a little bit. She posted it for me on Saturday, so I should get paid soon. That's why Ali didn't phone to tell us where she was. She hasn't got any credit on that phone you so kindly bought her. It wasn't her fault. I shouldn't have made such a fuss. But I expect that's why she's so fed up.' She put her knitting down and rose to her feet. 'I'll go and make her a nice cup of tea. Would you like one, Elsie? Perhaps I can persuade her to come down and watch *The Weakest Link* with us.'

Elsie, now deep in thought, said nothing.

'Li-ver-ree lord madam I took him for a captain he's so be ... be ... diz ... diz ...' Stephen swallowed. He was hating every minute of this.

'Bedizened.' June was getting impatient. 'He's so bedizened with lace.' She sighed heavily. 'Just do the moves, Stephen; then skip to Mrs Sullen's cue. Oh, I do hope we find someone to play Scrub soon. This is really slowing us down.'

Stephen flushed. He hated reading in for missing actors. They still hadn't managed to cast Scrub, the manservant, and it had fallen to him to walk through the part so that the rest of the cast could accommodate the missing character. Every time he opened his mouth, Stephen, struggling with the unspeakable text, sensed that the actors were either laughing at him or growing impatient. His only consolation was that the scene in which he was making this guest appearance involved Nicola as well, and it was her encouraging smiles that kept him from throwing the book down and refusing to be humiliated further.

He had been very subdued since the farm meeting. The possibility that they might lose the farm had horrified him; he knew of no other way in which he could earn a living. Although he and Charlie rarely discussed it, he knew that the herd was not the money-earner it once was, that they might make more if they concentrated on cereal production, but the thought of the farm without animals was appalling. He loved his beasts and would not consider letting them go, however counterproductive that might be. He didn't have a great imagination, but Jenny's suggestion that they might think about rare breeds had stirred him. He had read about ostrich farming some while ago and had only suggested it because, at that point, he had no other contribution to make. He had been surprised when the others took it seriously, and when the meeting was over, he resolved to consult Jeff Babbington.

He confided a little of what had passed to Angela when he gave her a lift to the rehearsal. She was interested.

'Do you want me to look up ostrich farms on the internet – see if there are any nearby? Then you could go and check them out. I could look up rare breed farms, too – see what there are ...'

'That's really kind of you, Angela,' Stephen replied warmly; he was touched. 'You've got enough to do.'

'No, really, I'd love to help. And it's easy, being at the library.' Angela went slightly pink. 'You've been so ... so unlike yourself; I knew you were worried about something. If only I could do more.'

Stephen made no reply and glancing at him, Angela saw that he was shyly smiling in the direction of Nicola, who was standing in the road, flagging them down. Their conversation ended there.

Stephen pulled over and they both got out.

'Oh, Stephen.' Nicola's eyes were wide with relief. 'I'm so pleased to see you.' She was standing beside a bright red Golf convertible. 'It's my stupid car; it's broken down. Can you give me a lift to the rehearsal?'

'Of course I can.' Stephen flushed at the touch of Nicola's

hand on his arm. She looked so pretty, in a simple cotton dress that showed off her tan and her long shapely legs to perfection. He stammered a little. 'But what about your car? Do you want me to look at it, see if I can sort out whatever's wrong?'

She smiled fetchingly. 'You're so kind, Stephen, but it's full of complicated bits of technology. I've given my brother a ring and he's going to come over later and tow it to the garage. It should be safe enough if I leave it here. But if you could give me a lift? Oh, hi, Angela.' Nicola acknowledged Angela for the first time.

These days, Stephen drove the farm's only Land Rover and a battered old affair it was, too. It had just two seats in the front. Stephen opened the passenger door. 'I'm afraid it will be a bit of a squeeze, but if you don't mind squashing up?'

'Of course not. Neither of us is particularly large, are we, Angela?' And Nicola climbed into the cab, leaving Angela to follow after. Stephen shut the door and resumed his position in the driver's seat in a state of bliss. The two girls sharing the passenger seat meant that although Angela obligingly squashed herself as much against the door as she could, Nicola was almost on top of Stephen. Her scent filled his nostrils; every time he changed gear his hand brushed her thigh and he'd blush his apology; if she turned her head to address Angela, which was rarely, her hair tickled his face, and when she turned back to say something to him (Angela getting a faceful of hair every time) her breath softly patted his cheek.

Before they arrived at the church hall, in a rare demonstration of assertiveness, Stephen offered to give her a lift home when the rehearsal had finished. She accepted his offer and Stephen had arrived at the rehearsal in a state of euphoria.

That had evaporated when Scrub was inflicted on him. He threw agonised looks in Angela's direction, hoping to catch her eye, knowing that she would sympathise, hoping that she might offer to take his place. But she was always looking in the opposite direction, or busy doing something else.

At the end of the evening's rehearsal, Stephen's humiliation was compounded by June's dismissive: 'You've all done very well this evening, darlings, but please, please everyone, be on the lookout for a Scrub. We're not looking for a Laurence Olivier, just someone who can read the Queen's English. I know dear Stephen won't thank us if he ends up having to don make-up.'

There were titters and then the cry went up: 'Who's for the pub? June? Nicola? Gerald? And how about our little Cherry?'

Angela hovered, waiting for Stephen as he rushed around clearing up. Nicola had gone off with the rest of the company, and for a moment, the two of them were alone in the hall. Stephen, crestfallen, registered this and joining Angela, he said indecisively, 'Do you think Nicola expects us to follow them to the pub? I thought I was going to give her a lift back.'

'Perhaps she's got a lift from someone else, and forgot to tell you. But we could go to the pub, if you like?'

'No, I don't think so. I'm tired. What about you?'

'I wouldn't mind giving it a miss. I'm tired myself and we've a new exhibition to put up tomorrow.'

'Stephen, where are you?' It was Nicola, standing by the exit. 'I hope you've not forgotten you're giving me a lift? Come on. It's Robin's round and I don't know what you drink.'

Stephen beamed. Angela, suddenly feeling the tiredness she had feigned moments earlier, refused to join them and walked home alone.

'I can't believe you didn't phone me up straightaway – what sort of friend are you, Ali Tucker? I can't believe it!' Hannah shrieked away at the other end of the phone. 'You've been out with Al twice, and you didn't tell me!'

Alison was curled up on a battered old sofa in the sitting room, the phone pulled through from the hall on an extension lead that Alison had bought with her earnings the year before, so that she could conduct her telephone calls with a degree of privacy. It was late. Her mother and Gran had gone to bed, as had, as far as she knew, Stephen and Charlie. Alison had just finished an essay and, needing some contact with the real world, had slipped downstairs to have a chat with Hannah.

'The first time was by chance. There was nothing to tell, and Sunday, well, nothing happened. We just went out on his bike for the afternoon, nothing more.'

'Well, are you going to see him again?'

Alison sighed. 'He's gone off for a few days, but he's given me his mobile number.'

'Great, so text him!'

'Easier said than done, Hannah. It's a sod, but earlier this evening he sent me a message to meet up on Saturday ...'

'Wicked. What's the problem? Have you changed your mind or summat? You don't sound too happy about it.'

'No, I *am* ... it's cool; what's not cool is that I've no money, not a cent, and no credit on my phone, so I can't text him back. What's he gonna make of that?'

Hannah whistled. 'I see your point, Ali. D'you want me to text him for you?'

'No, it's early days. I don't want him to know I've told anyone else about him in case he gets the wrong idea; and in case *I* have, if you see what I mean. I guess, if it comes to the worst, I'll have to phone him from home, and pretend there's something wrong with my mobile. It's so humiliating!'

Hannah commiserated but then shrieked, 'Hey, Ali, you've got to get some money from somewhere. Remember I told you Nick was babbling on about a disco event the other evening? Well, it's happening. He got a call this evening. He's on a commission to sell tickets. It'll be wild!'

'When's it happening?'

'A week next Saturday, the bank holiday weekend. The tickets are twenty quid.'

'Wow, that's a lot.'

'Maybe, but Nick says they bring in top DJs, and it's all night, Ali. You've got to come. Hey, why don't you see if Al wants to come? That would be really cool.' She sounded plaintive. 'Ali, you can't not come – it's gonna be the best thing.'

'Yeah,' said Ali, wretchedly, 'it sounds fantastic. I'll ask Al when he gets back.'

'Great. Nick gets a bonus if he sells more than a hundred tickets.'

'Does he know a hundred people?'

'You'd be surprised. It's all done by word of mouth. When the word gets out, the tickets will be gold dust. Oh, Ali, you've got to come!'

'Don't wuz; I'll get the money somehow. Do we know where it's gonna be held?'

'No, not yet. They don't distribute the tickets and say where it's gonna be held till the last possible moment. They keep the venue a secret in case of objections and gatecrashers, that sort of thing.'

'Are you gonna tell your mum?'

'You must be kidding. There's no way she'd let me—'

Their conversation was interrupted by a loud crash from the direction of the kitchen.

'Blimey! What the bloody hell is that? Hannah, I've got to go. I'll ring you tomorrow.'

Charlie, barely able to see through the Jack Daniels swishing round his brain, had fallen through the kitchen door and landed on Gip in her basket. The dog, woken so violently, set up a howl, and Charlie, unable to get out of the basket, started giggling helplessly.

Alison rushed into the kitchen and tried to quieten Gip. She regarded her eldest brother with fury. 'It's not surprising the farm is going to the wall with you in charge. How much did your little booze-up cost tonight, eh? How are we ever going to make money if you're gonna drink it all away? You make me sick!'

Charlie looked up at her, grinning lopsidedly, his knees framing his chin. 'If you knew what *I* knew ...' he sang, then placed a wavering finger to his lips. 'Shush, Charlie boy, not a word. Not a word unless it's Mum. Hey, I like that – Mum it is ...' Alison turned on her heel and stalked out of the kitchen, turning the light out as she went. Charlie held out his arm plaintively and called after her, 'Ali, Ali, don't leave me like this; give us a hand, I'm stuck!'

Paula was deep in dreamland when Lenny landed on the bed. She was not best pleased.

'Gawd, you stink, Lenny Spinks. Where the hell you been?'

'Sorry to wake you, my little flower. You just turn over and gets back to slumberland and I'll—'

'Get your bloody boots out of my back. Aw Lenny, you're still in yer overalls! I've got a mouthful o' barley dust. Where 'ave you been? You was meant to be back here at six to go and see Mr Lester.'

'Sorry, my darlin'. Me and Charlie had to have a little celebration and by the time I remembered Hughie, I thought he wouldn't be so pleased to see me. So I decided to cut my losses and have another Jack Daniels.'

'Jack Daniels? You've been on Jack Daniels? Why didn't you come and get me? We could've got Mrs Long in to sit with the kiddies. I've been stuck here all evening, wonderin' where you was, with old Hughie belly-achin' down the phone 'cos he waited ages for you to turn up. What was you celebratin'?'

'Can't tell you; it's a secret. Charlie's sworn me to secrecy ...'

Paula unzipped Lenny's overalls. The moonlight filtering through the uncurtained windows glanced across her naked, glistening body, deep shadows silhouetting the full outline of her breasts. She buried her head in the soft hair below his navel.

He groaned.

'If you don't tell me,' she whispered, 'you can sod off and sleep on the sofa downstairs.'

10

From Tuesday to Thursday, Stephen found his attention torn between animals and Nicola.

She had been so nice to him in the pub, insisting Gerald O'Donovan make room for him on the banquette next to her, and including him in the conversation, although he had little to say.

He hadn't wanted it to end, but the best of the evening was to come. When she had finally consented to be driven home, she had leaned across the passenger seat and kissed him on the cheek. Her lips were soft and cool, her scent the fleeting fragrance of primroses, and her soft, dark curls drifted lightly across his face as she leaned on his shoulder. He didn't know how he managed to drive in a straight line, let alone change gear. His whole body underwent a sort of metamorphosis: he tingled from head to toe, as if he was undergoing a mild electric shock; his genitals gently throbbed; small drops of perspiration welled up on his brow and top lip, and his armpits prickled. When she had said goodnight, she had kissed him once more, briefly, lightly, before sliding from the car into the dark.

Stephen didn't remember a single thing about the journey back to Marsh Farm. Too excited to sleep, he had lain in bed reading a book on rare breeds that he'd found on the kitchen table, and when he'd finally fallen asleep, his dreams were a jumble of cattle, Nicola, Angela, and rehearsals of *The Beaux Stratagem*. Trying to put milking teats on the udders of a temperamental Longhorn, the long-suffering cow had lowed, 'I'll open his breast, I warrant you', and, turning her massive head, had revealed the face of his Dorinda, his Nicola.

The alarm woke him.

He decided that Nicola had given him an unequivocal message: she had kissed him, twice; she had leaned against his arm. If that was not her saying she liked him, then ...

But Stephen had never had a girlfriend, had never undergone the cut and thrust of the flirtation game, had never had sex. Oh, he'd heard about it often enough from Charlie, who'd cheerfully shared with Stephen the details of his sexual encounters ever since he had first got laid at the age of fifteen – by Aggie Pruett, a cheerful twenty-year-old doing a holiday job, one summer, at The Forester's Arms. But Aggie had long gone by the time Stephen was ready for the experience, and there was never anyone else to oblige, so taking himself in hand, sex for Stephen was a lonely, secretive affair.

He decided the time had come to ask Nicola out – not in any bold way ... perhaps just to visit the farm, have tea, show her his cows, and the river, and ...

He washed with great thoroughness before Thursday night's rehearsal, determined to remove any lingering whiff of farmyard. Patting his chin with some of Charlie's aftershave, he anxiously scrutinised his face in the bathroom mirror. Yes, perhaps he was a bit on the plump side, but he had a good colour, his hair was thick and wavy – unlike Gerald O' Donovan's – and his mum said he had lovely eyes. Could Nicola possibly fancy him? Not knowing whom else to consult, he thought that perhaps before he took the plunge he would ask Angela's advice.

Angela had spent the time since the last rehearsal scouring the internet for information about ostrich farms. She climbed into the cab of his Land Rover and beamed at him, triumphantly flapping a large envelope in her hand. 'I've got lots of info, Stephen.' He looked at her blankly, but not noticing, she enthused on. 'It's been terribly interesting finding out. There aren't any ostrich farms nearby, I'm afraid, but there are about twenty in Britain and the nearest one is near Monmouth, as far as I can discover. It's not so very far – we could go there, if you like, check it out?'

'What? Oh yes, ostriches ... er ...'

'And there's lots about all the other sorts of animals that are bred now. Not necessarily farming them, of course, but keeping them as visitor attractions. There's so much you could do, Stephen.'

Stephen tried to match her enthusiasm, but was too distracted by the thought that he would soon be seeing Nicola, wondering where he would find the courage to ask her out. 'Thanks, Angela, that's great. I'll have a look, later. I've been reading this book on rare breeds ... Ange, do you think I should ask Nicola out?'

Angela gaped at him, temporarily bereft of speech. Not noticing, Stephen ploughed on. 'Thing is, last Tuesday she kissed me. Twice. On the cheek. It might mean nothing, of course, but if it doesn't ... mean nothing, I mean ... I mean, I don't want her to think I don't care, when I do, if you see what I mean.'

Angela was silent and, glancing at her immobile profile, he carried on. 'Thing is, Angela, you're my best friend and you're ... a girl, too, so I thought you might know and I know you wouldn't let me make a fool of myself, would you?'

'No,' said Angela in a small voice.

'Well, what shall I do? What d'yer think?'

'When did she kiss you?'

'When I took her home after the pub; when we got into the car, then again just before she got out.'

'Did she say anything?'

'Like what?'

'Like,' there was a slight edge to Angela's voice, '"Thank you"; or, "That was nice, do it again"; or,' she continued, rather cruelly, Stephen thought, '"I love you."'

'No,' he replied rather huffily. 'Nothing like that. In fact, I don't remember her saying anything except, 'You can drop me off here.' I've been wondering what to do ever since. I was wondering about inviting her over to the farm on Saturday.'

Angela, who had hoped that she and Stephen might make a trip to Monmouth on Saturday, sadly answered, 'Yes, why don't you? That's not too pushy. Then you'll be able to work out how she feels.'

'How?'

Angela was silent for a while, then turned to him with a bright, encouraging smile. 'Well, if she says no, you'll know where you are; if she says yes, you'll know at least she's interested in you; then, if she says yes, you can take her for a walk round the farm and hold her hand; if she won't let you do that, you'll know she likes you, but perhaps she doesn't fancy you; if she does let you hold her hand, then you can try kissing her.'

Stephen went bright red, and to their mutual relief, they arrived at the hall.

He had nerved himself to speak to Nicola as soon as she arrived, but she was late and by the time she walked in, the rehearsal was well under way and he had no opportunity to get her alone until they had finished.

'Nicola,' he croaked, as she was about to leave. She turned. He gulped. 'Are ... are you going for a drink, Nicola?'

She smiled sweetly at him. 'Are you?'

'Yes, probably.'

'I don't think I will tonight. I drank too much last time and felt awful the whole of the next day.'

'Oh, well ... actually, I think I won't tonight. Got a busy day tomorrow.'

He knew he was flannelling. He had to ask her, now. Now! He was conscious that Angela was coming over to him and that every-one else was leaving. It had to be now. 'Er ... I was wonderin ...' Damn, he had dropped the end of the word ... Ever since he'd joined the Merlin Players he had become conscious of his accent and had done his level best to speak RP when he was with them. 'Wonder-ring ... I was wondering, Nicola ...'

'Yes?' She smiled at him patiently, waiting.

'I was wonderin' if you'd like to come out to the farm on Saturday.' It came out in a rush.

'Why?' she asked, puzzled.

For a moment, he was floored. This was not part of his script.

He struggled on. 'You've never been there, and it's ... it's nice this time of year ... and you could have some tea and meet my mum. It don't matter if you don't want to. Really. It's just that . . . I thought it'd be nice.'

His voice trailed away and he desperately wished he were somewhere, anywhere, else.

She looked at him coolly for a few seconds, a little frown creasing her brow. Then the frown cleared and for a moment he thought she was going to laugh. However, she smiled demurely. 'That would be very nice, Stephen. This Saturday? Give me your number and I'll ring you for directions.'

'What's got into Stephen this morning?' asked Alison, looking out of the kitchen window at her brother, in the yard, having a mock tussle with Gip.

'He seems horribly cheerful, considering we're staring ruin in the face.'

'Don't say such things; you give me goosebumps,' tutted Jenny, trying to transform a lump of very hard margarine and some granulated sugar into a smooth paste, in a mixing bowl that kept sliding away from her under the pressure of her spoon. 'I must say it does me the world of good to see him looking a bit more cheerful. And you, too, Ali, you've cheered up since you went off with your gran yesterday. I'm glad you're friends again. I hate it when there is quarrelling in the family; you and your gran have always been close.'

Elsie had taken Alison to one side the previous morning and very hesitantly, it seemed to Alison, asked for her help. Taken by surprise, Alison had forgotten to remain cross. 'Of course, Gran. What is it?'

'It's a little job I need to do and you can help me. I'll pay you for it, of course. A labourer is worthy of his hire. Bring that phone of yours and I'll explain in the car.'

'But my phone won't be any use – it's run out of credit. And where are we going?'

'To Bath. We'll get the phone filled up, or whatever it is you have to do to it, when we get there.'

In the car, a little red Rover 100 that she had bought at a bargain price from a friend who had decided he was too old to drive, Elsie had explained to Alison that she had to collect some rent from an elderly tenant. Over time, unfortunately, his mental faculties had deteriorated to the extent that, occasionally, he didn't know who she was and had accused her of trying to extort money from him.

'The last collection day I called, he waved his fist at me; I was afraid he was going to hit me. So it seemed sensible, the next time the rent was due, to take someone with me for protection.'

'Like a bodyguard, you mean? Gran, is this a good idea? Shouldn't you get someone else to collect the rent? You're really exposing yourself to trouble, you know. And wouldn't it have been better to ask one of the boys, rather than me? No one's gonna be frightened of me.'

'That's the point. My tenants are also my friends. *I* don't want to frighten them. He's a poor old soul. With you there, I'm sure he won't get violent, and introducing him to my granddaughter will probably help calm him down; perhaps he'll remember who I am. If things go wrong, then you've got the phone. I must say, it's the first time I've ever seen any use for them.'

'You should get one yourself, Gran.'

'Don't be daft, girl. I couldn't see the numbers, let alone work out how to use the silly thing. Not a word about this to anyone, mind,' she added sharply. 'I don't want your mother fussing every time I have to collect, and I don't want your brothers trying to borrow money off me when I do.'

After a few minutes Elsie, having manoeuvred the car out of a country lane onto the main road that would take them directly to Bath, resumed the conversation in a slightly different tone. 'Now, my girl, there's one other thing we need to talk about before we go much further. We need to clear the air, don't we?'

'Yes, Gran.'

'So tell me, truthfully, how often do you sneak out at night like that? Where do you go? I've not told your mother – I think she'd have hysterics – but I'm not having you pull the wool over my eyes. Is that clear?'

Alison sighed deeply. She had been expecting this. 'It doesn't happen often, honest. It's just that most of my mates live in town and so they meet up all the time; they don't have to worry about how they'll get home. Summerstoke is miles from anywhere if you don't drive. So when we have a get-together, I'm picked up from the end of the drive and brought back again. That's all.'

'Wouldn't it have been better to ask permission?'

'Gran!'

'Well, think about it – supposing something happened to you and we thought you were safely in your bed. These days it's just not safe for a young girl to be out on her own in the early hours of the morning.'

'I'm not, Gran, I told you – I'm with friends.' A note of desperation entered Alison's voice. 'Look, I know you think I'm off out all the time and not doing any work, but that's just not true. I hardly go out at all and if I didn't escape sometimes, I think I'd go stark staring mad! I'm the only one of all my friends who hasn't been away. Do you realise, this is the first time I've gone out in the car this summer, apart from the odd trip to Summerbridge with Stephen?'

Elsie harrumphed. 'Very well, I'll say nothing further, on condition that the next time you go off to one of your parties, you go out of the door and return the same way, and you let me know. I won't stop you, but I want to know. Do you understand?'

'Yes, Gran. Thanks.'

Stopping only to buy credit for Alison's phone, they eventually arrived in front of a crescent of Georgian houses in a suburb of Bath, beside the river.

The crescent was imposing; clearly the houses must have been very handsome in their day. One or two of the buildings, cleaned and restored, gleamed honey-gold; others, blackened and peeling, contributed to a pervasive air of depression. Windows were flung wide and from within the sounds of human activity drifted out. A group of children were playing with bikes and scooters on the green in front of the crescent. The ground was parched and cracked, the grass thin and patchy and spotted with litter. Iron railings, flanked with straggling buddleia and other tired shrubs, prevented any access to the riverbank.

Alison stared up at the terrace. 'Do you own one of these, Gran?'

Elsie did not reply but climbed up the flagstone pavement and stopped in front of a house, not as shabby as its neighbours, but from the state of the stained stonework, not recently restored either. Alison caught up with her just as she produced a key and opened the door, pressing one of a row of bells as she did so. Inside, the house was cool and sang with echoes. A stone staircase stretched up in front of them; on one side, a long, bare corridor ran to the back of the building, providing access to two doors set into the wall a little way apart, each with its own doormat.

'There are two flats on every floor,' explained Elsie as she started to climb the stairs. 'There's no lift, so it's a bit of a climb. Mr Bates lives on the second floor.'

'Blimey,' said Alison, puffing slightly from the steepness of the staircase. 'You said he was quite elderly. How does he manage to get up and down these stairs every day?'

'He manages. He's used to it. There are lots of houses like this in Bath, many occupied by elderly people.'

'How long have you had this house? Did you ever live here?'

Elsie ignored her questions. 'Here we are. Come along, Ali; stand close behind me. Got your phone ready? Good.'

She pressed a doorbell. For a moment they stood there, waiting, listening. No sound.

'Perhaps he's out?'

'He's not out,' replied Elsie grimly. 'He doesn't go out much.' She rang the bell again.

Straining her ears, Alison could hear a faint shuffling on the other side of the door. 'He's coming!' she whispered, suddenly nervous.

There was the faint sound of scratching.

'He's looking at us through the spyhole,' hissed Elsie, then tilting her head, shouted, 'Mr Bates, it's me, Elsie Tucker, your landlady. Open the door, please.'

'Why should I?' The voice was aged, querulous, suspicious. 'I don't know you. Bugger off!'

'You do know me. You've known me for a long time. I'm Elsie Tucker. Open your door.'

'You can't make me. I know your game, so bloody well clear off out of it before I call the police.'

'You can call the police if you want to, Mr Bates, and they will put you in prison for being a nuisance—'

'Gran!'

'Who's that with you? Who've you got there?'

'My granddaughter, Alison. I've shown you her photograph. You said you'd like to meet her one day. Well, open the door and you can.'

Somewhat to Alison's surprise, Elsie's words seemed to have the desired effect. After a slight pause there came the sound of a latch being lifted, a chain unhooked, and the door opened on a rotund, bald head, with a pink, shiny face and round blue eyes, red and watery, but shrewd. He was a bent old man, and Alison, having no notion of age, thought he looked ancient.

'My dear Mrs Tucker, how lovely to see you. Do come in. And is this little Alison? My, my, isn't she a pretty thing. You must be very proud of her. Do come in.'

Alison was spooked by his complete change of manner and would rather have stayed outside, but Elsie took her firmly by the arm and marched her into the flat.

The corpulent figure of Mr Bates led the way into a comfortable, overheated, old-fashioned little sitting room. A faded leather armchair stood by the window, a tidy pile of newspapers folded up on the parquet floor next to it; a large Persian rug covered most of the floor, and next to the sofa, by the gas fire, was a small coffee table bearing a fruit bowl containing one apple, one pear and one banana.

He was evidently a man of some education, for a large bookcase occupied the whole of one wall, the shelves of which were crammed full of books, principally hardbacks, including a whole section devoted to an author bearing the name of Ronald Bates, for he had been a prolific and popular writer of adventure stories for boys in the 1950s. The prints, covering the walls of the little room, were the originals of the frontispieces to these books, depicting his boyish heroes in a variety of valiant or perilous situations.

The whole episode, for Alison, took on a surreal air. Mr Bates gushed, simpered and fluttered. He insisted on giving Alison a glass of lemon barley water, something she'd never had before in her life, and poured Elsie a glass of sherry, making them sit down whilst he looked for his rent book. He chatted the whole time, swooping in on Alison from time to time with: 'The little granddaughter, well, well, well', and turning to Elsie with, 'So like you, my dear Mrs Tucker, so like you.'

Alison could have sworn that Elsie was enjoying herself. 'He's absolutely nuts!' she thought. 'One minute completely abusive, now this!' On balance, she thought, she preferred him abusive. She found this attentiveness really creepy, and watched him closely in anticipation of the moment when his manner would change again and he would lash out at her grandmother.

It wasn't until business had been concluded to Elsie's satisfaction and they were back in the car that Alison relaxed.

'Well,' said Elsie brightly, 'that wasn't so bad after all, was it, dear? Thanks for coming with me. You made all the difference. Sweet as honey, once he knew who you were.'

'It was horrible, Gran. He's bonkers! You shouldn't be going alone, collecting money off people like that. He's a psychopath! I know I should feel sorry for him, being old an' all that, but supposing I hadn't been there and he'd gone for you. Really, Gran, he shouldn't be living alone there. He should be in care.'

'It would kill him. He likes his independence. He has his moments, I grant you, but he doesn't mean any harm.'

Alison turned to her grandmother. 'Gran, promise me you won't see him alone again. Please. I'm not fussing, I'm really not, but I don't think it's safe for you to be collecting money from nutcases!' At that, she could have sworn she detected a look of amusement flit across Elsie's face.

'Ah well, Ali, you might be right. I'm not as young as I used to be. Anyways, thank you for coming with me. I said I'd pay you for your time. Will twenty do?'

Twenty pounds!

Not only did Elsie give her twenty quid, but with her phone now in credit, Alison was able to text Al back and put an end to that particular torture, for Al had followed up his initial invitation with further text messages and was clearly puzzled, if not put out, by her failure to reply.

With money in her purse and a date with Al on Saturday night, no wonder Jenny had detected a change in her daughter's mood.

'I'm going to pick some blackberries for Gran, Mum.' Alison looked across at her mother wrestling with the mixing bowl. 'Do you want me to get any extra for you?'

'That'd be nice, dear. I'll make a crumble. We could have it at teatime tomorrow.'

'Teatime? Crumble? What on earth for?'

'Stephen's got a friend coming to tea. A girl. I'm making a cake, but she might prefer blackberry crumble.'

Alison chewed over this unexpected revelation as she walked up the track to the road. Stephen ... a girl! Wonders will never cease. It's been such a weird week! I meet Al; Stephen invites a girl round; Gran parts with hard cash ... Whatever next?

Crossing the road, she waved at Jeff Babbington as he turned his car into the farm's entrance. She was heading for fields alongside the river on the other side, where the marshy, tussocky grassland and swathes of thick bramble bushes rendered the land unfit for much except cover for rabbits and pheasants and, at this time of year, an abundance of blackberries. A permanently muddy footpath ran alongside the river and it was a popular walk for villagers exercising their dogs, and for Sunday afternoon ramblers.

Inevitably the lower fronds and the bushes in easy reach had already been picked clean, but Alison had come dressed for the

battle of the brambles, in jeans and a denim jacket. Thus protected, she was able to press bodily into the depths of the bushes.
Her fingers were soon stained purple and her pile of berries
grew.

As she picked, she thought about her twenty-pound windfall
and the dilemma it posed. It was enough for a ticket, the one
thing she had really wanted. She would be able to go to the event.
But, and it was a big 'but', she had this date with Al on Saturday.
Last Sunday he had insisted on treating her. She couldn't let him
do that again, and she had no idea what he was planning for Saturday night. If they went to the cinema, if they just went to the
pub, if they went out for a meal somewhere – it would all cost,
and she would pay her way: bang would go the twenty quid and
she'd be back where she started.

She edged around a bush growing close to the river's edge,
knowing from experience that the most luscious blackberries
always hung over the water, just out of reach. The raucous clatter
of a pheasant startled her. It flew out of the undergrowth straight
for her head and as she ducked to miss it, a dog hurled after it,
straight between her legs. Blackberries flew into the air and Alison
and the dog toppled into the water.

Fortunately for Alison it had been a long dry summer, so the
water level was quite low. Even so, the force of the dog's impact
took her right down to the reedy, muddy bottom. The water was
cold, and clouds of disturbed silt billowed around her. Shock
gave way to instinct and she struggled to break the surface, but
the denim was now cumbersome and heavy.

There was a disturbance in the water beside her and she was
aware of someone grabbing her arm, shouting and thrashing, then
of being held securely round her chest and of being pulled up out
of the murk into the sunshine and onto the riverbank, where she
lay gasping and choking.

'Oh God, I'm really sorry. Are you okay?' It was a male voice,
a nice voice, quite posh, like someone from a TV drama rather
than a soap. Alison looked up at the man bent anxiously over
her. She felt pretty bloody awful: shaking and shocked, soaked

through, mud and weeds trailing from her hair, her clothes, her mouth.

'I'm okay,' she replied feebly. 'Thanks for dragging me out. I'm not quite sure ... a dog ...'

'Yes,' he said wretchedly. 'She's mine. I'm really sorry. Normally she's very good, but at the sight of a pheasant, she goes mad. I'm really sorry.'

'Is she all right? I think she landed in the water with me.'

'Oh, she'll be fine. She's probably swum across to the other side. She'll be back when the stupid thing finally realises she won't be able to catch the bird. Look, I don't live far from here. Not only are you soaking, but you're in a state of shock, which is hardly surprising! Please, come back with me. You can have a hot bath or whatever; a hot toddy or a cup of tea, whichever takes your fancy, and I'll get your clothes dried. Then I'll run you home. It's the least I can do. Please.'

Alison looked at him rather dubiously. Truth to tell, she was feeling very cold and shivery and close to tears. If he lived locally, she'd never seen him before and she wasn't sure ... Her instinct was to go straight home. Then the dog, a joyous brown and white spaniel, dragged herself up over the bank, came straight up to them, and to add insult to injury, shook herself, spraying the both of them with dank river water.

Alison started to giggle helplessly. He looked at her anxiously, and then catching her mood, he joined in. He was, Alison reckoned, about the same age as Stephen, possibly younger. Even with mud and water weed streaking his face and body, staining his white cotton shirt and probably ruining for ever expensive-looking linen chinos, she could see that he had a pleasant face, with laughter lines etching his tanned skin.

'I feel a bit like Alice in Wonderland,' she expostulated, hiccupping, 'but instead of following the White Rabbit down a hole, I've followed a dog into the river and come up again into a world I don't recognise. Who are you? I've lived here all my life and I don't think I've seen you before.'

'You wouldn't have. I've just rented a cottage on the outskirts of the village. I moved in a couple of weeks ago. Look, you're shivering badly. I'm entirely responsible. Come back with me. I promise I won't eat you.'

Jenny beamed when Jeff poked his head round the door. She hadn't seen him since last Sunday, but then, she hadn't expected to.

'Not disturbing you, am I?'

'Don't be daft. Cup of tea?'

'Love one. Shall I put the kettle on? You look busy.'

'No, I could do with a break. My arm's aching something rotten trying to beat this marge.'

'What are you making?' He unearthed the kettle from under a damp woollen jumper. (When Jenny couldn't afford to buy wool, she would salvage old jumpers from the jumble sale, wash, and then unpick them.)

'A cake,' said Jenny proudly. 'I haven't made one for ages, but Stephen is bringing a girl home for tea tomorrow, so I thought I'd do some baking.'

Jeff, raising his eyebrows with surprise, digested this news. 'Stephen gave me a ring asking about rare breeds, so I've brought over a bit of stuff. I'll leave it here, on the dresser. So,' he continued thoughtfully, 'Elsie's threat has had an effect after all. Stephen's got a girl, eh? That's a first, isn't it?'

'Yes, and I so want us to make a good impression. Fortunately, as it's Saturday, Elsie will be off with her friends in Bath.'

'So she won't be around to put the fear of God into the poor girl! What about Charlie? Can you find something for him to do to keep him out of the way as well and stop him taking over?'

'Jeff! Charlie's not that bad.'

'Hmm, if you say so. What sort of cake is it?'

'I haven't decided yet. I'm a bit low on ingredients. I haven't got quite enough cocoa for a very chocolatey cake, so I thought I'd add some coconut I've found in the back of the cupboard.' She rested her arm. 'Whew – that will have to do.'

Jeff looked at the unprepossessing mixture of margarine and sugar in the bowl.

Jenny was cracking eggs into a cup. 'I think I can get away with just two eggs if I add some milk, only I'm a bit low at the moment.'

'Why are you doing it by hand? Haven't you got one of those electric mixers?'

'I used to have one, but it broke and I never got it fixed. I expect that's why I don't make cakes more often. It's quite hard work, all this beating.' She concentrated hard on the mixture, silent for a moment. 'Jeff ...' she said, shyly, 'Would *you* like to come to tea tomorrow, as well? We'll all be so nervous; at least I know I will, and poor Stephen ... with you here ... If you've got the time, that is.'

Jeff remembered the last cake of Jenny's he'd eaten. The memory sat heavily on his digestion. He sipped his tea, watching her ineffectually beating in the eggs and milk, and formulated his excuse. Then he remembered their trip on Sunday. He had offered to take her out of pity but then he'd really enjoyed her company. Released from the confines of her family it was as if she'd woken up; she'd come alive; she'd been good fun. She needed more trips like that, and, he admonished himself silently, he was being selfish by ignoring her request for help. After all, he didn't have to eat the wretched cake! Also, he realised, with a flash of inspiration, he could do his bit to help secure the success of the tea party.

'Thanks, Jenny. I'd like that. I tell you what – I'll bring some chocolate biscuits or something. Contribute to the feast, eh?'

Far from being tempted to 'take over', Charlie was heartily relieved to hear his family would be occupied in this fashion. Knowing that he was going to be very tied up the following week, working for Dark Glasses, he was desperate to get the harvest finished.

They had just started cutting the last field, the second of the two that Dark Glasses wanted to hire, at the furthest point from the farm, when the tractor had conked out and had to be towed back the whole length of Weasel Lane to the yard for running repairs.

'A tea party, I ask you!' he expostulated, waving a grease gun. 'Stephen's barking up the wrong tree if he thinks a tea party is gonna impress a bit of skirt.'

'Who is she?' Lenny emerged from the depths of the tractor engine and retrieved the gun. 'S'nearly fixed – she'll be singing like a bird in a minute.'

'I dunno, some bit of stuff from his am dram. Might be that mousy little four-eyes that he brings back from time to time to make stuff with.'

'Does he make it with her?'

'Stephen?' Charlie laughed. 'Lenny, you're kidding!'

'Still, he's bringing back the crumpet. That's the way your gran'll see it. You better watch out, mate. Tortoise and the hare! Before you know where you are, the year'll be up and Stephen will be nice and settled with his little wifey, crumpet or four-eyes, it won't matter 'cos he'll have your share.'

Charlie stared at him, unsettled. 'What are you talking about? What a load of rubbish! What do you mean, the tortoise and the hare?'

'Some story the kids had on a video. The hare and the tortoise are gonna have a race; the bets are on the hare of course. He's a cool dude, really fast. Thing is, he's so busy giving interviews and having his picture taken, he don't notice the race has started and by the time he gets the picture, the race is over and the slow guy, that's Stephen, has won. So which piece of crumpet are you taking home to Grandma, Charlie? As I understand it, you've ditched Sarah and ain't goin' nowhere with Beth. Got anyone else lined up?'

Charlie didn't like the turn this conversation had taken. 'Don't you worry about me, Lenny. Just get this fucking tractor fixed. We need to be finished by tonight, secure the field tomorrow morning and stand by to take delivery in the afternoon.'

'Yes, boss! Right y'are, boss. I can't stay late tomorrow,

though. Paula's gotta be up at the Lesters' for the evening and her mam can't babysit, so I've gotta.'

'Have you seen old man Lester yet?'

'Nope. Seems he was steamin' after I failed to deliver. Not my problem. If he wants me, he knows where to find me!'

Warmed by the most luxurious shower she'd ever had, Alison, her feet tucked under, was curled in the depths of a large arm-chair, wrapped in a thick towelling dressing gown, her hair a fluffy golden halo framing her face. Her cheeks were pink from the hot water and her green eyes bright with the excitement of this unexpected adventure. She nursed a large hot chocolate laced with brandy; in the distance, her clothes could be heard grinding round in a tumble dryer.

Simon, for such was his name, had put on some music before going off to the shower himself, and Alison, enchanted by the unfamiliar, haunting notes of a trumpet, looked around the room for some hints about the personality of her rescuer.

His cottage was on the outskirts of the village, at the end of a back lane where it petered out into a footpath. On the brief jour-ney back they had introduced themselves and she learned that his dog was called Duchess, that he was renting the cottage from an elderly aunt, and that he had come to stay in the area for a while, because of business.

The room was very comfortably furnished, but in Alison's opinion quite old-fashioned. The only things in the room that seemed to belong to the tenant were a number of boxes clearly full of books; there were piles of CDs everywhere, what must be a state-of-the-art sound system, a widescreen television, and again, piles of DVDs. Whatever else, she concluded, he wasn't short of a bob or two. There was no sign, either in here or in the bathroom, of anything feminine.

She had put down her drink and padded over to inspect the closest pile of CDs when Simon reappeared, freshly clothed and drying his hair. She could see that he was definitely the same age as her brothers, but better preserved and obviously fitter, good looking too, with wavy blond hair and brilliant blue eyes – but definitely too old to be in her league, which was something she found reassuring.

'I really like this music; what is it?'

'You've got taste. It's "Ascent to the Scaffold" – Miles Davis. Have you heard of him?'

It took an hour for her jeans to dry, an hour that passed all too quickly. Alison entertained Simon with spiky little portraits of the people who lived in the village; he told her that he was a management consultant who worked as a troubleshooter for companies in difficulties; she told him about the troubles they were having with Marsh Farm and of her grandmother's solution to the problem, which made him roar with laughter.

'I'd like to meet your gran – she sounds great. And how are your brothers reacting to the suggestion they should find brides?'

'That's the funny thing. Stephen is bringing someone home to tea tomorrow. Stephen! I wouldn't have been surprised if it had been Charlie. He's much the better looking and he's always got some girl or other on the go, but Stephen, I swear, is a virgin. He's never had a girlfriend in his life.'

'What about you, little Alison? Have you got a boyfriend?'

Alison found she didn't want to answer the question. She prevaricated. 'Not really. What about you?'

He paused, then said ruefully, 'Not really, either. I'm just emerging from a rather messy divorce and quite honestly, I'm not too keen to rush into another relationship.'

'Oh, I'm sorry. Have you got children?'

'No, I haven't.' He stopped abruptly. 'It's a painful subject. I'll tell you about it some day. Let's talk about something else. Tell me about the Lesters.'

'The Lesters? Why on earth would you want to know about them?'

'I play squash so I've joined the local club. I met Veronica-call-me-Vee Lester, there. She phoned me a couple of days ago to make up numbers at a dinner party she's giving on Saturday. I thought you could brief me.'

'My God, you don't want to go there!'

'Why not? Fishing you out of the river has been the first exciting thing to happen to me since I got here and I can't expect adventures on the riverbank every day. I've not got much else to do with my spare time, so tell me, why I should avoid these Lesters?'

'I'm sorry, it wasn't fair of me. Of course you should go. You might find you like them. It's just good old prejudice on my part. They represent the fat cat side of farming—'

'And you, the poor-but-honest toilers of the soil?'

Alison thought of her brother Charlie and grinned. 'Well, Stephen is. The thing is the Lesters aren't really interested in farming in the traditional sense; they just want to make as much money out of it as they can.'

'And you dislike them because they are succeeding in doing what you would like to do – making money out of farming?'

Alison was stung. 'No! I ... we dislike them because they're what they are: greedy, selfish, stuck-up snobs. What they do isn't farming! Hundreds of horses, beautiful though they are, ultimately ruin good pasture, and Hugh Lester pumps so many chemicals into his fields they probably glow luminous at night.'

'And your Charlie doesn't do the same to his crops?'

'No, as it happens. But we're not in the same league and if we were, quite truthfully, he might. He hasn't the same feel for the farm as Stephen. But Simon, honestly, the Lesters aren't very nice. I know someone who works for them. She's normally very easy going, but get her to talk about her employers and it's another story.'

'You don't have much to do with them on a social level, then?'

She grimaced. 'They've certainly never invited us round to dinner, and I've never had much to do with their two children. Cordelia's younger than me, anyway, and the oldest, Anthony, I don't think I've seen since we went to a party at the vicarage when I was five and he must have been about eight. Poor sod was sent away to school after that; his parents must have worried that he'd catch something nasty from the village children.'

'Well, I look forward to an interesting evening. I'll be fed, at least. I get sick of eating out of the microwave. Talking of food, what's the word on the pub in the village?'

'The Forester's Arms? I worked there last summer, doing the washing up. The scraps they threw at us were always very tasty.'

'Great; we should try it. How about tonight?' He grinned at her astonished look and rose to his feet. 'The dryer has stopped so I think your clothes are ready, and I can hear Duchess whining. She's fed up with being confined to the kitchen; I'll let her through; she should be dry by now and she can make her apologies.'

He opened the kitchen door and the spaniel shot across the room, making a huge fuss first of her master and then, turning her attention to Alison, tried to climb into her lap. Alison laughingly fought the dog off, but her mind was fully occupied with the implications of Simon's invitation. She'd never been taken out to dinner before; she really liked his company, but how would they get through a whole evening without running out of things to talk about? He was so much older than her – what would people think? What should she wear? And what about Al? Should she say no?

'Here're your things,' he said, returning. 'Bit stiff, I'm afraid. They probably need washing properly. I'll give you a lift home.'

'You don't have to do that. I can walk. It's not far.'

'I won't take no for an answer. I want to meet your family; they sound fascinating, and now I'm a neighbour … And anyway, if I'm going to take you out to dinner tonight, I need to know where to pick you up. That is, if you'd like to come, and if you're not doing anything else?' He could see that she was hesitating. 'I'd like to make proper amends for nearly drowning you. Besides,' he added simply, 'I've really enjoyed the last hour, but I feel that I'm definitely in need of a more detailed briefing before I go to dinner with the Lesters tomorrow night.'

*

It was in an unusually thoughtful frame of mind that Charlie took himself off across the fields after his supper, to have a drink with his mates at The Bunch of Grapes as he always did on a Friday night, and to see if he could pin Beth down to another date.

Although he might pretend otherwise, Charlie was disconcerted by Lenny's teasing. Sarah had phoned him earlier and he still hadn't the heart to tell her it was all off. She had sounded very tearful and said she had to see him – she had something to discuss – but she wouldn't say what over the phone. With a sense of foreboding, Charlie had agreed to meet her after work the following evening.

The way he saw it, he didn't have to take Elsie's threats seriously, not just yet. He had a whole year to find a piece of crumpet he fancied enough to marry, or to find some way to persuade Elsie to change her mind, and he was confident of doing one or the other.

However, the problem that preoccupied Charlie was not Elsie, but how he was going to meet the bank's demands. He smiled sourly when he thought of the three thousand he was about to earn from the hire of the field. It would give him great pleasure to be able to slam down the wads in front of that slimy bastard Mr Gordon White, who clearly thought he'd not be able to find the wherewithal. But it was a bitter pleasure. He consoled himself with the thought of the other two K. That was a nice consolation prize and he was blowed if the bank was going to get its sticky paws on that!

But there was no ignoring the problem that, come the end of October, he'd have to find another three K, and where was that going to come from? They needed to do something big, something drastic, to pay off the debt and get the bank off their backs for good. But what?

In his opinion, diversifying was playing kids' games ... rare breeds, what bloody good would that do? No, they had to think big. If only the farm wasn't so flat. In his mind's eye, Charlie could see the whole of Marsh Farm laid out as a motocross circuit, with the farmhouse in the middle. 'We could shift some earth, build hillocks, plant a wood,' he said aloud in his enthusiasm. 'Bugger the bank, we'll sell some land for housebuilding and get started ... we'll get big business investing and then, when we're not using it for motocross, we could use it for paintballing. Brilliant idea!' Charlie had been paintballing, once, for a friend's stag party, and next to motocross, could think of no better way to spend his time.

Putting his dream to one side, Charlie returned to the immediate problem of the farm, and Stephen. Without making a big deal of it, they both knew the cows weren't paying their way. If they got rid of the herd, Charlie reasoned to himself, they could turn the entire farm over to cash crop and cereal production. That was where the money was these days, not in milk. If they were to do that, they could cut their overheads – they wouldn't need the Merfield meadows for a start – and start making a profit instead of feeding it to the cows. That would see off Gordon White. But could he persuade Stephen to see the sense of it? He was devoted to those bloomin' animals. But he'd have to, 'cos if he didn't, the whole shebang would go to the wall, cows an' all.

With that depressing thought Charlie arrived at The Grapes. Pushing open the door to the public bar he was greeted with hoots of laughter, a cracked rendition of 'The Farmer Wants a Wife', and someone playing 'I'm Getting Married in the Morning' on a kazoo. Six or seven of his friends and drinking companions, Spike amongst them, filled the bar. As they completed their cacophony, Spike thrust a glass of Babycham into his hand and Robbie, a mischievous, red-headed pig man from a nearby farm, whom Charlie had known since he was a child, liberally sprinkled him with confetti. Dusting himself down and spitting stray bits of paper out of his mouth, he demanded to know what the hell his mates were playing at.

He should have known.

With shouts of laughter, led by Robbie, who had himself married a year ago, and Spike, who had once vowed no woman would ever tie him down, they demanded to know whether what they'd heard on the grapevine was true: that his gran had said he was to find himself a wife or she'd cut him out of her will.

Charlie sat down, a sickly grin on his face, and tried to bluff it out. 'I don't know who's been saying things. Whad'ya mean? Wife? Me? You must be joking!'

But they were not to be fobbed off and the noise grew more raucous. Inwardly, Charlie seethed. How had they found out? Who'd blabbed? Lenny – he weren't there, but he was Charlie's best mate ... Lin? Surely not?

Stan came bustling over from the bar. 'Okay, lads, I don't know what the joke is, but you've had your laugh. Keep the noise down now, please; you're disturbing the rest of my customers.' He saw Charlie dejectedly picking confetti out of his hair. 'What's all this then, Charlie? You getting married or something? Are congratulations in order?'

'No, no they're not,' said Charlie through gritted teeth, but inwardly relieved, for if Stan didn't know, then it wasn't Linda who'd spilt the beans. 'I don't know what they've heard, but the word seems to have got about that my gran has told me I've got to get a wife.'

Stan chuckled. 'That's a tough order. And are you?'

'Not bloomin' likely!' said Charlie fervently. 'Me? Lookin' for a wife? No way!'

A little later, having recovered his sense of humour, Charlie pushed his way to the bar in search of a pint and Beth. When she saw him, she grinned.

'What's this I hear, Charlie? You're looking for a wife?'

'No I'm not,' he said, for the umpteenth time that evening. 'I'm looking for a pint of Sam, Beth, and another date with you. How about tomorrow night? We could go out after you finish here, like last Saturday.'

'The pint of Sam is easy, Charlie, so long as you've got a couple of quid. The date, well, that's not so easy.'

'Why?'

Beth pulled him his pint and set it on the bar before she replied. 'Two reasons, Charlie. One, I'm not the marrying kind, leastways not yet, and if I go out with you, everyone knowing you're looking for a wife—'

'But I'm not!' he expostulated loudly.

'If I go out with you – the way things are – anybody *I* might be interested in having a good time with will think *I'm* in the marriage market too, which I'm not.'

'That's crazy logic, Beth.'

'Nevertheless, that's what I think. And the other thing against my going out with you, Charlie ...'

'Yeah?'

'Is your whiskers.'

Charlie was flabbergasted. 'What?!'

'Your whiskers. You're great fun, Charlie, and underneath all that hair, you're probably quite good looking. I just couldn't bear the way everyone was looking at you the other night and sniggering. I know you don't care, but I felt stupid. I don't want to go out with a guy I have to apologise for.'

'I don't want you to apologise for me – I can take care of myself, thank you.'

Beth shrugged her shoulders. 'Well maybe you can. It's just that if I go out with a bloke, I want to feel proud of him; I want other girls to look at my fellah and think, "He's a bit of all right". The more good looking, the greater my kudos – get it? With those whiskers, I can hear them thinking, "What a clown." And then they feel sorry for me and I'm rock-bottom. There's no way I'm gonna be put in that position. And Charlie, while we're about it ...'

'Yes?' said Charlie, feeling wretched.

'Have you ever thought what it must be like to kiss someone with all that facial hair? Ugh – gets up your nose and turns your chin red as a beetroot.'

Charlie's ego was shrivelling by the second. 'No one's ever complained before.'

Beth tossed her hair and her eyes flashed with contempt. 'So? I'm me, and I'm telling you why I don't want a date. I'd better go – Linda's firing daggers at me for talking to you for so long.'

'Beth, wait ... Gran's ultimatum apart, would you go out with me if ... if I shaved my sideburns?'

'I'd consider it,' was the unsatisfactory reply, and he didn't manage to speak to her again the entire evening.

I I

Elsie wrapped Ron's silk dressing gown tightly round her thin frame and carefully carried the plate into the bedroom.

'I've got a dark chocolate torte this week, Ron. It's a reward for being a clever boy!'

Ron beamed happily from the bed. He had a very mischievous streak, and had had great fun devising the elaborate little charade. 'I was afraid I'd give the game away. I just wanted to laugh. My, I'm glad you're not my landlady, Elsie love, you'd terrify the daylights out of me. She didn't guess, did she?'

'Not for one minute. She thought you were absolutely bonkers and couldn't wait to get away. Maybe you were a bit too convincing – she thinks I ought to report you to social services, and now she's fussing about how safe I am with my other tenants.'

She climbed into bed and cuddled up to Ron. The physical side of their relationship was not quite as active as it used to be; inevitable, perhaps, considering their age, but they still derived great pleasure from touching and caressing each other, and celebrating the occasional conjugation. Their affair had begun a couple of years after she became a widow. They had known each other for some time when both were happily married to their respective partners. Ron's wife died first and then, when Thomas Tucker died, Ron and Elsie had grown close. When they first became lovers, they talked about marrying, but Elsie, more forcibly than Ron, rejected the idea, having no wish to become involved in any way with Ron's offspring, or to complicate the various legal settlements in place. No one knew about their affair, which added a certain spice to the relationship.

'Perhaps you should employ her on a regular basis,' Ron suggested, gently stroking her cheek. He loved this fierce little old lady and secretly worried about her, but knew far better than to give her any hint of it.

'Twenty pounds a time, I couldn't possibly afford that! I made an exception this time because I realised the poor child was going through the entire holiday without a farthing, but I couldn't possibly do it on a regular basis.'

'Once a month, love. It's not much, really. I know you worry about the family taking advantage of you, but quite frankly, Elsie dear, they wouldn't dare.'

'That's probably true, Ron, but as I've explained to you before, I worry that if they know just how much they will have when I am dead, they won't try hard enough now. Thomas and I made Marsh Farm what it was without any help from my father and we were proud of what we achieved. I want to see Charlie and Stephen, and Alison, too, get somewhere by the sweat of their own labours.'

'Well, you know your family best, and maybe you don't want to ask either of the boys to accompany you, but I repeat what I said: I do think you might employ young Alison to help you. I know you like to do the rent collections yourself, but I think it's important not to take unnecessary risks. I realise she is only a slip of a girl, but just having someone else with you is a good idea. After all, if you got knocked over and were robbed, the insurance company would take a very dim view of your lack of protection.'

Business sense was always the best sort of sense as far as Elsie was concerned. 'I'll think about it. Now, how about a piece of that torte?'

The kitchen clock showed that it was nearly three-thirty. Half an hour before Nicola was expected for tea. Jenny hummed happily to herself as she smeared olive oil spread on the sliced bread (Weight Watchers had convinced her that anything containing olive oil would help her lose weight). Gran might threaten, the bank might threaten, but life seemed suddenly to have changed for the better. Not that they were any the less broke, far from it. In fact she was worried because she had not heard anything from Mrs Moorhead, who was normally extremely punctual about paying. Still, she thought, looking at the kitchen table with pride, she wasn't going to let Stephen down, or Ali, come to that.

Now that had been unexpected, Alison coming back with that nice man. He had seemed so concerned about the accident, even though Alison seemed none the worse. And lucky Alison – being taken out for dinner like that. Jenny couldn't remember the last time anyone had taken her out to dinner. Jim must have done once, but she really couldn't remember. And Simon seemed so interested in the farm, asking her all sorts of questions, really politely. It was only natural for her to invite him to tea this after-noon as well. She could see Alison was uncomfortable about it, but he'd accepted.

It was lucky I found that old tin of sardines in the back of the cupboard, she thought happily to herself. I'll mix them up with a bit of low-calorie mayo for sardine sandwiches. The cake had sunk in the middle, but Jenny sacrificed the bar of chocolate she'd set aside to treat herself with after her Weight Watchers weigh-in, and iced the cake with it. With the biscuits that Jeff said he'd bring, some scones she'd rescued from the deep freeze, and a pot of her own strawberry jam, 'Why, it's like a proper farmhouse tea!' she exclaimed.

That was Jeff's reaction when he arrived armed with an M & S carrier bag a short time later. 'And I've bought one or two little things to add to the feast,' he added.

Jenny's eyes popped. It wasn't just chocolate biscuits. Jeff had bought three different packets of fancy biscuits, some crumpets, and a large, rich fruit cake.

'I'm rather partial to fruit cake,' he said apologetically, 'I hope that's all right.'

Jenny, misty-eyed, silently vowed to make him a fruit cake at the first opportunity.

*

167

To say that Stephen was nervous would be an understatement. Normally the alarm for the early morning milking dragged him reluctantly to his senses. Today he had left the house before the alarm had gone off. He'd been unable to eat anything at breakfast or lunch. He'd sat under the shower attachment in the bath and washed his hair and every inch of his body. He had raided Charlie's supply of cologne, changed his shirt three times, brushed his teeth at least twice and then had waited and sweated.

He was dimly aware of his mother's effort in the kitchen and was grateful. He was dimly aware, too, that there would be other people to tea. Not Gran, to his great relief, and probably not Charlie, who had reacted to the idea with a snort, and the sentiment that he'd better things to do. The thought of Charlie turning his charms on Nicola had made Stephen uneasy, so he did nothing to encourage his brother to change his mind. He barely registered the fact that Alison's new boyfriend would be there, or that Jeff was also coming.

All he could think about was Nicola on his farm. He would show her the cows, and the lovely little heifer calf that had arrived the day before – he was going to call her Nicola; that is, if the real Nicola didn't mind. He would take her for a walk along the river – most of the best wild flowers were long gone, but purple loosestrife, great willowherb and himalayan balsam were growing in profusion along the bank, and the water lilies, gold and yellow, could be found in the still margins of the river. Maybe then, remembering Angela's advice, he would try and hold her hand. And if she didn't draw back, then, under the old grey ash tree on the riverbank, he would lean her against the trunk and kiss her ... At that his imagination failed and panic set in. What if he kissed her wrong ... his breath smelt ... she wouldn't hold his hand ... she didn't like his cows ... she didn't turn up!

Alison sat at her desk, anxiously inspecting her face for any sign of spots. Today was too important for any unexpected eruptions. She still found it hard to get her head around the way events had moved in the last week. First Al, then Gran, then Simon.

Her head was still spinning from the previous evening. It had been fabulous. She had eaten steak, and prawns, and a wonderful lemon tart, and drank wine, and brandy, and coffee. She and Simon had laughed and talked so easily. 'And I worried that we might run out of things to say,' she marvelled. 'It was like we'd known each other for ever.' And then he had driven her home, kissed her hand and told her to take an aspirin to ward off any possible hangover.

'And he didn't try anything on!' she said aloud, exultantly, which meant that she could look forward to her evening with Al with a completely clear conscience.

The thought of meeting Al again had been uppermost in her mind when she had woken that morning, and although initially she'd not been terribly enthusiastic when her mother had invited Simon to tea, now she was glad because it would be a welcome diversion during the countdown to seeing Al again, a prospect that was making her increasingly nervous as the day wore on.

She heard the sound of a car arriving in the yard and went to her window to check who it was. It was Jeff Babbington. She decided to slip out of the house and walk up the track to wait for Simon.

On her way out she caught sight of Stephen sitting on a hay bale in the shadow of the barn. Gone was the carefree figure of yesterday. He looked positively haggard. Alison had never paid much attention to her brothers' feelings. They were so much older than her and so had always seemed emotionally remote, self-sufficient, not needing or wanting her sympathy or understanding. Sitting there, Stephen looked so vulnerable Alison suddenly felt differently about him. She changed direction and went and sat beside him.

Replete with rich chocolate cake and wine, Ron and Elsie were lying in each other's arms, dozing, when their quiet comfort was shattered by the sound of the doorbell.

'What was that?' Elsie, startled out of her slumber, was momentarily confused.

'The doorbell.' Ron sat up in bed. 'That's odd.'

'What is?'

'It's my front door bell. Not the one downstairs.'

'Perhaps it's a neighbour, wanting something. Leave it, dear. They'll go away.'

But a moment later they heard the scraping of a key in the lock and Ron shot out of bed. He had barely time to whisper to Elsie, 'It's June!' when they heard someone call 'Dad? Dad?' and move across the living room in the direction of the bedroom.

Elsie dived under the duvet, taking with her the remnants of the torte and the wine, and Ron just had time to don a dressing gown and with great presence of mind, throw a jacket over Elsie's clothes on the chair before the door opened.

Elsie, lying half suffocated under the duvet, and flattening herself into the mattress as much as possible, trying not to move, could visualise the thin, sharp features of Ron's daughter peering suspiciously round the door.

'Dad? What are you doing?' Her voice was sharp. 'It's not like you to go to bed in the afternoon. Are you all right?'

Elsie could hear Ron moving towards the door. He sounded irritated. 'Yes, of course I am, perfectly all right. Mayn't a man have a snooze, if he feels like it?'

'Yes, but ... it's just not like you, that's all. And don't you normally see friends on Saturday afternoon?'

'I do. So what are you doing here?'

Elsie felt a tickle in her nose. 'This is ridiculous,' she thought, half way to panicking and half way to collapsing with laughter at the absurdity of the situation.

With relief, she heard June say with some hesitation, 'I'll go and put the kettle on. We need to talk, Dad. You get dressed and we'll have a cup of tea.'

Ron shut the door behind her and pulled back the duvet.

'Thank God for that,' muttered Elsie. 'I thought I was going to suffocate. Get dressed, Ron, and get rid of her as quickly as possible. I'll put my clothes on and hide in the wardrobe till she's gone.'

'Why don't we just tell her, Elsie? For goodness' sake, we've got our own lives to lead.'

'And the less other people know of our business, the better. Go on, find out what she wants. Why did she come here if she thought you were out? That daughter of yours doesn't do things without a reason.'

They dressed as rapidly as they were able; Elsie ensconced safely in the wardrobe, Ron went to face his daughter. Elsie could hear the rise and fall of their voices, but although they were clearly having an argument, she couldn't make out what was being said, try as she might.

It was some time before she heard the front door slam and Ron came to release her. Elsie, even though she had left the wardrobe door open a crack, was feeling faint through lack of air and having to sit in such cramped quarters. Ron sat her in a chair and, giving her a glass of water, anxiously rubbed her feet and hands until she could move comfortably again.

'I felt like a teenager all over again. Fancy hiding under the duvet at my age!' She chuckled, but Ron remained serious. She looked at him, concerned, 'What was that all about, then?'

He pulled a face. 'She was here because a neighbour asked her to call round this afternoon. Walls have ears, my dear. Our little scene with Alison the other day was overheard and it would seem all the neighbours have got together to enjoy the gossip and decide what is to be done with me. June suspects the onset of senile dementia and nothing I could say would persuade her there was a perfectly simple explanation. Being in bed on a Saturday afternoon has further reinforced her suspicions. She's on the warpath, Elsie, and I'm going to have to watch my step or I'm going to find myself clapped in a home!'

By the time they arrived in the kitchen for tea, Nicola was regretting the impulse that had led her to accept Stephen's invitation.

The farm wasn't anything like she thought it would be. It was a hot afternoon and the heat seemed to accentuate the smell, the dust and the flies. The farm buildings were tumbledown;

the milking parlour, which he showed her with pride, was of no interest at all. The barn, where the calf had been born, smelled oppressively sickly and strange. The little calf was sweet, but she'd hastily backed away when the mother made a loud 'don't touch' noise the moment she had tentatively put her hand out.

Stephen then suggested they went and looked at his herd, which was grazing in a field quite close to the farmyard. They walked down a rutted farm track, the afternoon sun beating down, remorselessly hot, on her head and back, there being no shade of any sort from the sparse hedgerow. While she made polite conversation, he was almost inarticulate in his replies. She was wearing a short, thin, cotton dress, and she could feel a trickle of perspiration running down her spine.

When they arrived at the field, the cows were over on the far side, huddled together in the shade of a large chestnut. Nicola would have preferred to admire them from a distance, in the safety of the lane, but to her alarm Stephen opened the gate and ushered her into the meadow. The size and proximity of the cows worried her, though she did her best to hide it. When one vast black and white monster lumbered slowly to her feet, Nicola couldn't help squeaking with terror and did her best to conceal herself behind Stephen's broad back.

He looked at her with concern. 'It's all right, Nicola. She's only being curious. She's a good milker, that one; gave me a pair of calves six months ago.'

'Oh ... how nice.' Nicola's voice came out high and thin with fear, and in spite of Stephen's inclination to linger and extol the virtues of every individual cow, she couldn't get out of the field fast enough, feeling the cows' eyes on her back all the way to the field gate.

'Er ... would you like to go for a walk along the river? It's pretty nice at this time of year.'

Anything, Nicola thought. Anything so long as he doesn't show me any more cows. This afternoon is turning out to be the longest in my life. Why, oh why ... She attempted a smile. 'That would be nice, Stephen. Will it be cooler there, do you think?'

He looked at her with concern. 'You do look a bit hot. Are you all right?'

The path along the riverbank was hard and uneven – her sandals were not really up to it – and she had to concentrate to avoid the thistles, nettles and cowpats. She tried to draw Stephen out, but he had no conversation and went red whenever he put more than two words together which, after a while, she found very trying.

Climbing a stile, he took her hand to help her over and then tried to hold onto it. She managed to disengage herself by pointing at a bird on the river. 'Oh look, what's that? Isn't it handsome?'

'It's a mallard, a drake – they're pretty common really.'

Nicola walked in front of him, putting the hand he had clutched in the pocket of her skirt, giving him no opportunity to take it again, and hardening her heart against the look of despair she saw pass across Stephen's face.

They reached a huge old tree, its roots stretching over the bank into the river as if it were dipping its toes in the water. They paused for a moment under the shade of its branches and she became aware that he was trying to pluck up courage to say something to her.

That Stephen had a crush on Nicola was not a secret among the Merlin Players and it had caused her, and the rest of them, a great deal of amusement when she had returned on periodic visits to catch up with her friends in The Players. Nicola liked being adored and was used to it and rarely, to her credit, took advantage of it. But this summer, she was bored. She had come back to her parents' house because there was no work in London and her funds were very low. She had broken up with her most recent boyfriend, at his instigation, which had left her sore. She had agreed to take the star part in *The Beaux Stratagem* as her ego needed stroking, but she was out of their league and she knew it, which added to her general feelings of frustration. So she had been teasing Stephen, leading him on for her amusement and that of her friends in the company.

She had anticipated having great fun, reporting back to the

others her experiences of Marsh farm and Stephen's family, none of whom any of them had ever met. But what had started out as a frivolous game was turning into an ordeal, and for one awful moment she feared, under the grey ash tree, that Stephen was about to declare his passion, which was more than she was prepared to deal with. So she gave him no chance to say anything and talked about the river, the view, the heat, rehearsals, anything that came into her head. He seemed to deflate even more and, almost in silence, finally led the way back to the farmhouse and to the tea that awaited them.

Jenny beamed. Everything seemed to be going so well. True, nobody except Stephen seemed to have much of an appetite; there were a lot of the sardine sandwiches left and Nicola was taking a long time to eat hers. What a pretty girl she was, with those lovely blue eyes and glossy dark curls; Jenny could understand why Stephen was so smitten. She reminded Jenny of a heroine in a Georgette Heyer novel she'd just finished reading.

When she had first arrived in the kitchen, Jenny was nervous. Nicola had seemed a bit quiet, cold even. But then Simon had appeared with Alison, and Nicola appeared to come out of herself and sparkled. 'Poor girl, I expect she was just shy,' Jenny thought sympathetically, and cut her an extra large piece of chocolate cake.

Simon was a great hit with all of them. Jenny had liked him from the moment Alison had brought him home. It wasn't just that she was impressed by his appearance and by his charming manner, but there was a kindness about him that made her feel relaxed and comfortable. She beamed at him across the table. He certainly was good looking. Jenny marvelled at the good-fortune of her two children to have attracted such a glamorous pair. It was just such a pity neither of them seemed to eat anything. Simon had managed one sandwich and a scone, had praised her strawberry jam but had refused anything else. But then he had told her he was going out to dinner that evening. And Nicola … well, she was such a slim creature and an actress – they did have to watch their figures, didn't they?

Sitting by Jenny's side, Alison nibbled at a sardine sandwich. The bread was slightly dry and the filling was very fishy and slimy, so with the practice born of years, she waited till her mother's attention was elsewhere then slid the sandwich under the table into the eager jaws of Gip, who had long since learned to sit patiently under the table by Alison's knees at mealtimes. Alison was concerned about Stephen. He was very quiet and there was a defeated air about him — the way he sat with his shoulders hunched and rarely looked up at anybody. True, he hadn't lost his appetite, but then, Alison reminded herself, Stephen had always stuffed his face, however miserable or worried he was. Then Simon turned to talk to him and to her relief, she saw Stephen respond and become more animated. The conversation led on to the Tuckers' plans to regenerate the farm's fortunes. Stephen brightened, helped himself to another large slice of chocolate cake and turned to talk to Jeff, animatedly, about what they might do with rare breeds.

Alison felt guilty. With everything that had happened over the last few days, she had given very little thought to the farm's future. She said as much, and added, 'I guess, since I don't know too much about farming, I ought to look at other ideas for using what we've got.'

'Like what, Alison?' Simon smiled across at her. He was sitting in Charlie's chair, next to Stephen; Nicola sat in Jenny's place, next to Alison, and Jeff occupied Elsie's huge wooden chair at the head. Jenny had pushed the heap of paraphernalia on the table further down one end, to make room for herself next to Alison, and from here she jumped up periodically to fill the kettle or teapot, cut cake, and press more food on her guests.

'I don't know,' Alison replied thoughtfully. 'We had a few ideas the other day: clay pigeon shooting; paint-balling; pick your own; ostrich farming; a farm shop; weddings ... I really don't know, but we've land and we've got a nice setting. We should be able to think of doing something that people want, and if it could happen alongside Stephen's rare breeds—'

'Sounds like a recipe for a circus!' Nicola laughed.

'Yeah, well, I'm sure even circuses will pay good money for a site,' retorted Alison sourly.

'Talking about sites ...' Nicola sparkled. The arrival of the man sitting opposite her had been as unexpected as it was welcome. Simon was just the sort of man she liked; the sort who brought out the best in her; the sort of man she would very much like to have and *would* have, if she put her mind to it. 'I've heard there's going to be some sort of rave near here. You should get onto that bandwagon – I bet the organisers would pay well for the land. They charge enough for the tickets.'

'Yeah well, raves are old hat,' replied Alison, 'but letting the land out for a music event was one of the ideas I thought we might consider.'

Her mother looked up, alarmed. 'Event, what sort of event? We might need the money, but I don't want anything illegal going on. I've heard about those raves and I'm not having one on my land.'

'But Mum, they're not what you think—'

'How do you know? I've heard all about them. Can you imagine how your gran would react if we were invaded by hippies, rolling around in the dirt; dogs and alcohol; weird music; drugs for sale, and goodness knows what else? If there is going to be such a thing round here, they'd better keep well away from our land or I'll set the police on them.'

'Raves have changed, Mum. They're not like they used to be – they're more like huge discos; they're not for hippies.'

'You're not going to get me to change my mind about them, Ali, and I hope you're not planning on going to this one. I've heard about them discos and teenagers takin' those E tablets, dancing all night and dying from thirst. Terrible!' And she shook her head, visibly distressed.

Jeff leaned forward and patted her hand. 'I'm sure raves would be the last thing Stephen would want here.' He smiled encouragingly at her. 'I've got another idea: how about a golf driving range? There are a number about and they seem to do quite well.' Jeff liked golf.

176

'Or a pitch and putt.' Jenny cheered up at the thought and helped herself to a piece of fruit cake. She had played pitch and putt once, on the seafront at Weston.

'What ideas has Charlie come up with?' Jeff took a nibble out of the large slice of chocolate cake Jenny had insisted on giving him. It was like eating clay. Nicola, he noticed, had just taken a bite and was staring at her piece with dismay.

'Oh, he would like to set up a motocross circuit, of course,' said Alison contemptuously. 'Apart from that, he hasn't come up with anything.'

'He's busy with harvesting at the moment. He probably hasn't had time to give it much thought. More tea, Nicola? Are you sure you won't try my cake, Simon? Have another scone and some strawberry jam ...'

The conversation drifted onto other things. Nicola questioned Simon about where he lived, his reasons for moving out of London, and his job. She then started exchanging London reminiscences with him, which rather cut the rest of them out, Alison noticed. She was beginning to dislike Nicola.

Alison's mobile buzzed, and excusing herself from the party, she went outside to check the text message.

'Probs. Held up. CU 8. Al.'

For some reason she felt gutted. All day she'd been pitching for seven o' clock. It was only a delay of an hour, but ... Meeting someone at eight rather than seven ruled out so many possibilities: it would be too late to eat, too late to go to the movies, too late to go anywhere very far. Alison ground her teeth in vexation.

When she re-entered the kitchen, Simon, casting a quick glance in her direction and sensing a mood change, stood up. 'I really ought to go. Mrs Tucker, thanks very much for inviting me. It's years since I've had a tea like this. Stephen, I don't know anything about farms or farming, but if I can help with business plans, tell my mate Alison here, and I'll do what I can.'

Alison, deep in her gloom, registered the implication of what Simon was saying. She warmed a little.

Simon smiled round the table. 'Bye, Jeff, nice to have met you.

Bye, Nicola. I look forward to seeing your Dorinda; perhaps I'll be able to persuade Alison to take me. Ali, are you going to show me this little heifer of Stephen's before I have to go and sample the high life of Summerstoke? I've a strong feeling it's not going to be nearly as much fun.'

It was late afternoon by the time the last of the deliveries had been made and stashed in the field neatly alongside the hedge, invisible from the road. A small caravan was installed next to the newly padlocked gate, again out of sight of the road. With the fencing that Charlie and Lenny had completed that morning, the field was secure and the man in dark glasses (anyone giving orders wore dark glasses, Charlie noticed) grunted his satisfaction before going off to give a last-minute briefing to the two men who were going to live in the caravan for the next week.

'Care for a pint, mate?' Charlie asked affably when, business concluded, Dark Glasses rejoined them.

'No, thanks. Early start tomorrow.' Watched by the two of them, he got into his car, started the engine, then wound down the smoked-glass window. 'Remember what I said. Not a word to anyone. Any publicity is bad publicity. If this gets out, the deal is off. Clear?'

'As daylight.' Charlie nodded, the windows slid back up and the car slipped noiselessly down the lane and was out of sight in seconds. 'I wonder how much he can see, wearing dark glasses and with a smoked windscreen.' He turned to Lenny. 'You heard what the man said, Lenny. Mum's the word, eh? Time for a quick one?'

Lenny, remembering a drunken conversation with Paula, felt a twinge of guilt. 'Sorry, mate, best get back or Paula'll kill me.'

Charlie decided to give The Grapes a miss until after he'd met Sarah and found out what she wanted, so he took off back to the farm to clean himself up. He turned into the farm track and met a Golf convertible driven by a pretty brunette. As he reversed into a passing space, Charlie goggled and whistled to himself. 'Blimey, if that's Stevie's crumpet ... maybe Lenny has a point!'

As the two cars crept past, he leaned out of the window, flashed her a smile and enquired sociably, 'You Stephen's friend?'

The girl looked at him coolly. 'Yes, I suppose so.'

'Sorry I missed tea, then. I'm Charlie. His brother.'

'Oh.'

'So they were all there, then, all the family?'

'There seemed to be a lot of them, certainly. Well, nice meeting—'

But Charlie hadn't finished. Driven, possibly, by his humiliation of the night before, Lenny's words, the thought of Sarah, or simply unnerved that Stephen could attract such a classy girl, a spirit of mischief entered his soul.

'So you met our grandmother?'

'No. She wasn't there. Now if—'

'No, thinking about it, she wouldn't have been. She and Stephen had a bit of a ding-dong last Sunday. He was right pissed off. Still ...' he paused and looked at her meaningfully. 'He's a fast worker and no mistake. Didn't think he had it in him.'

Nicola was growing impatient. She'd had enough of Marsh Farm and the Tuckers, and she didn't like the way this man, with his lean brown face, mocking eyes and ridiculous whiskers, was looking at her. But she couldn't get past until he'd moved his car forward. 'I don't know what you're talking about. Please, I'm in a bit of a hurry and—'

'So he didn't tell you, then?'

'Tell me what?'

'That his grandmother said he had to get married or she'd cut him out of her will. That was last Sunday and here you are, coming to tea the following Saturday. That's what I mean. Fast worker!'

'What?' Nicola was aghast.

'So he hadn't told you. Well, maybe he had his reasons. Look, you better not say anything to him about our little chat. I don't want to queer his pitch. I'm sure he'll tell you, when the time is right ...'

He pulled his car over to allow her to get past and chuckled as, grinding the gears, she accelerated up to the main road.

'Well, what did you think?' Jenny had her hands in the washing-up bowl and didn't notice Jeff clearing the table and sweeping the remains of her cake into a rubbish bag.

'Of what?'

'Of Stephen's girl, Nicola. She was very pretty. How old do you think she is? Twenty-three, twenty-four?'

'Oh, older than that. I thought she was okay, but Jenny,' he tried to be tactful, 'she didn't pay much attention to Stephen, did she?'

Jenny slowly turned to look at him, her hands dripping suds. 'No,' she said sadly. 'I know you think I'm hopelessly stupid over the boys, but even I could see that she was, well, too pretty for Stephen. But she must see something in him; why else would she accept his invitation?'

'Lord only knows. I just think he's out of his depth, old girl.' He squeezed Jenny's shoulder. 'I liked Ali's boyfriend, Simon. He's a real find.'

'Oh, he's lovely, isn't he? But ... you don't think he's a bit old for her?'

Before Jeff had time to reply, they were interrupted by Alison's return.

'I was just telling your mother here that I like your boyfriend, Ali—'

'Boyfriend?' Alison snarled. 'Are you talking about Simon? He's *not* my boyfriend. For one thing he's far too old. He's just someone I met and we've become friends and that's all there is to it, for Chrissake!' And she banged out of the room, almost knocking Stephen over.

Stephen, in his overalls and on his way to do the evening milking, was miserable and confused. Miserable because he had failed all Angela's tests; confused, because as she left, Nicola had kissed him on the cheek, thanked him for a lovely afternoon and said she would see him on Sunday. And when he had asked her if she would come again, she had said, 'Of course!' He really didn't know what to think, but grasping at straws, he was allowing that tiny glimmer of hope to light his way to the milking shed and inform his communion with the cows.

As he crossed the yard Charlie's van screeched to a halt, but Stephen didn't feel up to any more conversation and hurried on to collect his cows.

Watching his dejected frame disappearing around the barn, Jenny sadly observed, 'He'd be better off going with someone like little Angela, poor lamb.'

'That little mouse! She's got as much sex appeal as Gip's blanket. No, Jenny; you've got to let him have a go. It might wake him up!'

'I had such high hopes: Stephen bringing her, and Ali finding Simon. Seems we're back where we started.'

Jeff turned to see Jenny staring gloomily into the bin. 'And my cake wasn't very nice, either, was it?'

She looked so deflated, Jeff was moved to console her. 'Cheer up, Jenny. I'm sure things will work out. Look, I normally go down to my local on Saturday night. There's always a bit of live music. Why don't you clear up here and we'll pop down for a pie and a pint. What yer say?'

12

'Right,' snapped Veronica. 'Everyone's here – champagne cocktails for the next half hour and then we'll go into dinner. Don't let the sauce boil; I'll be back to cook the ravioli in twenty minutes. Have the plates ready, as I showed you. In the meantime, you can start tying up the beans into little parcels, and for heaven's sake, Paula, try not to make a mess of them.' She swept out of the kitchen in a scented waft, ignoring the face Paula pulled at her and the resentfully muttered, 'What did yer last slave die of?'

Vee crossed the hall, fluffed her hair and checked her make-up in a large oval, gilt-framed mirror hanging above an escritoire. She smoothed the irritating tic in the corner of her eye, an inevitable consequence of any conversation with Paula, checked her dress, a short, black, backless shift made from raw silk that had, inevitably, cost a small fortune, and schooled her countenance into a more agreeable expression with which to greet her guests. The sound of conversation, the clinking of glass and the loud braying laugh of the editor of a local newspaper – Vee always invited him when she wanted to impress – floated from the drawing room.

She entered the room, which was tastefully furnished – in her opinion – with wall-to-wall pale gold carpeting complementing the even paler gold paint of the walls and the long white drapes with a gold leaf design that framed the windows, from which her guests could look down over the river valley. They had all been thrown open to offset the warmth of the evening, and a gentle breeze dispersed the scent of the huge lilies displayed in the fireplace. Smiling gaily, and taking a glass from Hugh, Vee went to join her guest of honour, Harriet Flood, who was standing in the bay of one window talking to her son. Vee insisted that her two children join their guests for pre-dinner drinks as part of her effort to 'introduce them to society' as she put it.

Cordelia, fourteen, loud and self-possessed in spite of being short and inclined to pudginess and spots, needed no encouragement. She loved grown-up parties and had smothered her acne in foundation, brushed her waist-length blonde hair till it crackled with static, and wore a sleeveless, multi-coloured chiffon blouse with a matching skirt that parted company every time she moved, revealing a comfortable little roll of flesh for a waistline. Vee could hear her loudly enthusing about her latest mount to Gavin Croucher, the ex-Olympic show jumper and Isabelle Garnett, married to Richard Garnett – he of the braying laugh.

Anthony, however, was the antithesis of his sister, and had refused to attend at first. It wasn't until she had lost her temper, all cajoling having proved ineffective, that he had backed down. He stood, in a white shirt she'd pressed on him, and jeans, which he had insisted on wearing as a condition of his presence, a lanky, glowering, rebellious, mute nineteen-year-old, on the edge of a small group that included Harriet Flood and Vee's best chum, Marion Croucher, Gavin's wife. Marion was an interior designer, short and plump, but very well dressed, and Vee thought that she would be a good conversational match for Harriet.

At the sight of his mother Anthony made his excuses to leave, to the clear disappointment of Harriet Flood. 'I'm so sorry you're not joining us for dinner, Anthony. I'm sure your mother could squeeze you in. I'd love to have a chat about dear old Durham. I'm sure it's changed a lot since I was there.'

But with a polite smile he was gone.

'I do so love young people,' drawled Harriet. 'They have such a refreshing attitude to life, don't you think? He tells me he rides. He must look quite something on horseback. Don't you agree that men on horses look really sexy? You will persuade Anthony to show me round the stables tomorrow, Veronica, won't you?'

When Veronica Lester met Harriet Flood for the first time that evening, she had found the *Country Homes and Gardens'* lead feature writer disconcertingly intimidating – an unusual experience for Veronica. Harriet was in her early fifties, taller than Veronica, and she had shaken her hostess's hand with an air of veiled contempt. She had malicious dark eyes that flickered everywhere, registering, assessing, mocking, and Veronica, used to being in complete control of any situation, was unnerved by this. Veronica had been very put out when, contrary to what they had arranged, Harriet had turned up only just before the other guests were due. Originally, she had planned to impress the writer with a tour round the house and gardens before the dinner party, but having met her, it was with some relief that she turned Harriet over to Hugh and had made good her escape to the kitchen. So if Harriet liked the look of Anthony, so much the better. Anthony could look after her tomorrow.

'Of course, whatever you want,' she said smoothly, smothering the alarm bell that had sounded off somewhere in the brain where her maternal instincts were meant to lie. 'And please, call me Vee. Now, have you met Richard Garnett? He's our local newspaper man and a great friend, and Gavin Croucher, the Olympic show jumper. We've known him for years!'

Vee loved dinner parties; loved showing off her prowess as cook and hostess; took pride in the selection of her guests and in keeping them stimulated. For her, a successful evening was measured by non-stop conversation and endless praise for her culinary achievements. Hugh was generous with the wine, and the loquacity of her guests this evening left nothing to be desired.

Having sat her guests down at the long table in the elegant, high-ceilinged dining room that glowed with polished wood, sparkling crystal, silver candelabra and flickering candlelight, Vee served them first with crabmeat ravioli.

(Paula had tasted a rejected misshapen one and had spat it out in disgust.)

Then a champagne sorbet.

('Give me Ben & Jerry's anytime – tasteless or what! What are they doin' eatin' ice cream in the middle of a meal?')

Paula was kept out of sight of the guests.

Vee was clear that all credit for the seamless presentation of the feast was to be hers. So the dishes came and went amid satisfying little crows of delight and appreciation.

She sat at one end of the table and glowed.

Paula, standing at the kitchen table, struggling to tie little parcels of fine green beans with chives and dropping a large proportion of them onto the floor, glowered.

Charlie's departure to meet Sarah was delayed by an unexpected telephone call.

'Is that Charlie? Charlie Tucker?'

It was a female voice, faintly familiar, Charlie thought.

'Yeah, this is Charlie Tucker. What can I do fer you?'

'It's Tricia. Tricia Stevens. You remember. We went out together when we was at school ...'

Charlie struggled to remember. He thought he recognised the name, but he couldn't put a face to the voice. 'Er ... yeah ... How are you doing, Trish? Long time no see.'

'I'm fine.' She paused slightly. 'I've been away and now I'm back, I thought I'd look up me ol' mates. I got yer number off've Skip. He said to give you a ring.'

'Oh?' A warning bell went off faintly in the back of Charlie's brain.

'Yeah. Look, I know yer busy with the farm an' everythin' – but d'ya fancy comin' out for a drink, for ol' times' sake? It would be nice to meet up again, wouldn't it?'

'Yeah. Sure. Why not? Thing is, I'm a bit busy right this minute but give us your number, Tricia and I'll give you a ring. Fix something up.'

Tricia Stevens. No, it was no good. He couldn't remember ever going out with a girl of that name. He supposed he might have snogged her; he'd snogged a lot of girls by the time he'd left school. Linda might know. He'd ask her.

Sarah, who worked in a travel agency, lived in a small semi-detached house near the centre of Summerbridge, which she rented with two other girls. Charlie had toyed with taking her out for a pub meal somewhere in the country, but then changed his mind in favour of a Chinese, in the town, on the grounds that service would be quick and it would enable him to get Sarah home and himself to The Grapes before closing time, and also if things turned nasty and she wanted to leave, she would be able to walk home, leaving him free to scoot off to the pub.

What did she want to talk to him about? The question occupied his thoughts as he drove to Sarah's place. 'Pregnant?' Even the thought sent a cold shiver through him, but he thought it unlikely. She had told him she was on the pill and she wasn't the sort of person to do the dirty. Perhaps, he thought optimistically, she's found herself another fella. That would let me out, nice and dandy.

Sarah was ready when he arrived and fell in with the idea of going for a Chinese meal. While she was studying the menu, he studied her, surreptitiously. She looked all right. She had her hair up, which looked nice, and that blue dress suited her — it was plain and straight and she certainly had the figure for it. For a moment he felt regretful, but then a picture of Beth, laughing and teasing, flitted across his mind.

They ordered the food.

They chatted about work, the harvest, the weather, how they each were. Charlie was puzzled.

The food was served. Charlie, trying to make his chopsticks work in a coordinated way, suddenly thought of a question he wanted to ask.

'Sarah? May I ask you something?'

She looked up and smiled, anticipating. 'Yes?'

'Be honest, now, what do you think of my sideburns?'

She looked startled. 'Er ... they're fine, Charlie. Very distinctive. Why?'

'Do you think I should shave them off?'

She hesitated. 'Um ... if you want to, then yes.'

'But I don't. I just wanted to know what you thought of them.'

'They're fine.'

'Good. That's all right, then.'

Then Sarah looked up from her chow mein and regarded him seriously. 'Charlie,' she began, almost shyly, 'I said on the phone that I wanted to talk to you about something.'

'Talk away,' he said, with a nonchalance he wasn't feeling. 'I'm listening.'

'It's just that I've heard your news.'

'What?' For a moment Charlie's brain went into a spin – what news? Which bit of his life had she heard about? Beth? The event? His visit to the bank?

'I thought you were a bit subdued last Saturday. You said it was because of the harvest, but I worried that you might be going off me, and then I heard.'

'Yes?' said Charlie, still needing enlightenment.

'I just want you to know that I understand what you must be going through. It's terrible.'

'Yes?' Whatever it was, she wasn't planning to go off with somebody else; it clearly wasn't anything to do with the event, and it didn't seem very likely she would be this sympathetic if she'd found out about Beth.

'It's not fair on you. One can't make these things happen.'

'No?'

'I just wanted you to know that you've got my support.'

'Thanks, Sarah.'

'And if we get married sooner rather than later, that's fine by me.'

'What?!' Charlie's reaction was so loud and explosive, all the other diners stopped talking and stared, and the entire Chinese family who owned the restaurant emerged from the kitchen or left off serving to congregate in a tight, watchful group by the kitchen door.

In a state of shock, Charlie lost no time in telling Sarah he had no intention of getting married to her, or anyone else, whatever his grandmother might order. Their evening out ended even more abruptly than Charlie had planned, with Sarah finally jumping up and marching to the door of the restaurant where she turned and shouted, 'And as for your whiskers, Charlie Tucker – they're a joke! They are stupid and revolting, like you!'

Charlie arrived at the pub still in a state of shock and in desperate need of a few sensible words from Linda. The pub was busy and there was no sign of her. Stan and Beth were too busy to engage in anything more than passing back-chat with him, so Charlie decided to bide his time with Beth and took his pint over to a table where other regulars were playing a noisy game of cribbage.

'Where's Linda?' he asked casually of Skip. 'Not like her not to be in on a Saturday.'

'Stan says she's off looking after her mother. Not well or something.' Skip was clearly not interested.

'I thought that was Stan's mum?'

'What?'

'Last time I saw her, when I helped behind the bar, she said that Stan's mum was ill and he'd gone to sort her out. She weren't here on Tuesday either.'

'Well, maybe it's Stan's mum she's gone to look after. I don't know. Why are you so bothered about which mum Linda's with?'

'I'm not.' He sipped his beer and watched the cards being slammed on the table. He suddenly remembered the curious phone call that had started his evening and nudged Skip again. 'Here, Skip, who's this Tricia Stevens?'

'Who?'

'Tricia Stevens. She gave me a ring this evening, said she'd got my number from you.'

'Oh, her.' Skip smirked. 'I was just giving you a helpin' hand, me ol' mate. She's footloose and fancy free at the moment so I thought, what with you in your predicament—'

'Thanks for nothing, Skip. I can do without help of that sort. Anyway, who is she?'

'Search me. Met her with a group of mates the other night,

when we was plannin' your little surprise. Said she was at school wiv you; that's all I know. Ask Linda.'

'That's what I was going to do, but she ain't here,' and Charlie, puzzled by Linda's absence, took his pint back to his perch at the bar and watched Stan and Beth bustling, laughing and flirting with their customers and with each other.

As the last orders were called and served, he finally managed to speak to Beth.

'How about tonight – fancy going on somewhere?'

She looked at him coolly. 'Maybe I would, Charlie, but you're forgetting one thing.'

'What?'

'I'm not going anywhere with those whiskers.'

Once the main course had been served, Vee was able to relax and take stock of her guests. Hugh, at the far end, was in close conversation with Gavin Croucher, a tall, loose-limbed man with a bulbous nose and a high colour. Their conversation was always on horses: the current lack of talent in show jumping, the inadequacies of the Beaufort course, and the problems encountered with 'Johnny Foreigner' in stud farming.

Marion, on Hugh's right, was talking across the table to Harriet Flood about 'paint authenticity' and Vee strained to catch their conversation, but she knew she could rely on Marion to give her a faithful account of Ms Flood's opinions.

On Vee's right sat Simon Weatherby. Vee had met him only a week ago and had invited him, on impulse, to make up numbers. He seemed pleasant enough; quite quiet, but that was not surprising since he didn't know anybody. 'He's a good-looking man,' thought Vee to herself. 'Quite yummy, in fact. I wonder how old he is.' He had honey-blond hair and quite the bluest eyes she'd seen, a straight nose and good jaw, with white, even teeth. He was quite tall, lean and tanned. He rarely smiled, but when he did, his face crinkled and illuminated. He was listening to the conversation between Issy Garnett, on his right, and Richard Garnett, on Vee's left.

Vee liked Richard Garnett. As editor of the local paper, he could be relied upon for an endless supply of good gossip. He had a sharp mind but had grown lazy in the provinces rather than throwing himself in the deeper end of mainstream journalism where his talents could have taken him. Now nearly fifty, he'd left it too late to make the move, he confided to Vee, so he was making the most of being a large fish in a small pond. His salt and pepper hair was cropped really short and he always wore black, whether casually dressed or not. He was tall, with a stomach that was starting to swell from good living, and a strong-featured face that habitually wore a mocking expression.

Isabelle, or Issy as she was called, was Richard's second wife, nearly twenty years younger than him and the youngest around the table, apart from Simon Weatherby. She had been an artist of some note before she had married and had two babies in quick succession. She was not Vee's type and although their husbands were good friends, Vee, apart from acknowledging her slightly distrait prettiness, thought little of her. She was a thin, nervous woman in a floating, diaphanous dress. She wore lots of silvery bracelets on her arms, which chinked and clinked as she talked and waved her hands. When Vee sat down, having served the duck, she became aware of a tension in the conversation between the Garnetts.

'Well, I think the sort of naming and shaming campaign run by your newspaper is horrid.'

'We have a lot of support for it. Don't you think people who drink and drive ought to be identified, Issy, darling? After all, they could easily kill someone.'

'The fact that they could kill someone is taken into account by the punishment they receive from the courts. Why should you take it upon yourself to punish them further? What you're doing is little better than shoving them in the stocks, and the only reason you're doing it is to sell newspapers.'

'And if we sell newspapers because of our campaign, doesn't that mean we have the public's support?' There was little warmth in Richard's expression as he fenced with his wife.

She grew more heated. 'You're playing to the lowest common denominator, to the prurient spectator who gloats in the discomfiture of others whilst probably offending in the same way himself. I bet,' she said, looking round at the rest of the table who had fallen quiet, 'There's nobody here who could say, hand on heart, they haven't driven under the influence of alcohol.'

There was an uncomfortable silence.

Harriet sipped her wine. It was unusually good: an appellation, Pecharmant, possibly. That's why she put up with the extraordinary tedium of these occasions – she loved good food and wine with a passion, and if people were prepared to lavish their hospitality on her in return for the exposure of their pretentious houses and boring lifestyles, she had the stomach for it. The fawning and flattery left her unmoved; she did and said what she liked, but did not go out of her way either to be liked or disliked. She felt under no obligation to her hosts and it was not uncommon for the promised feature not to materialise. The desire of people to show off their houses meant that there were always more invitations than she could accept, so she was selective. Nevertheless, there was an incredible sameness about them all, and this house, these hosts and this dinner party were no exception.

There was an extraordinary inevitability about the guests, as well. The hostess would pull in a friend who was an interior designer; a journalist who either wrote for the national press, or who was at least the editor of the local rag; a local minor celebrity, although Harriet had to admit she hadn't met many ex-Olympic show jumpers; and usually an artist or musician to add a refreshingly bohemian touch.

The only conundrum in this evening's gathering was the rather good-looking young man sitting at the far end who, as far as she could tell, had come alone and knew nobody else around the table. She had been about to break off a very tedious discussion with the interior designer and interrogate him, when the girl's challenge hijacked the conversation. To Harriet's experienced eye, the bohemian element was in her cups rather early on in the proceedings and the hostess, Veronica-call-me-Vee, was doing her best not to show that she was annoyed.

Harriet had absolutely no intention of responding to the challenge. She was only fifty, but she had given up driving years ago, having been banned for three years after one particularly heavy session. She had not reapplied for her licence, having enjoyed three years of other people chauffeuring her about and being able to drink as much as she liked.

Yes, the wine was good; definitely a Pecharmant. She finished her glass and looked to her host to replenish it. Hugh was too involved joining in the general humiliation of the young woman to notice, so she helped herself, preening a little when she read the label: Château Corbiac. The food was good too, though a bit fussy (it always was). It amazed her how many times she had been presented with puy lentils that summer. She sighed inwardly. She didn't like her hosts and only the fact that, for once, this was a feature she might need, stopped her making her excuses and taking a train back at the earliest opportunity.

It was a Victorian house, decorated and furnished with discreet and expensive good taste. 'Anywhere would look good with that sort of money thrown at it,' she thought, her eyes drifting over the deep red Persian rugs on the highly polished oak floor, heavy silver-grey drapes in the tall window recesses, and the glistening chandelier suspended over the long mahogany table at which they were sitting. If it had just been the house ... but her editor was clear. They wanted to break the mould, hook the reader – a makeover series with a difference, and what could be better than to follow the creation of a stud, with lots of photogenic horses and lovable long-legged little foals?

'How are your plans for the stud coming on?' she asked, breaking across the conversation.

Hugh answered her guardedly. 'Oh fine, one or two problems to sort out; land, that sort of thing. Our business plan—'

'Land? What's the problem with land? You seem to have plenty.'

'Yes,' interjected Vee smoothly. 'We have, but expansion

inevitably means more land. It's all in hand, however, and we don't envisage any problems.'

'I didn't know you were going to buy more land.' Gavin raised bushy brows and leaned forward, interested. 'There isn't any for sale around here as far as I know. Whose are you going to buy?'

Vee was caught. She didn't want to reveal their plans for Marsh Farm too soon, but equally, she wanted Harriet Flood to commit to that series. She made a quick assessment and gambled on her guests' partisanship. 'I know you'll all be discreet until it's happened, but we're planning to buy Marsh Farm.'

Simon looked up.

'Marsh Farm?' persisted Gavin. 'The Tuckers' place? I didn't know they intended to sell.'

Hugh frowned across the table at Vee. She avoided his eye and laughed lightly. 'We have it on good authority that they are about to go bankrupt; Hugh has already given them a good offer … but please, everybody, not a word. I've said too much already and now Hugh is cross with me!' And she laughed again.

'Wasn't the Tucker fellow the one we photographed straddled across that polar bear, drunk out of his brain and howling for his mum because he was afraid of heights and couldn't get down?' Richard Garnett brayed with laughter and retold the story to the rest of the table.

Simon was shocked. He had dismissed Alison's portrait of the Lesters as adolescent prejudice, but the whole evening had served to confirm what she had told him. At first he had been inclined to give them the benefit of the doubt. He hadn't immediately warmed to them or to the other guests, but he had been to dinners like this in the past, when still married to Helen, and they had been made more tolerable by the humorous post-mortems they would have afterwards.

The thought of Helen still gave him pain and he pushed her out of his thoughts; he was getting good at that. Alison, he decided, would enjoy his description of the dinner and until the mention of

Marsh Farm, he had settled back to absorb as much as he could, to amuse her.

Alison and her family had arrived so unexpectedly in his life. Their topsy-turvy world, their whole background, cultural, social, economic, was so different from his that, ordinarily, he would never have met them. When Alison had taken her tumble in the river, he had been gloomily deliberating if moving to the country had been such a good idea after all: he was bored and lonely, wondering whether he would ever recover from losing Helen, ever stop trying to imagine what she was doing at that particular moment. Would he ever stop remembering what she looked, sounded, and smelled like, or stop hoping that she might have some regret, that next time his phone went off, it would be her?

Alison somehow dispelled those wraiths – she was quirky, fierce and funny, and he enjoyed her company immensely. When Helen left, he had found himself surrounded by predatory women, all professing to want to help, all with sexual agendas. Alison had made it clear he was far too old for her to worry about and though he experienced a certain amount of pique at this realisation, it had enabled him to relax with her.

It was an instant rapport and in the short time they had become friends, he had grown very protective of her. This was a new feeling for him; Helen had never wanted protecting. He had been curious to meet the Tucker family and in spite of Alison's clear objections, had wangled that invitation to tea. He had succumbed to their kind, unquestioning acceptance of him. With the exception of Stephen's girl, who was a type he recognised of old, he liked them all. It was clear they were struggling and he wanted to help them, but he wasn't at all sure how he could. And even though he'd never met Charlie, or the extraordinary grandmother for that matter, they were part of his newfound treasure trove and he couldn't bear these people laughing and sneering at them. It was clear that they were prepared to take advantage of the Tuckers' difficulties, and were unscrupulous enough to nudge them towards disaster.

He resisted the urge to wipe the smirks off the faces of his hosts and guests and embarrass them by declaring his allegiance. He decided, for the moment, the best he could do was to cultivate the Lesters. He would keep his ears and eyes open, he thought to himself; he would be a sleeper. He smiled ironically to himself. How appropriate – he was too much a man of the world to be unaware of the interest of his hostess in him.

He glanced across at Harriet Flood. Not an attractive woman, he thought: tall, unnaturally black hair, heavy body with white pudgy skin and malicious dark eyes. She was Veronica Lester's Achilles heel, he surmised, and probably worth cultivating. He leaned across the table with a smile.

Panting, they reached the top of the tor and flung themselves down on the grass. Traces of the sunset could still be seen in the western sky, but the stars were out in force, mirroring the twinkling lights from the homesteads and hamlets that dotted the Levels below them. In the distance, they could see the faint dark profile of a line of hills.

'Is that Exmoor?' Alison pointed.

'Probably the Quantocks. Have you ever been there? We should take a day out and go there on the bike.' Al unzipped his leather jacket and produced a bottle of wine and a bag of crisps. 'I hope these aren't too squashed.'

Alison laughed happily. This had been worth the week's anguished waiting. The night air was warm and still, carrying the murmurings of other people on the tor; somewhere, a guitar struck up; somewhere, the sound of low drumming; somewhere someone started singing. There was a gentle pop as Al eased the cork out of the bottle. 'Here, have the first swig. You don't mind sharing the bottle, do you? The crystal glasses wouldn't fit in my jacket pocket.'

Alison had a mouthful of warm, rather fusty, wine and lay back on the grass, cupping the back of her head in her hand. She watched Al's profile, silhouetted against the stars as he tilted his head back to take a swig. She had never felt so churned up by any previous boyfriend. He was such a mixture – remote, aloof, silent, like now, then warm and funny and talking non-stop, like last weekend. She found his physical presence disturbing, too. A slight breeze flattened his T-shirt against his chest, showing the contours of his muscles, and his arms, draped over his knees, were brown and strong. The moonlight threw strong, angular shadows across his face and he looked, she thought, like some romantic hero from an archaic work of fiction.

He hadn't said much when they had met, had made no attempt to kiss her, either then, or when they arrived at the foot of the tor, but he had held her hand as they scrambled up and she could sense that the anger, or whatever it was that had been driving him, had dissipated. They had asked so few questions of each other since they met, Alison hesitated to start now, but, she reasoned to herself, if there was to be any sort of future in this relationship, they would have to know more than each other's names.

'You seemed a bit pissed off when we met,' she began, lightly.

'Yeah, sorry. Nothing to do with you. I have as little to do with my parents as I possibly can, but sometimes I get caught. That's why I had to delay meeting up with you tonight.' He turned to look at her, his expression completely unreadable in the dark. 'I've thought a lot about you, this week, Ali.'

Alison managed a small, inarticulate reply, before he leaned over her and kissed her.

Some time later, lying enfolded in his arms, Alison picked up the conversation. 'Do you live with your parents?'

'Only when I can't make other arrangements during the holidays. I've got a bar job that sees me through most of the Christmas and Easter breaks, but this summer they laid me off; not enough in the way of seasonal visitors.' He laughed, without amusement.

'You know, Al, you've told me so little about yourself. Do you have brothers and sisters? What do your parents do?' She paused, then drove on. 'And I don't know, and rather feel I should, whether you've got a girlfriend or not.'

Al was silent for a moment, but did not draw away from her. Then, in a slightly mocking tone he replied, 'No, it's true, I've told you very little. Perhaps it doesn't seem so very important. We've got along well enough so far without each other's life histories. After all, you've played the same game. Have *you* got a bloke?'

'I wouldn't be up here on a Saturday night with you, if I had; I wouldn't have let you kiss me the way you did. I don't two-time people.'

'No, I don't believe you would.' Again he fell silent. 'It's strange,' he began in a low voice, 'how things happen and everything changes. I returned home to work off a debt and promised myself it would be one of the last times I came back. I was away last week because I had to sort out some permanent accommodation for myself and go for a job interview that would at least make me financially viable until I finish my course. That way I would have an excuse not to ... And then I meet you.' He sighed.

Alison didn't know whether to laugh or cry. Her arm, tucked under his body, was going numb, but she didn't want to move.

He continued so quietly, she had to concentrate to hear what he was saying. 'I won't lie, Ali; I do have a girlfriend. She's on the same course as me. Nothing serious, but—'

Alison pulled away and sat up, her arm tingling with pins and needles, her emotions jangled. She was so disappointed – she didn't know what she'd been expecting. After all, if she thought he was cool, then others must do so, and it would be pretty odd if he *was* unattached. It was just that ... oh, sod it, she felt so pathetic!

Al sat up beside her and pulled out his cigarettes. He lit one and as the thin stream of blue smoke vaporised in the night air, he said simply, 'Ali, I really like you. That's what I'm trying to tell you. When we met, I thought you would be good fun for a brief fling, help pass the time here. But you're better than that. When I was away, I kept thinking about you. I didn't want to, believe me, 'cos it changes things and I thought I'd got everything so sorted. But I just wanted to come back and see you. I was amazed how fed up I got when you didn't text me, and then when you did ...'

'What about your girlfriend? Where's she? Are you sharing this accommodation with her?'

'No. It's with three other blokes. We're going off grape picking in France the week after next, on our bikes, so we had to get the house sorted before the start of term.'

Alison digested this second piece of unwelcome news. 'You're leaving – what, after next weekend?'

'Yeah, it's been planned for a while. We'll be off for about three weeks.'

Alison felt close to tears. It seemed so hopeless: girlfriend; away for the next three weeks; then off back to his university and everything that entailed. What was the point?

He stroked her back. 'Ali, I have to sort things out. Please, give me a bit of space. I didn't think you'd be so ...' he paused.

'Stupid? Easy? A pushover?' She spat out the words.

'No, no, nothing like that at all.' He turned to her. 'Ali, all I want to do is kiss you, and kiss you, and kiss you, and ... oh, and make you laugh. I don't feel like that about anyone else.'

'Not your girlfriend?'

'Rachel? No. I don't think I do.' He pulled her to him and kissed her. She didn't resist, didn't want to. When they finally broke off, he sighed. 'But I'm not an easy two-timer, either, Ali, so I think I'd better go and see her before I go away.'

'Where does she live?'

'Wrexham. In North Wales. It's a sod of a way, but I need to see her. That means I'm going to have to work flat out for my dad to make up the time. It's gonna be difficult to snatch more than a couple of hours together before the weekend.'

'Next weekend Hannah has told me there's going to be an event, held somewhere locally – an all-night disco. She's pressurising me to go and asked if you'd like a ticket. Nick's selling them.'

'All night? Cool. How much?'

'Twenty quid.'

'I guess my holiday money will run to that ... Yeah, put me down for one. Will you be there?'

Alison's voice was small, and she hated herself for her lack of pride. 'If you want me to, I will.'

'Of course I do. Look, Ali, I'll be honest with you – until I see Rachel, things won't be clear. But I'll be back before Saturday, and I'll tell you then how things are. You have to trust me. I'm sure everything will be sorted. So we'll have the whole night, Ali, the whole night, and then you can tell me all about yourself, and I'll tell you about me.'

He kissed her again, hard, passionate, and she responded, her brain fizzing.

Elsie reread the letter she'd just opened, a frown deepening on her face. It had arrived that morning, but, being Saturday, she'd left home before the post had arrived. It was late, and she was tired and couldn't work out why she should have been sent it. The note was short.

> *The Manor House,*
> *Summerstoke.*
>
> *Dear Mrs Tucker,*
> *My sisters and I would welcome the opportunity of discussing a matter that has been brought to our attention and is the cause of some concern. If it is convenient to you, we would be pleased if you would accept an invitation to tea on Tuesday, at 3.30 p.m.*
> *Yours sincerely,*
> *Mrs Elizabeth Merfield.*

'Pah! What do they want? It is certainly not an invitation without fire, that's for sure.' But it would never occur to Elsie to refuse such a summons. However, it was received without pleasure, and brooding over what it might mean, thoroughly disconcerted by the unexpected turn the little deception she and Ron had practised on Alison had taken, Elsie went to bed completely out of sorts with the world.

13

'I'm dreading this, Rita,' whispered Jenny, as the queue shuffled forward. Jenny hadn't been to Weight Watchers for a couple of weeks and would have ducked out of tonight's weigh-in, pleading poverty, if Rita had not insisted on lending her the session fee.

'Pie and pints!' smirked Rita. Jenny had told her about her trip to the pub with Jeff on Saturday night. Jenny smiled guiltily back.

'It was worth it,' she whispered. 'Though I'd give anything to have lost something, if only a pound. I hate this!'

The leader, tall, thin, bright, with an everlasting smile, made Jenny feel as if she were back at school again. The smile never wavered, even when Jenny put on pounds rather than lost them. But there was an edge to her consolatory comments that made Jenny feel faintly humiliated. She had put on as little clothing as she could get away with; even taking off her tights and going for a pee before Rita had picked her up.

She persuaded Rita to go before her in the queue waiting to take their turn on the scales. Although the results of the weigh-in were meant to be totally confidential, Jenny knew that the next person in the queue, could, if she listened hard enough, hear the leader read off the results. Whereas Jenny was slow, plump and rather dreamy, Rita was wiry and energetic, and Jenny knew that Rita secretly liked the fact that Jenny weighed more than she did, and that, in spite of every encouraging remark, Rita didn't want Jenny to lose too much. After they had both been on the weighing machine, she would seize hold of Jenny and insist on sharing the exact amount of any gain or loss; Jenny seldom disappointed her.

In spite of that, and in spite of the awful moment when she had to step on the scales and stop pretending that she was getting slimmer, Jenny enjoyed these evenings.

They were held in the hall of the primary school that all of her children had once attended. Jenny had spent countless hours there in the past, listening to little concerts or the school nativity play; being dragged around by one child or another to admire their artwork stuck on the wall; helping out with school dinners, the faint whiff of which still seemed to linger; or sitting waiting in the hall nervously, as she'd had to do countless times, summoned to the headteacher's office to face the fall-out from some piece of mischief one of the children – usually Charlie – had got up to. Very little about the school had changed: the pictures drawn by the children looked the same and the air still smelled of stale plasticine, and Jenny felt that in lining up with the others, in turns apprehensive and rebellious as they waited to see their teacher and receive a gentle ticking-off, there was little difference between her and the children.

The others were a mixed bunch, mainly women. Men were rarities who received huge emotional support from the rest of the group when they did turn up, but who seldom lasted more than two sessions. The women were of all ages, mainly married, with families to run and busy lives. Sometimes they brought their children with them and almost all came with a friend. There was a camaraderie amongst them that arose from the shared experience of bulge and fat, the inevitable lapses, and the desire to put the clock back and be as thin as they once thought they were when they were young and careless.

After the weigh-in, the ladies would pull their chairs into a semi-circle and the leader would give them a lecture on the topic of the week. It was a living manifestation of the magazines Jenny devoured, when she could afford them. As well as the more serious aim of getting them to eat less and eat well, there was a lot of joking and backchat, and Jenny, although generally quiet, loved the feeling of belonging to the group.

Once she had married Jim she had left her friends behind, and even Lizzie, her sister, rarely came to visit. She was often very lonely on the farm, and if it hadn't been for Rita, life would have been miserable. Rita was very much more gregarious than Jenny and swept her along in her wake, joking and chatting, for which Jenny, smiling shyly in the background, was grateful.

The queue edged forward. Progress was slow; there were nearly thirty of them to be weighed and their results entered on their progress charts.

'I bought myself a cream doughnut to eat when I get home tonight,' the girl behind Jenny in the queue whispered. 'Naughty but nice, innit? Why not, wiv a whole week before we gets weighed again?'

'Yeah,' whispered another. 'I always have sausage 'n chips after. Best meal of the week, it is!'

It was Rita's turn. Jenny kicked off her shoes in readiness; her insides turned to water and she tried to distract her thoughts. She'd had a lovely time on Saturday night. Jeff had introduced her to a number of his friends and they'd made her feel as if she'd known them all her life. There was a folk group playing. It was a new experience and one that affected her in a way she'd never been affected by music before. Jeff and his friends had laughed at her excitement.

She had tried to explain how she felt. 'Here am I, a shabby, borin' old middle-aged woman, finding out about things I never knew existed, and here they were all the time on my doorstep. Have I been going round with my eyes tight shut? Have I been asleep all my life? I feel as if I'm just waking up.'

And she didn't know whether it was because he'd drunk a few, or because of what she'd said, but Jeff had put his arms around her shoulders and given her a hug and said he didn't think she was shabby or boring, and that he'd bring her to hear another group.

But yes, she'd had a pie, fat and juicy – forbidden food; and worse, a pile of glistening golden chips and at least three Bacardi and Cokes. She was quite tiddly by the time she got home. He hadn't kissed her when they said goodnight, but that hadn't stopped her fantasising. Then, as she undressed for bed, she had caught sight of her body. That had brought her to earth with a sobering clunk.

'Jenny, how nice to see you. We've missed you the last couple of weeks. How have you been doing? Oh – we seem to have put on a bit, dear; nearly seven pounds. What have you been celebrating?'

Nicola had scarcely spoken to Stephen at the Sunday rehearsal. In spite of his shy attempts to engage her attention, she appeared to avoid his eye and surrounded herself with the other actors. They seemed to sit in gossipy huddles more frequently than usual and at one point, something Nicola said initiated such a gale of laughter that June Pagett became annoyed and threatened to call a halt to the rehearsal since clearly their attention was elsewhere. After that, Stephen became convinced the others were looking at him in a different way. At the end of the afternoon Nicola had rushed off, not even pausing to say goodbye to him and Angela, unusual in that she had once declared 'as a professional, one should always remember to thank the stage crew, without whom nothing would happen'.

Tuesday night was even worse. The whispering started before the rehearsal began. June Pagett made him read in for the wretched Scrub and every time he opened his mouth a suppressed titter went round the room. Finally a break was called for coffee and with relief Stephen went to help Angela. Her chin was red and wobbly and she looked upset.

'What's up, Ange?' he whispered, spooning in the instant coffee.

'I don't know how you put up with it!' She was unusually fierce. 'I don't know what's got into them tonight.'

Just then, Gerald O'Donovan piped up in a loud voice, 'I say, I'd die for a piece of chocolate cake with my coffee.'

Someone sniggered, 'Oh, you don't want to die, Gerald, least-ways, not such a horrible death.'

Someone else chimed in, 'I hear your mum makes chocolate cakes, Stephen.'

And another added, 'Bring a piece in for Gerald – he's longing to taste it.'

'Death by chocolate!' And they all laughed.

'Does she make wedding cakes?' another asked, at which there was hysterics.

Stephen felt hot and uncomfortable. He wasn't sure where this was going and looked across at Nicola for some sort of reassurance. She picked up a coffee and turned away from the group, laughing lightly. 'She's probably got one baking in the oven right now. Believe me, Stephen's mum's cakes are an experience. They're obviously made of stern stuff "down on the farm".' The last she drawled with an unmistakable imitation of Jenny's round West Country tones.

Stephen flushed and moved over to Angela, pushing past Robin Roberts who was engaged in a flirtation with Roxanne.

Robin Roberts looked up. 'Phew, what's that pong?'

Roxanne giggled. 'You naughty man. Eet ees the cowshed, you know. My father, 'ee says 'ee can smell the cowhands five kilometres away.'

For a moment Stephen stood there, clenching his fists, helpless.

Angela came to his rescue. 'Stephen, I've got loads of stuff to show you. Come over here; we've not got much time now, but I've brought in all this stuff on rare breeds I got off the Internet. You can take it with you, if you like.' Her enthusiasm helped and somehow he got through the rest of the evening.

When June finally called a halt to the rehearsal, she addressed them all, coldly. 'I have a feeling that tonight's rehearsal has not been taken seriously by a number of you. It was bad enough on Sunday. There's too much whispering and giggling going on at the back of the hall. We cannot afford not to have everyone focusing on what is going on on the stage. How you expect me to concentrate, I do not know. We've not got much time left, so please, everyone, next rehearsal, concentration, concentration, concentration. Do I make myself clear?'

'Yes, June,' they all replied dutifully and left, still sniggering and surreptitiously making the odd mooing sound. Someone even started humming loudly a tune that sounded a bit like 'Here Comes the Bride'. Nicola was one of the last to go and Stephen, rushing around putting the hall back to rights, felt his heart flutter into his mouth as she floated over to him, ruffling a hand through her curls, her eyes wide and bright as she sought him out.

'Oh, Stephen.' She smiled at him so sweetly, he almost swooned. 'Can you give me Simon's telephone number?'

'Simon's?' he croaked wretchedly.

'Yes,' she said, still smiling. 'I'm going back to London as soon as this pantomime is finished and I thought I'd look him up.'

Breakfast at Marsh Farm that Wednesday morning couldn't have been a more depressed affair. Stephen, gloomily moving his spoon around a mess of soggy cornflakes, remembered how, a week ago, he had been over the moon because Nicola had kissed him. Everything lay before him, his world rosy with possibility. Now ...

Last night had been awful — what was that all about? He felt he'd been singled out as the butt of some joke that everyone was in on, except himself. And Angela. If it hadn't been for Angela, he didn't know how he would have got through it. She had chatted away about rare breeds, asked him lots of questions, made suggestions and carried him along with her evident interest. More importantly, when Nicola had swept out of the hall, leaving him more wretched than he had ever felt in his life, she hadn't questioned him about Nicola, or about the tea party for that matter, for which he was very grateful.

Never had he looked forward to rehearsals with less enthusiasm, and as he munched his cornflakes, for the first time since he had joined, he chewed over the possibility of leaving the Merlin Players.

Alison sat slumped on the other side of the table, slowly peeling an apple. She, too, felt really fed up. Al had managed to make one more date before he went off to see her-in-Wrexham, and it hadn't been the most satisfactory evening.

They had teamed up with Hannah and Nick and gone bowling, which meant that Alison's precious twenty pounds had become depleted. It was difficult to speak to Al in any meaningful way, although, if she had, she wasn't sure what she would say. She didn't like the fact that she cared he was going off, that she was anxious about the outcome of his trip, and that he was buggering off for three weeks after the disco. The only compensation was that when he'd said goodbye, he'd taken her in his arms and kissed her with such passion, she still felt faint thinking about it. She had walked home when he had dropped her outside the village shop, her knees wobbling, wondering how she was going to get through the next four days.

She had looked Durham up in her school atlas. It was an awfully long way from Summerstoke, further even than Wrexham, which she had also checked out. If they were going to get it together, it was going to be a difficult relationship to maintain. As an additional dampener, she'd had one brief text saying he'd be in touch when he got back, which, she felt, was as good as telling her not to text him.

He told her he was leaving early on Tuesday. How the day dragged! In need of distraction she had wandered over to Simon's cottage, but there had been no sign of him; the cottage was locked, and squinting through the letterbox, she could see a pile of mail on the floor.

She had gone to bed early but could not sleep, so this morning she felt even more out of sorts. Gloomily she assessed her financial position. She still had some cash left, but she was going to have to find a way to make up the ticket money by tomorrow when, Hannah had told her, the tickets for the event were going to be issued. It was almost, she thought morosely to herself, like being back where she had started.

Hearing the postman's van in the yard, Jenny abandoned her toast. She returned moments later, sifting anxiously through a small clutch of letters. Her shoulders sagged. There was nothing from Mrs Moorhead. She mentally ticked off the days. It was twelve days since Alison had posted the parcel: there should have been a cheque by now. Her appetite, hardly titillated by the dry toast and black tea that was part of her new dietary regime, disappeared altogether. She passed a small bundle of circulars and letters over to Stephen and a postcard to Alison, and started to clear the table.

The door opened and Elsie walked in. She glanced at the assembled members of her family. 'Where's Charlie?'

Stephen, with a total lack of interest, shrugged his shoulders. 'I dunno, Gran. In bed?'

'No, he's not,' Jenny intervened. 'He went out a good hour ago, when you were still in the parlour, Stephen. He's really busy, finishing off the harvest. Making the most of this fine weather.'

'With this fine weather,' Stephen snorted, 'he should've finished days ago. Why hasn't he?'

'I don't know, dear, but I'm sure there's a good reason. I know you don't think Charlie always pulls his weight, but he's as concerned about the farm as you are. All the hours he's been working the last few weeks just shows you.'

'It shows me nothing but that we're gonna have to pay Lenny Spinks an awful lot come the end of the month. Why's the harvest taking them so long, that's what I'd like to know; what's he up to?'

'Well whatever he's doing, it had better not be anything to embarrass us,' retorted Elsie tartly. 'I'll have a cup of tea, thank you Jenny.'

She turned to Stephen. 'I know it had nothing to do with you, Stephen, but your brother's drunken exploit has affected us all. The Merfields asked me to tea yesterday. Someone had taken it upon themselves to show them a picture in the newspaper of your brother making a fool of himself. That, by itself, was of no great concern to them, but they were led to believe that his behaviour is symptomatic of his, of your, general behaviour these days, *and* of the declining fortunes of the Tucker family. And that, apparently ...' she continued, remorselessly, as Stephen let out an indignant shout, 'we're on the verge of bankruptcy. All of which makes them inclined not to give us the meadows when the lease comes up for renewal next month.'

Stephen was speechless for a moment; all he could do was gape at his grandmother. Then he stuttered back to life. 'What are they on about? Gran, you know how hard I'm working – those meadows – we couldn't survive without them; they're the best grazing we've got. If we lose those, then I'm stuffed! Bloody Charlie – it's all his fault. Just wait till I get my hands on him. I'll kill 'im!' Despairing, his head dropped onto the great balls of his fists, elbows slammed on the kitchen table.

Alison, equally taken aback by her gran's news, looked at the despairing set of her brother's shoulders, his face hidden by his hands. 'He's crying,' she thought with a shiver; her brothers didn't cry. She turned to Elsie. 'Gran, who told them all this crap? What did you say? You didn't just sit there and take it, did you?'

Elsie certainly had not. 'My grandson might make a fool of himself when he's in his cups, but that does not make him a bad farmer. On the contrary, both he and Stephen work extremely hard—'

'Please understand, Mrs Tucker,' Mrs Merfield continued. 'We have no wish to change the present arrangement. Our families have had a long association and I'm a firm believer in respecting traditional ties. However, I do have to put the interests of my family first.'

'Yes, of course.' Elsie was cold and as dignified as the matriarch presiding over the tea table. 'But I don't see how ...'

The five ladies were taking tea on the terrace. Although they were shaded from the sun by the house, the two Miss Merfields each sported little lacy parasols. The air was warm and sweet with the scent of roses and newly cut grass. Sitting upright on wrought-iron chairs, with nearly four hundred years between them, the women made a curious tableau. Ranged on one side, the three Merfields were tall, thin, heavily made up, immaculately coiffured and groomed – elegant creatures from another age, with plain, scrubbed Nanny, inscrutable, at their side; and on the other, Elsie Tucker, the archetypal countrywoman.

'I shouldn't be sitting here drinking tea like this,' she thought to herself. 'I should be standing up, bobbing curtsies, being ever so humble.' Her eyes glinted at the thought.

Her relationship with the Merfield ladies was ambivalent, to say the least. She had first encountered them when she moved to Marsh Farm as a young bride. Mrs Merfield had also recently married and had moved into the Manor House to take care of an invalid in-law. Their social circles were worlds apart, which Elsie, fresh from the city and much feted as her father's only child, resented.

When the elderly Mr Merfield died, followed very shortly by his son and heir, the manor was in poor condition and the estate's survival was threatened by the double death duties. Thomas Tucker's offer for Marsh Farm was therefore timely, but the young Mrs Merfield did not like seeing the estate broken up at all and resented what she saw as Elsie Tucker's opportunistic 'pushiness'. However, her sister-in-laws had a soft spot for Thomas Tucker, a gentle, unassuming man, and the farm was sold.

In later years, Elsie got to know the two sisters through a bridge circle, but she and Mrs Merfield had little to do with each other. Over time, however, both women had earned the other's respect. By determination and skilful management, Mrs Merfield had turned the estate's fortunes round, and it was Elsie's drive that had been instrumental in making Marsh Farm a successful dairy farm. It was logical, therefore, that before they decided what their next move should be over the meadows in question, the Merfield ladies would send for Elsie.

Mrs Merfield sipped her tea and pressed her point. 'The estate will pass, in time, to my grandchildren, and I would be irresponsible if I did not ensure that every arrangement in place has a solid financial basis. Your grandson, Charles, came to me last year to ask that the rent be paid per quarter rather than annually. Something to do with what he called cash flow problems. I must say, I agreed somewhat reluctantly, but if my informant is correct and the cash flow dries up, I could see valuable land tied up with no return.'

Elsie digested this in silence. Then, as if on cue, the two other Merfields joined in the conversation.

Louisa Merfield, the youngest, opened with, 'Elsie, there's an easy solution. If you were to underwrite the farm, there would be no problem.'

'You must be able to afford it, after all,' drawled Charlotte, the other sister. 'I know it's terribly vulgar of me to ask, but how many houses *do* you own in Bath?'

Elsie was furious. She could easily provide them with the reassurance they sought, but she didn't see why she should. On the other hand, she knew how critical those meadows were.

'It would be simply ghastly if we let that Lester person have them.'

'He wouldn't stop with the meadows.'

'No, once he got hold of a bit of our land, he wouldn't rest until he moved into the Manor.'

'It would be over my dead body.'

'He'd probably arrange that, too, dear!' The sisters shrieked with laughter.

Neither Elsie nor Mrs Merfield joined in.

'So Hugh Lester's behind this, is he?' Elsie was grim. 'Quite frankly I'm surprised you believed anything he told you.'

'He showed us the newspaper story,' said Mrs Merfield coldly. 'He was merely reinforcing concerns I've already felt about your grandson.'

'He does appear to have grown up into a very rackety young man, Elsie.' Nanny was blunt. 'And we hear he spends most Sundays racing motorbikes and drinking with his friends. Hardly the behaviour one would expect of a farmer. He's in his thirties, isn't he? Surely he should have got over the wildness of his youth and settled down by now.'

Since this was an exact echo of her own sentiments, Elsie could not defend Charlie. She sipped her tea, trying to think of a way to pull them back from the brink of this disaster. She came to a decision and turned to address Mrs Merfield. 'Have you met Stephen, my other grandson?'

'No, we haven't. We understood Charles ran the farm.'

'Well, you understood wrong. Mrs Merfield, as you yourself said, our two families go back a long way. May I take you into my confidence?'

Elsie looked across at her grandson. Her expression softened slightly, but not the tone of her voice. 'You give in to things far too easily, Stephen. Trouble is, you're soft. No good being soft if you're going to run a farm. You've got to start standing up for yourself. Everyone pushes you around. You've got to start fighting for what you want; if you don't, you'll lose it.'

It wasn't just the thought of the meadows that made Stephen groan: 'What can I do? What ... tell me, what?'

Elsie was brisk. 'Well for a start, you can take proper control of the dairy. It's you that should be dealing with the Merfields, not Charlie. You use the meadows – why is Charlie dealing with them?'

Stephen started mumbling about Charlie being better with figures, better at dealing with people, better at business.

'Rubbish. I see absolutely no evidence of that. The farm's in a mess because you've let Charlie run it his way. Well, it's time, my lad, you started taking more responsibility and you can start by sorting out the next year's lease with Mrs Merfield. She is expecting you to call on her next week. You, mind, not Charlie.'

Stephen looked up at her with horror on his face. 'But Gran, I've never spoken to her in my life. She terrifies the daylights out of me. Charlie—'

'She's expecting *you*, Stephen. If those meadows matter to you, then you will go. Do I make myself clear?'

Stephen muttered, 'Yes, Gran,' and unable to bear her steely gaze, distractedly started opening a letter.

'Good. Jenny, this tea is stewed. How long has it been sitting in the pot?'

'I'll make you another one, Elsie. Won't take two ticks.'

'No thank you. I'll make my own, in my room.' And she swept out of the kitchen leaving the three behind her, shaken and silent.

Jenny tried her best to lighten the atmosphere. 'Who's your postcard from, Ali?'

'Simon. He's been away, working. Wants to know if I'm free tonight.'

Alison was pleased to hear from Simon, but oh, if only it'd been a card from Al ... But of course, that was stupid – he'd no idea where she lived.

'That's nice, dear, do you good—' Jenny was interrupted by a strangulated cry from Stephen, who sat staring, a deep frown creasing his brows, his mouth dropped open, at an official-looking letter he'd just opened.

'I don't believe ... I just don't believe ... someone tell me I'm dreamin' ... this is just not on! What are they playin' at?'

'What is it, love? What's wrong?'

Stephen was too overcome to answer; his normally ruddy cheeks had turned ashen. Alison removed the letter from his nerveless fingers and quickly read it.

'It's from the Dairy Hygiene department at Defra; they want to come and inspect the dairy. They accept the last inspection was less than a year ago, but they've been alerted to the fact we've had a few problems and so they're obliged to make another visit. They don't say when they are coming, but it could be any day over the next couple of weeks.' She looked at her brother. 'Do we have problems in the dairy?'

Stephen groaned. 'I keep it going, but we need to buy a new thermostat for the water heating unit. It's developed an occasional fault. I think it sticks, but if I don't spot it in time, the bacterial level in the milk goes up and it ends up by being rejected at the depot. I've had a couple of warnings from them already. You can be sure, the way my luck is, it'll break down when the dairy's being inspected.'

'Would it cost a lot to replace?'

'More than I've got.'

'How much?'

'Five hundred, a thousand – depends if I've got to replace the whole unit.'

Alison was aghast. 'Couldn't we borrow?'

'Who from?' Stephen looked back at her, bitterly. 'The bank – you heard what they said to Charlie, not another penny … Gran? Don't make me laugh. Nope, it's hopeless. I've just got to keep the thing going and hope they don't notice.' He pushed his chair back and got heavily to his feet. 'If you want me for anything, Mum, I'm in the dairy. At least I can make sure they don't find anything else to get me for.'

'What would they do?' Alison was getting more and more anxious.

'At the end of the day, they'd call Health and Safety in and close me down till I fix whatever it is they find wrong. That would be the end of us. Mum, I'm gonna give this evening's rehearsal a miss.'

He slammed the kitchen door, dislodging the cork board hanging on the back of the door and sending it, and the various notices, invoices, and postcards stuck to it, slithering in different directions over the kitchen floor.

'My goodness me.' Jenny distractedly picked up the board – it was shaped like a strawberry, not a particularly efficient shape for its job, but Stephen had given it to her as a birthday present some years ago – and hung it back on the door. 'It's not like Stephen to bang the door like that. And what did he mean, "not go to the rehearsal this evening"? There isn't one tonight, and anyway, he's never missed a rehearsal before, not even when there was foot and mouth …'

Alison was rereading the letter.

'Someone alerted them; can you believe it?' exclaimed Alison, her mouth full of prawn cocktail, which was quite the yummiest thing she'd ever eaten. 'Who would do that? And the bank's cutting back our overdraft and refusing to lend us any more. And, if that's not bad enough, Gran says the Merfields are thinking of taking the meadows away from us because they've heard we're going bankrupt! Seems we're up shit creek without a paddle.'

Simon had picked her up earlier that evening, and they had driven some way into the country to a large old pub, which, he told her, had the best reputation for food, for miles around.

He poured her a glass of wine. 'So what can you do about it?'

'Dunno. Charlie'll get mad at Stephen, but we're going to have to find the money for the dairy somehow. Without the milk cheque, we'd be sunk.'

Simon sipped his wine thoughtfully. Alison glanced at him. 'I didn't mean to bend your ear with our woes. How was your trip? Did you take Duchess?'

'Yep. She always travels with me if she can. She didn't like Birmingham though, and nor did I. I never thought I'd say it, but I was quite pleased to see the cottage again.'

'Blimey – you'd rather be in boring old Summerstoke than the big city! Must be the people you mix with.' She grinned. 'You haven't given me a debriefing on your evening with Hughie and Veronica-call-me-Vee.'

'No.' Simon hesitated. He hadn't decided whether he would tell Alison about the conversation concerning the Tuckers. 'I agree with you.'

'What, that they're stuck up, conniving creeps?'

'Definitely that; worse, if anything.'

He then embarked on a graphic and witty demolition of the other guests, their hosts, and the evening's conversation. 'So there you have it: the husband and wife team ready to kill each other over the ethical behaviour of the local rag; the hag in black helping herself, less and less surreptitiously, to Hugh's very expensive wine, under his outraged nose, till she finished the lot, and completely ignoring the interior designer who was desperately trying to engage her in a discussion about the Victorian use of colour; Veronica-call-me-Vee furious with her husband because he wouldn't open any more wine to pour down the hag's insatiable throat; and the Olympic champion summing up the evening for all of us by letting out a loud snore over coffee and brandy.'

Alison convulsed with laughter. 'Wicked! So you're not aiming to go visiting the Lesters again?'

'On the contrary,' Simon said casually. 'I'm playing tennis with Veronica-call-me-Vee tomorrow.'

Alison gaped at him.

'There's a reason, and I'm going to take a chance and tell you. But for the moment, I think it'd better be just between the both of us. No sense, at this stage, in upsetting your mother or Stephen.'

'What the hell has your ... your friendship with the puky Lesters got to do with them? Or me? I've no claims over you; do what you like—'

'I do, and I like you, and your family, so don't get spiky with me. Listen, Alison, describing your run of bad luck just now you said "someone told them" both about the dairy *and* about the Merfields ... and the bank suddenly getting heavy – doesn't that all seem a bit coincidental?'

Alison stared, 'What do you mean?'

So Simon told her about Veronica and Hugh's plans for Marsh Farm.

'The bastards!' Alison shrieked, slamming her glass of wine on the table and spraying the white linen cloth with splashes of red wine. 'The conniving bastards!'

Other diners turned to stare and a waiter hurried forward. 'Is everything all right, sir? Miss?'

'Fine, thank you. My niece has just had a bit of a shock. Sorry about the mess.'

'No problem, sir.' He removed Alison's abandoned prawns, cutlery and glasses and deftly replaced their linen. Alison looked on, simmering with fury. When they were finally alone, she hissed, 'I don't believe it – you sat and listened to all that crap and didn't *say* anything? And now you're gonna play tennis with the arch bitch? They're gonna destroy us, Simon, and you're gonna play ball games? What sort of friendship is that? If we weren't in the middle of the soddin' country – an' I've no idea where we are – I'd leave, right now!'

'Alison, listen to me. Listen! If I'd've jumped up and said,

"Leave the Tuckers alone; they're decent people, trying to earn an honest crust, unlike you shitheads", where would that have got me ... you ... us? I'm on your side, see? Because I kept quiet, they spilled the beans in front of me. Dearest Ali – I've met people like them before; they know what they want and they've the money and influence to get it.'

'And they want Marsh Farm – well, they won't soddin' get it!'

'How are you going to stop them? If the dairy is closed, Stephen loses the Merfield meadows and the bank forecloses because you can't meet their repayments—'

'Gran would intervene. She wouldn't let the Lesters take us over.' Even as she said it, Alison could hear her grandmother's voice: 'Not a penny more ... no point in throwing good money after bad.'

'Would she, could she? Does she have that sort of capital?'

Alison stared at him, appalled. 'I don't know, Simon, I don't know. I know she owns at least one property in Bath – she might own more, but how much capital she has, and whether she'd be prepared to sell, to save Marsh farm, I just don't know ... What am I gonna do? I can't just let this happen.'

'No, *we* can't. The thing is, Alison, by befriending the ghastly duo I'm more likely to learn what they're up to than by declaring myself a friend of the enemy. Undoubtedly, they are responsible for the Merfields getting cold feet and for the tip-off to the dairy inspector. And I wouldn't be at all surprised to find they'd nobbled someone at the bank.'

'But banks are meant to be confidential, aren't they? Surely that would be ... well ...'

'Bad practice? Yep, and I'm sure if we could prove that had happened, we could make the situation very embarrassing for a certain bank employee ...'

'But how would you find that out?'

For a moment, Simon thought of the momentary flicker of Veronica's tongue in his ear when she kissed him goodnight. 'I'll find a way. Everyone has their Achilles heel.'

'Their what?'

'What do they teach you at school these days?' he mocked. 'Achilles heel – weak point. Haven't you seen the film *Troy*?'

'No, Uncle Simon,' she said, somewhat maliciously, as the waiter placed their plates in front of them. 'So, what's their heel?'

'Not what, but who. The features writer from *Country Homes and Gardens*.'

'That awful lady who was at the dinner party? Harriet?'

'Harriet Flood. They are desperate for her to write about the development of their stud – brilliant publicity, after all. But it was clear that if they don't get Marsh Farm, the stud won't happen, and no stud, no story – Harriet's not interested in doing a feature on the house and stables as they are. It's my guess she didn't altogether like our two, and it wouldn't take too much ingenuity to persuade her to drop the story. I've an idea about how it might be done, too, but I won't say anything more at this stage, in case it doesn't happen.'

Alison laughed. 'Wicked! Serve them right. If you pull that off, Simon, I wouldn't know how to repay you.'

'Oh, I'll think of something,' he lightly replied. 'But Alison, in the meantime, not a word to anyone, except … yes, I think it's time to meet Elsie.'

'Gran – why?'

'From what you've said, she plays her cards close to her chest. I think we should get her on side, if only to find out how far she is prepared to let things go. From what you say, Marsh Farm means a lot to her. It's important she knows that the greatest threat to its survival is not the bachelor state of her grandsons.'

'Hmm,' said Alison, thinking about how her gran might get on with Simon. 'It's not going to be that easy. If she takes against you, or gets the wrong idea about you, it'd make life very difficult …'

'What's *her* Achilles heel?'

'That's not difficult – Mum and cake,' replied Alison. 'Wow!'

She had taken a good look at the food in front of her. Having been reared on Jenny's cooking, she couldn't believe her eyes. 'Is this lamb?'

14

'Morning, Stephen. How are things? Could do with a drop of rain, no doubt?'

Stephen's stomach had turned to water at the sight of Mr Curry's vehicle. He knew that once Defra had decided to do an inspection, it would happen quite quickly – but not this quickly. He had just finished cleaning the dairy and was going in for a late breakfast when he heard the car. He knew Mr Curry of old, but not the tall, thin youth with thick spectacles and pale, spotty skin, who also climbed out, carrying a file and clipboard.

'Oh, hello, Mr Curry.' Stephen tried to sound as if the bottom had not just dropped out of the day. 'Yes, can't believe this weather. We're just waiting for it to break. I got your letter yesterday mornin'.'

'Yes, sorry to be so quick off the mark, but better not to keep you in suspense, eh? This is my colleague, Richard Tyrer. He's a student. You've no objection to him assisting me?'

'No, of course not.' Stephen didn't much like the look of Richard Tyrer. He had the look of a ferret about to kill a rabbit and Stephen suspected that he, Stephen, was the rabbit in the ferret's sights. Mr Curry, on the other hand, was a nice bloke, in Stephen's opinion. Firm but fair and to the point.

'You'll be off to have your breakfast, no doubt,' Mr Curry said, looking at his watch. 'Why don't you do that? I know my way round, after all. Then you can come and join us for a chat.'

But Stephen had lost his appetite. 'No. It's all right. I'll come with you. I'll just let Mum know.'

Mr Curry and his companion spent about an hour checking

around the dairy. Stephen looked on, hardly breathing, as they checked surfaces, tested the equipment, turning things on and off, testing the controls, the temperature of the cooling system, the general cleanliness of everything, making notes the whole time. When they tested the water heater and the temperature of the water, he had to leave and rush to the lavatory.

Finally, they finished.

'Well, Stephen,' Mr Curry was cheerful, 'you keep your dairy spotless. Normally we could give you a clean bill of health—'

Feeling slightly sick, Stephen said nothing and waited.

'Thing is, old chap, after we received this call – nasty things, anonymous phone calls. Nine times out of ten, they are malicious and time wasting, but we would be failing in our duty if we took no notice of them. So we checked up with your buyer and I understand they've rejected one batch and issued you with a warning. Seems the bacteria level has been creeping up. Now that would suggest to me, seeing as you're a careful dairyman and everything seems shipshape, that you've got a problem with your cleaning system. Most likely in the temperature of the water, although it seemed fine when we tested it today.'

Stephen felt wretched. 'Yes,' he mumbled, 'I think you might be right. But it seems to be intermittent and so it's difficult to correct. I am keeping a close eye on it, and—'

'But I think you're going to have to do more than that. I think you need to either replace it, or bring in a specialist to identify and cure the problem for you.'

The implications of what Mr Curry was saying filled Stephen with the deepest gloom. This was as bad as he had feared and he could see no way out. He was convinced there was a look of pleasure in the student's eyes.

'I'm not going to shut the dairy down, but I am going to issue you with an Improvement Notice. Now you know what that means?'

'Yes,' replied Stephen listlessly. 'You give me a time limit to do whatever it is that needs to be done and if I don't do it, then the dairy is closed down until it's fixed, or we go out of business.'

In the early afternoon, Charlie turned the tractor into the yard, jumped off and hurried into the barn.

'Do this, do that, bloody hell, I'm only human!' he muttered, starting to free the trailer he needed from under a pile of accumulated debris. He was tired out. Since the start of the week he had been trying to finish the harvest with Lenny, and to meet to the increasing demands of Dark Glasses and his cohorts in the fields. 'They're certainly getting their money's worth. I shall be glad when they bugger off and leave us in peace. Two and a half more days, and that'll be it. I can't wait.' The thought of all that lovely money mollified him though, as did the four tickets nestling in his pocket which Dark Glasses had given him that morning.

'Two for Lenny and two for me – that should stop Paula belly-aching about the late hours Lenny's been keeping,' he thought. 'If only I can get to The Grapes before closing time and give a ticket to Beth. Can't see her saying no, sideburns or no sideburns, and then, Charlie-me-old-fruit, you should be quids in there!' He should try and go tonight, he thought. It was now Thursday, and he knew from experience that girls liked to plan their Saturdays in advance; she might even arrange time off from the pub, although, since it was an all-nighter, that didn't matter so much.

He didn't hear Alison come into the barn. He'd been trying to avoid his family as much as possible – it seemed easier that way – so he was not pleased to turn round and see her standing there, watching him; the sort of expression on her face that experience had taught him meant trouble.

'Oh hi, Ali.' He tried to sound unconcerned. 'Can't stop, sorry – I'm busy.'

'With what?' She was cool. 'The harvest or the event?'

Heart sinking, Charlie tried to bluster. 'The harvest of course. Event? What event? What are you talking about? Ha ha ha ... me? Ali, what are you thinkin' of? When would I have time to go to an event, whatever it is?'

Unnoticed by either of them, Stephen had entered the gloom of the barn.

'Not *going* to an event, Charlie; helping to set one up. Or, let me be a bit more specific – hiring out our fields to the guys that are running the event this weekend.'

'What are you talking about? What event? If I find anyone has been squatting on our land—'

'Don't be daft, Charlie. This is a pro set-up. Hannah showed me her ticket this morning; the location map is on the back. How much dosh are you making, huh? Have you discussed this with Stephen?'

'No, he bloody hasn't,' came a growl from the shadows, 'and considerin' the mess we're in, and the fact that we're meant to be partners, you'd think he would've. Can you think of any reason, Charlie, why I shouldn't give you a good thumping?'

Both Alison and Charlie were shocked at this. Stephen hated violence of any sort and had never threatened anyone in his life, let alone Charlie.

He stood there staring at Charlie, looking strangely white and drawn, his fists clenching and unclenching.

Charlie had never before seen Stephen so upset and angry with him. And with good reason, he thought; he should have told Stephen as soon as the deal was proposed and not tried to cut him out. Squirming, he turned on the charm, smiled ruefully at Stephen, ruffled his hair in an abashed way and attempted to mollify him. 'Listen, mate, I was gonna tell you, honest. We had to keep it all deadly hush hush, or the deal was off. The bloke made us swear ... and then I thought, better you didn't know till it was all over, 'cos you'd only fuss. And supposing Mum or Gran found out and put a stop to it ...'

The fury in Stephen's face did not abate and Charlie, realising that he had taken his brother for granted once too often and sensing that their relationship was undergoing a seismic shift, that Stephen was now a force to be reckoned with, started to plead. 'The money's gonna save us, Stevie – just wait till we see the sick look on Gordon White's face when I deposit three K next month. He didn't think we could do it, and now we can—'

'Three thousand?' Stephen's voice shook.

'Yep. Perfect timing, ain't it?'

'Is that all?' Alison's voice was sharp. 'How much *are* you getting, Charlie?'

Charlie was not quite ready to give up on his potential profit, but shifted from one foot to the other, uneasily. 'Well ... a bit over three ... enough for me and Lenny to put our bike back in the running.'

'Enough to buy a new hot water unit for the dairy?'

'What?'

Alison pressed on. 'The thing is, Charlie, that while you've been busy sucking up to the big boys, things've been happening on the farm you've just not been around to notice. If Stephen doesn't replace that unit, like now, the dairy will be closed down.'

'What?'

'And what's more, due to your drunken tricks, the Merfields are thinking of not renewing our lease.'

'The old witches! They can't do that.'

'Oh yes they can – so what are they going to make of the news that you are holding a rave? They're going to love that, aren't they? Let alone Mum and Gran. They would've found out – how are you gonna explain things to them?'

Charlie started to perspire. 'It's not a rave, Ali. It's nothing like that. I'd have found some way of telling them. The bottom line is that we need the money; that's the way I see it.'

Stephen, having spent the last few miserable hours contemplating the ruin of his business, along with the death of all his hopes of Nicola, now felt almost faint with relief at such an unexpected rescue. Without hesitation he forgave Charlie and, turning to Alison, came to his brother's defence.

'It's a heck of a lot of money, Ali, just think – if we can get the bank off our neck and I can sort out the dairy – well, just think how great that would be. I'm sure Gran and Mum would see the sense in that.' He swallowed and straightened up, seeming in that moment to grow taller and older. 'I've got to see Mrs Merfield next week. I'll think of *something* to tell her. If we was able to pay the lease in advance ...'

'Good thinking, Batman.' Alison turned again to Charlie. 'So just how much money are we making?'

For all his faults, Charlie was not dishonest, and he crumbled. 'Five K.'

Stephen whistled.

'Three for the field they're using for the event, and two for the one next to it.' Charlie was alarmed, sensing the money slipping through his fingers. 'But don't forget, Lenny and I've been slogging our guts out for this the whole—'

'So you'll make some money.' Alison would not let him see how impressed she was, and continued crisply. 'But you know the farm must come first, Charlie. This is a farm enterprise, so you cover our outstanding debts, as far as you can, pay Lenny, give me my allowance, then divvy what's left with Stephen.'

'Divvy ... with Stephen? I'll end up with virtually nothing!'

'S'only right – I'm your partner!' The end of his immediate problems in sight, Stephen, stood tall, breathed out and with an authority he'd never had before, addressed his brother. 'One thing I'd like to know – when did you strike this little deal? Was it before our farm meeting or after? Did you know when you went to the bank that we were going to get all this money?'

There was a moment's tense silence as the implication of Stephen's questioning sunk home.

Not for the first time since he had come into the barn, Charlie wished the ground would swallow him up. 'It was after,' he said humbly. 'I struck the deal late last week. I was gutted by the bank and, truthfully, all the ideas we had at that meeting didn't seem to offer any real prospect of getting the bank off our backs. So when these geezers turned up and made their offer, I admit I leaped at it. I didn't tell anyone else, because I thought the fewer people who knew, the less likely it was to get out. I was wrong not to tell you. I'm sorry. If I'd known about the trouble you were in with the water heater, I would have, honest, Steve ...'

Alison had a strong feeling that Charlie was not altogether telling the truth, but Stephen looked mollified. The atmosphere eased and Stephen, with growing respect for his sister, turned to her.

'So what shall we do about Mum and Gran, Ali? Tell 'em?'

Alison shook her head. 'We can't take that chance. You heard how Mum was at tea on Saturday, and Gran will be ten times worse. No, we've got to find a way of keeping it from them until it's too late. Then, I think, the amount Charlie has earned will register. We can say we had to do it to save the farm – that it was a one-off thing. The problem is: how do we get them out of the way? Once things start hotting up, they're bound to notice.'

But there was no immediate solution forthcoming. The three worked together to release the trailer Charlie needed, and agreed to confer again the following morning.

Charlie set off on the tractor, trailer in tow, feeling very subdued. How was he going to break it to Lenny that there was not going to be a new bike, not even a reconditioned one, for the next moto-cross? Not only that, but Ali had guessed he would have been given some free tickets and insisted he gave her one, saying it was only fair that she should have *some* share in the spoils, and Stephen had taken her side. Charlie had ruled the roost with his brother and sister for the whole of their lives. Now they were dictating to him; he had been toppled from his perch and was wallowing in the dust, confused, shamed, and disorientated.

Simon was early for his game with Veronica Lester and so, to kill time, he wandered across to the courts where, he'd been told, she was playing with someone else. When he had joined the club, he had been given that year's league table and Veronica's name was high on the list. He had first met her when he found himself matched against her in one of the games he was required to play, as a formality, to assess his prowess. Veronica was good and his victory had been, in his opinion, a lucky one. He was therefore surprised, since she was one of the club's cream players, to eventually locate her on one of the more unpopular courts.

He was even more surprised at her play.

Gone was the intense, competitive stance – she was all floppy and uncoordinated; gone was the determined, focused stare – she laughed, looked everywhere but at the ball, tossed her head, pouted and flirted; balls that she could have easily punished home were banged into the net or missed altogether. It was an extraordinary performance and Simon, unnoticed by either of them, moved to get a better look at her opponent. He was a youngish man of nondescript appearance, pale of face, clean-shaven, hair sleeked back and receding at the temples, not plump, but clearly not very athletic; and he played very poor tennis.

The game was coming to an end and Veronica's partner was clearly the winner. For a moment, Simon was uncertain as to whether to make his presence known and thereby let her know he had witnessed her humiliation, or to pretend he had only just arrived. They were gathering racquets and balls and about to leave when Veronica noticed him.

'Simon. You're early. How long have you been there?'

He smiled. 'About five minutes.'

For a moment she looked disconcerted, then she laughed. 'So you witnessed the thrashing I got at Gordon's hands. He's some player ...'

'He certainly is.'

She turned to her tennis partner. 'So, you've beaten me again, Gordon.' She smiled at him sweetly and put her hand on his arm. 'I owe you a G and T at the very least. I've promised Simon here a couple of sets, but will I see you in the bar later?'

Gordon looked put out. 'Couldn't you take a break now, Vee? It's just that, well, I've no more games lined up and I'd rather hoped that we'd ... well, you know ... Go for a ride.'

'Another time, Gordon, I promise. But Simon, clever boy, has booked the number one court for us.'

Veronica had booked the court, but Simon said nothing, though anyone looking closely might have detected a gleam in his eye.

'See if you can book us a decent court for next week, Gordon. And if you want to wait for me, why don't you go for a swim or something?'

'The pool's always full of screaming kids at this time of day,' Gordon grumbled.

'Oh well, if I don't see you in the bar later, I'll see you on Saturday. You haven't forgotten? About eight. Come on, Simon, we don't want to lose our booking.'

Defeated, Gordon headed back to the clubhouse, watched, for a moment, by Veronica and Simon.

'What was all that about?' Simon enquired lightly.

'What?'

'Excuse me, Mrs Lester, but one would have to be completely stupid not to realise you had to work very hard to lose that game.'

'He's not stupid, but he's vain, and that makes it easier. Come along; I'll die unless I get a decent game in this afternoon.'

The game was hard fought and Veronica, working through all her frustrations, won, just. She was delighted. 'We're very evenly matched, Simon. That was thrilling. Will you partner me in the mixed doubles tournament?'

'But you've got a partner already.'

'He's not as good as you. Don't worry, I'll get rid of him.'

There was no sign of Gordon when they met again, freshly showered, in the club bar.

Veronica sat in an alcove and watched Simon as he made his way back from the bar with her gin and tonic. God, he was good looking, but there was something else about him that made her breath catch in her throat; something remote, something elusive that made him all the more desirable. She had been married to Hugh for twenty-one years and was not at all averse to flirting shamelessly and even having the odd sexual fling, but Hugh gave her more or less what she wanted in life and she would never consider embarking on a serious affair. Never, that is, until now, and for that reason, Simon Weatherby spelt danger, and there was nothing Veronica loved more than danger.

Dark Glasses had kept Charlie and Lenny hard at work on the site for the rest of the day and well into the evening, preparing the ground, moving beams and laying temporary flooring, so there

226

was little opportunity for Charlie to break the news to Lenny that not only would there be no money for a new bike, but precious little to do anything at all with.

Just before closing time, Charlie insisted he was going to take a break, and pausing only to change his shirt and smother his bodily smells with aftershave, shot off to The Grapes and to find Beth. He had reconciled himself to the loss of one of his tickets. After all, he would have a security pass, and although undoubtedly he would be expected to be on call during the night, he should have plenty of time to spend with her.

The Grapes was busy with last orders. Charlie squeezed his way to the bar, placed his order with one of the bar staff, and craned his head along the bar to see if he could see Beth. Linda was in the lounge bar, but there was no sign of Beth.

'Beth in tonight?' he asked the barman, handing over the money for his pint.

'Nope.'

'In tomorrow?'

'No idea. Ask Linda.'

Linda was unusually short. 'Beth's gone, and she's not coming back.'

Charlie was bewildered. 'But I thought she liked it here; I thought you and Stan thought she was good news—'

'I'm sorry; I'm busy. 'Scuse me ...'

Charlie was really put out. He sat on his stool and sulked. What a bummer of a day.

'Charlie? Charlie Tucker, ain't it?' He swivelled on his stool. A woman he didn't recognise stood at his elbow, smiling up at him. She was of average height, somewhere in her mid-thirties he guessed, but dressed younger. A small pink T-shirt was smoothed over a dominating bosom and rounded stomach, finishing a couple of inches short of a tiny denim skirt. Large, colourful ear-rings danced and flashed as she bobbed and nodded; her hair was shoulder-length and blonde, although not naturally so, judging from the darkness of her roots. She had a large round nose and round eyes, the lashes heavily impregnated with mascara, and her accent was unmistakably local. For a few moments he struggled, feeling he must know who she was – she had hailed him with such confidence. But it was no good; he'd no idea, as he confessed to her in what he hoped was a disarmingly honest way.

She was not at all put out. 'I'm not surprised. It's been a long time since we snogged behind the bike sheds. It's Tricia, Tricia Stevens. I rang you. Skip said you was a regular here. He said I'd recognise you, easy. He was right. Those whiskers certainly take the biscuit, don't they?'

15

'Look, Mrs Lester, it ain't my fault!' Paula was really fed up. 'Lenny's bin workin' flat out this last week and I've hardly seen him. He'll come and see Mr Lester as soon as he can – by Sunday at the latest, I promise.'

'One would think he's not interested,' said Veronica coldly. 'Really, Paula, it makes me think perhaps I'm paying you too much.'

Paula stopped polishing the dining table and stared at her employer, who was arranging some very odd-looking flowers in a tall glass vase.

'What?'

'Think about it: if Lenny can afford not to take up Hugh's offer, then clearly you are not as badly off as you pretend to be – ergo, I should pay you less, or employ you less.'

Paula felt ready to down duster and leave. It was only just after 11 a.m. and she had another two hours to get through at Summerstoke House before she could turn her back on the Lesters for the whole weekend.

There was a shriek of laughter from the garden and Veronica glanced out of the window. 'It's bad enough you bringing the children to work, but I thought I'd told you not to let them pick my flowers. For goodness' sake, they're ruining the gypsophila. Do something!'

Paula abandoned the polishing. 'I'll take them home. I told you me mam couldn't babysit today and there's no way I'm gonna work for you for less than I do.'

Paula knew that much as Veronica enjoyed baiting her,

Veronica's need of her was as great as Paula's need of the money she earned.

Veronica changed tack. 'No, don't go. I was only joking about your wages, for goodness' sake. Go and give the children some squash and biscuits in the kitchen. I'll come and join you when I've finished doing these flowers. Aren't they lovely?'

'They don't look like flowers to me; give me roses and carnations any day. What are they?'

'Protea, the national flower of South Africa – very sophisticated. I don't suppose you've ever come across them. They were a present from my new tennis partner.'

'Weird.'

In the kitchen Paula appeased her children who, turning their little noses up at the idea of squash, wanted to go home. With promises of ice-cream later, they were turned out into the garden once again, with strict instructions not to go anywhere near the flowers, even though they might look like weeds.

The kitchen was a long, light room that looked over the back of the house to the farmyard beyond. It was the antithesis of Marsh Farm's kitchen. It gleamed with cleanliness; even the deep red quarry tiles on the floor glistened. The Aga, a big double-ovened affair, occupied the old hearth and hanging from the mantle above it were a row of copper pans of various sizes, polished and gleaming, ready for use, although Veronica didn't use them for cooking – they were far too heavy. A large, beautiful old oak dresser occupied another wall, on which were arranged, in serried ranks, pewter platters, wooden platters and blue, willow pattern china platters, all of which were dusted or washed regularly, although Veronica never used them. The bottom shelf of the dresser was devoted to a long line of fashionable cookery books, which Veronica used a lot. All the pots, pans, crockery and cutlery, and other paraphernalia used by the family and usually associated with kitchen life, were stored away in deep purpose-built cupboards that lined the rest of the room. It was the sort of kitchen that one would find in a lifestyle magazine.

Veronica had followed Paula into the kitchen and was sitting at the long scrubbed oak table, flicking through just such a magazine, as Paula cleaned the Aga. She said, casually, without looking up, 'I've got people coming to dinner tomorrow night, Paula, and I need your help.'

'You had people to dinner last weekend!'

Veronica looked up in surprise. 'So?'

'I don't know why you do it, that's all. All that time slaving over pots 'n' pans, fiddle-faddling with itsy-bitsy bites of food that are gobbled up in a flash. Seems like a lot of work for nothing, to me.'

'I enjoy it, and people enjoy my cooking. I entertain – that's one of the ways in which we enjoy ourselves.'

'Well, I wouldn't do it, if it were me – not my idea of fun.'

'I think you need to take some wire wool to that hot plate – I dripped caramel on it.' Watched by Veronica, Paula moved, with ill-concealed annoyance, to the sink. 'What's your idea of fun, Paula?'

'Dancin'.' There had been almost no occasion to go dancing with Lenny since the children had been born and with a rush of excitement, Paula suddenly thought of the disco the following evening. 'I'm sorry, but I can't be here tomorrow night, Mrs Lester.'

Veronica was put out. 'Why not? I need you.'

'Well, I can't. Me and Lenny are goin' out. It's all arranged. Me mum's comin' over to babysit – that's why she's not got the kids today.'

'Paula …' Veronica hated having to beg and Paula secretly notched up a point when she was forced to do so. 'It's going to be very difficult.'

'I'm sure you'll manage. Sorry, but I can't do it.'

'What are you up to? Going dancing?'

Mindful of Lenny having sworn her to secrecy, Paula suddenly felt uncomfortable discussing Saturday night. 'Er … dancing? Er … yes, I s'pose so.'

Veronica's whiskers twitched, and Paula knew it. She just couldn't control the moment of hesitation that instantly roused

Veronica's curiosity. 'Where would you go dancing around here, Paula?'

Paula's mind went blank and she started to flounder. 'Er, there's nowhere really ... Me and Lenny, we're ... we're going to a party.' But the cautious nature of the sideways look she cast in Veronica's direction, and the extra vigour she applied to removing the burned caramel drips, was not lost on Veronica. Paula had something to conceal.

'A party! How nice. Where?' Veronica purred.

'I'm not sure really. Near here ... Lenny knows.'

'Friends of yours?'

'Who?'

'The people giving the party,' said Veronica. Paula knew she was patiently watching her face. She knew her employer had no interest in what Paula did with her free time, but she enjoyed playing cat and mouse, and the hapless Paula was becoming increasingly flustered, which greatly added to the sport.

'Er, Lenny knows them.'

'Many people going?'

'Er, I expect so.'

'Yes, people like dancing, don't they? So it's going to be a big party?'

Paula was feeling deeply resentful of this cross-questioning. She longed to tell the old bag it was no business of hers, but she wasn't sure whether this event was legal or not; she thought, knowing Lenny, probably not, so there was no way she'd let on about it to the likes of Veronica Lester, who, she suddenly remembered, was a magistrate. She decided to say nothing further and turning her back firmly on Veronica, started to clean the sink.

Veronica was not going to give up. 'So you've got your mum in to babysit so you can go dancing at a party, but you don't know who's holding it and you don't know where it is except it's somewhere nearby, and that it's going to be a big affair?'

Paula was silent, sulky.

Veronica moved in for the kill; Paula could sense it coming. 'I know we don't move in the same circles, Paula, so there's no reason, no reason at all why I should have heard of any party your Lenny would take you to, but I do have my ear to the ground and I know something is going on. Cordelia made some remark or other, only yesterday, but of course, the child denied anything when I asked her.'

Paula concentrated hard on her cleaning and did her level best to take no notice of her tormentor.

Then Veronica pounced.

'You know, it sounds to me like you might be going to a rave.'

In spite of herself, Paula started with alarm.

She'd given Veronica what she wanted. 'I thought something like that might be going on. The thing is,' she continued silkily, 'I think you should tell me all about it.'

'I don't see why.' Paula turned to face Veronica and said resentfully, 'What's it got to do with you?'

'A lot. We own most of the land round here. If there's going to be an illegal rave on our land, I want to know about it. Is this why Lenny has been too busy to see Hugh this week? We know he has a history with things illicit; is he involved in setting up this rave?'

Paula flushed and said nothing.

'Oh dear, I do wish you'd be open with me. I'm going to have to call the police and have them question Lenny.'

Paula was alarmed. 'Why, what's he done? He ain't up to anythin' illegal.'

'I don't know that,' continued Veronica, thoroughly enjoying her victim's discomfiture, 'but if the rave is being held on our land, then it is illegal.'

'Well it ain't,' muttered Paula.

'Ah, then you *do* know where it's being held?'

'Not exactly … I know it's not on your land though, and I promised Lenny I wouldn't talk about it.'

'Which suggests to me it's something the police would be interested in. If it's not our land, whose land is it on?'

Paula shrugged, but did not reply, her face mirroring the level of resentment she felt.

Veronica had not quite finished. 'Lenny works mainly for the Tuckers, doesn't he? And they're desperate for cash. Charlie Tucker is every bit as shifty as your husband, I hear ... is the rave going to be on their land, Paula?'

Paula would not be drawn, but from the expression on her face, Veronica knew that she was right.

Alison was all of a twitch, as Jenny put it, on Friday morning. The precious ticket in her possession, she had phoned round her friends, and there had been an excited discussion about the event; what they were going to wear, where they would meet beforehand, and whose house they would pretend to be staying overnight at, to fob off any anxious parent.

In addition, Al was due back on Friday. She had arranged to meet him outside the village shop at 7 o'clock, and she was counting the minutes. Then she received a text message:

'V. L8. CU 9 Luv Al.'

The postponement of their meeting by a couple of hours had a dampening effect on her spirits, which wasn't helped by the trouble she and her brothers were having trying to work out how to get Jenny and Gran out of the way until the event was well underway.

They had met in the dairy where Stephen was finishing cleaning up after the morning's milking.

'Gran's not such a problem,' said Alison. 'After all, she goes out every Saturday afternoon as it is. If we can persuade her that there's gonna be no one here in the evening, then maybe she'll stay out with her friends a bit longer.'

'But Mum'll be here, and we can't keep her locked in the house. One whiff of this ...' Stephen groaned. 'Any ideas, Charlie?'

Charlie was feeling physically and mentally battered. He had grabbed a quick break from the site where he had been working since dawn, to try and resolve this problem with the other two. 'Dunno. Ali's right, though: if none of us is here, Gran won't hurry back. Though Christ knows what she gets up to in Bath. Probably makes her money running a brothel!'

'There's only one thing for it,' said Alison decisively. 'Stephen, you've got to take Mum out for the day.'

'Me?' Stephen was alarmed. 'Why me?'

'Cos you're her favourite, that's why. She'd think it very odd if Charlie suggested it, and I can't drive. So it's gotta be you.'

'What about my cows? Where would I take her?'

'The last bit is easy; use your brains – Weston-super-Mare. It's bank holiday weekend, so there should be lots going on and hopefully you'll be caught up in traffic on your way home.'

Charlie managed a tired grin. 'Ali, you're a genius. Do the milking in the morning, Steve, and Ali and I will do the evening shift.'

But Stephen looked far from happy. 'How on earth am I gonna ask her? Supposin' she says no?'

But both Charlie and Ali brushed his doubts aside.

Alison had wondered, in the face of their newfound camaraderie, about telling her brothers about the Lesters. But she had promised Simon she would say nothing, and if they really did make all this money from the rave, then the Lesters' moves would be blocked, at least for the time being.

She thought a lot about Simon. She knew so little about him and couldn't fathom why he should show such an interest in her, or in her family. She trusted him, though. He had made no sexual overtures to her at all, which had been her first dread. And he made her laugh. She wondered, not for the first time, what Al would make of Simon and her friendship with him, and what Simon would make of Al.

The day passed slowly and Alison was periodically assailed by stabs of anxiety. Al had not been in touch, so she had no idea how his time with her-in-Wrexham had gone. He'd been there three nights. If he was going to split up with her, he was taking his time over it. Her fertile imagination, running the gauntlet of a three-day scenario featuring Al and the lovely Rachel – she had become a willowy, sophisticated, blonde intellectual in this scenario – found it hard to make the ending a happy one.

She collected Paula's helmet late afternoon. Paula looked more fed up than usual after a session at the Lesters and barely smiled at Alison, but upon being pressed, would say no more than how much she hated the 'Queen Bitch'.

Having changed her clothes, her earrings and her make-up twenty times over, the time finally arrived for Alison to walk to the village shop. Her stomach was knotted with nerves and as she reached the brow of the bridge, she nervously scanned the street in front of her. There, in the dusk, she could see the shape of the bike and a tall figure straddling it, waiting for her.

Motionless astride his bike, he waited for her to draw close, saying nothing. His face was cast in shadow; his eyes glinted at her in the dusk. She could feel her throat tightening and her breath came and went in nervous little gasps. He barely greeted her and she, aching for a deep, significant kiss, made a flippant reply.

As the bike sped through the country lanes, her arms round his waist and her head resting on his back, disappointment at the coolness of their greeting set a few tears to trickle down her cheeks and spin into the night air.

They stopped at a small pub, and finding their way into the dark and empty garden, sat at a ramshackle picnic table. By the time he returned with their beer, she had decided she couldn't bear the uncertainty any longer. As he put the glasses on the table and made to climb onto the bench next to her, she started to speak, just as he started to say something to her.

They both stopped and then laughed self-consciously.

'You first,' he said.

'No, you,' she replied. 'You're the one with things to tell. What happened?'

'In a minute, but first I want to—'

And taking Alison by surprise, he put his hand out and turned her face to meet his, bent forward and kissed her. At first it was a light, exploratory kiss, but the frustration, fears and longing of the last few days worked on them both: tentative kissing gave way to a hungry, passionate embrace.

They were rudely and forcibly interrupted by the rickety table, which overbalanced and hurled them to the ground. The glasses on the table flew into the air, showering them both with beer.

Alison lay on her back, giggling helplessly, Al on top of her, the table looming over them. He started to lick her face. 'Pity to waste good beer,' he murmured, then kissed her again and again, until her body was on fire.

The shifting of their bodies released the table and it crashed back to its former position, jolting them violently. Al paused, and looking down at Alison, said soberly, 'Okay, it's time for talking.'

They perched side by side on the table, their feet on the bench. Al put his arm around Alison's shoulder and she snuggled up to him, knowing that whatever had happened in Wrexham, the last five minutes had been magic and that she could swear he fancied her as much as she did him.

'So tell me. What have you decided to do about me? About Rachel?'

He took his time to reply, choosing his words with care. 'I could have rung Rachel, or texted her, or written a letter, but I liked her too much for that. We had a good thing going at uni, and to be honest, I didn't know whether what I felt about you was enough to make me want to finish with her.'

Alison held her breath. The last thing she wanted to hear was that their relationship was not going anywhere. And was she wrong? Kissing like that meant nothing?

'We'd planned for me to go over to hers anyway, before I went off to France, and I thought if I saw her, I would know more clearly how I felt about her, and about you.'

'And?'

'She's nice, Ali, really bright and funny. I like her a lot. But I realised I didn't want to kiss her the way I want to kiss you, and the whole time we were together, I found I was thinking of you, your green eyes and hair like silk; your oddness, your fierceness, and the way you laugh.'

Alison found breathing less painful. 'So what did you say to her? You were there for three days ...'

'No, I left after the first night. I got there so late, we had supper with her parents and then I went to bed. She said the next morning that that was when she knew something was up.'

'How?'

'Because I didn't go to her room.'

'You were ... you were sleeping together?' A spasm of jealousy – or was it envy? she wondered – resulted in the question coming out as little more than a whisper.

'Yes, which was why I owed it to her, to me, to go and see her.'

'Did you tell her about me?'

'As much as I could, which wasn't a lot. I couldn't even tell her your name. Ali what?' He fell silent for a moment. 'She asked if you and I'd slept together, and when I said no, she asked if I intended to.'

'And do you?' Why was her voice so shaky? It was what *she* had wanted, after all ...

'It's not just my decision, is it? The thing is, I don't know where we go from here. I'm off on Monday for three weeks, back here for two, then off north. Is this just going to be a quick fling? Shall we just make the most of the moment and draw a line? Shall we end it right here, because I can't make any commitments to you?'

She groaned. 'Why didn't you tell me you were back two days ago? There is so little time.'

'My parents weren't expecting me until today. I went to see a couple of mates in Lancaster. I needed to clear my head.'

They sat staring out into the darkness of the garden. The bushes rustled with a slight breeze; the air was sweet with the smells of cut grass and honeysuckle; a solitary street lamp cast shafts of orange light across the grass, picking out abandoned glasses, ashtrays and crisp packets; an owl called and was answered.

'So what do you want to do, Ali? Stop it here, now, before we go any further?'

'I so don't want to. But I don't want ... Oh Al, I don't know. I don't know ... Kiss me again, please!'

And he did.

When he dropped her off at the village shop, he had looked at her intently and had said, low and soft, 'I *would* like to sleep with you, Ali. Very much.'

Stephen had not gone to the rehearsal yesterday night, in spite of the fact that disaster had been temporarily averted. He had been through so much emotionally, had touched rock-bottom on more than one occasion, that he felt drained and not at all up to dealing with The Players. So he had held his breath and phoned Mrs Pagett. Fortunately for his resolve, her answerphone was on, so he left her the briefest of excuses. She had phoned to speak to him that morning, but Jenny took the call and Stephen sent a message that he was busy and would call her back. He hadn't done so.

In the evening, Stephen was in the sitting room watching a reality game show on the television with his mother. They were by themselves as Alison was out, as was Charlie, and Elsie eschewing 'such rubbish' had taken herself off upstairs. The sitting room was Stephen's favourite room. It was panelled in dark wood; old tapestry curtains, the lining in shreds, hung at the windows. The carpet was threadbare and the yawning fireplace smelled of old stone and wood ash. The furniture was as shabby as the rest of the house and the large sofa on which Stephen sprawled was a lumpy mixture of sag and broken spring. Jenny sat in an old Queen Anne chair, a small table at her side, on which sat her knitting basket. As they watched television she was carefully unravelling an old jumper, so when the telephone rang, she expected Stephen to jump up and answer it.

Stephen looked uncomfortable. 'Mum – you answer it. It might be Mrs Pagett again and I really don't want to talk to her, not now.'

Sighing at this strange state of affairs, Jenny put her wool down and went to answer the phone. One hand over the receiver, she hissed, 'It's Angela ... shall I tell her you're not here?'

Relieved, Stephen took the receiver from his mother. 'Hi, Angela.'

'Stephen, hello. Are you all right?' Angela sounded out of breath.

'Yes, I'm fine.'

'Oh, that's good … only :… you didn't come to the rehearsal last night.'

'No.'

Angela paused, waiting for Stephen to explain. He didn't.

'Oh, er … it shook everyone up, you not being there.'

'Did it?'

'Yes,' Angela continued cautiously, sounding disconcerted by this brevity of Stephen's. 'Mrs Pagett got into a right tizz and kept on shakin' her head and demandin' to know why you weren't there, and did anyone know if you were ill.'

Stephen digested this with a certain amount of pleasure. 'Did Nicola say anything?'

'Not really. She was a bit quiet, though, and when I was packing up she asked if I'd seen you. I told her I hadn't since the last rehearsal. Is … everything all right?'

Stephen was touched – she sounded so anxious. 'Yes, I'm fine, Angela. I went through a bad patch, but for the moment, things are sortin' themselves out.'

'Will you be there on Sunday?'

'Who read Snuff?'

'I did, in between prompting and things.'

'And settin' up and striking, and makin' the tea?'

'Yes.' Angela was obviously puzzled at the turn the conversation was taking.

'Hmm … Mrs Pagett needs to cast Snuff. I'm really busy this weekend and I might not get to the rehearsal on Sunday – it depends.'

'Oh, right …' Angela was clearly deflated by his stand, and Stephen was moved; she'd always been there for him. Whatever issue he had with The Merlin Players, it had nothing to do with Angela. 'Listen, I've bin' goin' through some of the rare breeds stuff you've got for me. I reckon we should take a trip out and go to some of these places.'

After he had hung up and resumed his place on the sofa, Stephen was thoughtful. So they'd all fussed about him not being there, but apart from Mrs P, Angela was the only one to take the trouble to phone. Most significantly, Nicola hadn't rung.

At heart, Stephen was a humble person; he hadn't expected his non-appearance to cause much of a stir, nor had he expected many concerned calls, but after his conversation with Angela, something like steel entered his soul and the phrase 'taken for granted' flickered through his brain. What I'd like to do, thought Stephen, in this unaccustomed frame of mind, is not to go on Sunday and persuade Angela not to go, as well. That'd show 'em.

He had no intention of giving up entirely on the Merlin Players, but he had been badly upset by Nicola and couldn't help feeling that her dalliance with him had been for some reason that had nothing to do with him at all. He had adored her for so long and had been so overwhelmed at being kissed by her, he had suppressed his common sense and allowed himself to become an object of ridicule. He blushed hotly when he thought of showing her round the farm and trying to hold her hand. He should have remembered what Angela had said: 'If she doesn't want to hold your hand, then she just wants to be friends.' Huh, some friend.

Unlike Angela.

The rest of the family had been in their beds for some considerable time when Charlie let himself into the farm kitchen in the early hours of the morning. They had worked without a break well into the night and he was exhausted and very hungry. His mother had left him out a plate of food and he lifted the cover to discover mashed potato, sausages and baked beans. She had once given him instructions, as he was often late in for supper, about how to reheat his food between two plates over a pan of boiling water, but he couldn't be bothered, so he sat at the kitchen table and ate his six-hour-cold supper.

He was not feeling very cheerful. Charlie was a spontaneous, impulsive person, full of energy, who would cheerfully discard without much regret ideas, schemes and even people if they didn't work out. He didn't often think long term about anything. But, maybe because he was as tired as he was, the events of the last two weeks had finally got under his skin and it was in a very depressed frame of mind that he sat and ate.

He still shivered when he thought of the awful shock he'd got when Sarah had suggested marriage. And then there was Tricia – what a bad joke! He fingered one of his sideburns thoughtfully. If Gran had wanted to really punish him she couldn't have thought of a more effective way of doing it. And what on earth had happened to Beth? The only way he'd been able to disentangle himself from the appalling Trish had been to leave the pub, so he'd not had the chance to question Linda further about that little mystery. He was disappointed, there was no denying it. He'd set great store on impressing Beth with a ticket for the disco and had planned that, during the course of the night, their relationship would be well and truly launched. Fat chance of that happening now!

But what was pulling him down more than all this was the farm and Stephen. It had really shaken Charlie to see Stephen so angry and he was finding it hard to lose his feelings of guilt over the way he had so casually treated his brother.

He really cares about this farm, he thought. More than me. It was an admission he rarely made, even to himself. And he's so grateful I've bailed us out with this cash. But what's gonna happen next, eh, Charlie boy? What's gonna happen next month? There won't be no events in September to provide the necessary … Then what are we going to do? And for once, the customary, 'Something will turn up, you'll see', remained unsaid, unthought, and it was a sombre, sober Charlie who took himself off to bed.

16

'He's not asked her!'
Charlie had just entered the kitchen, puffy-eyed after a poor night's sleep, to find his sister, arms akimbo, glaring down at Stephen, who was giving his full attention to a large bowl of cornflakes.

'Why not?' Charlie snapped. 'Bloody hell, you're cutting it a bit fine, aren't you?'

Alison tried a more cajoling tone. 'Stephen, only *you* can do this ... we agreed.'

'It's easier said than done,' Stephen, his mouth full of cereal, protested. 'How do I ask without her suspectin' somethin'? "Oh Mother," his voice went high and squeaky, "I was wonderin', would you like to go to Weston-super-Mare for the day?"' He shoved another spoon of cereal into his mouth, spitting the milk out as he spoke. 'She'd know straightaway we was up to somethin'.'

'Couldn't you say you wanted to visit a rare breeds farm or something, and you know she's interested in them? Then go to Weston?'

'Nice one, Ali. Well, Steve — you've been rabbiting on about them — why don't you do that?'

Before Stephen had time to reply, Jenny came in from the yard carrying a small bundle of post and a large parcel. She was looking at the label with concern, then she sighed and sat down at the table, the parcel in front of her. 'That's odd ...'

'Want a cup of tea, Mum?'

'Thanks Ali, that'd be nice. Charlie, have you had any breakfast

yet? You were in so late last night, and then up again this morning ... I've never known you work so hard over the harvest. Is
it finished yet?'

'Last push this weekend, Mum, then I'm done.'

As Jenny turned the parcel over and started to open it, Alison
and Charlie frantically made faces at Stephen. He turned red and
little beads of perspiration broke out on his top lip. His mouth
opened silently, like a goldfish, and closed again.

'Go on – now!' Alison mouthed at him, from behind Jenny's
back.

'Er—' he got as far as saying before a horrified exclamation
broke from Jenny.

'Oh no!' With a plaintive cry, she held up the rainbow sweater
she'd sent off two weeks previously. 'She's sent it back! Why? I
was wondering why she'd not paid me. Oh dear, oh dear. I don't
understand ... why's she sent it back?'

Alison reached over her mother's shoulder and from the remains of the parcel, extracted a folded letter. 'Mum, please, don't
be upset – there's probably a good reason. It's so beautiful, no
one in their right minds would send it back.'

Jenny opened the letter with trembling fingers, read the brief
note, and groaned.

'What is it, Mum ... what is it?' Stephen hated seeing his
mother in such a state of distress.

'She says,' Jenny looked up from the letter, quite miserable,
'she says she's very sorry, but she's returning the sweater because
it smells of something. She says it's affecting the rest of her stock.
She thinks it smells of vinegar.'

'It does, too.' Charlie sniffed the sweater. 'It reeks of it!'

'Green tomato chutney.' A tear rolled down Jenny's cheek.
'I'm so stupid – I should've realised. All that work, and when we
so need the money ...'

Her three children glanced at each other guiltily. They knew
that their immediate cash crisis had been solved, but there was no
way they could tell their mother that, not yet, and it made each of
them feel uncomfortable.

'That's the trouble, Mum — you've bin' workin' too hard and we just take you for granted!' Stephen suddenly sprang to life. 'It's time you had a break and I'm gonna give you one. How long do you need to get ready?'

'What for?' asked Jenny, faintly.

'I'm taking you out for the day. Angela's been loadin' me with stuff about alpacas and ostrich and the like. There's a farm near Weston-super-Mare — why don't we check 'em out, then go on to Weston. It's bank holiday weekend, so there should be lots goin' on. Maybe I'll give Angela a ring — she could do with a break too; you wouldn't mind her — you think she's all right, don't you, Mum?'

'Yes,' Jenny agreed, even more faintly. For a moment Stephen, in this unusually assertive mood, reminded her of Jim before they were married.

'Go on, then, Mum,' encouraged Alison. 'Don't worry about Gran — I'll make her breakfast when she comes down.'

'Best bib and tucker and don't worry 'bout the milking — me and Ali will do it, so don't hurry back.' Charlie was magnanimous in his relief.

In a daze, Jenny was virtually ejected from the kitchen to go and get ready, and as the door shut behind her Charlie and Alison almost cheered Stephen.

He blushed with pleasure. ''Twas nothin'. Poor Mum. I meant what I said — here's all of us moanin' our heads off when things go bad, and there's Mum, worryin' about the lot of us … I'll go and give Angela a ring.'

'Why on earth do you want to saddle yourself with her for?' Charlie was curious, rather than unkind.

It was a good question. 'I told you, she's looked all this stuff up for me on the computer …' was the only, very unsatisfactory, reply they could get.

Jenny rejoined her offspring in the kitchen, looking flustered and excited. 'We mustn't be too late back, though, Stephen,' she said, stuffing her handbag with lip balm, comb, face powder, rain hat, sun cream, hair pins, and other items indispensable for a day by the sea.

'Why's that, Mum?' Charlie was alarmed. There would be a huge number of cars turning down the tiny lane just beyond the farm's entrance and he wanted Jenny off the scene until the majority of the punters had arrived. 'I told you, me and Ali's gonna do the milkin'. Make a day of it. Don't hurry back.'

'Jeff is taking me to hear a folk group in Summerbridge tonight, so I've got to be back. He's pickin' me up about seventhirty, after supper.'

There was a moment of amazed silence. Jenny never went anywhere on a Saturday night, let alone to hear live music. If she returned from Weston-super-Mare in the early evening, she would run slap bang into the party traffic.

'I'll tell you what, Mum.' Alison thought rapidly. 'I'll give Uncle Jeff a ring and tell him you'll meet him at the pub. Stephen can take you directly there.'

'Yeah, Mum.' Stephen didn't give his mother a chance to object. 'That'll suit me, 'cos I'll have to drop Angela off.'

Stephen's car had just left when Elsie, in search of her breakfast, came into the kitchen.

'Where's your mother?' Elsie looked around the empty kitchen.

'Oh,' said Alison airily, 'Stephen's taking her out for the day. I said I'd do your breakfast.'

Elsie snorted. 'Going out for the day — that's not going to pay the bills, is it? Where are they gallivantin' off to?'

'Weston-super-Mare; then they're going to Summerbridge this evening, so they won't be back till late.'

'Why didn't they ask me? I would've enjoyed a bit of sea air.'

'Gran! The way you go on about Weston-super-Mare ... you'd hate it. And anyway, on Saturday you always meet up with your cronies in Bath. So why don't you stay on there and do something with them this evening?'

'Now why should I do that? Are you trying to get me out of the way by any chance? Are you up to something?'

Alison felt uncomfortable. Sometimes Gran had an unnerving

way of reading people's minds. 'Of course not,' she replied as blandly as she could. 'It's just that I'm going to be out tonight as well; I'm going to a party with Hannah and I'm staying overnight, so there won't be anyone here.'

'Well, that's nice – why didn't someone tell me?' Elsie was disgruntled. She sat at the table looking very displeased. 'I'll have a cup of tea, thank you, and a slice of toast, if it's not too much trouble.' She watched Alison fill the kettle and put a slice of bread under the grill then continued her grumble. 'I was going to do some bottling this evening, but if there's going to be nobody here to help . . . When's your mum coming back? I do think she might have told me she was off out.'

'I'm sorry, but it was very much a last-minute thing. She was upset and Stephen said he'd take her out for a treat. She's arranged to meet Jeff Babbington in Summerbridge this evening, so Stephen is going to take her directly there, so she'll be back late.' She placed a cup of tea in front of Elsie. 'I tell you what, I'll give you a hand with the bottling tomorrow afternoon, and then, later, I want to take you to meet a friend of mine.'

'Oh, who's that?'

'I'll tell you tomorrow. Here's your toast and some of that honey you like.' She placed the plate of toast on the table, helped herself to a cup of tea and joined her grandmother. She needed to establish that Elsie could be relied on not to come home dangerously early. 'So, what are you going to do this evening, Gran?' she began conversationally. 'It won't be much fun here by yourself.'

'Oh, don't fuss; there's plenty of things I can do. I would just like to have known earlier, that's all. Not too much to ask, is it?'

And try as she might, Alison could not pin Elsie down any further.

She reported as much to Charlie later, when he returned to grab a sandwich.

'Damn and blast – so she could come back right in the thick of it? I thought you were going to sort her out.' Charlie smeared margarine over the remains of the loaf in the bin, and looking round for something to put on the bread, finally unearthed a piece of cheese at the back of the fridge, slightly tinged with mould.

'Nobody sorts Gran out – she'll do her own thing, whatever we want. So what had *you* planned, eh, Charlie? Before Stephen and me tumbled your little scheme, how were *you* planning on keeping us all in the dark? Hoping we'd all go beddy-byes at six o'clock with cotton wool in our ears?'

Charlie, slicing the mould off the cheese, shrugged. 'I'd have thought of something.' He opened a jar of his mum's chutney (if nothing else, there was always plenty of that) and smeared it liberally on the cheese.

'Yeah, very likely! Well now, we've got to think about repairing the damage, because though we might be able to pull the wool over Mum's eyes, Gran's gonna find out; she'll sniff it out, even if she stays the *whole* night in Bath.' Alison's eyes narrowed, scrutinising Charlie's face. There was something else she wanted to check out. 'Is this event legit?'

'What do you mean?' He took a large bite of his sandwich.

'You know what I mean. Is this party, event, rave, whatever you want to call it – is it happening with the fuzz's blessing?'

'How should I know?' He took another large bite. 'I'm just renting out a couple of fields to a couple of blokes. Nothing against the law in doing that, is there? What they do is their business.'

Hugh Lester, having just returned from a business trip to London and hearing about the event for the first time, had just put a similar question to Veronica as they sat down to lunch in the dining room of Summerstoke House.

'I very much doubt it,' she replied with a smile. 'From Paula's reactions, I would say that there is a distinct possibility the police know nothing about this little party. Would you like salmon pâté, or wild boar?'

'Good!' Hugh smacked his lips with satisfaction. 'I'll take Black Jake out for a constitutional this afternoon; we could both do with the exercise, and do a bit of recceing – shouldn't be too difficult to find, and then … I'll have the wild boar, please, and some of the asparagus – that looks nice. Spanish?'

'Yes, it is. Then you'll contact the police?'

'I think we'll wait till it's well under way before we do that, my love. Much more satisfying to have a raid in the middle of the event, don't you think? And much more damaging. Hmm, this tastes jolly good. I'll take some of that tomato salad, too, please.'

Veronica passed him a dish of tomatoes, sliced and glistening with balsamic vinegar and olive oil. 'What a shame we've got dinner guests. I'd love to be there when the police move in.'

'And so you shall, my darling. These things go on all night. There's no one who particularly matters coming over tonight, is there?' Veronica shook her head. 'Good. We'll give everyone the heave-ho quite early, on the grounds that we've got things to do, and take ourselves off to observe the fun.'

Simon stood up and smiled as Harriet Flood reached his table. 'Harriet.' He kissed her on both cheeks. It was not a pleasant experience – London was sweltering and the extreme heat had caused her to perspire profusely; her skin felt damp and clammy. 'May I introduce you to Marcus Steel?'

A tall man, in his late thirties by Harriet's reckoning, with shaven head and piercing blue eyes, stood and shook Harriet's hand so firmly she almost winced.

Once they had exchanged pleasantries, Marcus Steel got straight to the point. 'I think Simon has explained a little about my interest in Marsh Farm. I work for a freelance television company, Laughing Jackass. You might have heard of us?'

Harriet had. She was impressed.

'I produce a mixture of programmes at the lighter end of the scale: light entertainment shows, comedies, and now, more and more makeovers and, of course, reality TV. The audience's appetite for that sort of programme seems endless!' He laughed wryly.

'And of course, you have to play to the lowest common

denominator?' Harriet sipped her cool white wine. What a treat to be entertained at lunch by two such striking young men.

'In the same way you have to write the articles your readers want to read, which is why, as I understand it, we might have a slight clash of interest.'

'Oh?' Harriet glanced across at Simon. He shrugged his shoulders. 'I haven't betrayed any confidences, Harriet. All Marcus knows is that you are contemplating a major series for your magazine, which would be dependent, in part, on the demise of Marsh Farm.'

'The thing is,' Marcus leaned forward, his expression intense, his voice lowered, 'in the same way you keep your projects close to your chest until the contract is signed, so do we, which is why what I'm going to tell you has to be kept completely confidential.'

'Of course.'

'We're working on a commission for a new series, working title "Up Against It". It's part makeover, part reality TV: a series that looks at little Britain and the little guys who are struggling against the odds to make it. Marsh Farm is struggling to survive in the agricultural jungle and the big guys are waiting to gobble them up. For this series, they are an ideal subject and they form the central platform of our proposal; our flagship, so to speak.'

'I see . . .' Harriet was thoughtful.

'So you can see why, when Marsh Farm was mentioned the other day,' put in Simon, 'I contacted Marcus. If it's not going to exist when he finally gets round to filming . . .'

'It would be a major setback. But I'm more inclined to get moving quickly. After all, it makes it a more interesting story, from our point of view, if there is an identifiable baddy, to put it crudely. The little farmer battling against the big stud!' He laughed.

Harriet cut a slice of steak and watched the blood ooze over her large white plate – nice and rare, the way she liked it. Much as she disliked Veronica and Hugh, she had decided to go with the story of the stud, so the television interest was unwelcome news. Had she worked on a different sort of publication, the adverse TV coverage might have been seen as a bit of a coup. As it was, *Country Homes and Gardens* was a magazine for the nice people of middle England. It featured nice people in their nice houses, with their nice gardens and their nice lifestyles. Her editor would not thank her if the stars of their first long-running feature – designed to broaden the magazine's appeal and boost circulation, after all – were exposed on television as the greedy land-grabbers they were. If the television programme happened, she could guarantee that the series on Summerstoke House Stud would be axed.

'Well, thank you for that. I will of course say nothing. I need to think about it – do you have a card?'

Marcus produced his card. Barely glancing at it, Harriet coolly surveyed both Simon and Marcus. 'One thing puzzles me, Marcus – what's Simon's role in all of this? I understood he works for a management consultancy. If programme proposals are as hush-hush as you say, how did Simon know of your interest in the farm? Call me a cynical old hack, but this whole thing does smell a little. What *is* Simon's interest in all of this?'

There was a moment's silence, then Simon answered smoothly. 'I have no interest, Harriet, apart from the fact that Marcus and I are old friends. I knew the gist of the idea he was working on, and because my work takes me into many such trouble spots, he approached me to look out for suitable subjects. I found Marsh Farm.'

Harriet was satisfied. She was thinking rapidly. If she consigned Summerstoke Stud to the rubbish bin, she would have to find something else. '*Country Homes and Gardens* is an upmarket mag. One that reflects the desirable side of living in the country,' she began slowly. 'Occasionally we do before-and-after features, but the property has to be worth it. What's the house like? Most farmhouses are a ghastly disappointment, in my experience.'

Simon shrugged his shoulders indifferently. 'As far as I can tell it's Georgian. On three floors, with one of those shell canopies over the front door – far too grand for the likes of the Tuckers, the family in question – and very shabby. They've let it go. The kitchen's a shambles. Large, of course, but with peeling paint, and linoleum-covered flagstones. It could be a lovely place, but would take a helluva lot to do it up.' He grinned at Harriet. 'Not your sort of place at all.'

Harriet turned to Marcus. 'Thinking on my feet, is there any mileage in a collaboration?'

'What sort of collaboration?'

'I need a series – this could make a good one. From the moment your camera goes in – house, garden, desperate, shabby – I write about what you show, pick out the decent features, advise what can be done, monitor the transformation. Then, if they do go to the wall, we could get the house sold at auction – make a nice little finale to my series and yours, I'd have thought. Anyway, I'll give you a call. I'm sure there's a whole lot more we could feature.'

'They're thinking of starting a rare breed collection,' Simon chipped in.

'Better and better.' Harriet was starting to feel tingly, the way she used to in the early days of her career, when a scoop was at her fingertips. It was very difficult to have a scoop in the world of houses and gardens. She raised her glass to these delicious and stimulating young men. 'This is a very nice Sauvignon. I think we should have another bottle, don't you?'

'I think she bought it,' said Marcus, watching the taxi carrying Harriet Flood drive off.

'She bought it. Thanks, Marcus. In fact you were so convincing I started to believe that you actually had such a series.'

Marcus laughed. 'I almost convinced myself. You know, it's not such a bad idea. We're assembling our pitch for the next round of offers at the moment. Maybe I should think of submitting it for discussion at the company's next meeting.'

'Anyway, thanks.'

'I enjoyed myself. What a revolting woman. Now, Simon, like it or not, you owe me an explanation.' He firmly steered Simon round the corner, through the portals of The Groucho, ordered a pot of coffee and two large brandies, then sat back in his armchair and lit a slim cigar. 'Well, what was that all about?'

Briefly Simon sketched for him the story of Alison and her family and of the threat they faced from the Lesters.

'I still don't get it, old man. What's it got to do with you? So it's a shame that this nice-but-hopeless family is going to be driven off their farm, but it's an all-too-familiar story. You can't single-handedly ride like a white knight to the rescue. And why should you want to? There's no sex interest, is there?'

'No. Alison has indicated I'm far too old for her.' Simon swirled the brandy in his glass. 'Thing is, Marcus, I left London 'cos I couldn't hack the tension any longer.'

'Helen?'

'Yes.' Marcus made to speak but Simon interrupted him. 'Dealing with my friends' sympathy is one of the hardest things to bear and until ... until everything is sorted, it gets worse. I can hear it on the tips of everyone's tongues: "Have you heard anything definite, yet? You never know ..." Well, I do know, but until I hear finally from Helen, everyone insists on being relentlessly optimistic. So I followed work down to the West Country and just as I thought I would have the screaming ab-dabs from living in the country, this ... this dryad falls into the river and stops me from drowning in my own self-pity. Call it a displacement activity, call it occupational therapy, call it what you like ... but they're nice people and if I can stop one rotten thing happening to them, then I will.'

Marcus was watching his friend's face closely. When Simon had finished speaking, he said softly, 'Hey, Simon, welcome back.'

'What do you mean?'

'You've been half-alive since Helen dropped her little bombshell. For a moment, just then, you looked more like your old self. They must have something, these Tuckers.'

Simon smiled faintly. 'The ones I've met are very decent. The granny sounds wonderful – I'm planning, on Alison's advice, to seduce her with the biggest gooey chocolate cake Valerie's can supply; Charlie, the oldest brother, sounds like an aspiring Pa Larkin.'

'H.E. Bates?'

'That's it. In fact, the whole set-up, along with Gran's ultimatum that the boys find themselves wives or she'll cut them out of her will, is like an old-fashioned TV sitcom. Trouble is, unlike the Larkins, they live in the real world.'

'Simon, I've had an idea!' Marcus sat upright in his chair, his eyes glinting with excitement. 'It could be just what I'm after. May I pay your Larkin family a visit? ASAP?'

'Have fun at your party tonight, dear.' Elsie kissed Alison goodbye. 'And don't do anything you'll be ashamed of later. It's never worth it.'

'I won't. Have a nice time with your friends. Bye. See you tomorrow.'

Watching Elsie drive off to Bath, Alison wondered, in the light of the advice she had just given her, whether her grandmother had any inkling of what was going through her mind. Ever since Al's return the night before she had been struggling to unscramble her brain and think clearly about her next move.

'So where do I go from here?' she thought to herself for the hundredth time, mooching back to the house, which suddenly seemed very empty.

She hadn't told Al she was a virgin and she didn't know when or where the consummation of their relationship would take place. Tonight? And then he was off? 'Wham, bam and thank you ma'am!' she muttered with disgust. That was not how she envisaged it at all. But if he suggested it, would she say no? Could she? And would she tell him she'd never done it before? And how would he react to that? Run a mile?

Perhaps it would be better if she did say no. He'd respect that, particularly as he was off the next day and, as he'd said, they didn't know where things were going; with time and distance so much against them ... Better to wait till things were clearer. After all, what did she know about him? Sweet FA! And what did he know about her? Ditto!

But the one thing Alison did know was that unlike anyone she had gone out with before, her body and mind melted under his touch, and that, more than anything, she wanted him to make love to her.

17

There had scarcely been a drop of rain the whole of August, for which Charlie, squeezing in a second cut of grass for silage and harvesting his barley, had been grateful, but the ground was hard and parched. Opening the gate for the cows, Charlie shook his head at the poverty of the pasture. Stephen had been moaning for days that they needed rain, but Charlie, caught up with the fortunes of the event, hadn't sympathised. Dark Glasses had confessed to Charlie that as far as he was concerned the only thing that could go wrong would be rain, and on site today, looking up at the clear blue sky and blazing sun, he gleefully predicted record numbers.

It was now nearly seven, and as if affected by the heat, the cows had taken their time strolling back to the meadow. Wiping the sweat from his brow, Charlie cursed. He was running late and he wanted time to change into party gear and to dowse himself in a new aftershave that guaranteed his irresistibility to women, before he was needed back on site. It seemed as hot now as it had been at midday, although the sky, Charlie noted, was covered with a milky film. The last lethargic beast had just ambled through the gate when his mobile rang.

'Charlie? How are the cows? Finished the milking all right? Did you check the water temperature?'

'Yeah, yeah. Everything's fine, Steve. I'm just closing the gate on the old ladies now. Christ, they took their time getting here.'

'They don't like it this hot. But at least they've got access to the river in that field. Well, since you asked, we're stuck in a lovely traffic jam.'

'Sorry, mate, all in a good cause. You are going straight to Summerbridge, aren't you?'

'If we ever get there.'

'Listen, Stevie, I've had an idea – why don't you ask Jeff if Mum can stay the night at his?'

There was a silence at Stephen's end of the phone, followed by a desperate, disbelieving, '*What?*'

Patiently, Charlie spelled out what he saw as an inspired solution. 'Ask Jeff if he'll put Mum up for the night. Then there's no way she'll find out.'

'And how do I do that?'

'You'll think of something. Don't hang around so she can get a lift back with you, mind ... I know, point out to Jeff that if she stays, he'll be able to put away a bellyful. It's Saturday night, after all. If he has to take Mum home, he won't be able to drink.'

At about the same time in the evening, as Charlie was talking to Stephen, a large black stallion trotting down a tiny country lane was reined in to a standstill. 'Bingo,' drawled Hugh Lester. He stood up in the stirrups to get a better view of the site. He was impressed. 'The boys in blue are going to love this!'

It had taken him some time to find. It was two miles or more down Weasel Lane. The site had been well chosen. A bend in the river and a convenient line of trees screened it from the sight of Summerstoke, or any houses on the other side of the river, and on this side the fields were bordered by an almost vertical hillside covered with hornbeam, birch and hazel, and thorny, inaccessible undergrowth.

'Quite an operation,' Hugh murmured. 'Tucker must be making a tidy sum out of that. Well, well, boy.' He caressed the neck of his black stallion. 'We'll just have to make sure it's a night they won't forget, eh?'

The stallion's ears flicked in response.

With great satisfaction, Hugh looked around him. 'Black Jake, between you and me, it's in the bag. After tonight's little operation, it shouldn't be too long before these fields will be full of your chums ...'

'There he is!' Beaming, Jenny waved across the crowded pub at Jeff, who was chatting to a group of friends. He waved back, broke off and pushed through the crowd to greet them.

'Here you are at last. I was beginning to think you'd miss the first set. Had a good day? Hello, Steve, Angela.'

He took Jenny's arm and guided her across to his group of friends. Stephen and Angela were introduced and Stephen was quite taken aback by the warmth with which Jeff's friends greeted Jenny. It was clear that he was not going to be needed to stay and look after her.

Jeff pushed a pint in his hand. 'Going to stay for this set, Stephen? Good little group.'

'Er, no ... I, er ...' Angela was at his elbow, sipping a pineapple juice. He took a decisive plunge. 'I thought I'd take Angela out for a bite. We went to a rare breeds farm – she did all the leg work, so I thought ... it'd ... be nice ...'

Angela looked up at him, her face suffused with pleasure. Stephen looked at her with some surprise. For that moment, he thought, she didn't look plain at all. Maybe that was the trouble – she didn't have much to make her happy.

Jeff had lost interest. 'Okay, fine. Don't worry about your mum. I'll see her home.'

Stephen remembered Charlie's request, closed his eyes and took the plunge. 'Er, don't want to ruin your evening, Jeff ... you won't be able to, you know, drink much ... Saturday night ... seems a pity ... can't you, you know, er ...' Totally ineffectual, his voice tailed away.

'Don't worry, Stephen. I'm used to restricting my drink – on call often enough, after all. Leave Jenny to me. It'll be a pleasure.'

Stephen floundered. 'No, no, what I mean is ...' He had known Jeff all his life and had known nothing but kindness and support from him. He took a deep breath, dropped his voice and whispered in Jeff's ear, 'The thing is, Uncle Jeff, it'd be better if Mum didn't go home tonight, so if you could, like, put her up for the night ...'

It was the rare use of the infantile epithet as much as the extraordinary proposal that caused the smile to vanish from Jeff's face. He stared for a moment at Stephen's red and sweaty face, guileless and concerned, then took him by the elbow and whispered back, 'See you in the gents', in five minutes.'

Having taken the decision to come clean to Jeff, it didn't take long, in the privacy of the gents, for Stephen to put him fully in the picture. 'The thing is,' he said, finally, 'we need this money, like right now. If I'm to keep the dairy going, if we are to get the bank off our backs for another month, we need it. But Mum is so dead against the whole idea of raves, she'd be really upset, and I don't want her to be.'

'Nor do I.' Jeff thought for a moment. 'Well, thanks for trusting me, Stephen. I can't say it's a form of farming I understand or approve of, but if it gets you out of a hole ... I don't promise anything, but I'll suggest to your mum that I've got a very nice little guest room, with a bed ready made ... but if she says no, then I'll make sure she gets home, whether I drive her or not. Is that understood?'

'Yes, Jeff. Thanks, thanks very much.'

'One other thing, Stephen. This rave – is it legal?'

It was not a question that had occurred to Stephen and he was, for a moment, totally confused. 'Legal? Why shouldn't it be? Charlie never said ... I assumed ... do you think it might be ... bloomin' heck, Jeff; what if it's not?'

Jeff patted him on the shoulder. 'It's obviously too late to go into those sorts of niceties, but I think I'll persuade Jenny to take advantage of my spare room. You take that little Angela out and try and forget all about it. But I will say this, Stephen: if you're going to try and make a serious go of Marsh Farm as a legitimate business, this racketeering of Charlie's has got to stop.'

*

259

'Wow!'

'Hey! Wicked!'

Hannah and Alison had just clambered out of the battered old van Nick had borrowed from his dad and were staring, with increasing excitement, at the transformation of the field.

From the improvised car park, they could see across the hedge into the adjacent field. Three large marquees, more like inflated canopies than tents, sat like alien spaceships, side by side. Illuminated from within, they emitted a glow that throbbed rhythmically to the music, spilling out across the fields, light and sound reflecting off the dark hillside behind. Laser beams danced across the site and raced into the evening sky, which was competing with its own colourful display. The sun was just below the horizon, and the sky to the west was an intense red and gold, but the last of the blue sky above was almost drained of colour, and a strange dirty yellow cloud was creeping across, followed by an inky black curtain drawing in from the east.

Alison stared at the sky and for a moment she felt uneasy. But the music was already loud and insistent, the car park was filling rapidly and somewhere by the entrance, Al would be waiting for her.

'Come on, Ali, what are you waiting for? You look great. Let's go find Al ...'

Alison had gone over to Hannah's after she and Charlie had finished the milking. The girls were going to be picked up by Nick shortly before nine and so they had a glorious couple of hours swapping clothes, make-up, and gossip. Alison had known Hannah since they were in Junior school together. An only child, Hannah had been indulged by her parents, and Alison had benefited from a continuous flow of unwanted clothes. Hannah was smaller than Alison, dark-haired, with big brown eyes, quite plump and full of fun, and brimming with self-confidence. Her face was carefully smothered with pounds of foundation, her bulging midriff was displayed without dismay, and she chattered and laughed with the greatest good humour.

Hannah's bedroom was completely different from Alison's ordered one. Chaos reigned: every available wall space was plastered with pouting, posturing posters of her favourite musicians and movie stars; the mirror on her dressing table was liberally smothered with photos of Nick, and on the dressing table itself, tubes of foundation cream without caps, tubs of moisturiser without lids, lipsticks without tops, eyeliner, mascara and eye make-up of every hue mingled in one glorious muddle; one drawer hung open and contained myriad earrings, necklaces, bracelets, brooches entangled with a variety of different coloured scarves and tights, camisoles and scraps of lingerie. The thickly carpeted floor was invisible under layers of discarded clothes, bags, trainers, sandals, books, DVDs, and magazines. A stereo, balanced on the top of a television set, belted out *Schizophrenic*, Hannah's favourite album of the moment, and the two girls chatted, laughed and sang as they tried on clothes and swapped gossip. Alison was not as forthcoming about Al as Hannah would have liked, but then, she was used to her friend.

At one point, however, looking into the mirror and concentrating on applying a lip liner, her eyes followed Alison, who was critically surveying her slight figure in a silky boob tube and dusky pink skirt, and casually she asked the question she'd been dying to put all evening. 'So are you going to make it tonight, Ali?'

Alison went slightly pink and studied the pair of high-heeled sandals Hannah had suggested she wear. They were purple satin, the toes long and pointed – not at all what she was used to – and decorated with a gold rosette. A bit over the top, possibly? Al had never seen her in anything but jeans and T-shirts. What on earth would he make of her dolled up like this?

She mulled over her reply to Hannah's question. She had told Hannah of her determination to lose her virginity when they had broken up for the summer, but they had not discussed it since.

'I don't know, Hannah. I feel a bit strange about it all. I thought it would be easier than it is. I mind more than I thought I would, if you see what I mean. I mean, it's nothing, is it? People do it all the time. So why am I making such an issue of it?'

'People talk about it more than they do it; you must know that. There's an element of trophy-hunting amongst our lot, but I reckon that's so much hot air.' She turned to face Alison, and Alison realised the usually dizzy Hannah was serious. 'You've got to like him, and I reckon it's got to be more important than a quick fling, otherwise you'll regret it. You do like Al, don't you?'

Alison blushed under her friend's direct gaze. 'Yes, yes I do. He's the first person I ever thought I would ... It's silly, Hannah, but because I said I was going to find someone and do it ... I wouldn't have, you know, if I didn't find the right person. And then *he* turns up and I'm all confused because I want to, but I don't, if we're going nowhere.'

'Have you told him this?'

'Sort of. And I think he feels the same way.'

Hannah suddenly grinned. 'Well, you're in for an exciting night. Will we, won't we? Lights, music! The scene is set. Let the ritual dance begin!'

'Let the ritual dance begin.' Hannah's words echoed in Alison's mind as they teetered across the grass in their heels. 'That's what this whole thing is, a bloody ritual. And there are the lights, and there is the music ... And there's Al!' She suddenly felt very excited. He was standing by the entrance. His hair was spiked and he was wearing a loose white linen shirt, the sleeves rolled up. He turned and gave an appreciative smile when he saw Alison, her blonde hair loose over her shoulders, wearing a dark plum, satin boob tube and dusky pink, silky skirt.

'See you later.' Hannah gave Alison a quick hug. 'Have a great one, Ali. Here – take this. You might need it.' Laughing, she pressed something into Alison's hand and grabbing Nick, disappeared among the crowd pushing into a tent. Alison opened her hand.

It was a condom.

*

Charlie was not having a good evening. Late back on site, he'd had to endure a bollocking from Dark Glasses which had taken place in front of a group of dancers he'd been flirting with earlier. Then, when he'd finally managed to gain some free time to play the field, he'd found the music so loud it hurt his chest and made all chat-up impossible. In one tent he'd spotted a group of girls gyrating in a circle around a pile of handbags, had gone to join them only to be driven off with the words 'Bog Off, Granddad' ringing in his ears. Added to that, it was almost unbearably hot in the marquees and there was only piss-poor lager on sale, at what Charlie considered to be a rip-off price. He decided to cut his losses, take a break and quench his thirst with a real pint.

The Grapes was surprisingly empty for a Saturday night. Linda was serving a customer and Charlie noticed that there was only her and a relief barman, Tony, behind the bar.

'You're quiet tonight, Lin,' he remarked as she pulled him a pint.

'Yeah.' She sounded tired. 'Word is there's some sort of disco event on and that's where most of my customers will be.'

He took a long, appreciative slurp. 'Where's Stan tonight? Not off visiting his sick mother again, is he?'

Linda stared at him. 'You are joking, aren't you? I'd've thought better of you, Charlie Tucker. I thought we was meant to be friends.'

It was Charlie's turn to stare. 'What've I said? Last time I asked, you said he was looking after his mum. Of course we're friends, Lin. You're one of my best mates. What's going on?'

She put both elbows on the bar and her shoulders sagged.

'Stan's gone, Charlie,' she said, her voice low and dull. 'We've split. Things haven't been great since Jessica came along. I dunno, I think Stan resented the time it takes to look after a baby. He'd flirt with the bar staff – nothing serious, done to make a point, I think. Then Beth joined us.'

'Beth!' Charlie was stunned. 'But she was … she and I … I thought …'

'You weren't the only one she made eyes at, Charlie. She's

very clever at spinning people along. She was good for business. But then I found out that she and Stan … and Stan told me it was serious. It had been going on for some time.' A wan smile flitted across her face. 'Charlie, you must be the last person I know not to have put two and two together.'

Charlie was shocked and angry. 'He must be fuckin' mad. He don't know his luck. You're the nicest person I know … and bloomin' good looking too.'

Linda gave a faint smile, but Charlie noticed the tears in her eyes. 'Not good enough to compete with Beth, though.'

Chagrin at the realisation Beth had taken him for a ride and the flicker of regret that he'd never got any further with her, was swept aside by his indignation at the way Linda had been betrayed. He stood up on his stool and leaned across the bar to put his arms around her. 'You're a million times better than that little shagger, Lin. He'll see sense in no time. Don't you—'

But his mobile interrupted his attempts to comfort her. It was Dark Glasses, urgently needing him at the entrance to the site, to sort out a bit of bother between the police and a local.

'Bugger, I've gotta go. Listen, Lin, I'll pop round tomorrow lunchtime. Give you a hand, if you like. You can give me the low-down then.'

'Well, this is nice!' Ron beamed across the plate of ganache, floating in a sea of raspberry coulis and cream, which he was sharing with Elsie. He had secured them a table tucked in the corner of their favourite restaurant in Bath.

'We don't often get to come here in the evening, these days. I like it noisy and bustling. More French, somehow.'

'You're right, Ron. We should come more often. We're getting lazy in our old age.'

Ron sighed, put his spoon down and placed his hand over Elsie's. 'I'm afraid, love, that this might be one of the last times we're going to be able to go out with each other. I've been dreading this moment, but it looks like the end of our Saturday afternoons, as well.'

Elsie was speechless with shock. When she finally found her voice, it sounded thin and shaky. 'What do you mean, Ron? I thought you enjoyed them as much as I do.'

Ron held her hand tightly and his eyes glistened with unshed tears. 'I do, Elsie, love, I do. I wish I could continue seeing you in this way, there's nothing I want more. But it's just not going to be possible.'

'Why not? Oh, I see.' Elsie became grim. 'It's not what *you* want, is it, darling? Has this got something to do with that daughter of yours?'

'She's wearing me down. Even before the incident with Alison, she'd been going on and on about how I shouldn't be living on my own; I might have an accident; I might get ill; I don't feed myself properly.' He gave an involuntary chuckle. 'Although considering the size of me, I don't know how she can say that! Then after she called round and nearly found us in bed together, she's become convinced that I'm drifting towards senility. She's even sent some snooper from social services to "assess my caring needs".'

'What cheek!' Elsie was appalled.

'Yes, but she's determined. Her last little lad has gone off to college and she says she's got room for me. She wants me to sell up and—'

'Use the money for her own advantage, I've no doubt. Property prices in Bath are good at the moment. Your flat will make a tidy sum.'

'Yes, she's made the point it would be a good time to sell, and it is true that, with three children all in higher education, she could do with whatever I can give her. She's my only child, Elsie.'

'But you don't like her?'

'No.'

The two sat in miserable silence, the chocolate treat unfinished, unwanted.

Elsie was the first to rally. 'Who are our children to tell us what we can do and what we can't? There's a way round this. Don't give up too soon. I'll put my thinking cap on. I'm too tired and too full of rich food to think clearly this evening, but I'm not defeated, and I don't want you to be, either.'

'No, Mrs Tucker,' he said meekly and bent to kiss her fingers. 'Now I think it's time you got off home to that family off yours. Find out what they're up to.'

Stephen and Angela sat side by side on a bench on the banks of the little muddy river that gave Summerbridge its name. Every now and then, the darkness was lit by vivid shiverings of sheet lightning. The dull yellow glow of the distant street lights was their only other illumination. After promising Angela a meal out, Stephen discovered the day in Weston had made heavy inroads on his cash and what he had left was just enough for fish and chips. Angela was very understanding. Nothing had prepared her for the day, and then to spend the evening in his company as well – she would have happily shared a stale crust with him.

So they sat eating their chips, chatting about Weston, about rare breeds and Stephen's problems with the dairy, about his impending visit to the Merfields and, of course, about the Merlin Players.

'It was chaos without you there on Thursday, Stephen. Honestly, I think if *you* left, then *I* wouldn't want to stay. Ooh, look at that! Isn't it weird the way the whole sky is lit up, just for a moment, but there's no sound? Does it mean we're going to have a storm?'

'Not necessarily. We could do with the weather breaking, though. The ground is that parched, there's hardly any new grass coming through.'

Stephen was no longer fretting about the event and the question of its legality. He'd no intention of going to it himself – he couldn't think of anything he'd rather do less – and if it *was* illegal, he couldn't stop it even if he wanted to, so he had relaxed and was enjoying himself in Angela's company. In spite of the years he had known her, they had not really spent much time together that was not locked into some Merlin Players activity or other. Taking her to Weston-super-Mare had been a decision made on the spur of the moment, but it had turned out very successfully. She and Jenny had got on well and when they had finally parted, Jenny had invited Angela to join the family for Sunday lunch before they had to go off to the afternoon rehearsal.

'Do you know, Angela, after you told me about Thursday, there was one part of me that thought it'd be brilliant if neither you nor me went to Sunday's rehearsal.'

She turned and stared at him.

'I just think they take us for granted, Ange, and it wouldn't do them no harm to see just how much we do.'

'Don't you enjoy it any more?' she asked, her voice small with anxiety.

'Yes, yes I do, don't get me wrong. I'm not talkin' about givin' it up. I just would like to be appreciated a bit more, that's all. And you. It makes my blood boil the way Mrs P treats you, sometimes.'

'Does it?' Angela murmured happily.

'Yeah. It'd be no good if I didn't turn up, 'cos they'd make you work harder – look what happened on Thursday. So we'd both have to skive.'

'Shall we go and visit an ostrich farm?'

It was his turn to stare at her. This was unexpected; she was normally so timid, so responsible.

He grinned in the dark. 'Shall we?'

'I don't think you're taking this seriously enough.' Hugh Lester's voice was getting shrill with indignation, and he threw himself forward in the armchair in which he had been lounging when he first made the call, nudging a small coffee table and splashing coffee over the floor. 'I phone you up with news of an illegal rave taking place outside our village and all you can say is you've made a note of my complaint! Don't you know what goes on at these raves? Illegal substances of every variety, underage drinking, that's what, quite apart from the noise ...'

'Give me the phone,' hissed Veronica, putting down her glass of cognac and crossing the sitting room to take the receiver from

Hugh. Putting on her most imperious voice, she addressed the bored policeman at the other end of the line. 'Good evening, officer, Veronica Lester here. I'm a Justice of the Peace. I think the Chief Constable would take a very dim view of no action being taken against this rave. You must be aware that we have a zero tolerance policy towards drugs and underage drinking, quite apart from ... oh, you have. Good. And they're on their way ... they're there already. Excellent! Thank you. Good night.' She put the phone down, looking very smug. 'Sometimes being a JP has its advantages. Let's go. I wouldn't miss this for the world!'

Stephen drove into the yard a second behind Elsie. She had got out of her car and was listening intently to something. When Stephen turned his engine off, he could hear it too, a deep, electronic throbbing. She fixed him with such a stare that he didn't need the shuddering light from the lightning, still periodically illuminating the sky, to tell him that there was no escape.

'Well, Stephen, perhaps you would be so good as to tell me why there are so many cars using Weasel Lane and what that noise is?'

In the same way he had taken a gamble with Jeff, Stephen decided to come clean with his grandmother. Sitting in the kitchen, over a cup of tea, he told her how close they had come to disaster and how this event, however much she and Jenny might disapprove, would keep the bank off their backs for another month and save his dairy from closure.

After a long silence, Elsie looked up. 'Thank you for being so honest with me. You're a good boy. There's a lot of your grandfather in you. I accept that necessity makes strange bedfellows, but if you're going to put Marsh Farm back on track in a serious way, this sort of activity has got to stop, and that's something you've got to make clear to Charlie.'

Charlie, his heart racing, arrived at the entrance to the site in time to see Hugh Lester, in a large Range Rover, shouting at a policeman standing by the side of the vehicle. 'What d'yer mean, move on? You should be closing this down! It's totally against the law – I phoned a short while ago. I was assured you were taking action.'

Veronica, sitting at his side, caught sight of Charlie. 'There is – arrest him! He's the owner of this field. He's responsible for this. Arrest him, officer!'

A stab of lightning and almost simultaneous crash of thunder drowned the policeman's reply, and Charlie, his heart sinking to the soles of his boots, thought he was well and truly for it. As the occupants of the Range Rover seemed to find it hard to understand what he was saying, the policeman repeated himself, loudly and clearly.

'Move on, please, sir. My instructions are to keep this entrance free of all obstructions. What this gentleman does with these fields is his own affair. Unless you've a ticket, or business on site, you've no business here.'

Snarling, protesting, with Veronica shrieking in outrage, Hugh stalled the engine. As two burly policemen leaped forward to push the offending vehicle out of the entrance to the field, Charlie, in sheer relief, threw back his head and hooted with laughter, gave his neighbour an exaggerated V sign and sauntered back onto the site, feeling better than he'd felt for weeks.

Hugh's humiliation didn't quite finish there. Before he was allowed to retreat, one of the policeman asked him to get out of the car. 'It's just that I can smell alcohol on your breath, sir, so if you wouldn't mind coming with me for a moment ...'

Knowing that they planned to visit the site and witness the Tuckers' humiliation at the hands of the police, he had, in fact, drunk very little that evening. Nevertheless, it was with nervous dread that Hugh blew into the bag. He registered just under the limit, but his humiliation at having to undergo the process at all left him raging. He blamed the Tuckers and swore, as he drove home, that he would not rest until he saw them leave Marsh Farm, destitute.

18

The same crack of thunder that had silenced the policeman momentarily startled Al and Alison, who were lying entwined under a hedge in a corner of the stubble field furthest away from the tents. The heat, the urgent throbbing of the music, and the growing intensity with which they had clung and swayed together as they danced, had fanned the flames of desire to such a point they had finally slipped away to join an indeterminate number of couples who had also abandoned the dance floor for a spot of amorous activity in the anonymity of the dark.

Their kissing had become increasingly passionate, when Al broke off and sat up. Alison lay on the ground looking up at him silhouetted against a troubled night sky. He looked down at her. 'Well?' His voice was thick, as though he found it hard to speak.

'Well what?'

'Do you want to go on?'

'Oh, Al ...' She sighed deeply. The moment she had dreamed of had finally arrived. She knew, but didn't know, and was puzzled and mortified by her indecision.

'I know.' He spoke gruffly. 'I realise it'd be the first time for you and I don't want you to ... unless you do. It'd make no difference to the way I feel about you, Ali. I really want to make love to you, but I'm prepared to wait, if that's the way you want it.'

A flash of lightning briefly, starkly, illuminated both them and the whole surrounding hedgerow. Alison groaned. Her groin throbbed and her back arched involuntarily, thrusting her breasts forward, longing for his touch. She put out her hand and touched his erection.

'Please, Al,' she whispered, 'please …'

A violent crack of thunder went unnoticed as he bent over her, slipping his hand under her boob tube, pulling it up and exposing her breasts, small and round, the nipples hard and erect. His other hand slid up her skirt and under the edge of her pants; his fingers parted her pubic hair and found her pulsating, sexual core.

A vivid streak of lightning skeetered across the sky as Alison, fumbling, undid his belt and moved her hand down to touch shyly, for the first time, his warm, hard penis.

He groaned deeply and started to remove her underwear. She had just managed to pull his jeans over his backside when the skies opened. The rainfall was vertical, heavy, unremitting, and unlike the thunder and lightning, could not be ignored. Within seconds, they were drenched.

The interruption was violent. Distracted, shrieking with shock, the sexual frustration racing around their bodies like electricity trying to find earth, they pulled their clothes back on and laughing hysterically, ran back, hand in hand, to the shelter of the nearest marquee.

Pushing into the crowded, hot interior, they came face to face with Paula and Lenny. Paula's eyes widened with shock.

'Alison, I didn't realise … blimey … you and Anthony … I'd never 'ave guessed.'

'Hello, Paula,' said Al, without enthusiasm.

Without any warning, it seemed to Alison, she had passed into a strange dimension of time and space. The overwhelming throb of the speakers drowned all sensation; conversation was conducted at the edge of audibility: nuance, all subtlety, was a waste of time, and her brain was so numbed, everything she heard and perceived seemed to take place in slow motion.

'I never expected to see you here, Anthony. I never put two and two together … you and Alison …' Paula shrieked.

'What are you talkin' about, woman?' Lenny shouted in Paula's ear. 'What's it to you who Ali goes out with? How do you know this bloke, anyway? *I've* never seen him before.'

'He's Anthony Lester, you great ape. He's Veronica's son; I've known him since he was ten – and it turns out he's Ali's mysterious biker boyfriend! I'd never've guessed.'

'How very sweet,' bellowed Lenny. 'Come on, darlin'. I like this number; let's go strut our stuff!' And the crowd swallowed them up before another word could be uttered.

Alison stared at Al, the blood draining from her face, her body, leaving her shaking and weak.

'You're Anthony Lester?'

'Yes.' Al immediately guessed from the strain in her voice that something was wrong. Her long blonde hair, dripping with rain, clung to her face, emphasising the wildness in her huge green eyes as she stood staring at him. 'What's wrong, Ali?'

'Why did you say your name was Al?'

'That's what my friends call me. I don't like the name Anthony. Never have; so when I went away to school, they put my initials together and called me Al. My parents are the only people to call me Anthony.'

Alison backed away to the entrance of the tent. The rain was a solid curtain beyond. Thunder rumbled and cracked. Tears started to stream down her face. Distressed, puzzled, Al put out a hand to comfort her.

'Don't touch me!' She screamed so loudly, she topped the output of loudspeakers and storm combined. A few people, gazing out of the marquee at the rain, turned and stared.

'Ali, what is it? What's the matter? What the fuck does it matter if my name is really Anthony?'

'What the fuck does it matter?' she shrieked back at him. 'You're fuckin' Hugh and Veronica fuckin' Lester's son – that's what matters. They're gonna destroy us, however they can; and they probably will because they've got money and influence and we've got nothing, except this snivellin' little farm, which means everything to us. But they don't care, oh no. They want it, so they'll get it – their sort always do – and you're one of them and I very nearly gave you what you wanted. I was about to sleep with the enemy – give you my ...' She hiccupped with anger and misery. 'I thought you cared about me. How bloody stupid can you get! The Lesters don't care about anything, except getting what they want.'

Confused by the turn of events, Al started to get angry himself. 'What are you talking about, Alison? It's fucking rubbish—'

'Is it? Is it? I don't believe you don't know who I am. I don't believe you didn't think it would be a bit of a laugh to screw me at the same time your parents are screwing my family. I hate you, Anthony Lester – go boil your head in hell!'

And so saying she turned, ran out of the tent and disappeared into the darkness and the torrential rain.

It was still raining hard nearly twelve hours later, but Jenny, happily bustling around the kitchen, hardly noticed. Jeff had dropped her off earlier with a bagful of groceries, promising to return for the lunch she was now busily preparing.

The house seemed unusually quiet, but as Alison had spent the night with Hannah and she presumed both Stephen and Charlie were busy about the farm, Jenny was not worried. In fact she was quite glad there was no one about to witness her late return, to see Jeff kiss her goodbye, or to notice the fact that Jenny, today, was a very different person from Jenny, yesterday. She felt she was about to burst with happiness, but she wasn't ready yet to share it with anyone, not even Rita.

Charlie, suddenly poking his head round the kitchen door, didn't notice anything different. 'Oh, hi, Mum. I'm gonna give lunch a miss today. Lin's a bit short-staffed so I said I'd give her a hand. I'll catch something to eat at the pub. I'll see you later. Bye.' And not giving her a chance to say anything, just in case she had caught a whiff of the event and was waiting to give him an earful, he was gone.

*

The onset of the storm, far from being a disaster, had delighted the event's organisers. As Dark Glasses explained when he counted out the money owing to Charlie, virtually all the punters who were going to come, had arrived, and the rain meant they didn't hang on till the last possible moment, which made the clearing up operation swift and efficient.

'Nice doing business with you.' Charlie had never had so much money in his possession before and although he knew most of it was destined elsewhere, for that particular moment he felt exhilarated. 'You planning any more of these ... these events?'

'Not around here. We'll be in touch when we do. It's a good site.'

'The fuzz ...' Charlie was curious. 'Gave me a nasty turn when I saw them.'

'Look, mate, the days of those sort of parties are over. It's strictly legit. These days we get a temporary licence and we pay the fuzz for their policing. It's in all our interests to keep it quiet – reduces the risk of gatecrashers, bikers, druggies, all those undesirable elements, as well as complaints from people like your neighbours.'

As Charlie drove his van through the pouring rain to The Grapes, the expression on Hugh Lester's face when the police had ordered him to move on, floated across his thoughts. He chortled aloud. 'One up to the Tuckers!'

Linda looked tired and pale when she opened the door to him and Charlie, who was not by nature very sensitive, felt a strange mixture of sympathy and protectiveness. She was one of his oldest friends. In his opinion she deserved better than this. He put his arm round her. 'Come on, Lin,' he said gently. 'You tell me what to do and I'll do it. And then – only if you want to, that is – then you can tell me how things are with Stan.'

A short while later, at Marsh Farm, the kitchen door opened again and Stephen ushered Angela in. They were both drenched from the short run from the yard to the house. Angela looked like a half-drowned mouse, thought Jenny to herself, with her hair plastered to her head and rivulets of water running down her cheeks and down her specs. Stephen fussed around her and, finding a towel, vigorously rubbed her head, in much the same manner, Jenny thought, as he would dry Gip, his dog.

Angela glowed, and watching her, the 'new' Jenny recognised the symptoms. 'She really loves him,' she thought. 'She's just what Stephen needs. Jeff's wrong about her. Such a nice little girl …' And she sighed to herself, thinking of Nicola and Stephen.

'It won't be long till dinner,' she said brightly. 'I've got the meat on. Just the veggies to do. Uncle Jeff is coming, too,' she added as casually as she could, acutely aware of how unnatural her voice sounded.

Stephen didn't notice. 'That's nice. Did you stay there last night?'

It was all Jenny could do to nod.

'That's good. Ange and I will give you a hand with the veg, if you like. I'm afraid we'll have to shoot off straight after, Mum.'

'For the rehearsal. It's going to be the first run without scripts,' piped up Angela.

'We weren't goin' to go …'

'We thought they could manage without us …'

'We were goin' to visit an ostrich farm that Ange had found …'

'But with this rain …'

'It's not worth it …'

'We can go another time, can't we, Stephen?'

'First bit of clear weather, Ange.' And he smiled at her.

Jenny stared. Something was different about them, too.

Alison lay on her bed, dry eyed, staring at the ceiling. For hours she had stormed and wept, then a deep lassitude overcame her. She didn't want to see or speak to anyone. She had turned her phone off and locked her bedroom door. Headphones on, the music thudded in her ears, the lyrics irrelevant and unheeded, an effective sound barrier between her and the outside world.

Her mind still churned over the events of the night before,

the revelation of Al's identity and all the implications; all the different times they had spent together; what he had said; what she had felt ... There were moments when she felt she might have been too hasty in her judgement – he genuinely might not have known who she was ... After all, until bumping into Paula, she'd had no idea who he was or where he came from. But then she would scold herself out of this softer train of thought by reminding herself that he knew Nick and Hannah, and *they* would have had no hesitation about filling him in on her details. 'He must have been laughing up his sleeve, watching me swoon all over him, the wanker!' she said aloud, bitterly.

The track on her CD came to an end and in the interval between that and the next, she became aware of a knocking on her door.

'Ali? Ali? Are you in there?'

It was her mother. Reluctantly, wearily, Alison pulled off her headphones, sat up and tried to sound as normal as possible.

'Yes, Mum, what is it?'

'I thought you were still over at Hannah's, dear.'

'I came back early. Party was boring.'

'I'm sorry to hear that, love, and you was so looking forward to it. Hannah's on the phone now. She says she's tried your mobile but you've got it switched off.'

'Tell her I'll phone her back later.'

'Won't you come and have some lunch? It's on the table.'

'No thanks, Mum, I'm not hungry.'

'Uncle Jeff's here.'

'I'm not hungry.'

'You must eat something, dear.'

Motherly concern – Alison would have sworn if she'd had the energy. 'I'm all *right*. I'll eat later.'

'I'll save you some meat and veg, then. Ange, Stephen's friend, has made some lovely-looking roast potatoes.'

Alison gritted her teeth. 'I'll have some later, Mum, please!'

'All right, love. Oh, Gran says you're planning to take her to Simon's for tea this afternoon? That'll be nice.'

Alison cursed. She had completely forgotten the arrangement, and in this mood, the last thing she wanted to do was see Simon. Or her Gran, for that matter. She hunted for an excuse, a reason to cancel. They would spot something was wrong and the last thing she wanted to do was to have to explain anything.

She was saved, temporarily, by Jeff, at the bottom of the stairs, shouting for Jenny to come and eat her lunch before it got cold.

'Must go, dear; Jeff's calling me. We're going to the cinema this afternoon, so I'll leave you some food in the oven.'

Alison listened to her mother's footsteps receding down the stairs, then turned to the window and stared at the rain cascading down the panes. How different everything was from yesterday.

She couldn't remember ever having felt so flat and miserable. And she had been so looking forward to the time when Simon should meet her Gran and they would plot against the dastardly Lesters. The bastards ... the bastard! A lick of anger at the thought of how near ... of how she'd been conned, brought a flush of colour to her face. She clenched her fists, ground her teeth and growled.

She'd show them!

Lunch at Summerstoke House was a bad-tempered affair. Both Veronica and Hugh blamed the other for the humiliations of the night before. Veronica's ill-humour had been further exacerbated by not being able to get hold of Simon since last Thursday, to fix another tennis date. The more she thought about him, the more she wanted him and the more frustrated she became at the lack of contact – and the more irritating she found Hugh and the rest of her family.

Cordelia was sulking because the unexpected change in the weather meant that a planned ride and picnic had been called off, and Anthony, apparently deaf to the exhortations of his mother, had not come down to join them, which further added to the tension at the table. And in the kitchen, Paula, who had arrived very late that morning to clear up after Veronica's dinner party of the night before, clattered and banged her way resentfully through the piles of pots and pans.

'Why can't we have Sunday lunches like everyone else?' complained Cordelia, trailing her spoon through her soup.

'What do you mean?' snapped Veronica.

'I like roast meat and vegetables. That's Sunday lunch. Not soup and cheese. It's boring!'

'If I spend Saturday evening slaving over a dinner party, I don't want to spend Sunday morning cooking a roast dinner, thank you, miss!'

'Stop playing with your food, Cordelia. Be thankful for what you've got,' Hugh growled. 'Does Paula have to make so much of a bloody racket?'

'She's in a mood – says she didn't get much sleep last night.'

'She's not the only one. Do you know what time Anthony came in?'

'No, but I've no doubt you're going to tell me. Cordelia, Anthony should be here. It's virtually our last meal together before he's off to France. Go and bang on his door, would you?'

'Do I have to?'

'For goodness' sake,' Hugh exploded, 'why do you make such heavy weather of anything you're asked to do? Go and fetch your brother. Now!'

With bad grace, Cordelia left the table, passing Paula on her way out of the room.

'What is it?' Veronica was in no frame of mind to humour Paula.

'It's Lenny,' Paula said sulkily. 'You said you wanted to speak to him, Mr Lester. He's waitin' in the kitchen.'

'I wanted to speak to him two weeks ago!'

'He's bin busy with the harvest. But with this rain, he thought he'd take advantage and pop up to see you. Still, if you don't want to see him, I'll tell him—'

'You bloody well do that. Who does he think he is? Farting about with my time. I'm a busy man, Paula, and—'

'Tell Lenny to wait in the study, Paula. Mr Lester will see him in a few minutes.' With a glare at Hugh, Veronica silenced any further objections on his part until Paula had left the room.

'I don't want to employ that man!' Hugh snarled. 'He's given me the runaround and I don't like it!'

'I know, I know,' replied Veronica, soothingly, 'but it doesn't alter the fact that he is important to us.' She didn't notice her son, a haggard shadow, standing in the doorway. 'You said last night you wanted to see the Tuckers on their knees. If we're to get Marsh Farm, we have to keep the squeeze on. Offer Lenny Spinks double his current rate on condition he doesn't work for anyone else. He'll jump at it. His sort always do. It will be the last straw, I guarantee it. The bank has already hauled them in and imposed conditions on their loan they won't possibly be able to meet. Gordon personally put the noose around their necks. He told me as much the other day. The Tuckers will not be able to meet their repayments, so, with or without the Merfields' meadows, they're done for. Helped, my darling,' Veronica was positively purring, 'by a little call I made the other day.'

'Who to?' Hugh smiled, his bad mood melting in the face of his wife's ruthlessness.

'To the local Dairy Hygiene Inspector. I told them the Tuckers were having problems with their milking parlour and were struggling to keep the dairy up to scratch. They took it *very* seriously.'

'God, darling, you're brilliant!'

'Brilliant is not a word I'd have used.' Anthony finally made his presence known.

Veronica looked up at her son. He was leaning against the doorframe, as if the effort of standing without support was too much for him. His face was startlingly white, his eyes dark and sunken.

'Darling, you look ghastly! Why on earth did you stay out so late last night? You look exhausted. Come and have something to eat.'

Anthony shook his head. 'No thank you. I think the food would choke me.'

The venom in his voice disconcerted both of his parents. Nobody noticed the kitchen door open and Paula appear, about to show Lenny to Hugh's study. She froze, motioning Lenny to remain silent as Anthony raised his voice.

'Tell me, Mum, Dad, why do you want the Tuckers' land? We have so much already. Why do you want their tin pot little farm? From what I heard you say, Mum, you are stooping to really devious measures to get it. Why?'

Hugh started to bluster. 'Come now, Anthony, you shouldn't talk to your mother like that. It's business, not devious at all.'

'All we are trying to do is expand, darling.' Veronica sensed confrontation was imminent. 'We want to develop a stud, but without more land that's just not going to be possible. Marsh Farm is the only viable proposition.'

'It's failing; the Tuckers are hopeless farmers; they'd be glad to sell—' Hugh ignored Vee's signals for restraint.

'But from what you said, you're setting out to make sure they fail,' Anthony stormed on, his face still livid, his eyes flashing with anger. 'I didn't believe it. Even knowing you, I didn't believe it … and I was wrong. You're rotten to the core, both of you. You have everything and yet you want more and you don't care who you hurt or destroy in the process.'

'You don't know what you're saying!' Hugh jumped up and bawled, 'You ungrateful little tyke! In the long run, you'll benefit—'

Simultaneously, Veronica stood up and chimed in, trying a different tack. 'Darling, the Tuckers aren't worth fretting over. They're peasants – they'd be as happy in a council house—'

'What do you know about people like the Tuckers? You've never made any effort to find out. You just set about destroying people's lives without bothering to know the first thing about them. Greedy! Avaricious! That's what you are.' Veronica put out a hand towards him. He looked at her contemptuously. 'And don't pretend you're doing it for me, that you care about me. You don't. The only thing you care about is what you want, then doing whatever you can to make sure you get it and bugger the rest of the world!'

Hugh pushed his chair over with a crash and lurched at his son, bellowing, 'Apologise! By God, apologise!'

But Anthony ran back up to the staircase, ignoring his father's shouts and his mother's cries of 'Anthony, come back; you don't understand ...'

In the middle of the pandemonium, the telephone started to ring.

'Answer that, Paula, and tell whoever it is we're busy and we'll ring back later,' snapped Veronica. 'Hugh, calm down. Let me deal with this.'

Paula left Lenny standing by the kitchen door, crossed the hall to pick up the phone, and delivered Veronica's message to the caller – Mrs Merfield – making no effort to shield the receiver from the sound of Hugh, who had dashed into the hall and was bellowing up the stairs for Anthony to come down and apologise. Veronica had followed and was doing her best to calm him down, to no avail. Paula replaced the phone and went back to join Lenny at the kitchen door, with a smirk.

Moments later Anthony reappeared, his leather jacket half on, and a bulging rucksack over his arm. Attracted by the noise, Cordelia came out of her room.

'Why's everyone shouting? I've got a headache. Anthony, you're not going already, are you?'

Anthony ignored her and started down the stairs. Veronica, standing at the bottom and looking up at him, made a huge effort to bring the situation back under her control. 'Darling, what *are* you getting so upset about? I don't know what you thought you overheard, but really, it was nothing!'

Anthony stopped in his tracks and regarded his mother with lip-curling contempt. 'Nothing? Bribing Lenny Spinks is nothing? Bad-mouthing the Tuckers' dairy in an effort to close it down, is nothing? Somehow getting the bank to put pressure on them, is nothing – Gordon, who's Gordon? Some tame little bank clerk you've flattered with your sexual favours?'

With a howl, Hugh rushed at his son brandishing his fists, but Anthony, rapidly descending the last few stairs, punched back, hitting him in the face and sending him sprawling at Veronica's feet. With a shriek, she went to Hugh's aid.

He opened the front door to a vertical sheet of rain, paused for a moment and turned to address his parents, who were shouting at each other and him. There was such vitriol in his voice, both Hugh and Veronica fell silent, and Paula, watching in the background, involuntarily clutched Lenny's arm.

'It's as well I'm going to France tomorrow. I'm not coming back. I'll send you my address in Durham. If you want to send anything on, that's fine. If not, burn it all. I don't care. I'm ashamed of you. I'm ashamed of myself. You're poison and you've poisoned me, and everything I care about!' As he turned to leave, he suddenly had a clear image of Alison about to disappear into a curtain of rain, staring at him, the tears streaming down her cheeks. 'Go boil your heads in hell,' he said, a sob welling up from deep within his breast.

The door slammed and he was gone. Moments later they heard the motorbike burst into life and the throbbing engine fading rapidly into the distance until they could hear it no more. For a moment they stood, frozen.

'Blimey!' said Paula.

'Bloody 'ell!' said Lenny. 'What was all that about, then, eh?'

'That's it, Ange – spread your arms out and shout at 'em. Give 'em a good slap if they try to get past. You're doin' great. Come on! Come on, girls! Come on yer stubborn ol' things ... Come on!'

Standing on the edge of the riverbank, up to her knees in swirling brown water, trying to herd Stephen's cows to the safety of higher ground, Angela had never been so wet. About to leave for the Merlin Players rehearsal, Stephen thought he had better check on a small herd of cows that were grazing in a field next to the river on the Summerstoke side.

'They're in between milking, so I ain't seen them today and what with the storm and this non-stop rain ... It'll only take a couple of minutes, and I'd just like to know they're okay.'

But the cows were far from okay. The river had broken its banks and they were marooned on a patch of higher ground. Refusing to stay in the shelter of the Land Rover, Angela had found an old Mackintosh and a pair of wellingtons, far too big for her, in the back and had gone to help Stephen dismantle the electric fence that confined the cows to one section of the field, and then had waded with him through the muddy water to try and herd the frightened, stubborn creatures to safety.

'Come on, old girl!' she shouted, trying to imitate Stephen's tone. 'Move on there!' And she slapped the sodden rump of the nearest cow. Uncomfortable though she might be, she was ridiculously happy, and not for one moment would she have exchanged the discomfort of their situation for the warmth and dry of the rehearsal room.

Slowly, lowing loudly to emphasise their displeasure, the cows started to move. Angela could scarcely see anything through her rain-spattered glasses, but she heard the relief in Stephen's voice as he shouted, 'They're shiftin'! Great stuff, Ange, keep 'em goin' but watch their backs. Don't get too close ...'

Too late. A cow suddenly stopped and backed into Angela. She was sent flying and landed, with a squelching splash, on her back in the marshy shallows of the flood, her boots flying off in different directions.

'Ange, Ange, are you all right?' Stephen was by her side in seconds and pulled her to her feet.

Drenched through and now muddy from tip to toe, the water swirling over her ankle socks, Angela smiled mistily up at him. 'I'm fine, Stephen, really. Don't worry about me. Stay with the cows.'

'Oh they're all right; they're on the move. You've been brilliant. I couldn't have managed without you.'

Angela, retrieving her boots, blushed with happiness. 'Anyone would have done the same.'

'No they wouldn't.' Stephen looked at her seriously. 'They wouldn't 'ave, Ange. You're one in a million.' He suddenly broke off, looking alarmed. 'Oh my God!'

'What is it? What's wrong?'

'Come on, we'll secure the electric fence — the girls'll be safe up here — then we'd better get over to the Manor. Look at the way that water is spreadin' ... If we don't alert everyone, the whole of Lower Summerstoke could be under water and the Manor will be the first to get it.'

So it was that the youngest Miss Merfield, staring out at the rain, saw a battered Land Rover career through the gateway, screech to a halt and two bedraggled figures jump out.

She had barely time to murmur to her sisters, 'A diversion, what fun!' when the thunderous sound of the knocker reverberated throughout the house. Nanny's voice could be heard, reproving at first, then silenced by the urgency of the other voice. The sitting-room door opened and Nanny came in. Following behind her in the hall, the ladies could see Stephen and Angela, dripping onto the polished flagstone floor. Stephen's face was ruddy with anxiety and embarrassment. His hair, dark with the rain, clung to his somewhat chubby features, and his large red hands, hanging by his side, opened and closed nervously. He towered over the diminutive creature by his side, who was in a similar waterlogged state, wearing an outsized mac and boots, blinking across at the ladies through a pair of huge spectacles. Signalling for them to stay where they were, Nanny addressed Mrs Merfield. 'It's Mr Tucker, ma'am. He says the river is rising fast, the meadows are flooding and we could be next.'

Mrs Merfield rose to the occasion.

The Manor had been flooded before, and after the last occasion, some ten years ago, a good supply of sandbags had been stored in the cellar. 'The only thing is,' she explained to Stephen, 'I know they are terribly heavy, and I doubt if my sisters and I could lift them.'

Stephen looked at the frail old ladies and at tiny Angela. 'No, Mrs Merfield, you couldn't.' Overcoming his shyness, the urgency of the situation made Stephen decisive in a way that would have surprised his family. 'We must get some help. A bit of phone bashing is what we need. If you can ring round, Mrs Merfield, please, and explain the situation, people'll help out. We need to alert the lower part of the village in any event, 'cos the flood's heading their way. I'll get hold of my brother, Charlie. He can drum up a few of his mates. Meantime, p'raps you should take some of the lighter things up to the next floor. Ange'll help. I'll go and make a start on those sandbags.'

'I'm coming with you, Stephen. You can't do it by yourself.' Angela moved determinedly to his side, bedraggled and shivering.

He shook his head and put his arm around her thin shoulders. 'No. It'll be too much for you. Besides, you're soaked through. I don't want you to catch your death. You stay here and help Mrs Merfield.'

'The first thing your young lady's going to do is take those things off and put something dry on,' said Nanny firmly. 'Come along, my dear.' She took Angela by the hand. 'Your fellah's right and we best get a move on. We've got a lot to do!'

Outside, staring through the downpour across the lawns, Stephen could make out the spumey tendrils of the water, still at some distance, but creeping closer. He had tried Charlie's mobile without success, then Lenny's, with the same result. In desperation he phoned Marsh Farm. Alison answered and he filled her in.

Jeff had already left with Jenny for the cinema, but Alison said she would phone around and then come over herself. Making his way back to the cellar, Stephen reflected that he was beginning to see his sister in a different light; her readiness to help was in stark contrast to the absence of his older brother who was, he thought, probably still at the pub. Hoping help would come soon, he started to heave the sandbags out.

Mrs Merfield sat by the phone and made a succession of calls. When she had finished, she went to the basement and reported her results to Stephen. 'My great-nephew will be here shortly. Fortunately he has a friend staying who has volunteered, too. Mr Featherstone at the Forester's Arms is sending two of his staff.

The vicar has a heart condition, but has promised to try and drum up more support. I tried the fire brigade, but they said they were very sorry, they are fully occupied. At least we've got sandbags, they said, and they should hold the water at bay for a while. They will get here when they can.'

'Did you try Hugh Lester? He could send some of his men.'

Mrs Merfield's voice became cold. 'I tried, but was told they were busy and would phone back later.'

Within a short time, much to his surprise, Stephen was joined by Simon and another man, who was introduced to him as Marcus.

Then Alison turned up. 'I can't get hold of Uncle Jeff,' she told Stephen. 'He must have turned his mobile off in the cinema. But four or five of my mates are on the way. Oh hello, Simon.' She was even more surprised than Stephen had been to see Simon, staggering from the depths of the cellar, carrying a sandbag. 'What are you doing here?'

'My aunt sent out an SOS.' Simon grinned. 'So I had to stop making the chocolate cake we're having for tea and ride to the rescue.'

'Mrs Merfield's your aunt?'

'My great aunt, to be exact. I don't think you can lift these sandbags, Alison, but see if you can get hold of a wheelbarrow and then you can trundle them into position. You'll find my mate, Marcus, outside, putting them in place.'

Within the space of half an hour, Alison's friends had arrived, a cheerful group of teenage boys in leather and denim, sporting nose rings, earrings and shaven heads, the sort of lads whom the Merfield ladies would normally have crossed the other side of the road to avoid. Three kitchen staff from the pub also turned up. A chain gang was formed and the bulky sandbags were moved swiftly from the cellar to the outside. By the time the water started filtering through the rose garden and onto the terrace, every sack was in place and every possible entry point into the house blocked.

19

The vicar might have had a heart condition (which was why, as he had explained to puzzled friends, he, with all his intellectual abilities, had been content to settle in a backwater like Summerstoke) but deep down he saw himself as a man of action as well as a man of God, and this man of action was deeply bored. Guiltily, he had prayed for something exciting to happen, something to lighten his days, dull days spent listening to the litany of woes his parishioners knew he was helpless to do anything about.

Therefore, when he heard of the impending flood, he was secretly thrilled. Visions of marooned villagers rose before his eyes: children calling for rescue from first-floor windows, families gathered on rooftops, old Mrs Long floating by on an upturned table. It was his duty to save them if he could!

Fired by the challenge, he startled his churchwardens with a firmness of purpose he had never displayed before. He ordered the church bells to ring the alarm, despatched the wardens to warn those living in Lower Summerstoke of the danger, and rang the fire brigades of Wiltshire and Somerset. Unlike Mrs Merfield, he was not to be fobbed off with promises of 'later' and peremptorily brushed aside any question of delay. They had to come immediately, bringing sandbags, ladders, pumps and 'those silver foil hypothermia bag-things to wrap the victims of the elements in.'

Thus it was that Paula, hurrying down the High Street in the drenching rain, wondering why on earth the church bells were making such a racket, stopped in amazement at the sight of four fire engines (two from each county – both would have sent more, but the service really *was* stretched that afternoon). She joined a small group of villagers standing under their umbrellas watching the action.

'Bloomin' 'eck. What's goin' on?' she asked Rita Godwin.

'It's the river, Paula. It's flooding. You better get on home. Who's looking after your kiddies?'

'Me mum, till I get back. But Lenny'll be there. He should've got back half an hour ago. Oh, bloomin' 'eck!' And she ran as fast as her four-inch heels would allow.

She turned down the garden path, shaking her head at a group of locals who had gathered on the bridge to watch the rising waters. 'Last place I'd stand to watch a flood. Supposin' those arches gave way – they'd be for it!'

As yet, there was no sign of the flood in her garden, apart from the huge puddles of rain forming on the broken path, but from an upstairs window she heard her mother shout, 'Up here, Paula, we're up here. Quick, before you're swept away! I've got the kiddies safe.'

She found her mother sitting in the main bedroom in a state of nervous collapse, clutching a teapot and the kettle. Far from being frightened, her four little children were rushing excitedly between the three rooms, jumping, in turn, on each of the beds to check which would make the best boat on which to sail away when the house was flooded.

'What's goin' on, Mum? Quiet, you kids. How many times have I told you not to jump on the beds? Where's Lenny?'

'It's a flood, Paula. This man came bangin' at the door. Said the vicar said we was to put sandbags out, then take our valuables upstairs. I couldn't find no sandbags; leastways nothing to put the sand in – the kiddies' sandpit is nearly empty – so I grabbed the kettle and teapot and come upstairs.'

'We ain't got no sandbags, Mum. Don't be daft. Where's Lenny? Why ain't he here?'

'He come in about half an hour ago, got a call on his mobile and said he had to go. Didn't say what it was. Said he was needed, urgent, but he wouldn't be long.'

'He better not be, 'cos he's needed here, urgent. I'll just zip downstairs and pick up one or two other things.'

Over her mum's moans not to be too long and not to take any chances, Paula rushed downstairs, rescued the copy of her favourite Joan Collins movie, *Tales from the Crypt*, grabbed the bottle of Jack Daniels that Lenny had been given for his work by the event people, a carton of milk, some teabags, a large bottle of Coke and a jumbo pack of crisps for the kids, and then dashed back upstairs to await the arrival of the flood.

'Thanks, Charlie.' Linda turned out the bar lights. 'Thanks for everything, this afternoon. You've been great. I owe you.'

'No you don't. It's what friends is for,' said Charlie gruffly. 'And I meant what I said, Lin: I'll be here whenever you need me. I enjoy this bar lark and I can do any humping and fixing you need.'

'You've got enough to do already. Don't worry. I'll look out for a temporary barman until Stan and I decide what to do about the pub. I shall be sorry to see The Grapes go, though. I like the life, but I can't afford to get a place on me own and no brewery is going to employ a single mum.'

'What you need is a partner to buy Stan out.'

Linda smiled wanly. 'If only – they don't grow on trees.'

'Maybe not. But don't give up.' He gave her a brief hug. 'I'll be back this evening.'

About to let himself out, he hesitated and turned to her, 'Lin, do you mind if I ask your advice about something?'

'Of course not. You've been saying all afternoon that's what friends are for.'

'Yeah, I know, but this sounds … well, a bit silly, really, compared to what you're going through, only it's starting to bug me.'

'What is?'

'My whiskers. What do you think of them?'

Linda's face lightened and for a moment, Charlie was afraid she was going to laugh. But she didn't. 'They are magnificent, Charlie.'

'So you don't think I should get rid of them?'

'You've had those whiskers ever since we left school. You're like my little brother – as soon as he got hair growing on his face, he grew whiskers. My mum hated them, the school banned them, his girlfriend moaned, but he wouldn't shave – he thought they made him look older.'

'Yeah, right.'

'But do you need to look older, now you *are* older? As I remember, you're quite good-looking under all that hair. Perhaps it's time to see what Charlie Tucker really looks like.'

The rain lashed down as Charlie shot across to his van. Blimey, he thought to himself, wiping his face dry and staring at the windscreen teeming with water. Nothing I could do on the farm today, even if I wanted to ... He had been planning to make a start on ploughing, but the long night and then working in the bar had left him feeling tired, and he relished the fact that the rain gave him an excuse to have a kip in front of the telly instead.

Visibility was so poor, he drove back slowly, thinking about his whiskers, and about Linda and her plight. If only *he* could afford to buy Stan out. Be Linda's sleeping partner. He cackled coarsely at his pun. But then, he thought wistfully, she was a bit of all right. Stan was bloody mad to have thrown her over for a pair of big bazookas and bed-me eyes. Charlie no longer had any regrets about Beth, and contemptuously wrote them both off.

He thought of working on the farm. He thought of working in the pub. I could do both, he thought. Perhaps I should get Lin to train me as her relief barman... If only, he sighed wistfully, if only *I* could make enough money and buy Stan out.

His daydreams came to an abrupt halt when he turned off the road. Even through the deluge, the track to Marsh Farm brought the riverbank and fields on either side clearly into view and he could see that the river was in flood.

'Bloody hell!' he exclaimed aloud. 'What's caused that?' Although it had rained solidly since the night before, the summer had been long and dry and the water levels had been very low.

Even with the run-off from the hard ground, the river shouldn't have been that high. The storm must have brought a tree down, damming the river somewhere.

He abandoned his van, ran into the barn and collected the chainsaw, ropes and a chain, then jumped into a tractor. He found his mobile, turned it on and was just about to phone his brother when he remembered that Stephen always turned his phone off when he was at his rehearsals. 'Bloody Norah!' Charlie snorted in disgust and phoned Lenny, instead. Lenny, who had just got home from the Lesters, groaned, but came out immediately.

The two of them set off in the old tractor, crossed the yard, drove behind the house and bumped across an empty pasture down to the river. The rain blotted out the windscreen of the cab; the wipers had stopped working ages ago and Charlie had to peer out of his window to see where he was going, so by the time he arrived at the river's edge, his head and shoulders were already soaked. Trundling along the river's bank, keeping just clear of the edge of the flood, they crossed several fields before Lenny let out a shout and pointed. 'Over there, Charlie ... On the bend ... Bloody hell, this is gonna be some job!'

The culprit was a huge old ash that had completely upended and now straddled the river.

Leaving the tractor, Charlie and Lenny waded through the flood, which swirled ankle-deep around their boots, and stared up at the huge root ball, which was easily six foot high. Charlie was aghast and for a moment quailed at the size and difficulty of the task in front of them. 'Blimey, Lenny, you weren't wrong. Well, come on, no point in hanging about – it's not going to get any better.'

'How on earth are we gonna shift this? We can't do it by ourselves. We're gonna need help.' Lenny, completely bedraggled by now, his hair a dripping rat's tail hanging down his back, stood gaping up at the tree.

'From whom? You can try raising the fire brigade, or the Environment Agency, but by the time we get help, the river will have flooded as far back as Summerstoke. But you'd better put in a call to 'em both, while I check it out. As sure as eggs is eggs, we're gonna have to do this ourselves.'

Leaving Lenny punching numbers into his mobile from a list in the tractor cab, Charlie waded a little way upstream along the bank to get a clearer view of the tree, which straddled the river completely, with half of its branches submerged. In a short time he was joined by Lenny, shaking his head in disbelief. 'The Agency just had an answerphone; the fire brigade says they're busy – they'll come when they can, but they've got a lot of calls to deal with and it's people rather than trees that have to have priority. Morons! If this tree ain't shifted, there're gonna be a lot more people with water in their sitting rooms, includin' ...' his eyes widened with sudden shock, 'my missus and the kids. Blimey – what are we waitin' for?'

'Okay, this is what we do – see that big branch there, clear of the water? First thing we do is get a rope round that. I'll have to shimmy along the trunk, cutting off the other little branches first, so tie a length of rope to the chainsaw handle, will you, in case I drop it, and start it up for me.'

With water dripping off the end of his nose, trickling through his scalp and running down his neck, he attached one end of a rope to his waist and Lenny attached the other to the tractor. He placed a muddy boot onto Lenny's knee, then his back and climbed up onto the ball. Lenny handed him the chainsaw once he was aloft, then, straddling the trunk, Charlie slowly edged forward, cutting off the branches in his way with the chainsaw as he went.

The tree was slippery with the rain and once or twice he nearly slid off. The water churned and boiled only a few feet below and Charlie, who had absolutely no head for heights, even little ones, kept his attention grimly focused on the next branch in front of him. After what seemed eternity, but was probably only half an hour, he reached the substantial branch he had identified earlier, which was approximately halfway along the trunk. By this time he was sweating profusely, his hands were numb, and his thighs and calves were trembling convulsively with the effort of keeping himself balanced. He carefully lay the chainsaw down on the tree trunk behind him and slowly untied the rope from around his waist. Up to this point it had been his lifeline in case he fell, but now it was needed. Feeling incredibly vulnerable, he pulled at the rope until the chain that Lenny had tied to the other end was in his hand. Feeling as scared as he'd ever been in his life, he leaned forward and attached the chain securely around the branch. His heart in his mouth, still not daring to look down, he felt behind him for the chainsaw, then slowly, slowly, edged back along the trunk, occasionally snagging on the sawn-off stumps of the branches. He finally got to the top of the root ball and half jumped, half fell to the ground where he landed with a huge splash. He lay there for a moment, trembling with the effort, limp with relief, sodden and muddy, but past caring.

Lenny started the tractor. Slipping and spluttering on the sodden ground, spraying Charlie with mud, he drove the tractor downstream, pulling the trunk in the direction of the river current. Charlie could do little more than watch and guide the tractor's path until, finally, the combination of the tractor pulling and the force of the current pushing against the trunk became irresistible. The tree swung on its axis, releasing the swollen waters, which then swept through, fast and free. The flood reversed its flow, sucked back over the banks and almost immediately the water level started to fall.

Charlie weakly climbed back into the cab. He was so covered with mud he was barely recognisable.

'You're a bloody hero, Charlie Tucker,' Lenny said, gruffly.

'Thanks, Lenny.' Charlie stretched and groaned. 'I owe you a pint. See you at The Grapes, later?'

'I'm knackered. Maybe not tonight. But mate, wait, there's summat I've gotta tell you—'

'Not now. I've promised Lin I'd help her open up and if I don't get some shut-eye, like right now, I won't last five minutes.'

'Blimey, you've got some stamina – up all night, all afternoon shifting that bloomin' tree, then down at the pub for opening time. Surprised yer don't sleep there.'

*

At the Manor, sandbags in place, the workers, drenched and exhausted, gathered in the kitchen where they were served mugs of tea and thick slices of fruit cake by Nanny, aided by Elsie who had insisted on accompanying Alison. The next task was to be the evacuation of the furniture from the ground floor of the house, should the waters continue to rise.

'Where's Stephen?' Angela asked Alison anxiously.

'He's outside, keeping an eye on the water level,' Alison replied. Like everyone else, she was tired and wet. She had earned both Simon and Marcus's admiration for the way she tirelessly ferried the wheelbarrow full of sandbags from the top of the cellar steps to wherever they were needed. The urgency of the situation and the strenuous physical exercise had temporarily banished her unhappiness, but it lurked, a great, black, throbbing bruise.

Taking him a mug of tea, Angela went to find Stephen. It was still raining hard and she could just make him out on the terrace, standing at the edge of the flood, staring down at the water. She called out to him and he turned, beaming with relief. 'It's stopped, Ange. It's stopped.'

'What has?'

'The waters have stopped rising. Look, you can see from the line of sticks and foam, it's retreating.'

Angela stared in disbelief. 'But how? It's still raining hard. Why should it stop, just like that?'

All afternoon, the inhabitants of Lower Summerstoke had waited for the disaster to strike. Many had taken the vicar's advice and had pulled out sandbags lying, long forgotten, in garden sheds or garages; others had panicked and left their homes for the higher ground of Upper Summerstoke, congregating anxiously in the shelter of the church (where they found the vicar, in unusually high spirits, helping his long-suffering wife dispense tea and biscuits to the refugees); others had struggled to take television sets, DVD players and other items of inestimable value, upstairs.

When it became clear that the danger had passed and the fire crews, not having needed to hand out a single sandbag or wrap a sole shivering body in a thermal suit, had cheerfully departed (stopping on their way out of the village to have a quiet 'word' with the vicar), the ungrateful villagers, muttering darkly about 'a false alarm' and 'what a waste of a Sunday afternoon' and 'what was the vicar playing at, giving us all a fright like that?' returned to their homes, and returned their homes to rights.

Lenny, returning to his home, found Paula and his mother-in-law halfway through his bottle of Jack Daniels and shrieking with laughter at *Tales From the Crypt*.

The kitchen at the Manor was warm and convivial. A huge old white Aga popped and burped one end of the long, low-ceilinged room and was the source of the welcome heat. Gigantic cream-painted dressers lined the walls, filled with at least three different dinner services and hung with pots and pans of every description. A vast porcelain sink and wooden draining board sat under a casement window that looked out over the lawns; a long refectory table dominated the centre of the room and a battered but very comfortable assortment of armchairs were scattered around.

The danger over, Mrs Merfield, erect, gracious and utterly formidable, wanted to express her thanks to her rescue team. The staff from the Forester's Arms hadn't stayed – they were keen to get back to collect their afternoon's tips – and Alison's friends had made good their escape just in case 'the stiff old bird in black' was to get it into her head to ask for the sandbags, which were twice as heavy now they were wet, to be taken back to the cellar.

Angela's clothes were still drying, so the party from Marsh Farm had been persuaded to linger longer. Simon volunteered to go and collect the chocolate cake he had planned for Elsie, and he had returned with it and Duchess, who immediately made a bee-line for Alison, nuzzling and licking her.

Marcus, who knew Simon's dog of old, raised his eyebrows. 'She obviously likes you, Ali. She's a fussy old hound and picks her friends carefully.'

Alison, buried in the depths of an old armchair, damp,

exhausted, was pleased. She liked Marcus and so his approval mattered. He was obviously a bit older than Simon and very tall. His bald head seemed to emphasise his eyes, which were bright and shrewd. When they had first met, she felt herself being appraised by him and had felt oddly nervous, until he had smiled with a warmth that touched even her frozen soul.

But now a growing melancholy was taking her over and she felt distant and detached from the general activity in the kitchen. It was certainly an odd bunch assembled round the kitchen table. Mrs Merfield sat at the head, upright, imperious, but chatting to Stephen, who was becoming less awkward by the minute. Angela sat at his side listening, head cocked like a scraggy little bird, thought Alison. Nanny was helping Simon divide the chocolate cake and Marcus was entertaining Elsie and the other two Merfields, an incongruous duo, in their chiffon dresses, high strappy sandals and carefully applied face-paint, amongst the muddy, soggy gang who had fought the flood. Elsie, Alison noted with amazement, was flirting with Marcus. She had never seen her formidable old gran like this before, chatting animatedly with the other two old ladies, digging Marcus in the ribs, and dimpling when he roared with laughter at some acerbic remark she'd made.

Simon brought her over a piece of chocolate cake. 'Penny for them, Ali?'

'Nothing, really. I've just never seen Gran like this before.'

'You're right, though; she's a rare old bird.'

Elsie turned in her chair to look at them. 'Now that we've had your chocolate cake, Simon, and very nice it was too, are you and Ali going to tell me what you want from me?'

Simon was taken aback, but Alison was never surprised by her gran's perspicacity. 'It's family business, really, Gran, and I'm not sure that we should—'

'It also involves my aunt,' Simon reminded her.

'Me?' Mrs Merfield was curious. 'What is all this? Why are you both being so mysterious? Explain.'

'Yes, what's this all about, Ali?' Stephen was equally curious.

'But we don't want dirty linen washed in public!' Elsie interjected sharply.

'Where else should it be washed?' tittered Louisa Merfield. She was ignored.

'It's nothing for the Tuckers to be ashamed of, but it's important that you know what's going on before it's too late.' Simon was sombre, and the company fell silent as he and Alison described what they knew and what they suspected of the Lesters' plot against the Tucker family.

By the time they had finished, the mood had shifted from polite attention to disgust and anger. Amid an eruption of indignation from the rest of the company, Stephen groaned and held his head in his hands. 'They'll succeed, I know they will. They've got money and power – they'll get what they want. So I'll manage to get the milking parlour up to scratch, but then it'll be something else ... and if the bank is against us, what hope do we have? We pay them what they ask this time, then they just up the stakes. It's hopeless.'

'No it's not!' Alison was angry. 'I knew you'd react like that, Stephen. Are you really just gonna lie down and let them walk all over you? You're such a wuss!'

'No, he's not!' Angela leapt to Stephen's defence. 'Your brother's not a coward. It's just that he can see all the problems and that's what upsets him, but he'd never let anyone walk over him. He wouldn't!'

It was the first time Angela had spoken since they had assembled in the kitchen and everyone, including Stephen, stared at her. She blushed. 'I know it's none of my business, but you're kind, decent people, and it makes my blood boil to think of those horrid people trampling over you.' Stephen found her hand over the table, squeezed it and did not let go.

'I agree with Angela.' Simon smiled at her.

'And so do I,' chipped in Marcus. 'I've only met you this afternoon, but the way you rallied round to help ... we could all do with neighbours like you.'

'I quite agree,' said Mrs Merfield. 'We are very fortunate. And we saw this afternoon just what sort of neighbourly support the Lesters give! My sisters and I have never liked them and when *he* came here to besmirch your brother's reputation and suggest we hand over our meadows, we were as one in sending him away with a flea in his ear.'

Elsie, having experienced a different version of the event, raised her eyebrows. She turned to Simon. 'Let me get this straight – this woman who wanted to write an article about the Lesters' stud has been put off by some yarn you've spun with Marcus here?' Simon nodded. Elsie continued, 'But that's not going to stop them, is it? Stephen's right. So, young man, what are you suggesting? And how do you see my role in all of this?'

Alison spoke up. 'Gran, you've got the best business head of anyone. Stephen needs a business plan. He's got to be able to show the bank how he can make Marsh Farm viable. You did it once, with Grandpa. You told us often enough how you transformed the farm from a depressed tenancy into a humming, prize-winning dairy farm.'

'What Alison says is true.' Simon turned and spoke earnestly to Stephen. 'You're going to have to beat the bank at their own game. In reality, they don't want their customers to go bankrupt. This guy, whoever he is, is going to push you to the limit, but not over; then the Lesters will step in and make you an offer you'd be only too grateful to accept. So we need a two-pronged response. One is to present them with an attractive, watertight business plan and ...' He paused, his brow furrowed.

'And the other?' Elsie asked.

'Oh, I don't know, but it would help us if we could find out who it is at the bank the Lesters have nobbled. What he, or she, is doing is bad practice. If we can find out who it is, then maybe we can nobble them ourselves.'

'And how do we do that?' demanded Stephen, squeezing Angela's hand.

'Who did Charlie go to see at the bank? Do you know his name? Maybe it was him...' Alison asked, looking across at her brother. He looked different, somehow. It was odd, she thought to herself – here they were discussing the fate of the farm and she could swear he looked ... well ... happy.

'I dunno,' he replied, 'but we can find out.'

'And I suppose I'm going to have to play a bit more tennis!' Simon sighed. 'But in the meantime, Elsie, as Alison said, what you can do better than anyone is help Stephen put together a plan for the development of the farm.'

'I'll help,' Angela volunteered shyly.

'And I'll check it over so that financially it's viable and water-tight. I've got some bumpf I brought back to show you, Stephen. A sort of prototype the banks'll recognise, and a few other things. I was going to give them to Elsie at chocolate cake time. I could drop them round this evening.'

'Thank you, Simon.' Elsie nodded in approval. 'Bring your friend with you and then he can taste my cordials.'

'Haven't we forgotten something in all this cosy scheming?' Alison suddenly felt bleak and weary. 'Where does Charlie fit into all of this? Surely he'd have to be part of any business plan and I'm not at all sure he'd be in favour of some of the ideas we discussed. We can't ignore him. After all, he's the one that's saved the farm from immediate closure.'

There was a moment's silence, then Elsie said thoughtfully, 'You're right, Ali, of course. I have an idea about Charlie, but I need to have a good think about it.'

Reluctant as they were to leave the warmth of the kitchen, the time had come to go.

'Well, Stephen,' said Mrs Merfield, shaking him by the hand and thanking him for the umpteenth time, 'you're very fortunate to have such support behind you. I certainly hope, and I know my sisters agree with me, that you are successful in overcoming the threat imposed by the Lesters.'

'Slimy bastards!' said the youngest Miss Merfield cheerfully.

Mrs Merfield ignored the interjection and continued, 'I'll give the whole matter careful thought. We want to be able to help you in any way we can. Please come and see us, as arranged, on Tuesday for tea. And please bring your girlfriend.'

Nanny, who had taken a particular shine to Angela, gave her a squeeze. 'It'll be nice to see you again, flower,' she said quietly. Then, casting a glance at Stephen, whispered, 'You'll be fine, don't worry. See you on Tuesday.'

Veronica slammed the phone down and angrily tossed her head. Hugh, sunk in the depths of one too many glasses of brandy, looked up from the sofa where he was stretched out with a cold compress on his eye. 'Who was that?'

'Gordon White,' she snapped, stalking back across the sitting room to stare out at the prematurely darkening sky and unrelenting rain.

'What on earth does he want?'

'He wanted to say how much he enjoyed dinner last night.'

'That's more than I can say about him. He's a creep, Vee.'

'Well, that creep is going to get us Marsh Farm, Hugh, so for the moment we'll just have to put up with him. He is dreadful, and I could see Gavin and Marion staring at him, wondering why on earth he'd been invited. But we'll ditch him the moment he gets us Marsh Farm.'

'There's no way I'm going to let him ride one of my horses. They'd never recover from the experience.'

'But you promised him.'

'Listen, I'm not stupid! It's not the riding he's interested in. He made that perfectly obvious last night. It's you.'

'So?'

'So, darling, it's up to you. Play tennis with him. Flatter his almighty ego. Get him to deliver us Marsh Farm, and then we'll drop him.'

Veronica regarded him coldly. 'It comes to something when you are prepared to sacrifice your wife rather than your horses. I've spent as much time with him as I want to. It's time you did your bit. I don't see why you can't find some old nag for him to ride.'

'I don't possess any old nags!' Hugh was outraged.

'And you don't possess me. "Play tennis with him ... flatter his ego ..."' Veronica was furious. 'You sound like a pimp! And I am certainly not going to act as your tart! Maybe Anthony was right about us.'

'Anthony's a stupid little boy. He'll soon realise which side his bread is buttered; he'll come crawling back.'

Veronica turned her back on Hugh. Staring out at the unrelenting sheet of rain, she thought of Simon, of Gordon, of Hugh, and then of Anthony and felt a tinge of ... concern? Regret? Shame? Of course not! Her principal feeling was one of frustration: that bloody Simon still hadn't returned her call.

Charlie leaned across the avocado green washbasin to wipe the condensation from the mirror. He stared at his face long and hard, trying to imagine what he would look like. He felt like a man going to his execution. Lovingly, he fingered the condemned whiskers. Could he really go through with this? He didn't have to – after all, Sarah and Beth were history ... but Linda's words – 'Do you need to look older, now that you are older?' – had struck an uncomfortable note and he couldn't forget the mocking tones of the girls at the disco. 'Bog off, Granddad!' Granddad! Nope – it was no good; they had to go.

When he finished, he was aghast. He just didn't recognise the face that stared back, looking horrified. What made the face look so odd was the two dead white scimitar shapes framing that face. He'd never seen anyone with leprosy before, but that's what he thought it looked like. It was all very well telling himself that in a few days the marks would have disappeared and the skin would become as weathered as the rest of his face. For the moment he looked really strange. I'm going to be a laughing stock at the pub tonight, he thought grimly. For a moment he toyed with the idea of phoning Linda and making some sort of excuse. After all, what with being up all night, helping Linda at lunchtime, and clearing that ruddy tree, he was exhausted. But Linda needed him and he'd said he'd go. Perhaps his mum or Ali might have some instant tan or make-up that he could rub on to make it less obvious.

He went down to the kitchen in search of Jenny, but the kitchen was empty. He peered into the little mirror hanging on the wall next to the sink, to check how bad he looked in a different light. As he did so, his mother came into the kitchen. Charlie turned and was just about to speak when she gave a hysterical shriek: 'Jim!' and collapsed into the nearest chair.

Charlie had gone by the time the rest of the family with Simon, Marcus and Angela descended on Marsh Farm. Jenny, completely recovered from the shock of mistaking her eldest son for her long-dead husband, was overwhelmed. With Angela's help, she undertook to make cheese on toast for them all. Marcus appeared to be entranced by everything and with Gran's permission rushed here, there, and everywhere with his digital camera.

As the smell of burnt toast and animated chatter filled the kitchen, Alison could bear it no longer and slipped away. Simon noticed her going and his brow furrowed. Something, he realised, was wrong with Alison, but now was not the time to find out what.

'This is such fun!' Jenny beamed at them all. 'What a pity Charlie's not here. He was here earlier. Came in covered in mud and soaked through – that old ash tree, Stephen, in Home Field; it'd come down in the storm and was damming the river. He and Lenny spent most of the afternoon clearing it. He was tired out, but he wouldn't stop – said he was late for opening time. He looked dreadful; I've never seen him look so pale, but maybe that's because he'd shaved off his whiskers. Gave me such a shock. He's the spitting image of Jim!'

'It's a pity he's not more like him in other ways, then. That boy lives in the public house!' snapped Elsie. 'Why on earth doesn't he move in there?'

'The answerphone is full of messages.' Jenny turned to Stephen. 'Hannah moanin' because Ali hasn't phoned her back, but mainly Mrs Pagett wonderin' where you was, and where Angela was. Said without you they was gettin' nowhere and not like you to be so unreliable ... said to give her a ring as soon as you got her message.'

Stephen and Angela looked at each other, overcome for a moment with guilt: they had both totally forgotten about The Merlin Players. Then Angela started to giggle and after a few seconds, to the amazement of the rest of the company, Stephen joined in, and laughed and laughed till his eyes watered.

The night had descended prematurely. The rain continued to lash down and visibility was poor. Al, having downed a scalding cup of black coffee and checked his mobile phone for the message that wasn't there, was in no mood to linger. He had planned to meet his mates at Ashford the following day, and to head on into the tunnel with them. Having left home earlier than he'd planned, he thought he'd land up in Maidstone and find a B&B for the night.

He turned out of the motorway services car park and headed down the slip road. A car, mistaking an entrance for an exit in the foul weather, pulled across his path. He swerved, skidded on the wet surface and went under the front wheels. Mangled metal mingled with blood as Al's body went skidding one way, his bike the other, and his mobile phone, flying out of his pocket, went in another and was crushed under the wheels of an articulated lorry transporting cattle to a slaughterhouse.

20

After the activity of the weekend, Elsie was tired and slept in far later than she usually did. She felt stiff and old, and when she finally got up, she selected her underwear with less enthusiasm than usual. What did it matter what she wore? No one could see it and if Ron were taken from her, then there would be no one to admire her in it ever again.

Ron.

In all the excitement of yesterday, she hadn't given a thought to his predicament. She stood in front of her mirror, looking at her thin, withered body in its lace trappings. Ron loved her body, he said. He loved touching her. He made her feel that age didn't matter. If he went, there would be no one to take his place. It wasn't just Ron's predicament, she realised. It was hers, too. Without Ron, life would become extremely dull; there would be nothing to look forward to on a daily basis. She would shrink into old age, become a cantankerous old hag, then die, to everyone's relief.

And what of Ron? Plump, cheerful, kind, dear, dear Ron. His daughter had inherited none of his softness. 'She'll eat him alive,' whispered Elsie sadly, 'and spit him out when there's nothing left. He'll end up in one of those awful old folk's homes. It'll kill him and that'll be just what she wants.'

Elsie knew that for years she had taken Ron for granted. Now it was likely she would no longer be able to see him, she didn't want to lose him. Was it just habit? Was it love? It was so long since Elsie had thought about such a thing, she felt confused. Maybe it was. Not the sort of love that had driven her into Thomas's arms all those years ago, or the sort that found its way on to the television, or expressed itself in the books she read. Was it possible for someone so near eighty to experience love, in this way, for someone else?

Whatever it was, she wasn't going to give Ron up without a fight and having made that decision, she felt better. She smoothed her hands over the lacy cups of her bra and started to dress for the day ahead.

Resolving to make a start on her wine-making, Elsie headed down the stairs and tapped on her granddaughter's door.

'Ali?'

Alison padded over to the door and opened it. She looked, Elsie thought, as if she hadn't slept. Her face was pale, with huge, dark shadows under her eyes.

'Yes, Gran?'

'I'm going to drain the blackberry juice and start making a marrow rum. Do you want to help?'

Since childhood Alison had helped her grandmother brew wines and cordials and had always enjoyed the whole process as much as Elsie did. Today, however, she shook her head.

'Sorry. I've only got a week left before I'm back at college and I've got this massive biology essay to write. I'll give you a hand later, when I've broken the back of it.'

'You look peaky, my girl. Are you all right? Nothing troubling you?' Elsie didn't really expect a truthful answer and she didn't get one.

'I'm fine. Just a bit tired. I'll be down later.'

It had finally stopped raining and a damp, misty morning greeted Elsie as she walked round the back of the house to the old dairy that had been converted, long ago, for her brewing activities. She stopped at the sight of Jenny on her knees at the strawberry patch, a large bucket by her side into which she periodically dropped a snail.

'Oh hello, Elsie,' said Jenny, more cheerfully than Elsie could ever remember. 'I'm just replacing this sodden straw and collecting the snails. D'yer know, I think we've got a good crop of strawberries here. It's funny, I would never have thought of growing strawberries for the end of summer, but Jeff was right. He gave me these runners last year and they're fruiting beautifully!'

Elsie, preoccupied with thoughts of Ron and Alison, for once couldn't think of an acerbic put-down.

'Good. If you have a large crop, we could think about making a strawberry liqueur.'

'That'd be lovely.' beamed Jenny. 'What a treat!'

'Why are you collecting the snails?'

'I'm doing my bit to earn some extra. Ali said strawberry-flavoured snails would be a delicacy.'

'Ugh!' Elsie searched Jenny's face for some hint that she might be joking. But Jenny, completely guileless, looked up and nodded in agreement.

'That's what I think, but Ali suggested it. People these days . . . they'll eat anything.'

For a moment Elsie toyed with asking Jenny if she knew what was troubling Alison, but Jenny, she felt, was not blessed with great insight as far as her youngest child was concerned, and from her cheerful demeanour it was clear that nothing was worrying her and therefore nothing would be gained from making the enquiry.

She left Jenny to her task and went into her little distillery. Strawberry-flavoured snails! Whatever next! Now, country liqueurs, distilled on the farm; that would be a much more viable proposition.

She erected a muslin cradle over a bucket and poured the blackberries, which had been soaking for four days, into the muslin. As she worked, her mind cleared. The answer to the question of Ron was obvious and she mentally kicked herself for not having suggested it to him on Saturday night. Obviously the lateness of the evening, the wine and rich food had impaired her faculties.

Alison? She was not so sure. On Saturday she had been as skittish as a bulling heifer. Perhaps that was what was wrong – boy trouble – but until Ali took Elsie into her confidence, there was nothing to be gained from pushing her. Elsie wasn't aware of any boy in particular. She had wondered about this Simon. She was aware that, in the short time Alison had got to know him, a strong bond had formed between them and Elsie had been very curious to meet him. She liked what she saw when she met him yesterday. He was good company, affectionate to his elderly relative, and generally attentive to the needs of everyone, but he had the shuttered look of a person in pain. It was also clear that whilst he was fond of Alison, there was nothing romantic going on between them. No easy solution there, then.

So she turned her mind to the problem of Marsh Farm.

She left the blackberries dripping and went to rinse and dry the long straight marrow she had rescued from the ravages of the slugs that lived in Jenny's vegetable garden.

She had been shocked by Simon and Alison's revelations. She certainly was not going to sit by and watch the Lesters destroy them, but how to do it without going back on her ultimatum and bailing her grandsons out? Stephen was a good boy, and with her help, and the help of his little girlfriend, and with Simon's guidance, Elsie was sure he would come up with a good business plan.

The trouble was Charlie.

With a sharp knife, Elsie sliced the top off the marrow.

She loved her grandson. He was a loose cannon; he'd always been the naughtiest of the three grandchildren, with far too much undirected energy for his own good. But he was charismatic and charming. However, and on this point she was certain, Charlie's heart was not in farming.

With the aid of the knife and a long spoon, she dug into the centre of the marrow, pulling out the seed and membrane.

The trouble was, he farmed because he had never thought of doing anything else.

She discarded the seeds and gave the marrow a sharp tap on its bottom, ensuring all the seeds were out.

Charlie was not without abilities. In many ways he was a lot brighter than his brother. The trouble was, he lacked direction, and farming didn't seem to be providing it, which was why Elsie had told him to find a wife.

She stood the marrow on end and started to stuff it with soft, golden demerara sugar.

However, unlike Stephen, it didn't appear as if a wife was in the offing, and she couldn't have him jeopardising Stephen's plans and exposing Marsh Farm to the likes of the Lesters.

She poured a cup of liquefied yeast into the neck of the marrow.

There was no help for it. She would have to intervene.

The top of the marrow was replaced, sealed down with sticky tape and placed in a tall glass jug, the top then covered with a cloth.

Grunting with satisfaction at the outcome of her morning's labours, she washed her hands and went back to the house to telephone her solicitor.

After the heavy rain the day before, the ground was sticky and very slippery underfoot. Walking along the river, with Duchess racing here, there, and everywhere, in pursuit of pheasants, real and imaginary, Simon felt relaxed and cheerful. It's not just being out of London, he thought, looking with pleasure at the steam rising from the sodden ground, at the drops of water suspended, sparkling, on leaf and berry, and at a flock of martins squeaking shrilly just over his head as they swooped and dived in a frenzy of feeding, the change in the weather having produced an influx of insects. No, it's the Tuckers. They think I'm the one that's doing all the helping; if they only knew how much they're helping me.

Marcus shared his enthusiasm for the family, and said as much to Simon when he had left that morning, at the crack of dawn. 'They're great – particularly Granny - anything else I can do to help defeat the enemy, Simon, I will. I won't say anything more for the moment, but if my idea comes off, we can ensure the future of Marsh Farm for a while at least.'

The next thing for Simon to do was find out what was troubling Alison. It had been obvious, even to Marcus who had never met her before, that she was unhappy.

It's a pity I've got this meeting today, he thought, but if I get back early enough, I'll take her out, see if I can persuade her to tell me what's wrong. I'm pretty certain it's nothing to do with the Lesters.

The Lesters. He sighed, whistled for Duchess and headed for home. He didn't have to see Harriet Flood again, for which he was heartily grateful, but Veronica Lester … She had left four or five messages on his answerphone and he'd been in no hurry to get back to her. But he had to maintain this charade of being interested in her, until he had found out who her contact was at the Tuckers' bank.

Veronica was handsome enough, though at least ten years older than Simon, and her nose was too long and sharp. Her assumption that just because she found him attractive he would become her toy boy, disgusted him, and he had experienced at first hand how devious she could be in getting whatever she wanted. His mind lingered on the image of the man she had lost her game of tennis to. He was clearly infatuated with her and she, equally clearly, held him in contempt. Why had she deliberately lost? To put him off wanting to play tennis with her again? Or because she wanted something from him?

He reached the back door of the cottage.

'In you go, Duchess, there's a good girl.' Simon pulled off his muddy boots, left them by the kitchen door and padded over to the front door mat to pick up his post. Duchess danced around him with as much energy as she'd had at the start of their four-mile hike. He laughed, threw the letters on the kitchen table and looked ruefully at the mud on the floor. 'I should have hosed you down before letting you in, you filthy animal. I'm going to have to advertise for a cleaner if we stay here. Okay, okay. I'll feed you, don't worry.'

He collected the can opener and a fresh tin of dog meat, took them over to the kitchen table and started to open the can. As he did so, his eye fell on one of the letters scattered across the table.

He froze.

Lenny didn't make The Grapes on Sunday evening. So exhausted was he by dancing all night on Saturday, having to get up early to go and see Hugh Lester on Sunday, then drive his drunken mother-in-law home and put both Paula and the children to bed, not even the thought of a free pint could keep him awake.

Charlie left him a message on his mobile to meet at the pub on Monday lunchtime, after which he proposed they should spend the afternoon clearing up after the storm. When Lenny walked into The Grapes on Monday he stopped and stared. His astonishment at seeing Charlie behind the bar was surpassed only by the fact that the Charlie he had last seen struggling with the ash tree the day before was a substantially different-looking Charlie from the one behind the bar. At first, Lenny couldn't work out what was so different, and then he realised. 'Your whiskers! Charlie – you shaved your whiskers! Why on earth have you gone and done that?'

Charlie, very self-conscious and looking, in Lenny's opinion, about ten years old, said, 'Yeah, Lenny. I decided it was time for a change. I've had those whiskers since I was a kid. What do you think?'

Lenny stared hard at Charlie before he gave his reply. Charlie's face, lean and brown, was flanked by two strange, broad, triangular white shadows, making him look both very young and very gaunt at the same time. Like someone returning from overseas with a strange disease, Lenny thought. But what was gone was gone, and there was no sense, in Lenny's opinion, in giving Charlie any unnecessary grief.

'Well, mate, I wished you'd asked me before you stripped them off. I liked them – they was you. But what's done's done. I'll get used to it. Now, Charlie, cop a load of this . . .'and at long last, he told Charlie what he'd seen and heard at the Lesters' on Sunday.

Charlie's reaction was loud and furious. 'You're kiddin' me!' He shook his head with disbelief. 'Nobbled the bank? You've gotta be jokin'?'

'And tried to bribe me into not workin' for yer – as if he could. Desert me ol' mate, Charlie Tucker. He don't know nothin' about me an' you; we go back a long way, we do … Now where's this pint you promised me?'

Charlie fumed as he pulled Lenny a pint. 'I know he wanted us to sell, but to stoop to those sorts of tricks – he must want Marsh Farm really bad, the bastard!'

'Lucky fer you Paula and me was there. Whad'yer gonna do, Charlie?'

'Apart from putting my hands round his scrawny neck and squeezing the life out of his stinking body, I dunno. But what really gets up my nose is the bloody bank jumping to his tune.'

'That were his missus doing, as far as I could make out. Young Anthony as good as called her a tart – that's when old Hugh weighed in to wallop him and got a shiner for his trouble.'

'I'd give him more than a shiner if I get the chance … if they'd not nobbled the bank, we'd've had the money for a new bike. I tell yer, it breaks my heart havin' to pay that little lot over.'

'Yeah, what a bummer!' A deep gloom settled over the both of them. They had both dreamed of getting a bike that didn't fall to pieces at the end of every race; they had been so close, and they had lost their chance through no fault of their own. That hurt.

'So what are you gonna do? Just because me and Paula got wind of what they're up to, don't mean they're gonna stop.'

'No.' Charlie was thoughtful. 'Listen, don't say anything to anyone about this. Not yet. I've gotta think this one through.'

'Fair enough. Are you gonna stand me another pint, seein' as Linda's not about? Where *is* she by the way, and what are *you* doin' behind the bar?'

'She and Stan have split. She's off seeing her solicitor this morning, so I said I'd open up for her.'

Lenny whistled. 'Split, have they? It were pretty obvious he was having a fling with that tasty barmaid, but I didn't know things had got that bad. Well, Charlie, me ol' mate, you've lost no time gettin' yer feet under the table, 'ave yer?'

*

With a sigh, Alison put her book down. It was no use; she was finding it impossible to concentrate. Her mobile had jingled a number of times that morning, and Hannah could be put off no longer. She wondered, not for the first time, whether Al might have tried to get in touch. Today, presumably, he was on his way to France; but yesterday, perhaps? She no longer felt so angry – tired rather, and very low in spirits.

There was a text message from him, sent the previous evening:

I DIDN'T KNOW. BELIEVE ME. LOVE.

A shouted text. Alison shook her head. Perhaps he hadn't known? She so desperately wanted that to be the case, but that was her being weak and she hardened her heart – he *must* have known.

The other messages were mainly from Hannah, who couldn't believe that Alison hadn't got in touch with her and which ranged from the indignant to the plaintive. Alison braced herself for the inevitable cross-examination.

'Hi, Hannah, it's me, Ali—'

'Ali, thank God! Why haven't you rung me? What's going on? What happened with you and Al? He was fuming on Saturday night. What was he *on*? He wanted to know who you were! Talk about weird. Didn't he *know*? Then Frank phoned and said he, Rob, Ben and Ian had been over at yours, sandbagging the house against a flood. Are you all right? Are you under water?'

Alison felt a constriction in her chest. 'You saw Al on Saturday night?'

'Yeah. We bumped into him; he looked ghastly. Before I could ask him where you were, he asked me what your name was and where you lived. I thought he must be joking, but he was deadly serious. So I told him. Then he left without saying anything. What's going on, Ali, and what about this flood?'

'That happened yesterday, and it wasn't at ours. It was over at the Manor in the village, occupied by some old biddies. My brother needed help, so I called up the gang.'

'Why didn't you call me? Sounds like they had fun.'

Alison smiled in spite of herself. 'I knew you'd be out with Nick, and I don't think your nails would have survived those sandbags, Hannah … Listen, Hannah, this is really important, but I have to know – are you sure that, before Saturday night, neither you, nor Nick, told Al that my surname was Tucker and that I lived on Marsh Farm?'

By the end of the call, Alison had been convinced that, whether or not Al was complicit in his parents' scheming, he'd had no idea that she was a member of the Tucker family.

'Oh no!' she wailed, when Hannah had rung off. 'What on earth do I do now?'

She desperately wanted to talk to him; she needed him to tell her that not only was he not involved, but that he didn't know anything about his parents' plans; but Al would be in France by now, and she wasn't ready to text him with messages of contrition until she had proof he wasn't a conniving rat.

She regarded her text books with despair. She wasn't going to get any work done in this frame of mind. Simon's jumper lay over a chair. He'd lent it to her the evening before. She picked it up. He'd probably be at work, but she so wanted to talk to him. 'I'll go and see if Gran needs a hand with the wine,' she thought to herself, 'and if she doesn't, I'll take Bumble out. I'll go over to Simon's later.'

There was no sign of her gran, so she saddled up her fat old pony and went to see what damage the storm and the flood might have caused. She knew Charlie had been out first thing doing just that, so she wasn't surprised to see him and Lenny on the riverbank, stripping the fallen ash. Alison had a sentimental affection for all the trees on the farm and seeing the fate of the old tree, lying where it had been half-dragged onto the riverbank and stripped of its branches, her depression deepened. She turned Bumble away. She didn't feel like talking at the moment, least of all to Charlie and Lenny.

*

Lenny noticed her. 'Does Ali know about her boyfriend beating up his dad?'

Charlie, who was sawing a branch, momentarily stopped and shrugged his shoulders. 'I dunno. I tell you, it makes me sick to think my sister is going out with Lester's son. What's she on about? Sleeping with the enemy, that's what!'

Lenny gave a crack of laughter. 'Imagine havin' the Lesters as yer in-laws!'

'Over my dead body!' Charlie, not very amused, resumed his labours.

'Yeah, and over theirs too, I expect! I'd love to see their faces when their son and heir tells 'em he's courtin' a Tucker.' He chuckled at the thought and Charlie couldn't help grinning. 'So Charlie, 'ave you decided what yer gonna do?'

Charlie straightened up. 'The way I see it is,' he began slowly, 'Hugh Lester must want my farm real bad to go to all these tricks and the more he tries it on, the more we're going dig our heels in. It's a vicious circle, and unless we can catch him doing something illegal, I have a horrible feeling we might lose in the end. He's got money and a finger in every pie in this county on his side. And what have we got? Certainly not money, and who is there to give a toss about the fate of the Tuckers? So what I thought, Lenny, and you must keep this under your hat, is give him a price.'

'What? Sell out? Give him what he wants?' Lenny was flabbergasted.

'If it comes to it. But at a price, at *my* price. Thing is, if he wants it bad enough, he'll find the money.'

'But you wouldn't sell Marsh Farm! What would you do? What'd Stephen do? And Ali, and Elsie? They'd never agree.'

'Maybe not at the moment, but they might if the money is right. I know it's a gamble and it'll be hard to persuade them, but I've been thinking we could raise a fair packet – I know the farm is a bit run down—'

'A bit!'

'But the land is valuable and what's more, the house is. I know it's a bit shabby, but it's got six bedrooms. At today's prices, that's six hundred K, without blinking. I know Stephen's trying to think up ways we might save the farm, but nothing is going to be quick, is it? The bank has us in a stranglehold. Where's the money coming from to pay the extra three thousand at the end of October, and the month after that, and the month after that? So the way I see it, we could set our price, pay off the bank, divvy it up. Stephen should have enough, with the others as partners, to buy somewhere cheaper.'

Lenny stared at Charlie. 'And what about you? What would you do with your share?'

Charlie shrugged again. 'I'm thinking about it. Could be an opportunity to move into something different. We might set up a business together ...'

Lenny whistled. 'Blimey! What a turn up. I wouldn't never have thought that you'd even think of sellin' to that bastard!'

'No, and I tell you, I feel a bit sick even thinking about it. But we've got to be realistic. Someone's going to win out, and I don't want to end up a complete loser. I know it's a long shot, but it's worth a try. I phoned old Lester this afternoon to tell him I was onto his schemes. But he was out. I've arranged for an agent to come over on Wednesday.'

'What's Stephen gonna say?'

'It's market day. Stephen'll be out of the way.'

'Off you go, Snuffles.' Jeff lifted the fat little pug off the table and placed him on the floor. He patted Snuffles' owner, a plump elderly lady, on her shoulder. 'He should be fine now, Mrs Dunning, but you must be careful not to overfeed him. Cut out the tit-bits and you'll be doing him a favour.'

He closed the door behind Mrs Dunning and pulled a face at Monica, his nurse. 'She doesn't take any notice of me. One day that little dog will explode. Is that the lot for this afternoon?'

'Yes, Mr Babbington.' The nurse started to clean down the table.

Jeff glanced at his watch. 'That leaves forty-five minutes before this evening's surgery. No time for anything. I'll go out for fish and chips and bring them back here.'

'It's Monday, Mr Babbington. The chippie's closed.'

Jeff cursed under his breath. He was hungry; it'd been a long day. He should have thought ahead and brought in some sandwiches. He knew that's what his partner did, but then his partner had a wife who made them for him, and would have a nice hot casserole, or something equivalent, waiting for him when he got home.

He thought of this again when he was in the pub, the relic of a lunchtime roll sitting in front of him. His wife had died so long ago now that he'd become self-sufficient, but every now and then he thought wistfully of how it would be to have someone at home waiting for him. He thought of Jenny and grinned. If he was going to depend on her to make his sandwiches and cook him casseroles, then he'd better think again ... But just the thought of her made him feel different: warm somehow, tingly.

What had started out as an act of sympathy on his part, the visit to the rare breed farm that Sunday two weeks ago, had escalated rapidly and unexpectedly from a long-term companionable friendship into a relationship, which he was enjoying hugely, and which, he suspected, was going to make a substantial difference to his life. The occasional woman friend had shared his bed but it had never occurred to him that he might one day want to be with another woman enough to consider living with her; it certainly had never occurred to him that Jenny Tucker might be such a woman.

He remembered her when she was a girl of eighteen. He'd envied his friend Jim. Jenny was blonde and slim with soft blue-green eyes and the shyest of manners. But she was his best friend's girl, and even after both their spouses were dead, he still thought of Jenny as that. She certainly wasn't slim any more, or very blonde, come to that, but when he found himself in bed with her last Saturday night, a passion that he had been suppressing, unawares, for years, welled over.

He couldn't wait to share his bed with her again.

*

Alison peered through the cottage window into the sitting room. She was puzzled. Simon hadn't answered the doorbell, but she could see a light was on inside, and could make out Duchess lying on the floor, her head on her paws, next to an armchair. Simon wouldn't have gone out without Duchess. The dog, sensing the presence of someone at the window, lifted her head and looked in Alison's direction revealing, as she did so, a pair of feet. Simon was in – then why hadn't he answered the door?

Alison went back and tried the bell again. Again, no response. Remembering how still those feet were, and how mournful Duchess looked, Alison became anxious. She tried the handle and the door opened. She went in. Through the open kitchen door she could see a large can of dog meat on the table, the can opener stuck in it as if the opening of it had been interrupted. Post, largely circulars, was scattered on the table and floor, and next to the dog food was an empty bottle of whisky.

She turned into the sitting room and became aware of the mournful sounds of 'The Ascent to the Scaffold' and the bleeping of Simon's answerphone. Duchess's tail started to thump, but she didn't get up to greet Alison and as she neared the occupant of the armchair Alison had almost convinced herself she would find a corpse.

He was lying stretched out, unshaven, very pale, eyes shut. A strong, acrid smell assailed Alison's nostrils and resting on the floor, held loosely in an inert hand, was a another bottle of whisky, half full.

'Simon?' She touched his arm gently and his eyes flew open. They were red-rimmed and puffy. He's been crying, she thought to herself, shocked.

'Ali?' His voice was thick and unsteady. 'What are you doing here?'

'I brought your jumper back. You lent it to me last night. I rang at the door, but you didn't answer. Then when I saw Duchess in here I became worried. Are you all right?'

'Of course I'm all right – what do you mean?' He struggled to

317

sit up, but the effort was too much and he fell back into the chair and closed his eyes.

'Why are you drinking whisky?'

'Why shouldn't I?' He opened his eyes again. 'It's a good drink, Ali.' He waved the bottle at her. 'Have some; I can recommend it. It's a good an ... ana ... asthet ... it's a good painkiller.'

'No, thanks, not right now. *Are* you in pain, Simon? Why are you drinking it? I noticed there's an empty bottle in the kitchen. Have you drunk that much today? You'll kill yourself.'

'So much the better. Make everything a lot easier.'

Alison crouched by his side. 'What's wrong? Please tell me.'

He turned to look at her blearily. For a moment his drunkenness seemed to lift and he said, softly and sadly, 'Go home, go home, there's a good girl. You can't help me. I need to be alone. Go home, please.'

She hesitated. His request was direct and unequivocal.

'No.' She stood up and looked down at him. 'I won't. I'm not leaving you like this. For one thing, I don't know how long you've been drinking, but it doesn't look as if poor old Duchess has been fed.'

She turned and went to the kitchen. There was a sound behind her. Still clutching his bottle, Simon had staggered to the doorway. 'Alison,' he began, desperately, 'I don't want ...' But before he could tell her what he didn't want, his knees buckled and he passed out.

Simon was too tall and heavy for Alison to get upstairs, so she dragged him to the sofa and improvised a bed for him there. She sponged his face and body and provided him with a bucket when he recovered consciousness and started to vomit. Finally he fell into a deep sleep. Keeping one eye on him, Alison started to clean up.

The telephone rang and, not wanting Simon's sleep to be broken, Alison sprang to answer it. It was Marcus.

'Thank God you're there, Alison. Is he all right?'

'I hope so. I've never seen anyone so drunk. He's been terribly sick, but he's fast asleep now. I'm not sure what else I should do.'

'Stay with him for as long as you can. When he wakes up, give him plenty of fluids to drink. I'll be down as soon as I can get away, but it'll be later on this evening. I've got a production meeting.'

'What's it all about? What's wrong?'

'He hasn't told you?'

'What?'

'About Helen?'

'His wife? I'd thought they'd separated, divorce pending ...'

'Yep, but the tragic thing for Simon was that not only did he adore Helen, but before everything blew up in his face, she had become pregnant. He was so excited about the baby. He rushed around buying things for the nursery, read whatever literature he could get hold of, framed the first pictures of the foetus ...'

'So what happened?'

'A couple of months ago she broke down and said she couldn't go through the rest of her pregnancy living a lie. She was having an affair with someone, and the baby, she said, was his.'

'Marcus! That is the worst ... oh, poor Simon!'

'Yeah, horrible, isn't it? She left him and went off to live with this chap. We've all been waiting for Helen to give birth, and for proof, once and for all, that the baby is not Simon's. He, poor fellow, left London 'cos he couldn't bear the strain.'

'And now she's had the baby?'

'Right. Helen told Sue, my partner, that she had written to Simon to tell him. He would've got the letter this morning.'

Sitting by the sofa, looking down at the face of her sleeping friend, Alison wanted to weep for him. 'Poor, poor Simon,' she whispered. It put her heartache over Al in a different light.

21

The church clock was striking five as Stephen, swinging Angela's hand in his, walked away from the Manor. Tea with the Merfields had not been nearly as bad as he'd feared, and the reason for that, he'd concluded, was the presence of Angela. Timid herself, she had made him feel bold and protective. The Merfield women had been kind to her and her ease made him feel easy.

He laughed out loud. 'Old Hugh Lester would be as sick as a dog if he knew that it was because of him Mrs Merfield has given us tenure of the land. And for the next eight years, Ange, at a peppercorn rent!'

'It wasn't because of him,' protested Angela. 'It was because you went to their rescue and made nothing of all your hard work and bravery.'

Stephen wasn't sure where the bravery fitted in, but he glowed. 'No, but it helped that she's still cross with him for not phoning back and not sending any men. Things might have been different if he'd answered the phone and said, "You're in trouble, Mrs Merfield? No problem, I'll come over right away."'

'But he didn't, because that's not the sort of person he is. Mrs Merfield has the measure of him, and of you. You've only got what you deserve.'

He looked down at her and stopped. 'I don't deserve you, Ange,' he said shyly. 'How you've put up with me all these years … I didn't realise what a treasure I had under my nose all the time — kept on looking for the end of the rainbow somewhere else.'

Angela was so happy, great tears welled up in her eyes and slipped down her cheeks. Stephen was alarmed. 'Ange, Ange, don't cry. What have I said?'

Angela took out her handkerchief, dabbed at her glasses, then realising what she was doing, giggled, took them off and wiped her eyes. 'It's just that I feel so happy, Stephen.'

And to the amazement and very great excitement of Rita Godwin, outside whose shop they had stopped, Stephen, undeterred by inexperience or self doubt, and without any hesitation, took Angela in his arms and kissed her. Perhaps it was because they were both so untried and innocent, but it worked, for both of them, and it was some time later that, with regret, Stephen broke off.

'We've got to hurry if I'm to get the cows in and milked, and we're to eat before the rehearsal tonight.'

'I'll help.'

Mournfully, Alison considered the black-fringed eyes of the pink crash helmet staring back at her from the corner of her room. 'I suppose' she reflected, 'I'd better take you back. I won't be needing *you* again!'

She was tired. Marcus had arrived late the previous night and had given her a lift home. Simon had woken once, smiled at her and gone straight back to sleep, but looking a lot healthier. She had let herself in to a silent house, had gone to bed and grieved for Simon, and for herself.

There had been no further messages from Al. Not that she expected any. She hadn't responded to his text and now he was away with his mates, putting her out of his mind. Still, she wanted some news of him. It was this unacknowledged need that led her to think of returning the crash helmet to Paula. Paula, working as she did for the Lesters, might be able to throw some light on Al's relationship with his parents, might even have news of him.

So she decided she would go over to the Spinks' after supper when there was a greater chance of Lenny not being there.

Supper at Marsh Farm was a quiet affair, Elsie having gone off to Bath, Charlie out somewhere and Stephen and Angela at their rehearsal. Jenny seemed as preoccupied with her thoughts as Alison, so conversation was desultory. Alison asked her mother if she'd enjoyed herself at Uncle Jeff's over the weekend, but as she was concentrating on how to leave her cauliflower cheese (which was more like cauliflower with a lumpy grey sauce) without hurting her mother's feelings, she didn't notice the blush of colour that came to Jenny's cheeks.

The telephone rang and as Jenny went to answer it. Alison leapt to her feet and, disposing of the contents of her plate, shouted to her mother that she was going over to Paula's.

To her relief, there was no sign of Lenny. 'He's gone off to the pub with Charlie,' Paula said cheerfully, turning the volume of the television down a fraction. 'He'll be back later, drunk as a skunk, demanding a pizza. Sit down, Ali. 'Ave a cup of tea. Shove that helmet on the shelf over there. You don't need it any more?'

'No.' Alison's mind went a complete blank. How on earth could she ask about Al and his parents without coming straight out with it? Paula, returning with two mugs of tea, came to her rescue.

'That was a real shiner your boyfriend gave old Lester the other day!' Paula chuckled at the memory as she collapsed on the old sofa and swung her legs up, tossing an Action Man and a plastic tractor onto the floor as she did so.

Alison stared. 'What?'

'You 'aven't heard? He hasn't told you?'

'I haven't seen him.'

'But didn't Charlie tell you? He knows. Lenny told him. I'd 'ave thought he'd 'ave told you about their row – a real corker it was – and all that stuff about Mrs Lester screwing the bank manager so he could put the screws on you, so to speak?'

This was so unexpected, Alison's excitement grew and she could feel her heart thumping. She wanted Paula to tell her everything, straightaway, but Paula was scatty and Alison knew that if she fired questions at her, something important might get overlooked. So slowly, patiently, Alison teased out a more or less accurate account of the fight between Al and his parents on Sunday afternoon. 'And the man from the bank was called Gordon? You're sure of that?'

'Yeah. Ask Lenny; he heard it, too.'

'But no surname, no Gordon something?'

The frustrated film starlet, dormant in Paula's psyche, rose to the occasion. 'No, Ali. They were making such a racket. She was shrieking, he was bellowin', but I could hear Anthony, cold as ice. "Gordon?" he said. "Gordon. The bank manager you've had sex with?" That's when Hughie rushed up the stairs to hit him and Anthony laid him out cold.'

'And then he left?'

'It was straight out of the movies. He opened the door – it was bloody chucking it down – and he turned and told them they was poison and how they'd ruined his life and they'd never see him again. And then he vanished.'

Alison wanted both to weep and cheer.

'He didn't say anything else?'

'No. Just told 'em to go and boil their heads in hell. Brilliant!'

Her heart so full, her mind racing, Alison wanted, needed, to follow every last little detail of Al's movements. 'Then you heard his bike?'

'Yes, roaring off into the distance. And then ... nothing.' Paula's voice dropped dramatically.

'Has there been any word of him since?'

'No.' Paula was back to earth with a bump. 'They treat me like dirt, Ali. I went to work Monday morning as usual. House was locked up – Chubb locked, so I couldn't get in. And not a word. No explanation. Nothing. Same thing this morning. I tell you, I've had my fill of them and after I heard what they were on about with you lot, I told Lenny: "Lenny," I said, "I'm not workin' for them any more. They're fuckin' evil."' She lit a cigarette and inhaled deeply. 'I wonder why Charlie didn't tell you any of this.'

As Alison raced over to Simon's cottage, the same question jostled in her thoughts together with a tortured condemnation of herself. She had been so unfair. If she had stopped to think, to remember, Al, himself, had told her about his relationship with his parents. She went over and over all the conversations they'd had together, all the things he had let slip about his home life. 'He said he'd planned to go to Durham and not come back,' she whispered to herself. 'He said he had as little to do with his parents as he could ...'

She should have listened to what he was saying, she thought bitterly. He obviously disliked his parents, and she'd accused him of being like them, of conspiring with them, of planning to strip her of her virginity ... as if she hadn't got any say in the matter! She blushed, and in the darkness outside Simon's cottage, cried bitter tears of recrimination. It was some minutes before, sniffing deeply and wiping her face, she could ring on his bell.

Any embarrassment that Simon might have felt on seeing Alison vanished as, at the sight of him, she collapsed, weeping desperately, in his arms. He led her into his sitting room, sat her down and gently questioned her. Through hiccups and tears, she told him of Al and everything that had passed, including how she had nearly made love to him; and then of Paula's revelations including Gordon somebody at the bank. Simon sat her on his lap and rocked her in his arms, stroked her head and wiped her tears until she finally stopped crying.

He'd lit a fire against the damp of the early autumnal chill, and for a while they sat there, Alison sniffing occasionally, watching the flames flickering in the hearth.

'Alison.' His voice was quiet. 'You're the best sort of sister a man could have. Thank you for looking after me last night. I don't remember much, but Marcus told me what you did. And thank you for sharing this with me. I can't make any promises about your Al, but he sounds okay and while there's hope ... Have you tried to text him?'

'No.' Alison sniffed.

'Well, listen, I'll go and make us a cup of hot chocolate while you do that.' He nudged her off his lap and started towards the kitchen. 'Oh.' He turned. 'And as for Gordon, I've a good idea who he might be. Veronica Lester likes to wear the colours of her conquests for all to see. She introduced me to a Gordon the last time we played tennis.'

Stephen and Angela arrived ahead of the rest of the Merlin Players and were busy setting the stage when the actors started drifting in. Their presence was greeted with pleasure and some relief. 'Thank God you're both here.' There was a note of reproof in Gerald O'Donovan's voice. 'It was chaos on Sunday. Mrs P really had her knickers in a twist.'

If Mrs Pagett was relieved to see them, she didn't show it. 'The one thing I expect of my stage-management team is reliability,' she said coldly. 'Sunday's rehearsal was very difficult, very difficult indeed. If you're not going to turn up, I would appreciate a phone call, at the very least.'

'Sorry about that.' Stephen did not sound in the least sorry. 'We had a bit of an emergency.'

'We had to go and rescue Stephen's cows.'

'The river was in flood ...'

'The poor things were marooned ...'

'Too frightened to move ...'

'So we had to wade into the water ourselves ...'

'Took some budging, they did ...'

'But they finally moved. One knocked me over and Stephen rescued me ...'

'She was very brave; not everyone would have helped the way she did ...'

Someone giggled. June Pagett was slightly mollified. 'Well, well, as it was an emergency, I can understand. But please, don't let it happen again. We've got very little time to get this play off the ground.' She raised her voice. 'Quiet, everybody. May I have your attention, please! Thank you. Now, we're going to have a run through this evening. You should all be off your books; Angela will prompt. Stephen, when it comes to it, will you read Scrub?'

'No.'

June Pagett stopped in mid-flow, startled, and turned to stare at him, her face turning slightly pink. 'I beg your pardon?'

'I said no, Mrs Pagett. I volunteered my services as a stage manager. That is what I do, stage manage. I do not act. You must find someone else to read Scrub.'

The whole company stared at Stephen. This was a side of him none had seen before. Angela flushed with pride.

'Hurrah,' cried Nicola, mocking. 'The workers are revolting!'

June Pagett was flustered. 'Oh, well, if that's your attitude ... Angela, read Scrub, please.'

'No.' Stephen cut across Angela before she could agree. 'Ange has got enough to do, promptin', makin' the tea, doin' props and generally runnin' around after you. You've had long enough, Mrs Pagett, to find someone to play Scrub. It's up to you, not us, to fill the part. Come on, Ange,' he continued, turning his back on the speechless producer, 'I'll help you finish setting your props.'

No one had ever stood up to Mrs Pagett quite so openly before; her face turned from pink to a blotchy red, which seemed to accentuate the ginger of her freckles; slight beads of perspiration appeared on her top lip; her eyes, frog-like, protruded in their sockets, and although she tried to regain the upper hand by shouting and blustering her way through the evening, a number of the actors slipped over to Stephen's corner to congratulate him on his stand, including the amiable Mrs Brownsword who, rummaging in the bottom of her bag, pressed a handful of Quality Street on him 'to share with little Angela at the coffee break'. Nicola took him by surprise by putting an arm casually round his shoulder and whispering in his ear, 'I didn't know you'd got it in you. Well done. You put the old battleaxe in her place. Coming for a drink after?'

Stephen, aware that Angela was watching, agonised, removed Nicola's arm. 'No thanks, Nicola. I've promised to see Angela home. Did you know you're the wrong side of the stage for your entrance?'

*

Having put the phone down, Jenny had rushed into the kitchen to remove all traces of cooking and dirty crockery. If she wasn't tone deaf and very self-conscious about it, she would have burst into song. Jeff had asked her to go out with him, to a Chinese restaurant!

'I've only just got back from a call,' he'd explained. 'I don't feel much like cooking. Have you eaten yet? 'Cos if you haven't, I thought we could go out for a Chinese. Or an Indian, whichever you prefer.'

For a second, Jenny thought of the rather large portion of cauliflower cheese she'd just eaten. 'I'd love to, Jeff.' Visions of the last Chinese meal she'd eaten, years and years ago, swam before her eyes. All she could remember was some lovely soup, with bits of chicken and lots of sweetcorn, and as she didn't like spicy food at all, the decision was easy. 'Chinese, that'd be a real treat. Are you sure?'

He was sure, but there was no way that Jenny would jeopardise the invitation by letting him know she'd eaten already, so the kitchen had to be cleared before she got herself ready.

In the privacy of her bedroom, Jenny stood in her underwear and critically surveyed her body. She shook her head, despairing. What was she doing? Two meals in one evening – how would she ever lose weight? 'Look at you,' she scolded herself in the mirror. Her breasts were large, sagging rather than pert; her stomach bulging and crinkly – if she breathed in hard, she could almost flatten it, but she couldn't hold her breath like that for long; she had heavy dimply thighs, and legs criss-crossed with veins.

She and Jeff had had a bit to drink when they tumbled into bed together last Saturday night, so he couldn't have taken too much notice of what she looked like. But if, as she so hoped, they ended up back at his place after the meal, she'd have to make sure they went to bed in the dark. That, or she'd have to keep her clothes on.

In the pub after the rehearsal, it was inevitable that Stephen's stand should be a major topic of conversation amongst the Merlin Players. There was much laughter at June Pagett's discomfiture and shrieks when Nicola and Gerald, wickedly and accurately, mimicked Stephen and Angela's double act.

'But,' asked one girl, wiping the tears of mirth from her eyes, 'what does it all mean? Are Stephen and Angela an item? After having been so in love with you, darling, all these years, I wouldn't have thought he'd be so fickle.'

'No,' said Nicola coldly, remembering the afternoon at the Tuckers. 'But you forget, he's desperate.'

'The old granny's threat – of course! Spurned by the lovely princess, desperate, he casts around and then his eyes fall on the humble servant girl. She won't say no. This is better than *The Beaux Stratagem* any day, isn't it, my sweet Cherry?' Robert Robins nuzzled the neck of Roxanne, who was sitting on his lap, very much enjoying his attentions.

'Me? I think it is so romantic. He will marry her, no? And get the terrible granny's farm?'

'Do you think he's told her?' Gerald asked.

Nicola frowned. 'He didn't tell me, did he? I only found out because I bumped into his brother.'

'Don't you think she ought to know?'

'Of course she should, but—'

'Really, you'd have thought she was bright enough to have wondered at his sudden transfer of affections,' Gerald drawled. 'He's quite unscrupulous; I would never have thought it of him. He's a dark horse, all right. Do you think he plans to marry Angela, get the farm, then ditch her?'

'That's what I'd do in his situation,' chuckled Robert. 'Imagine being married to little Angela. One has to have sympathy for the poor fellow.'

'I don't agree. I think it's a really rotten trick to pull on anyone. Poor Angela. I think we should tell her.'

'Well you're the one to do it, darling. Give her a ring.'

Nicola sighed heavily. 'Well, I shall. I'm not going to let Stephen get away with it. Does anyone know her number?'

*

Simon walked Alison home. The sky was completely clear and full of stars; the balmy night air of summer had gone and as they talked, the vapour of their breath hung like ghosts on the air. Their mood was subdued. Alison had not been able to raise any response whatever from Al's mobile and though she tried to put a brave face on it, she couldn't conceal from Simon quite how miserable she felt.

'There's probably a simple explanation, Ali. Don't despair. And if his mobile is a no-through route, we can find other ways of contacting him. After all, when he's finished in France you know he's going back to Durham to study zoology. It won't be difficult to trace him.'

Alison was silent for a short while, then she said fiercely, 'You make me so ashamed, Simon. After all you've been through and here I am, whingeing and snivelling over what must seem to you a petty, adolescent affair.'

'I know how painful it is. It's not petty. You're not an adolescent any more and the first real love affair means a lot. I must have been about Al's age when I first met Helen.'

'How did you meet her?'

'We were at university together. We were studying such completely different subjects—'

'What?'

'Oh, I was doing modern languages and she was studying archaeology.'

'So how did you meet?' Alison was aware that Simon, picking his words with great care, was prepared to confide in her, and she was so touched, she didn't want to breathe in case he stopped. She held tightly onto his arm, leaning her head on his shoulder as they walked down the dark and empty high street.

'Through our grandmothers. My mother died when I was young. My father was a soldier, so I was brought up by my grandmother, Great Aunt Merfield's younger sister. Grandmother's great friend happened to be Helen's grandmother and when the two realised we were at the same university, the order went out that I was to invite Helen to tea.' He gave a low chuckle. 'I was so green. But she was very nice to me. She came from a large, jolly family, and before long I was in love with them and deeply in love with her.'

'Was she in love with you?'

He sighed. 'I thought so, but I don't think I stopped to find out. You know what it's like. You're going through it right now. The difference between us is that, in my own way, I was an arrogant little shit. I was an only child, you see, so I never really had to share, or think too much about what other people wanted. I wanted Helen. Ergo, she wanted me. In hindsight, she was undecided and I ... I convinced her that I was right, that we were made for each other. With the help of the grandmothers, of course, I finally persuaded her to get married. I was so sure that once we were together all the time, any doubts she had would disappear. Instead, I think they just grew.'

'So why did she become pregnant? I'm sorry, that sounds a bit ... but she must have—'

'I was dead keen to have children. Cement the relationship and all that. Then I had to go away on a six-week business trip. Whilst I was away, Helen said she'd have her coil taken out. She had decided to try and make our marriage work; to commit herself, once and for all. Thing is, Alison, the humbling thing is, I didn't know she was thinking like that. I thought she was as happy as I was.'

For a moment he stopped talking and, arm in arm, they continued until they reached Summerstoke Bridge, where they stood looking down at the black, rushing water. His face in shadow, staring down at the torrent, Simon quietly picked up his story. 'Shortly before I returned, she met someone at a party. He was an archaeologist, like her. They hit it off straightaway and became lovers almost immediately. She told me later she had never been more sure of herself.'

'Then why did she not tell you when you returned?'

'That was my fault again. I was so pleased to see her, so keen to start our family, I brushed aside any possible obstacle and she, feeling guilty in the face of my ... me, thought she would try.

330

The rest is history. She was probably pregnant before I returned.'

Alison's eyes were full of tears. She touched his arm. 'Simon.' He turned, and by the silvery light she could see the tears coursing down his cheeks. She flung her arms around him and hugging each other tightly, they both wept.

The vicar of Summerstoke, returning home after a solitary late night ramble (ever since the flood fiasco, he had resorted to taking his daily constitutional under cover of darkness), froze at the sight and sound of the sobbing couple on the bridge.

He retreated quietly, back over the stile onto the footpath below the bridge, out of sight, and stood there tortured with indecision about what he should do next. Should he intervene? Offer words of comfort? Supposing they had made a suicide pact and were about to jump into the river? His ears strained for the sound of a loud splash. What would he do if that happened? Should he try and pull them out, or run for help? And if they drowned, would the village blame him, like he'd been blamed for the non-appearance of the flood? He dropped to his knees on the muddy path and fervently prayed for guidance.

'Good evening, vicar.' It was a pleasant male voice. Looking up, the vicar saw the young couple staring down at him curiously.

'Don't you want to?' Jeff asked plaintively, as Jenny stopped him unbuttoning her blouse.

Jenny couldn't think of anything she wanted more.

'Oh yes,' she whispered, as if afraid someone else might hear in Jeff's empty house. 'It's just that ...'

'What?' He thrust his hand through the half-opened garment to cup her lovely round breast in his hand. 'What is it?'

'I'm so fat!' She hung her head. 'When you see what I really look like, you won't want ... you won't want it any more ... and I'd be so upset.'

'What?' Jeff looked at her in amazement. 'What are you talking about, woman?'

'I'm getting old. My body sags where it shouldn't. And I've

tried to lose weight, I really have. I looked at myself in the mirror before I came out. You don't want me.'

'Oh yes I do. Jenny, I've been thinking of nothing else since Saturday. All these wasted years. I can't wait to make love to you again. I think you're lovely. So you're fatter and wrinklier than you used to be. So am I. So what? I don't want some scrawny chicken – I want voluptuous maturity, and that's you. Come on, I'll race you, and you can see *my* paunch and *my* wrinkles. Last one with their clothes on has to make a cup of tea when the rumpty-tumpty is done!'

In another part of Summerbridge, outside Angela's bedsit, Stephen and Angela were in the Land Rover having a cuddle. They, too, were having a giggle at June Pagett's discomfiture.

'Well,' said Stephen stoutly. 'She's a bully. It's about time someone told her—'

Angela was quiet for a moment and Stephen knew what she was thinking about. 'You don't have to worry about me and Nicola, Ange . . .'

'It's just when I saw her come over to you and put her arm round you . . . She's so pretty. I—'

'Listen, she might be pretty outside, but it's prettiness inside what counts. And that's what you are, pretty inside. You're the one I want to be with. It took me a long time to realise it. I was bloody stupid, but you and Nicola – no contest!'

'Oh, Stephen!' Angela was almost faint with happiness.

It was Stephen's turn to fall quiet. Holding Angela in his arms, he felt not just happy, but more than that – excited, ecstatic. His life had taken on a new shape and the future became something that he could look forward to without dread. He felt lighter, stronger than he had ever done, and it was all due to this frail, brave little creature whom he had undervalued for years. He remembered the expression on her face last Saturday when he had suggested they go out after their visit to Weston. She had blossomed. The same thing was happening to him – he felt as if he was blossoming too.

He kissed her and whispered, 'Ange?'

'Yes, Stephen?'

'How about you and me? You know? You like the farm, don't you? And my mum? And the cows?'

'Yes, I like them all.'

'Then why don't we ...' He seemed to be finding it difficult to finish his sentence and Angela, for the first and only time in their relationship, did not help him out.

'Why don't we ... Oh heck, Ange, why don't we get married? I mean I don't know if you want to ... If you think it's a good idea that is ...'

'Oh, Stephen!'

22

For two days Charlie had tried to get hold of Hugh Lester, without success.

'Must have gone off on holiday,' he muttered to Lenny. 'S'all right for some.'

They were working in the yard, at Charlie's insistence, trying to tidy it up prior to the agent's arrival. Lenny was not his usual cheerful self. He disapproved of Charlie's latest idea and the suspicion that he knew what was behind his sudden enthusiasm for selling the farm exacerbated that disapproval.

'Are you sure you're doin' the right thing here? I can't see your family givin' up this place without a fight.'

'I've told you.' Charlie repeated his argument with a conviction he was far from feeling. 'Better to give it up with money in our pockets than be forced to give it up for nothing. When I tell 'em the lengths old Hugh is prepared to go to get it, they'll see sense. Particularly Gran. She's got a good business head, has Gran, and she'll see the time has come to put sentiment on one side.'

'I just can't bear the thought of Hugh Lester getting his grubby little hands on this place.'

'But at a price, my boy, at a price. We'll be the ones laughing.'

'I never thought you'd give in to Hugh Lester. I reckon it's your whiskers what done it.'

'What?'

'It's like that Bible story we was told at school: Samson and Delia.'

334

'Delilah. What are you rabbitting on about? What have my whiskers and Hugh Lester got to do with Samson and Delilah?'

'Lin tells you to get your whiskers cut off and you gives in to Hugh Lester.'

'She did *not* tell me to get them cut off; leastways, she wasn't the only one, and it's got absolutely nothing to do with my decision to sell to Hugh Lester. I've told you why, Lenny. I really don't see as there is any other way—'

Lenny was not convinced. 'Did Stephen go off to market?'

'Yeah, I saw him load up some calves straight after milking. He won't be back for a while yet.'

'What about Elsie, and yer mum?'

Charlie shrugged. 'Mum'll believe anything I tell her and Gran's gone off to Bath. Oh ho, here, unless I'm very much mistaken, is our man.'

A brand new, sparkling clean Mondeo splashed through a puddle and was clean no more. A suited man, every inch a salesman, got out of the car and looked around him with a faint air of distaste.

'I'll leave you to it,' muttered Lenny. 'I'll catch up in The Grapes later.'

The inspection of the farm and house went smoothly. Neither Elsie nor Stephen returned unexpectedly. Jenny was on the phone, deep in conversation with Rita, and although she looked puzzled at the sight of Charlie's companion, she didn't break off her call. However, possibly because he hadn't really seen her since Saturday, Charlie had completely forgotten about Alison.

After drawing a blank with Al's mobile last night, Alison had tried again this morning, but with the same result: 'number unobtainable' and 'message failed'. Puzzled, frustrated, and rather desperate, she couldn't understand why the text was not getting through – unless, of course, she speculated gloomily, Al, wanting to cut off any possible line of communication, had thrown his mobile into the sea.

Unable to get down to any school work, she had taken herself off to Bumble's small stable. She was giving her pony the most thorough grooming he'd had in years when she was disturbed by the sound of her brother's voice.

'It's a bit shabby, I grant you, but handsome. Built about 1810. Makes it Georgian, doesn't it?'

Alison couldn't hear distinctly what was said in reply, but then she heard her brother again. 'Yeah, well, this side of things is my brother's concern. It's been a good little dairy in its time and you've seen what prime grazing we've got.'

Something was said in response and then Charlie replied, clearly bringing the conversation to a close. 'Well, fine. As soon as possible. A rough figure is all I need to begin with. Thanks for coming out. Nice doing business with you.'

Feeling slightly sick, Alison put down the brushes and emerged to investigate. Charlie was just escorting a man back to his car.

'Charlie,' she called. 'Charlie – what's going on?'

At the sound of his sister's voice, Charlie almost bundled his companion into his car. Alison reached them just as the man released his handbrake and with a brief wave to Charlie, pulled away. She had time to register a large bundle of documents with an estate agent's logo on the car's back seat, before the Mondeo lurched and splashed its way back down the track.

She turned on her brother, hands on her hips, her jaw jutting aggressively. 'Okay, what was all that about? What was he doing here?'

'Nothing.' Charlie tried to sound as innocent as possible, whilst praying for inspiration. 'He just wanted to look round—'

'Look round? What for? He's an estate agent, isn't he? I saw his stuff in the back of his car. What's he here for?'

'He just wanted to look round, I told you ... He has a client who's looking for a farm this size and he—'

'Don't lie! I heard you: "thanks for coming – a rough figure is all I need" – what the hell do you mean? You're mad, Charlie! This farm does not belong just to you. We all own part of it, and, just in case you've forgotten, the Georgian farmhouse you were so admiring belongs to Mum!'

Charlie, perspiring slightly, tried reasoning. 'Listen, I've given this a lot of thought. You don't know this, but Hugh Lester wants this place something bad. I have it on good authority he's giving us a lot of grief ... So what I thought was, why not see how much the farm is worth, ask him something over the asking price and if he wants it that bad, he'll cough up and—'

'And what?' Alison was almost incoherent with rage. 'And what, you absolute and utter bastard? I can't believe you're thinking of selling out to the Lesters.'

'Isn't that what you've done?' Charlie shouted back, incensed at being wrong-footed.

'What do you fuckin' mean?' Alison screamed.

'You know what I mean – you've bloody slept with his son. If that isn't selling out to the enemy, I don't know what is!'

'You just don't know how wrong you are!' Weeping with fury, Alison lunged at her brother, but before their argument could descend into violence, Jenny called from the kitchen door.

'Alison, Alison! Come quick. Quick!'

Alison pushed her brother away, dashed the tears out of her eyes and hissed, 'Just you wait, Charlie. Just wait till Stephen and Gran hear about your plans for the farm!' Then she hurried over to join her mother. 'What is it, Mum?'

'It's Paula, dear, on the phone. She wants to speak to you urgently. Were you having a fight with Charlie?'

'Yes. With good reason. Why does Paula want to speak to me?'

'I dunno. Go on, pick up the receiver; she's waiting.'

As if the atmosphere at Summerstoke House on Sunday had not been bad enough, Wednesday threatened to be worse.

Paula had been summoned to work that morning and when she walked into the kitchen, a strange scene of desolation greeted her. The sink was full of unwashed pans and glasses, and on opening the dishwasher Paula found that it was full, and not only had the cycle not been started, but from the grungy state of the plates, it had been left like that for days. A loaf of bread, half eaten, sat on the table, crumbs everywhere; the butter dish had not been put away and the butter was half-melted; a slab of cheese had been cut into and left unwrapped, the edges hardening and cracked; a cloud of fruit flies hovered over a suppurating slice of watermelon; egg shells littered the counter next to the Aga, along with a pan that had clearly been used for scrambled eggs and been left to harden. Toast crumbs crunched under Paula's feet.

For all her faults, Veronica was a meticulous housekeeper, with exacting standards of tidiness and hygiene, so not only was Paula put out by the mess, but she was puzzled. She opened the door to the hall intending to announce her presence when the sound of voices in argument, floating from the direction of the sitting room, made her think better of it. She had nearly finished cleaning the kitchen when her employer stalked in.

'Are, there you are, Paula. Perhaps you'd make Mr Lester and myself some fresh coffee. We'll take it in the sitting room.'

Clearly there were going to be no apologies for the state of the kitchen or for the fact they had said nothing to her about being away on Monday and Tuesday. Paula was incensed. 'Excuse me, Mrs Lester, but would you mind tellin' me what's goin' on? You didn't say nothin' about goin' away and I do have my children to think of ... And the mess in here ...'

'I have no desire, or energy, to bandy words with you this morning. I don't pay you for that,' snapped Veronica. 'When you've finished in here, you can hull the strawberries I've put in the pantry, and then perhaps you'd be good enough to do the beds.' And she swept out of the kitchen.

Not only was Veronica more irritable than usual, but Paula thought she looked older, her body seeming to sag, and an aggrieved expression had settled like a permanent cloud over her features, making her nose sharper and her teeth more rodent-like than usual. Paula then caught a glimpse of Hugh when she carried the coffee through to the sitting room. He looked pale and haggard and his eye was a wonderful combination of purple and gold; his temper was no better than his wife's and the atmosphere between them was four-star deep freeze.

As she stripped the beds Paula wondered, not for the first time,

338

whether she could hack it any longer. There must be other people who wanted cleaners – perhaps she could persuade Lenny to fix her up with a little van and then she could have her own cleaning service, perhaps join forces with a mate, do people's houses when they weren't there … have a bit of a laugh. She'd rather be at home living on bread and water than be here, that much was certain.

The telephone rang and Paula went out onto the landing, wondering whether she was expected to answer it – Veronica liked to play posh sometimes and have her 'housekeeper' take calls. Veronica got there first and answered it peremptorily. Her tone changed when she recognised the caller. 'Mrs Merfield, how very … yes, Hugh is here. Just one moment, I'll … no, of course he's not too busy … oh, did you? I'm so sorry … no, it was my housekeeper; she didn't tell me that … I'm so sorry … I really am very sorry … look, here is Hugh now …'

Paula, fuming, headed back into the bedroom she was cleaning. So she was going to take the blame for them not phoning the Merfields. The cheek of it! A few moments later she heard Hugh bellowing for Veronica. She moved quietly to the bedroom door and opened it wide so she could enjoy the fireworks.

'Bloody old bag! What does she mean … when did she phone? "Actions speak louder than words" – that's what she kept on parroting, like some bloody mantra. We've lost the meadows, Vee. She's signed them over to the Tuckers for the next eight years and she has the cheek to suggest it was our fault!'

On and on he raged, and Paula could hear Veronica's voice getting shrill with fatigue, trying to calm him down. The phone rang again. Paula, again, went to the landing, but Veronica shouted up, a bit on the vicious side, Paula thought:

'I'll get it, Paula, since you don't seem to be able to pass on important messages.' Then Paula heard her cooing down the phone. 'Harriet! How are you? It was so nice … oh? I … I don't understand … but I thought … your editor changed his mind … just like that … but … I see. Well, thank you for letting me know … No, not at all … Yes, very nice to have met you, too.'

339

She slammed the receiver down – 'Cow!' – then pounded her fists on the little oak escritoire next to the phone, screaming at the top of her voice, 'I don't believe it! The cow! The bitch! She was spinning us along all the time.'

Paula was starting to find this all too much. She went into the next bedroom and shut the door. It was Anthony's room and now that he'd gone, she planned to give it a good clean out. To her surprise Cordelia was in there, sitting on his bed, shoulders drooping, head hanging.

Paula had known Cordelia since she was six and had watched her grow from a dainty, pretty child with blonde curly hair and big blue eyes, into a teenage blob with braces on her teeth, long straight hair that now verged on mousy, and a chubby, spotty face with small round eyes and a snub nose. In Paula's opinion, Cordelia was a horrible spoilt brat who took after her parents, and who treated Paula even more like a servant than they did, so Paula had as little to do with her as possible. But Paula had a warm heart, and the sight of the girl sitting there like a deflated balloon, hair hanging like a curtain around her face, looking so desolate, affected her. She went and sat on the bed next to Cordelia, putting an arm round her shoulders.

'What's up, Cordelia? What's wrong?'

To Paula's surprise, Cordelia flung her arms round her neck and sobbed bitterly. 'Anthony's not coming back. He's left, for good. And now he's in hospital – he could be dying ... they said he's badly hurt, but he won't see us. He sent them away and said he never wanted to see them again ... I'll never see him again ... and supposing he dies!' She wailed even louder, tears streaming down her podgy face, mascara and foundation smearing her cheeks.

Paula continued to hug her and utter soothing words of comfort until the loud sobs gave way to huge, disconsolate sniffs. Then she found her a tissue to blow her nose and when Cordelia had calmed down sufficiently, extracted the story from her.

Anthony had been in a bad crash at some service station on the motorway near Swindon. He'd been taken, unconscious, to Swindon Hospital and the police'd had to track his parents down. Cordelia had been sent to stay with friends while Hugh and Veronica had gone to the hospital. There they had waited the whole of Monday for him to regain consciousness. He finally came round on Tuesday and when he saw his parents at his bedside, he'd freaked and they'd had to leave. They booked into a local hotel, but he still refused to see them. Finally they had admitted defeat and came home that morning, picking her up on the way.

'Just because he says he doesn't want to see his parents, doesn't mean he don't want to see you, Cordelia.' Paula was dying to get away, but she was too kind to leave the girl in the state she was in. 'You could always go an' see him in Durham. Think of that – you could go with a mate; that's what I'd do.'

Cordelia, dabbing her eyes, started to cheer up. 'Hey, that would be really cool. I could go with my friend Tania. Mum doesn't like her, but she's keen and she's not afraid of anything.'

Meanwhile, downstairs, the screaming had subsided.

Paula decided the time had come to leave. Patting Cordelia farewell, she scooped up the sheets, walked out of the door, down the stairs and through the kitchen, ignoring Veronica's shouted 'Paula, come here a moment, would you?' She dropped the sheets in the middle of the kitchen floor, picked up her bag and jacket, kicked off the mules Veronica made her wear around the house, put on her high heels and was just about to leave when her eyes fell on the huge crystal bowl of glistening red strawberries that had tortured her nails when she had hulled them earlier. She skipped to a cupboard, took out a tub of fine sea salt and sprinkled it liberally over the fruit. Then she walked out of the kitchen door, away from Summerstoke House, for ever, as far as she was concerned.

She felt really good.

Then she remembered Alison. Whatever had gone on, Alison needed to know about Anthony.

*

Simon poked his head round the door and coughed politely. The secretary to the Country Club, who had been deep in a crossword, jumped slightly and looked up. 'Good morning, Mr Weatherby. Can I help you?'

Simon came into the large, light office that looked out across the tennis courts to a line of hills beyond. An oversized oil painting of the founder of the Country Club hung on one wall; on another, a picture of the Queen; and behind the secretary's desk hung an aerial photograph of the club buildings and grounds. Vying for position on the rest of the wall space were photographs of tennis players, golfers, and athletes of all shapes and sizes. A large display cabinet exhibiting numerous important-looking silver cups and badges stood in one corner, and in the other an elegant, bowed drinks cabinet.

Simon was politely apologetic. 'Sorry to disturb you, Mr Mackenzie, but I need to get in touch with a member. I have to ask him a favour and as I'm new here, I'm not one hundred per cent certain of his surname.'

'I'll do what I can. Can you give me any clues?' Mr Mackenzie swivelled round in his green leather chair and activated his computer. He was a small, neat man in his early sixties, who had taken up the appointment to keep himself busy after retiring from the armed forces, and ran the Country Club with exemplary efficiency. He kept a strategic distance between himself and the members, but there was very little he didn't know about them.

'His first name is Gordon. He was playing tennis with Veronica Lester last Thursday, on court number nine.'

Mr Mackenzie was surprised. 'Are you sure? Mrs Lester normally plays on one of the central courts.' He tapped on his keyboard as he spoke. 'The only two members called Gordon are Gordon Spence, one of our senior members, who rarely plays anything these days, and Gordon White, who joined shortly before you. He's not in Mrs Lester's league at all, so I can't imagine ... good gracious ...' He peered at his computer screen. 'Well, well, I must admit I am surprised. It's as you say: Gordon White is the chap you want.'

'Is there any way I can get hold of him? I've got to go off on a business trip within the next hour and I'd like to get him before I go.'

Mr Mackenzie tapped the keyboard again and in a matter of seconds Simon held a copy of Gordon White's details, including his daytime telephone number and his workplace address. Gotcha! he thought jubilantly, but his face was impassive as he politely thanked Mr Mackenzie and left.

A short while later, sitting in his car in the club car park, he was on the phone. 'Gordon, it's Simon Weatherby here. We met last week at the Country Club. You'd just thrashed Vee Lester ... well, thing is, I'm due to play her tomorrow evening at six-thirty on court number one ... yes, it was a lucky booking. Sadly, I'm going to have to cry off; I've got to go up north within the next hour and I won't be back, probably, till Friday. I know how much she enjoyed the challenge of playing against you last time and rather than disappoint her, I wondered ... you will? Thanks a lot, Gordon. Have a good game.'

As he rang off, a faint smile flitted across Simon's countenance. Faced with playing Gordon White on the court that always attracted spectators, would Veronica swallow her pride and continue her charade, or would she thrash the nasty creep? He turned the key in the ignition of his BMW convertible and drove out of the car park, away from the Country Club, for good.

Alison was devastated by Paula's call. Charlie's perfidy forgotten, she sat clutching the phone, white and shocked.

Jenny was worried. 'What is it, love? Bad news? You look dreadful.'

'Um, yes ... a friend of mine. He's been really badly hurt, in a crash.'

'Oh dear, I'm sorry to hear that, Ali. A car crash?'

'Yes, no. He came off his bike ... I don't know the details ...'

'Motorbikes are such lethal things. I'm glad Charlie doesn't ride one on the road any more.'

Alison stood up, desperate. 'Mum, I need to get to Swindon.'

'Swindon?' Jenny stared at her daughter.

'Yes, that's where he is. I need to get there.' Alison, distracted with grief, started to pace up and down the hall. 'I could get a bus into Bath and catch the train from there—'

'Yes, but—'

'Can you lend me the money? I know you're skint, but I've only got about five quid.'

Jenny shook her head, 'Ali, I spent the last of my housekeeping at the weekend. I've got nothing left till next weekend. I'm sorry, but you're gonna have to ask Charlie, or Stephen . . .'

Suddenly Alison remembered all the money Charlie had earned from the rave. Not only had he still not coughed up her allowance, as agreed, but he hadn't even found the time to give Mum a bit extra. She hated him; she couldn't bear the thought of having to ask him for anything, yet she needed money, urgently. 'Where's Stephen?'

'At the market; he had some calves to sell. If you wait for him to come back, I'm sure he'll lend you some, seein' as it's an emergency.'

Alison couldn't wait for his return. Swallowing her bile, she jumped up and rushed out through the kitchen into the yard to find Charlie.

But Charlie had made good his escape. He wasn't going to return until Alison had calmed down, and he'd thought of a better way of convincing the family that he had their interests at heart. If he'd looked in his rear-view mirror, he would have seen Alison running after him, shouting and waving her arms, trying to attract his attention. But he didn't, and he turned onto the road heading towards The Grapes without a backward glance.

Alison stood in the middle of the track, weeping helplessly. She couldn't think what to do. Simon had told her he was going to be out all day, so she couldn't apply to him, and Gran? She'd no idea where Elsie had gone.

She sank down onto the grassy verge and put her head on her knees.

'Please,' she whispered, 'somebody help, please!' She couldn't bear to think of Al lying in a hospital bed, badly injured ... Supposing he died before she could get to him? The tears flowed fast and furious. Such was her state of misery, she didn't hear a car approach down the track and stop.

'What's all this about then, Ali?' Elsie asked gently.

On the way to Bath station, Elsie stopped and made Alison top up her mobile.

'I want you to phone me the moment you get to Swindon. I'm going to give you enough money to take a taxi direct to the hospital. I don't want you wanderin' round, lost in a strange town. When you leave, you get a taxi back to the station and phone me so I know what train you're on. Is that clear?'

'Yes, Gran ... Gran, I don't know how to thank you. I tried to catch up with Charlie, but—' The mention of Charlie's name brought back the whole horror of what she'd overheard and what he was planning. 'Gran, Gran, you've got to stop him. He thinks he's doing it for the best, for all of us, but he's wrong—'

'Who are we talking about now, child? For goodness' sake, blow your nose. You don't want your young man opening his eyes and seeing you looking like that.'

'It's Charlie – I overheard him talking to an agent. He's getting the farm valued. He's gonna give a price to Hugh Lester—'

'Is he now?' said Elsie grimly. 'And how does he think he's going to persuade *me* to agree to the sale?'

'I don't know, but he's convinced himself it makes economic sense and that'll convince you and Stephen ...'

'That boy's always had his head somewhere else; always out for a quick buck, without thinking things through.' Elsie shook her head. 'Don't worry, Ali. I know what to do. Now, I haven't had a chance to tell you how much I like your friend Simon.'

'And his friend, Marcus.' Worried though she was, the fact that she was on her way to Al, and that Gran now knew everything, made her feel that life had stopped spinning out of control.

'Yes. Marcus was very nice, too. A bit of a flirt, though. Now tell me about Simon ...'

And so the rest of the journey was spent with Alison filling Elsie in on the details of how she'd met him, how their friendship had grown and the terrible circumstances that had led to him coming to Summerstoke.

'Poor young man.' Elsie shook her head. 'He's going to have to be very strong not to be destroyed by such goings on. How sad, how very sad.'

Having bought Alison's ticket, Elsie kissed her goodbye. 'One more thing, dear. I'm getting too old to drive back home and then back to Bath and then home again, all in one evening. I've got some business to sort out so I'll stay in Bath until I meet your train. You can contact me on this number.' She handed Alison a slip of paper. 'I'll phone your mother so she doesn't worry.'

But Jenny wasn't in a frame of mind to worry. 'Thank you, Elsie,' she said cheerfully. 'I'm off to the cinema with Jeff this evening, so I shall probably be home after you.'

Elsie sniffed. 'Seems to me, Jenny Tucker, you're seeing rather a lot of Jeff Babbington!'

'Angela ...' Nicola, after a great deal of effort, it seemed to her, had finally tracked Angela down in a corner of the children's section of Summerbridge public library. She had phoned the number given on the Merlin Players contact sheet a number of times. Finally it had been answered by an anonymous voice, identifying herself only as Angela's landlady, who had told her that Angela could be found at the library. The library refused to call Angela to the phone, so Nicola was faced with either abandoning her quest, or taking the trouble to go and confront Angela in person.

Left to herself, Nicola would probably have shrugged her elegant shoulders and moved on. But last night in the pub she had spoken long and eloquently about the exploitation of women and how Stephen was going to take advantage of the innocent Angela and it was up to them, to her, to prevent it from happening. To go back to the Players and say she couldn't get hold of Angela on the phone would be too feeble for words. So, she had turned up at the library and had been pointed in the direction of children's books.

Angela, who had been in such a state of rapture since Stephen had proposed to her that she could hardly think straight, was on her knees, ostensibly refilling the shelves. In fact she was reading *Northern Lights*, an experience so thrilling, she treated herself to five pages at a time whenever she could do so unobserved. When Nicola whispered her name, guiltily she snapped the book shut and looked up. Her eyes widened to see her rival, a vision of prettiness in a powder-blue linen dress with matching espadrilles, leaning over her.

'Nicola. What are you doing here?'

'Angela, we need to talk.'

'Why? What about? Are you having problems with *The Beaux Stratagem*? Don't say you can't do it —'

'No, no. It's nothing to do with the play. It's about Stephen.'

An alarm bell went off in Angela's brain. She sat back on her heels and looked up at Nicola.

'What about him?'

'Can't we go and talk somewhere else? Can you take a coffee break?'

Angela stared at Nicola. She looked uncomfortable and out of place, but Angela did not feel inclined to set her at her ease. 'No, sorry. I've had my break already. What do you want to say?'

Nicola hesitated, then squatting down on her heels by Angela's side, she launched into her speech. 'We couldn't help noticing, last night, that you and Stephen ... that you seemed to have ... that you and he ... seemed to have become an item.'

'So what business is that is yours?'

Nicola flushed. She had played this scene so many times in her head since last night, and had never envisaged any aggression or nastiness; rather a pitiful Angela, weeping with gratitude at having been rescued by her kind and beautiful ally. For a moment she looked at Angela with dislike. She really was a plain little thing.

Her white cotton blouse and dark blue rayon skirt emphasised the scrawniness of her figure; her skin was mottled; the glasses completely distorted the shape of her face and the sandy hair, scraped back into some sort of ponytail, was wispy and dull. How could Stephen have turned from worshipping her to proposing to…to this? Perversely, Nicola felt mortified, and was ready to lash out.

'Well, none, of course. But, Angela, darling,' she attempted to regain the high ground. 'There's something you need to know about Stephen. That is, if you don't know already.'

'I can't imagine there's anything else I need to know about Stephen. He tells me everything.'

Poor Angela. Her blissful certainty was her undoing.

Nicola pounced. 'So he's told you that unless he gets married within the year, his grandmother will disinherit him?'

Angela's eyes widened, her face went pink and her chin wobbled. Hiding her face from Nicola, she gave the pile of books, waiting to be put back on the shelves, her full attention.

Nicola knew she was on firm ground. She laughed, attractively self-conscious, a laugh she had worked at. 'The thing is, you must know that, until very recently, Stephen thought that I might … he was so in love with me, but …' She shook her head sympathetically and confided, 'Poor fellow, I don't know where he got the idea from that I might even be a little bit interested … I tried to let him down as gently as I could, and then I found out about his grandmother's ultimatum. He's desperate, Angela. And when you came into the rehearsal last night, apparently so sorted … I just wondered if he'd told you, that's all.'

Angela's flush deepened; *Anne of Green Gables* was pushed back on the shelf alongside *The Demon Headmaster*, and *The Sheep Pig* was placed upside down, its spine against the back of the bookcase, next to *Under Sea, Under Stone*. Nervously, she rubbed her chin. 'So when did Stephen tell you about … about his gran's threat?'

'I learned about it nearly two weeks ago now. He's kept it pretty quiet. I'm not surprised. What a thing to have hanging over you. Anyway, I just wanted to know that you're in the picture. It seemed such a dramatic changeover – first me, then you ... Poor fellow, he really must be desperate.'

The train journey to Swindon seemed interminable. Alison mentally blessed her grandmother for having insisted that she should take a taxi to the hospital, as it turned out to be a fair distance from the station. The longer she travelled, the more her anxiety grew and when she finally arrived at the hospital, she saw with dismay that it was a vast, modern construction. It took some time for her to finally locate the ward where Al had been put. It was a long, wide corridor, divided on either side by a series of partitions, each section containing four beds, some curtained off. At one end was a larger sitting area where a number of patients and their visitors sat chatting or watching the television. At the other was a series of small rooms and offices. Alison wandered up and down with growing desperation, unable to see Al anywhere. Finally she found a nurse and asked after him.

'Anthony Lester? Yes, he's here. But I'm afraid he's not well enough for visitors at the moment.'

It had never occurred to Alison that having finally tracked Al down, she might not be allowed to see him. 'Please,' she said, trying to hold back her tears. 'Please let me see him. I won't stay long, I promise.'

'You really should've phoned before you set out. For the moment, his visitors should really be just close family members. I'm not sure that includes girlfriends.'

'But I know he won't see his parents. If he doesn't want to see me, either, I promise I won't make a fuss.'

The nurse looked at her for a moment, then relented. 'Very well, but you mustn't stay long, and please don't get him over-excited about anything.'

She led Alison to a more enclosed section with four beds, close to the nurses' station, and pointed to one in the corner, half-concealed by a curtain. Alison, hardly breathing, walked softly over to where Al lay.

One leg was suspended in a hoist, an arm was in plaster and a long strip of tape stretched from his temple almost down to his ear, which, with his earring, gave him a piratical look. His face was very pale, smudged with bruising and grazes. His eyes were shut and his breathing was so light that for a moment Alison couldn't quite believe he wasn't dead. She knelt by his bed and touched his hand. It was warm.

'Ali?' His eyes were open and he was staring at her. 'Ali?'

23

Alison leaned forward and gently placed a hand on his cheek.

'Ali, I'm not dreaming, am I? Tell me I'm not dreaming.'

'You're not dreaming. It's really me. But Al ... I'll go if you want me to. I promised the nurse.'

'Why should I want you to go? Ali, you're the one person, the *only* person I wanted. But I didn't think I'd ever see you again.' His voice sank to a whisper and his eyes half closed, but he seized the hand that caressed his cheek and held it so tightly she couldn't withdraw it even if she'd wanted to.

'Ali ...' He opened his eyes again and stared at her. 'I don't know whether I'm asleep or awake, half the time. It *is* you, isn't it?'

'It is me.'

'Don't leave, don't go. I couldn't bear it if you left again. "Go boil your head in hell," you said, and your face ... I've never seen anyone so angry.'

'Al,' she whispered, trying to keep her voice steady. 'I was wrong, so wrong. I leaped to a conclusion and it was a totally wrong one. I should have trusted you; I didn't and I am so, so sorry.'

'No.' He gave a deep sigh and closed his eyes. 'I'm the one that's sorry.'

For a long while he lay there, his eyes shut, his hair dark against the pillow, his face so pale and drawn, Alison thought he looked close to death, but his grip on her hand was strong. The nurse popped her head round the curtain. 'Well, he looks a lot better, doesn't he? You can stay a bit longer, dear, if you want.

Don't worry about him dropping off like that – he's on morphine and it does have that effect.'

The afternoon ticked slowly by. It was quiet by Al's bed. The blue floral curtains occasionally rustled, lifting with a slight breeze from an open window on the other side of the room; in another bed, someone was snoring with a low, adenoidal rattle; there was the occasional murmur of conversation from the other occupants of the room, and beyond that she could hear the distant sounds of hospital life: the squelching of shoes hurrying along the corridor; electronic beeps; the telephone that seemed to sound off every few minutes; voices raised, briefly, in protest; the faint whine and clunk of the lift. Somewhere a clock struck four. The tea trolley shuffled in and out. Alison's stomach lurched – she hadn't eaten since breakfast – but she wouldn't have changed her position for anything.

'Ali?' He stirred, his eyes still shut. 'Ali? I love you. I love you.'

'I love you, Al.' She was so overcome, she could hardly get the words out. 'I love you.'

'Good.' A little smile flickered across his face, his eyes still closed as if the effort of opening them was too much. 'Even though I am a Lester?'

Alison's voice wobbled. 'You're nothing like your parents and I am so ashamed I ever thought you might have been.' She paused, unused to talking in this way, suddenly feeling shy, then continued, trying to be as light as she could. 'It's 'cos you got under my skin. I was falling in love with you and I think that's why I exploded, the other night. It was all too important. When I thought you'd betrayed me, I hated you. But I don't, I don't ... I realise that. And when I thought I'd lost you, when I couldn't get hold of you, I thought I'd go mad. And then, when I heard about your accident ... Oh Al, I love you, and I want you, I want you so much ... more than anything.'

At that he opened his eyes and gave her a lop-sided grin. 'Well, as to that, we might have to wait a while. But you can kiss me, if you like.'

It was the sweetest kiss of her life.

After his fight with Alison, Charlie changed his mind about going
to The Grapes. He had been unsettled by the confrontation and
didn't feel very sociable. Instead, he turned into Weasel Lane and
headed back to the field where he had started ploughing the day
before. He phoned Lenny and put off his promised pint until the
evening, then, just as he had climbed into the tractor's cab, his
mobile rang. It was the long-awaited call from Hugh Lester.

'What is it, Tucker? What do you want? I'm a busy man.'

'So we all are, Mr Lester. And it's not so much about what *I*
want, but what *you* want. You want my farm.'

There was a short silence from Hugh before he replied in a
guarded way. 'You know I do, Tucker. I've already made you
two offers, which you've turned down.'

'That's because you offered stupid money, and I'm not a fool,
Mr Lester. I just wanted to let you know that if you're seriously
interested, and I understand you are, then perhaps we should
meet and have a little discussion.'

A meeting was duly arranged for early the following evening.
Hugh suggested Charlie go to Summerstoke House, but Charlie,
feeling he had the upper hand, insisted that the meeting take place
in the lounge bar of The Grapes.

This was a development that should have pleased Charlie more
than it actually did. He was worried. His fight with Alison that
morning had been completely unexpected and he suspected he
hadn't handled it well. She was bound to tell Stephen about the
agent's visit and the prospect of having to face his brother's anger
did not appeal to him. Stephen had always been a pushover in the
past, but lately he'd been much more difficult to handle; Charlie
blamed Elsie and her schemes.

For the rest of the afternoon he concentrated on the ploughing.
The mist slowly lifted and by the end of the afternoon a milky
sun had pushed the temperature up and the weather had become
warm and humid. Charlie stopped at the end of his last furrow,
wiped the sweat off his brow and looked with satisfaction at the

neat rows of turned rich brown earth already occupied by flocks of argumentative seagulls. Stephen might be the better farmer, he thought, but he can't turn furrows as well as I can. He glanced at his watch. Not quite six. Rather than go and face Alison and a potential showdown at the farm, he decided to hop into his van and throw himself on Linda's mercy.

She was just opening up when he got to The Grapes and readily agreed to let him use her bathroom. 'Actually, Charlie ...' She stopped him as he was climbing the narrow staircase that ran up from the bar to the living quarters above. 'This would be a good time to do it. There's nobody about and it won't take long. Give me a shout when you've had your shower.'

Charlie looked at her, uncertain. 'Are you sure, Lin? Do you know what you're doing?'

Linda grinned. 'Of course I'm sure. You'll not regret it, I promise you. Don't forget, I trained as a hairdresser before I married Stan.'

A short while later, Charlie found himself sat in a chair, a towel around his shoulders, with Linda attacking his hair with comb and scissors. It seemed to him she was cutting an awful lot off. 'What am I going to look like?' he wailed. 'None of my friends will recognise me.'

'You took the first step shaving off those whiskers. It looked ridiculous keeping your hair so long and slapped into place with all that Brylcreem – so old-fashioned. I know you think you look odd, but that's because you're not used to it. One of my customers asked me who the dish was behind the bar, yesterday, and she wasn't referring to the dish of the day!'

Mollified, Charlie put up no further objections and told Linda about his fight with Alison, his worries about Stephen and his planned meeting with Hugh Lester.

She was interested and sympathetic, but sided with Stephen, which took Charlie by surprise.

'He'd be in the same boat as I'm in, Charlie. Stan wants to sell and if we do, that means I shall be homeless and jobless. Think about it.'

'I have, endlessly. And the more I do, the more sense it makes to sell. I really can't find any other way out of our difficulties. If Hugh Lester accepts my price, then it's a starting point; it doesn't commit us to anything. I couldn't sell without the rest of the family's agreement, anyway. But once they got over the shock, I'm sure they'd come round to the idea.'

'But it's more than a job for you all, isn't it? How would your family feel, not being at Marsh Farm any more? It's been in your family for years. What are they going to think of you, going to see Hugh Lester behind their backs?'

Charlie had no satisfactory answers. 'I'm just sounding out the ground.'

'So you say. However ... There. I'm done.' She held out a mirror to Charlie.

He stared at an unfamiliar image. The long sweep of hair, darkened and stiff with Brylcreem, had gone completely. His hair was a glossy nut-brown, now cropped quite short. He looked very much younger than his thirty-two years, but, he thought, he looked so odd ... maybe it was the white patches from his missing hair that were the problem. He fingered his face.

'What do you think?' Linda was enthusiastic. 'Looks cool, doesn't it? I always knew you were a good-looking dude under all that growth. Come on, put your shirt on and stop looking so mournful. Don't worry about the white skin – it'll tan soon enough.'

They were interrupted by a shout from the bar and Linda hurried down to serve.

When Charlie joined her, Lenny had just come in. He stopped in his tracks and stared and stared, open-mouthed, at his friend, until Charlie protested, 'Oh, come on – I've just had a haircut, that's all.'

'That's all! Blimey, Charlie, you've 'ad a complete makeover. Talk about the ugly duckling! You'll be wearing Armani suits next.'

*

Stephen had spent the day in a happy daze. He'd arranged for a specialist to come and sort out his water heater problems, cleaned the dairy till it sparkled, and had driven the cows back to their pasture after the afternoon milking. Angela finished work at five-thirty and they had agreed that he should pick her up from her lodgings with all the information on different approaches to farming that she'd been collecting for him. They were going to spend the evening together, working on the business plan. He glanced at his watch. No time to change – he'd do that after he picked her up. *She* wouldn't mind if he smelled of cows.

Driving to Summerbridge, Stephen contentedly indulged in daydreams about Angela, the farm and their future. Left to himself, he freely admitted, he would not have been up to the task of putting together a business plan, but with Angela helping him, he almost looked forward to it. 'She's a bit like Gran,' he thought happily, 'not afraid of forms and figures.'

From out of nowhere, the thought of his gran thumped Stephen in the solar plexus. Inadvertently, he swerved violently, causing the car behind to sound its horn. Stephen, shaking, pulled onto the side of the road. How could he have forgotten his gran's ultimatum? And Angela ... what on earth would Angela make of it when she found out? Perhaps she didn't have to know? After all, he hadn't told anyone, and he knew *that* wasn't the reason why he'd asked her to marry him. Far from it ... Why complicate matters?'

'Say nothing,' he thought, 'and maybe it won't arise. Say nothing, and maybe it will ...'

Miserably, he resumed his journey.

Unusually, Angela didn't come running out as soon as he arrived. The curtains in her window, which was on the ground floor at the front of the house, were drawn, and it was the landlady who let him in.

Angela finally responded to the knock on her door, and although she tried to smile brightly at him, she looked pale and her eyes were pink and puffy. She drew back slightly when he bent to kiss her and responded only with a perfunctory peck.

'Sorry, I didn't hear you arrive, Stephen. I was lying down. I've got a bit of a headache.'

'I'm sorry to hear that. Do you want to give this evening a miss?'

'No, no, it's all right. Simon says we need to get a move on.'

'But if you're not up to it ... you do look really pale.' He was concerned.

Angela flushed and Stephen could have sworn there were tears in her eyes. But she shook her head. 'No,' she said firmly, 'I'm fine. The stuff's all in that box, there, and I've bought some things for our supper.'

Her room was small and neat. The box she indicated was sitting on a table in the window bay; her sofa-bed was tucked against the wall, underneath a picture of Constable's *The Hay Wain* (her favourite painting, she had once told Stephen); the third wall was filled by a built-in cupboard divided into two, one half of which held her modest collection of clothes, and the other half a sink and an electric hotplate, with shelves below, for her food. A small chest of drawers, one dining chair and one armchair completed the furniture, all of which was serviceable, but dull and old-fashioned. The room was enough to pull anyone down, Stephen thought. Ange deserved better.

She was unusually silent all the way back to the farm and Stephen, stealing a glance, noticed her staring out of the window, a set expression on her face. Perhaps now would not be a good time to tell her about Gran; if she was not feeling well, she might completely misunderstand – particularly if she was having a period or something (he'd been alerted to the problems of PMT often enough, by the women in his household).

So instead Stephen set about trying to make Angela as comfortable as possible. She was so very quiet, it worried him and he fussed, making her endless cups of tea, assembling the lettuce, tomatoes, coleslaw, potato salad, cold meat and cheese that she'd bought for their supper, till finally, pulling up a chair next to her so that they could go through the business plan, he put his arm around her and said gently, 'Is there something wrong? Are you all right?'

Angela turned her head away and studied one of the forms intently. 'No, nothing's wrong. Really. You've been so kind to me this evening. It's just … it's just this headache.'

At the end of a busy evening in the public bar of The Grapes, Charlie washed glasses, wiped the bar, cleared tables and stashed empties, whistling quietly as if he'd being doing it for years. His new look had attracted many favourable comments, he had enjoyed lively conversation with a number of regulars and, although tired, he felt content.

Linda, seeing off the last few customers, threw him a grateful smile. 'Charlie, you've been a real asset this evening. Lots of people have complimented me on my new barman.'

Charlie grinned back. 'Any time you want me, I'm happy to oblige. Beats farming, any day.'

She had just gone into the kitchen to put their supper in the microwave when Charlie heard the outer door to the pub open. 'Sorry, mate, we're closed,' he called out.

'Well, well, well,' Stan said softly, his face cast in deep shadows by the bar light. 'If it's not Farmer Tucker, toes tucked behind the bar, all shorn and sheepish. What a pretty boy, eh? She didn't waste much time, did she? Giving me all that crap about being abandoned, trying to run the place on her own …'

'What are you fucking on about? I'm just giving her a hand.'

'Oh yeah? And what else are you givin' her? Didn't hang about, did yer?'

'I don't know what you're talking about. I'm not giving her anything but help running this place.'

'Come off it, Charlie, you've always fancied her. I'm not stupid—'

'Yes, you are.' Charlie was suddenly really angry and didn't notice Linda coming back into the bar. 'You're *really* stupid, Stan. You had something nice here and you threw it away. Linda's a really classy bird and you just didn't see it, didn't see what she was worth. Threw it all away for a bit of tit and big blue eyes, and the sort of skirt that would make eyes at the likes of me. Linda's not that sort, more's the pity for me. But you, you just snapped your fingers and turned your back on it, so don't tell me you're not stupid. Stupid ain't the word for it – you're fuckin' brain-dead!'

Stan growled deep in his throat and swung a punch at Charlie who, just in time, ducked down behind the bar. Stan's fist came crashing down on the counter, setting all the glasses jumping and tinkling.

'That'll do.' Linda was composed, icy. 'Charlie, you'd better go now. I'll lock up. Stan and I have business to discuss. If you'd like to call round tomorrow, I'll settle your wages. Thanks for tonight.'

Wages? Charlie was deeply offended. So Linda saw him as a hired hand, and *he'd* thought . . . oh never mind what he'd thought. He stalked to the door and Linda followed him, the keys in her hand. Stan stood at the bar and watched them.

Over the rattling of the lock, Linda whispered, 'Charlie, come back tomorrow, please. It's best if I deal with him on my own. I'll be all right, honest.'

'Your mum's back late from the cinema,' remarked Angela, rubbing her eyes with fatigue. 'I'm sorry, but I don't think I can do any more tonight. We've made a good start, though. I'll take this map of the farm and photocopy it tomorrow, then we can mark in what might be the farm walk—'

'I'm sorry, Ange. A full day at the library, then a whole evening working on this plan – and with a headache. You must be exhausted. I'll run you home.'

'Thank you.'

'Shall I make us a cup of tea before we go?' Stephen blushed. 'It would be nice to see Mum and tell her about us.'

Angela went slightly pink and looked distressed. 'Er, perhaps not tonight. We don't want to rush things, do we? Not until we're really sure.'

359

It was Stephen's turn to look distressed. He turned in his chair to face her and put an arm round her thin shoulders. 'I'm sure. Aren't you?' When she didn't reply but hung her head still further, Stephen was alarmed and put out a hand, gently touching her cheek. 'Have I done something to upset you? I wouldn't hurt you for the world.'

Before Angela had a chance to answer, Charlie stumbled in. 'Blimey, you'd never guess what I've just seen – Mum and Jeff outside, in the car, snogging!' He registered his brother's position. 'Strike a light! What's goin' on? Mum and Jeff, you and Four Eyes ... Somebody fill me in, please!'

'If you ever call Ange that again, I'll fill you in all right!' Stephen hissed, turning to meet his brother. His eyes widened. 'Blimey, you've had your hair cut – you don't look like Charlie any more; you look like ... like ...' For a moment his brow furrowed, trying to work out, without success, just who his brother reminded him of.

Then he took Angela's arm and self-consciously started to introduce his fiancée to his brother. 'Ange, I'm not sure how well you know my brother, Charlie. We're partners on the farm. Charlie, Ange and I have been working on a business plan. We've been looking at how we might introduce rare breeds, change farming practices, introduce things like farm walks and stuff; bringing the farm up to date and making it a more commercial proposition. Do you want to have a look over it? If you agree, we could submit it to the bank and maybe ...'

From the way Stephen was talking, Charlie realised that Alison hadn't told him about the estate agent. Overwhelmed with relief, he seized his opportunity.

'Steve, you should have talked to me before you went to all this trouble.' He picked up the document and flicked through it. 'It's great you've done so much, and I hate to pour cold water on it, mate, but it ain't going to work.'

Stephen stared at his brother. 'Why not?'

'Well, for one thing, the way things are with the bank at the moment, they're not going to look twice at anything like this. Be realistic, Stevie – they want us to cut our debt, not ask them for more money!'

'But Simon said, and Gran, that this was the best way to go. We've got to get them on our side—'

'I don't know who this Simon is, but Gran's still living in the last century.'

'I don't know how you can say that. She's as sharp as she ever was, and you know it.'

Charlie shook his head. 'Well, maybe, but the thing is, she doesn't know how things stand.'

'And you do?'

'Yes, I do – there's something I've found out that she doesn't know, and nor do you.'

'What?' Stephen's chin jutted belligerently.

'For a start, the bank is in the pocket of Hugh Lester. They'll turn anything down that we might come up with. He wants our farm.'

'We know—' Angela started to speak, but Stephen stopped her. He turned to his brother, a dangerous look in his eyes.

'So what are you proposing, Charlie? Do nothing and slide towards bankruptcy?'

'Of course not. I've given the matter a lot of thought, Stevie, and this is my plan: we sell to Hugh Lester.'

'What?' Stephen was almost beside himself with rage and disbelief.

'Hold on, hold on. Let me explain. Hugh Lester wants this farm so bad, he's prepared to go to almost any lengths to get it. I've had the farm valued and I'm proposing offering it to him at a bit above the valuation. He's unscrupulous. He'll get us out one way or another. This way it'll save him and us a lot of bother.'

'What?' Stephen leaped to his feet, knocking his chair over.

Charlie held up a hand. 'Makes sense. We collect a tidy sum, well over a million, with any luck. You can buy another farm somewhere else, cheaper than this. Everyone's selling at the moment, but we're lucky, we've got a buyer who's desperate, so we're quids in—'

'I don't believe I'm hearing this!' Stephen, furious, grabbed Charlie's jacket.

'Take your hands off me.' Charlie, getting annoyed in turn, pushed him back. 'For Chrissake, Stephen, don't be so bloody stupid. Can't you get it in your thick head that this is the best thing we can do – all that stuff with fluffy, cuddly animals just won't work.'

Incensed, Stephen pushed Charlie, hard, and before Angela could do anything to stop them, both men were rolling over and over on the kitchen floor. Chairs went flying and the table, crashed into once too often, collapsed at one end, sending years of accumulated paraphernalia slithering to the floor.

Gip, jolted out of her basket, added to the general mayhem by barking furiously at the fighting men and dancing round them, trying to nip any available ankle.

Amid the chaos, Jenny and Jeff came into the kitchen, followed closely by Elsie and Alison.

'What is going on?' Jenny shouted across the din to Angela.

'Oh, please stop them, Mrs Tucker. Stephen's bleeding. They're going to kill each other!'

Jeff attempted to intervene, but to no avail.

Jenny went straight to the sink, picked up a bowl of stagnating washing-up water and threw it over them. The fight stopped abruptly. Both men sat on the floor, dazed, water dripping off their faces, their hair, their clothes. Stephen had blood streaming from his nose and with a small scream Angela ran to him. Charlie had received a thump to one eye, which was closing rapidly.

'Well done, Jenny,' said Elsie approvingly. She turned to the two men. 'Now it's your turn. I think we deserve an explanation.'

24

'They calmed down pretty quick, after that, although they couldn't stop glowering at each other.' Alison, her arm linked through Simon's, chuckled.

Simon had rung her that morning. She told him about Al and the accident, and the agreement she'd made with Al that as Swindon was so far away, she would confine her visits to every other day. Awful though Al's injuries were, Alison was on a cloud of loving and being loved, and Simon was delighted. He had suggested that when he got back from work they should meet for a walk.

'Angela seemed pretty upset,' Alison continued, 'so Uncle Jeff took her back to Summerbridge, then Gran gave the boys a right ticking off. Gave us *all* a lecture on pulling together, not fighting – Mum'd no idea what was going on. She seemed more amazed by Charlie's haircut and how like Dad he looked, than anything … Gran wants us all to meet up this evening. She says she wants to talk to us.'

'Sounds intriguing.' Simon whistled for Duchess, who had lingered behind on the riverbank, fascinated by some smell or other. 'Wish I could be a fly on the ceiling.'

They were making their way along the riverbank, past the blackberry bushes where Duchess had knocked her into the water. 'Funny to think I never met Charlie,' Simon mused. 'Actually, apart from the fact that no one should *ever* give the Lesters anything, his plan was not without economic sense.'

Alison snorted. 'Any plan of Charlie's is doomed to failure. I wish you'd met him when he still had sideburns – he looked like a relic from the nineteenth century; now he just looks ordinary.'

Simon took a card out of his inside pocket. 'Here, give this to Stephen, Ali. I had a word with someone at your bank. He's working with me on this current project. I'm pleased to say he was horrified to hear of the somewhat non-professional practices of Mr Gordon White. He's instructed me to tell you that when Stephen is ready with his business plan, he must contact this gentleman. I think Stephen'll find the bank sympathetic.'

Alison's eyes widened. 'How did you swing that?'

'I didn't swing it. Banks don't like to think their employees behave unprofessionally. If you'd made a complaint, which we could have substantiated, they would be in a very difficult position. This is an easy way out for them.'

Alison shook her head. 'I don't know how to thank you. You've made everything come right for us. If only,' she added, wistfully, 'I could make things come right for you.'

Simon put his arm around her shoulders. 'Unfortunately you can't do that, but you and your family have made it easier, in all sorts of ways. Above all else, you've kept me sane.'

Alison slipped her arm round his waist and hugged him. She wanted so much to make him happy, but she knew there was not a lot she could do or say. Then a thought struck her. 'Talking about sanity ... is your friend Marcus entirely sane?'

The unexpected question made Simon laugh. 'Yes, I think so. Why do you ask?'

'He came over this morning and spent hours taking loads of photographs of everything – broken tractors, the old duck pond, even the stinking puddle round the silage bunker.'

'He works with pictures all the time. He sees things we don't.' Simon became serious. 'Listen, I want to tell you something and I need to ask a huge favour of you.'

'What is it?' Alison had a premonition it wasn't going to be something she would like very much, and she was right.

'I've been offered a job. It's going to take me overseas, to South Africa, in fact. There's an important company in trouble there and they want me to go as soon as possible.'

Alison went cold. 'When? How long will you be gone for? Oh, Simon!'

'They want me to go by the end of this coming weekend. I don't know how long for – could be six months, or could be longer. Don't look so stricken, Ali. Be pleased for me. It'll be a new country, new people, and I shall be far removed from any chance meeting with Helen and the baby. I'll be back, don't worry. I'll come and dance at your wedding to Al; that's a promise!'

But she couldn't raise a smile, even at that prospect. Simon stopped and turned her to look at him. 'I have to come back, anyway,' he said. 'If I didn't, Duchess would never forgive me.'

'Duchess! Oh, poor Duchess, she'll be desolate!'

'Yes, but I can't take her with me. Will you look after her, Alison?'

'Of course I will.' Alison suddenly felt weepy and flung her arms round Simon. 'Take care of yourself. Please take care. I'm going to miss you.'

'And I shall miss you; you and Duchess. You mean a lot to me, little Alison, and I don't intend to lose you. I'll be back.'

'No thanks, Mum. I haven't got time, and anyway, I'm not really hungry.'

For the first time in his life, Stephen had refused food.

Jenny, in the process of serving out a plate of sausage and beans, stared at him with concern. 'Are you all right, love? You've been hard at it all day; you must eat something before your rehearsal. Are you feeling unwell?'

'No, I'm fine. Ange wants me to pick her up a bit earlier, so I've got to dash.' And he left the kitchen almost at a run before his mother could question him further.

Stephen had spent a miserable day. Not only was he thoroughly upset by what he saw as his brother's perfidy, but he was worried about Angela. She had been so quiet the evening before. She'd not wanted to talk about anything apart from the farm proposals; she'd not responded to his attempts to kiss her, and then she'd suggested that she wasn't sure about marrying him. He, Stephen, was sure. He'd never been more certain about anything. Once the fog of his obsession with Nicola had rolled back, he could see clearly that Angela was worth a million Nicolas, that she would make him happy in a way nobody else could, and he didn't want anything to get in the way of their future together.

He had thought that Angela felt the same way. But it seemed he was wrong. Had something happened to make her change her mind? Was it something that he'd done? And then there was that threat of Gran's looming over his head. He'd have to tell Angela about that, and if she was uncertain already . . .

Then Angela had phoned him at lunchtime and had asked him to meet her a bit earlier than usual, so they could talk. About what, she hadn't said, so he had spent the afternoon in fruitless speculation. No wonder he wasn't hungry.

She was obviously looking out for him because she was out of the house as soon as he drew up in the Land Rover. To his great relief, when she climbed into the cab, she leaned across and kissed him on the cheek and smiled. He turned the engine off and turned to her. Whatever happened, there was never going to be a right time and he had decided to take the plunge, come what may.

'I know you want to talk to me about something, Ange, but first there's something I've got to tell you. Something I've told no one else and it might upset you. I can see that it might, anyway, if you didn't believe that I love you, which I do, love you, that is . . .'

Angela turned to look at him, her eyes bright. 'Do you? Do you really?'

He took her hand. 'Yes, I do, Ange. I really do. All that stuff I said to you on Tuesday, I meant it, all of it. It's like I've suddenly woken up to what I want.'

'You want the farm to survive more than anything, don't you, Stephen?'

He nodded. 'Of course, because that's my life, and yours, too, I hope. But if you didn't want . . . if you didn't want to farm, I'd rather lose it, than lose you.'

'Do you mean that?'

He sighed. 'Yes, I really mean that.'

She leaned across, took his face in her hands and kissed him. After a dizzying few minutes she let go and breathlessly asked, 'What was it you was going to tell me?'

He looked down at his hands, took a deep breath, and began. 'It's to do with my gran. She's quite strong-willed, you know ... an' she owns half the farm, an' ...'

He froze, suddenly overwhelmed by the realisation that Elsie's stupid ultimatum was putting his whole future in jeopardy. And he also realised that what he'd said to Angela was true: if it came to a point where he'd have to choose between the farm and her, there was no contest.

Angela took his hand in hers. 'Go on, Stephen, tell me.'

'A few weeks back, Charlie did something really stupid, which really got up her nose. Being the sort of person she is, she told us that unless we got our act together within the year, she would cut us out of her will. If we did, you know, what she asked us, then ... then she would give us her share of the farm.'

Silence.

Nervously Stephen cast a glance at Angela.

She was looking at her hands folded in her lap and he could not read her expression. 'What did she ask you to do?'

Stephen could find no way of making it less awful. 'Find a wife,' he finally blurted out. 'But Ange, that's not why I—'

'Stephen.' Angela looked up at him, her eyes sparkling. 'I've been thinking about it ever since I heard. I admit I was upset at first, but then, I thought, you've got more than eleven months to find someone else. It's like something from a Greek legend or a Grimm's fairytale. Do you want to take up the quest to find the perfect bride?'

'No.' Stephen was humbled. 'I've found her. I know you're the only one I shall ever be truly happy with.'

Angela, glowing, flung her arms around him. 'Kiss me.'

It was Stephen who broke off this time, panting and feeling a little puzzled. 'Hold on, Ange, you said "ever since you heard". How did you hear? I never told anyone.'

'Nicola told me. She came to the library to warn me.'

'How did *she* know?'

'She hinted that you'd told her. That's what hurt, Stephen. The thought that you'd told her and you hadn't told me, your best friend.'

'I would never keep anything back from you. I would never do anything to hurt you. You know that, don't you?'

'Yes,' Angela said happily. 'Yes, I know that. When Mr Babbington gave me a lift home last night, we talked and he helped to make everything clear. He's very fond of you, Stephen, and he said you were the most honest man he knew. That you would never say anything you didn't mean. I told him about Nicola and he said I should talk to you and not leap to conclusions. He was so kind. So that's why I phoned. I was going to ask you about your gran, but you got there first and I can't tell you how happy that's made me!'

'I wonder who told Nicola ...' But he found Angela's mouth on his, and that particular question never got answered.

It was inevitable that this conversation, and the long embrace that followed, meant that when June Pagett and the Merlin Players arrived for their evening rehearsal there was no sign of Stephen and Angela and the stage was bare of furniture and props. Mrs Pagett was loud in her annoyance and bullied the actors into setting up for themselves. Nicola found herself being questioned and then taken to task by Gerald and the others.

'Did you see Angela?'

'How did she take it?'

'Was she upset?'

'Do you think that's why she's not here tonight? Couldn't face us?'

'Or Stephen, for that matter. If she told him we knew, then maybe he wouldn't want to face us.'

'What about our rehearsal?'

'Supposing neither of them comes back?'

'What's going to happen to our performance?'

'It's really hard to get a decent stage manager.'

'And we've gone and lost two really good ones.'

'We shouldn't have interfered ...'

'Nicola shouldn't have interfered, you mean. What business was it of hers to say anything?'

'We're going to be in a right mess if one of them doesn't come back.'

'Nicola's really upset the applecart.'

It was with some relief that Nicola saw Stephen and Angela walk in, hand in hand, half an hour late, unapologetic and clearly very happy.

'You must be joking, Tucker, if you think that I'd be prepared to pay that much for your dump of a place.'

Hugh Lester, his eye now a glorious, autumnal yellow and brown, glared at Charlie, who sported a resplendent red and purple eye and who sat, unperturbed, sipping his beer. They had met as agreed. The bar, a comfortable red plush haven, smelling of beer and furniture polish, was empty apart from one couple tucked away on the window seat, engaged in an intimate conversation. Having served Charlie and Hugh, Linda had left them to it and gone back into the public bar.

Charlie had been very subdued all day. The fight with his brother had upset him, and the revelation that the rest of the family all knew about the Lesters anyway, and backed Stephen's approach to dealing with the farm's problems, left him feeling redundant and sidelined. The prospect of the meeting that Gran had called for that evening further added to his gloom. He hadn't had a chance to soften her up to the idea of selling to the Lesters, and she had indicated in the strongest possible terms last night that she did not approve of his proposal to do so. He had considered cancelling the meeting with Hugh Lester, but at the thought of everything Hugh had done to them, at the prospect of the struggles facing them trying to meet the bank's demands in the months to come, and at the thought that there would never be enough money for a reconditioned motocross bike, let alone a new one, Charlie was filled with an overwhelming desire to see Hugh Lester suffer in some way. So he had decided to spin him along.

Sitting opposite him, Charlie viewed his family's enemy dispassionately. He certainly was well preserved for his age – what was he? Fifty? He looked strong, clean-shaven with a firm jaw and prominent cheekbones; his hair was thick and black, and his eyes – such a cold blue. There was nothing soft or humorous in his face and it was not made any more attractive by the glaring, blood-shot eyeball. He was surprisingly short – Charlie had not met him often and then he was usually in his car or on a horse, so his lack of height took Charlie aback. 'That's probably why he's such a bully,' he thought to himself. 'He's a short-arse.'

He sipped his beer and smiled in response to Hugh's terse rejection of the figure he'd proposed. 'There's no need to be uncivil, Mr Lester. That "dump of a place" is our home, so it has a price. I've told you, I had the farm and house valued. You've told me you want Marsh Farm. I've told you what we want for it.'

'It's a preposterous amount. Way above the valuation figure, I'm sure. It's not worth it.' Hugh was getting impatient.

'No? But Mr Lester, it's what you're going to have to cough up if you really want it. And from what I've heard, you really want it.'

Hugh glared at Charlie. 'What do you mean?'

'I mean: interfering with my bank manager – sending your wife out to make love to him so he puts the screws on us. You must want it really bad, Hughie, or is that the way you normally do business – using your wife?'

With an explosion of anger, Hugh leaped to his feet and grabbed hold of Charlie's shirtfront. 'You little piece of shit; I don't have to take that from someone like you. Apologise!'

Charlie got to his feet and towered above Hugh. 'I think you should let go of my shirt, Hughie, or I'll colour the other eye for you.'

'You do that and I'll have you back in court for a bit more than being drunk and disorderly.'

'You do that and I'll have *you* in court. Nobbling the bank — I don't know what the courts call it these days, but I bet it carries a heavier sentence than my clocking you one would, particularly when I have been *so* provoked, and not just with your wife playing with my bank manager, but making malicious calls to the boys in white coats about our dairy, trying to bribe my hired man, and blackening my name in the village so we lose our leased meadows? As I said, you must want our farm really bad. Is there nothing you will not stoop to, Hughie?'

For a moment, Charlie watched Hugh change all colours of the rainbow, then he released his hold on Charlie's shirt and pulled himself back, knocking his chair over with a clatter. Out of the corner of his eye, Charlie saw Linda reappear in the bar. 'You'll regret this,' Hugh muttered thickly. 'I'll make sure of it. You'll regret taking me on—'

'Are we adding threats to our list of things we stoop to, Mr Lester? If so, allow me to make one of my own: if I so much as get a whiff of any action taken by you against my farm or my family, I shan't hesitate to take a full description of you and your wife's antics to the press. It's the sort of story they'd love!'

With an inarticulate cry, Hugh turned on his heel and charged out of the pub.

With an insouciance he was not feeling, Charlie picked up his unfinished pint and went to join Linda at the bar.

The meeting had been arranged for ten o'clock. The kitchen had been tidied, all traces of supper had been cleared away and the kettle was gently hissing on the Rayburn ready for demands for tea. Jeff, whom Elsie had also invited to the family gathering, was sitting at the kitchen table unpacking a box containing a food mixer. It had belonged to his wife and had been sitting at the back of a cupboard unused for years, he told Jenny. Stephen, and Angela who had also been invited at Elsie's request, were expected back from their rehearsal at any moment. Charlie had just returned from The Grapes, armed with a tube of instant tan that Linda had given him. He had disappeared off to the bathroom to touch up his white wings whilst they were waiting for Stephen and Angela to arrive. And Alison was sitting at the kitchen table with Jeff and her mother, telling Jenny about Simon's plans and about looking after Duchess.

'That'll be nice, dear – company for Gip. We shall miss Simon, though. What a friend he's been to us, eh? And how's that young man of yours doing?' She was knitting something that looked like a small tea cosy, in bright red wool, impregnated with little flecks of yellow.

'I spoke to him this afternoon. He says he feels a lot stronger today.'

'Good. I'm looking forward to meeting him. I must bake a cake for you to take in to him. Now I've got Jeff's lovely mixer to use, I'll be able to bake cakes every day. You know what they say about hospital food. How long are they going to keep him in?'

'He doesn't know. He's going to have to find somewhere to stay. He'll be on crutches, so he'll need quite a bit of care.'

'Won't he go home?'

'He'd rather die. Do you know, Mum, his parents had him put in a private room when he was still unconscious. When he came round, he ordered the nurses to put him back on the ward!'

'Goodness me; his poor parents! How they must feel – they'd only want the best for him!'

Alison realised that the whole Lester thing had passed her mother completely by. Maybe one day, before she brought Al home, she'd attempt to explain things to her.

The door opened and Stephen ushered Angela in.

'That's pretty, Mrs Tucker.' Angela sat down, admiring Jenny's dexterity with the needles. 'What are you knitting?'

'A strawberry.' Jenny held it up for Angela to see. 'Or rather, a hat shaped like a strawberry. I saw one for sale the other day for ten pounds and I thought: I could knit that for a fraction of that price. My friend Rita suggested I make a few and sell them in her shop and in the farmers' market. Oh, Stephen, here's a funny thing; I quite forgot to tell you earlier. A lady phoned this afternoon, Harriet something – I've written it down. She wants to come and see us. Something about an article for a magazine called ... now what was it called? It's written on that pad over there, Ali. Read it out, would you?'

Alison obliged. 'Harriet Flood, *Country Homes and Gardens.*' She grinned. 'Clever Simon!'

'What's that, Ali?'

'Oh, nothing, Mum. Where's Gran? We're all here.'

'Not quite,' said Elsie, entering the kitchen with Charlie following her. 'Jeff,' she produced two bottles of elderberry wine, ' – make yourself useful and open these, would you? Charlie, you get the glasses together. We're going to need eight. Ah!' The diesel chug of a taxi could be heard outside. 'He's here.'

She went to the door, followed by six curious pairs of eyes. 'Come in, come in, we're all waiting for you ...' And in through the door walked an elderly, stout, red-faced man with twinkly blue eyes and a polished bald head.

Alison gasped in alarm. 'Gran! What's he doing here?'

Elsie motioned to her to be quiet. 'Before I introduce you to our guest, I just want to say we've got a lot of family business to tie up this evening, so I won't waste any time and I'd thank you to all keep quiet! Now, first of all, let me introduce you to Mr Ronald Bates. He's a very old friend of mine and we've decided to get married. We're not inviting any of you. We're off to Scotland at the weekend and we're going to get married in Gretna. It's all arranged.'

The shockwaves in that kitchen might have registered eight point nine on an emotional Richter scale. Without exception, jaws dropped, eyes bulged.

Alison alone attempted to protest. 'But Gran, you can't marry him – he's mad – you said so yourself!'

Ron, sitting by Elsie's side, chuckled, looking anything but mad.

'No he's not,' said Elsie briskly. 'I enlisted his help in a little deception, for which, my girl, you should be grateful.'

Alison, puzzled, sank back in her chair, trying to assimilate the shock. There was a feeble chorus of felicitations, but Elsie held up her hand. 'We can celebrate later. Now then, next in seniority – Jeff Babbington, are you going to make an honest woman of Jenny?'

Jenny, startled, dropped her knitting. 'Gran!'

Jeff, taken by surprise for once, gaped at the full-on effrontery of the question, then threw back his head and laughed heartily. 'I'd love to,' he shouted, 'if she'll make an honest man of me!'

'Well, Jenny?' Elsie was in no mood for niceties.

Jenny blushed crimson and looked across at Jeff, who grinned broadly back at her. 'This is all very sudden,' she said shyly. 'We've not had much time to ... What I mean is ...'

Jeff came to her rescue. 'Thanks for the suggestion, Elsie. Jenny and I will let you all know when we're good and ready.'

At that, the kitchen erupted with excitement and Elsie had to bring them to order by banging the table with a rolling pin.

'We haven't finished. Stephen, have you got something to tell us?'

'Yes, Gran.' He took Angela's hand and turned to Jenny. 'Mum, Angela and me, we want to get married.'

There was a moment's stunned silence and then Jenny burst into tears, hugging Stephen and then Angela, then Stephen again. Jeff and Alison joined in enthusiastically and then, after an initial diffidence, so did Charlie. Ron sat and looked on, smiling benignly, squeezing the bony hand of their commander-in-chief.

'Right,' she said, calling them to order yet again. 'That's all the nuptial announcements over unless, Charlie, you've got something up your sleeve.' He shook his head, too shaken to make the sort of wisecrack he could boast of later.

'Now, to business – the farm. I'm going to be as good as my word. Stephen, I'm going to give you my share of the farm. That's your wedding present.'

Stephen went pink. 'Gran, I ... I don't know what to say – but what about Ali; what about Charlie?'

'Ali doesn't want the farm and neither does Charlie.'

Charlie went pale, opened his mouth to protest, but thought better of it and slumped down in his chair.

'But I want to be fair,' said Gran. 'I've talked it over with Ron and he agrees with me. We are nearly into our eighties and there's no point in hanging onto things until we're dead. Might as well make them work for our kin, as well as for ourselves ...'

This was such a radical departure from the view Elsie had rigidly espoused for years, Alison stared at Ron anew, full of awe.

'So I'm going to sell the two houses I have in Bath, and Ron is going to sell his flat and give the proceeds to his daughter. With your help, Charlie, Stephen, we're going to convert one of the small barns into a cottage for us both to live in. I'm going to put a sum of money into trust for Alison, which she can use once she starts her higher education, or when she's twenty-one, whichever comes first. And I am going to give *you*, Charlie ...' Charlie looked up, a flicker of hope lightening his dulled features. 'A sum of money proportionate to the value of the farm that your current share represents, if that's what you want, plus up to twice as much more if you present me with a business plan, or an investment that I approve of. Which means, Charlie, if you've been following me, I'm buying you out of the farm, but you're getting, if you're sensible, the same size inheritance as Stephen.'

Charlie's jaw dropped. He could say nothing. His mind was a jumble of all the dreams he'd had: of setting up a bike workshop with Lenny; of having the best motocross bike money could buy; of owning his very own motocross circuit; or maybe a pub, a pub of his own; of ... of Linda, looking for a partner ...

'Well, Charlie?'

Charlie spluttered back to life. 'Thanks, Gran,' he said meekly. 'Thanks. You're one in a million.'

And he meant it.

Unusually for a Saturday morning, the farm seemed deserted when Alison let herself out of the house. A taxi containing Ron had collected Elsie first thing that morning; Jenny had left instructions for lunch and had gone out with Jeff for the day; Stephen had finished cleaning the dairy and had gone with Angela to look at rings in Summerbridge; and Charlie had vanished shortly after breakfast. The sky was grey and a slight breeze felt cool on Alison's face. She stopped for a moment to pull on a hooded sweatshirt, then slid a small rucksack onto her back. She checked her watch. A little after eleven-thirty. By her reckoning it would take half an hour to walk through Summerstoke and reach the main road to Bath. Once there it would all depend on the lifts, but with luck on her side, it meant that she could be at the hospital shortly after the start of visiting time.

She had collected her allowance from Charlie yesterday and had used some of it to go and see Al. Unfortunately, the cost of the journey was prohibitive, and on fifty quid, she would only be able to make the journey once more. So, taking advantage of the fact that today there was no one to prevent her, she decided to try and hitch. She had told Al she might not be able to come again until Sunday, and her heart had shivered into little bits at the look of disappointment on his face. She couldn't think of anything else but what he had said: each tender word, every caress, the sweetness of his kisses, the touch of his hand on her skin ... She couldn't wait to see him again and watch his face light up, as it always did when she appeared at his bedside. She knew that nobody, not even Al himself, would approve her plan, but faced with the impossibility of getting there any other way, she blanked out all possible objections.

She had just passed the village shop when she was hailed from behind.

'Alison ... Alison. Just a minute.'

It was Mrs Godwin.

Alison groaned to herself. Her mum's friend was a complete gossip, and inevitably, given the events at Marsh Farm over the last few days, this conversation would be a marathon. She turned and smiled politely.

Rita Godwin was waving a large card in her hand. 'Oh Alison, I was hoping to give this to your mum, to pass on to Charlie, but ...' and she chuckled meaningfully, 'she's a bit tied up these days and I haven't seen her. Can *you* give it to him, there's a dear?'

'Charlie?' Alison was puzzled. 'It's Stephen who's getting married, Mrs Godwin. Don't you mean Stephen?'

'No. It's for Charlie. It's wonderful news about Stephen, isn't it? I've not met his fiancée, but your mum is very fond of her … and what about your mum, eh? Isn't she lucky? She deserves a bit of happiness after all this time. And your gran! Getting married at her age – eighty, is she? What a surprise for you all.'

'Yes,' Alison replied weakly, still staring at the card. 'I'm sorry, but why are you giving Charlie a card? It's not his birthday.'

'It's a thank-you card.'

'A what?'

'A thank-you card. The village wanted to thank him for saving us from the flood.'

Alison was even more confused. 'I think you mean Stephen.'

'No, dear. Charlie, definitely.'

Rita had learned from Paula, who had been told by Lenny, the extent of Charlie's heroism in crawling out along the fallen tree the previous Sunday. Inevitably, the story had been amply embellished with moments of high drama: apparently Charlie, whose fear of heights was well known, had escaped from the jaws of the raging torrent by the skin of his teeth and, undeterred, had battled on to save the village. Rita had been much affected by this tale and had started a collection amongst the residents who might have become victims of the flood. She had intended, as an expression of the community's gratitude, to buy him a bottle of Jack Daniels, Lenny having told her it was Charlie's favourite tipple. But the villagers didn't appear that grateful and she had only raised enough to buy a card.

She had just embarked on this explanation when a genteel cough interrupted her. It was the vicar, hovering apologetically at the door of the shop.

'He's come for his pear drops. Must go. Tell your mum I'm dying for a chat. Bye, dear.' And she whisked back into her shop, leaving a bemused Alison to stuff the card into her bag and continue on her way.

By the time she reached the main road it had started to drizzle. She pulled up her hood, then, sticking out her thumb, started to walk. It was dispiriting: nothing stopped, and the cars passed without reducing their speed, pulling out to give her a wide berth. She was very damp and thinking about giving up when a battered white van passed her at speed, then screeched to a halt. Alison didn't hesitate. She ran up to the van and opened the door. Her thanks died on her lips. It was Charlie.

'Get in.' He looked at her grimly.

For a moment she thought of making her escape, but the misery of the hitchhiking experience had dampened her spirits as well as her clothes, so sullenly she climbed in.

'What do you think you're doing?'

'What did it look like? I was hitching – or trying to. No one would stop.'

'Are you surprised? A young girl, hood up. You spell trouble. Anyone in their right mind would give you a wide berth and if they didn't, that would spell trouble for you. Are you mad, Ali? What are you about, for Chrissakes?'

Alison felt close to tears and the last person she wanted to talk to was Charlie. She swallowed hard. 'I was trying to get to Swindon, to see Al. I thought if I hitched into Bath I might get a lift up to the motorway.'

'You went to see him yesterday.'

'I know. But he is in such a state and I wanted to see him. He doesn't have any other visitors – he won't let his parents near him … So I thought I'd try hitching.'

'You got your money yesterday. Why don't you use that? Mum'd have a heart attack if she knew what you were up to.'

'Charlie, I used up half of it getting a bus to Bath, then a train to Swindon, and then another bus to the hospital. I've got to find some other way of getting there.'

Charlie sat for a moment, staring out at the drizzle. Then he put the van into gear. 'Come on. I'll take you.'

Alison was speechless.

Charlie was the first to break the silence. 'As it happens, I've been thinking about your fellah – or more particularly, about his bike.'

Alison was startled. 'Oh? What about it?'

'It was a classic, an old BMW, wasn't it? What happened to it?'

'I don't know. I think it was wrecked. Perhaps the police have got it.'

'If he's as mad on BMWs as I was, its fate will be eating him. I thought I might retrieve it, see if Lenny and I can fix it.'

Alison stared at her brother. 'You've changed.'

Charlie self-consciously rubbed his head. 'Yeah, about time, probably. Can't believe I held on to those whiskers for so long.'

'No, not your hair, you pillock. You. *You've* changed. You're being … nice!'

Some time later, having chatted over the events of the last few days, culminating in Elsie's surprise announcement, Alison suddenly remembered the card for Charlie. She rummaged in her bag and produced it.

'Mrs Godwin said this was for you, Charlie.'

It was Charlie's turn to be surprised. 'For me? Whatever for? It's not my birthday and I ain't the one getting married.'

'That's what I said, but she was adamant. Said it was a thank-you card.'

'A what?'

'A thank-you card. For saving the village, she said.'

'Blimey. What on earth's she on about? See what it says.'

Alison opened the envelope and pulled out the card. Bordered with balloons, flowers, streamers and overflowing glasses of champagne, it was embossed with 'Thank You' in thick gold letters. Alison opened it and read aloud: '"Dear Charlie, we, the residents of Lower Summerstoke, have heard how you climbed along the tree that had fallen across the river, risking life and limb. It must have been very scary, but because of your bravery, our houses were saved from the flood. Thank you, Charlie. Yours sincerely, Rita Godwin, Mavis Long, Francis Young …"

and a number of other signatures I can't quite make out.' Alison looked across at her brother. 'What's all that about, Charlie?'

Charlie shrugged his shoulders and grinned. 'Something and nothing.' And he told Alison how he and Lenny had struggled with the fallen tree.

Alison was impressed; more particularly because she realised that when everyone had praised Stephen for his role in preventing the flood, Charlie had said nothing about himself. She was beginning to see him and his actions in a new light, and it wasn't such a bad one after all. He might have crazy ideas and go about them the wrong way, she thought, but he does things for the right reason. He's not totally the selfish bastard I thought he was.

They finally arrived at the hospital and Alison agreed to let Charlie go with her to meet Al, so that he could put his proposal about the bike to him. He didn't stay long but the conversation between the two was animated, and when Charlie had left, having arranged to meet Alison in a couple of hours, Al looked at her with a pale but glowing face and said with enthusiasm, 'What a nice bloke your brother is.' And Alison could do nothing else but agree with him.

They spent a blissful time together. Al was still very weak, so Alison did most of the talking and entertained him with stories of her brothers and her grandmother. He held her hand tightly the whole while, and then together they whispered of love and the things they would do together when Al was back on his feet. So engrossed in each other were they, the arrival of another visitor went unnoticed, until they were interrupted by a polite cough.

'Anthony?' A slender, blonde lady with a slightly long, pointed nose, and smartly dressed in a casual way, stood looking down at Al enquiringly. She looked vaguely familiar, Alison thought.

'Yes, but nobody calls me that, if you don't mind. It's Al.' Al surveyed the newcomer warily from under drooping eyelids.

'Al.' The lady smiled slightly. 'I won't interrupt you for long.

I'm so glad you've got someone with you. I'd heard you've refused to see your parents. I didn't realise your girlfriend was here, otherwise I would have come at another time. You probably don't remember me, do you?'

'No, no I don't, sorry.' There was a suspicious note to Al's voice.

'My name is Miranda, Miranda Patterson. But my friends call me Andy.'

Again Alison detected an air of familiarity about her. She stared at her curiously. The woman had a bright, lively face. Her blonde hair was spiky and short, and she was, Alison reckoned, getting on for forty.

'I'm your aunt, and for what it's worth, your godmother.'

'What?' Al shrieked. 'Have *they* sent you? I don't want anything more to do with them! Haven't I made myself clear?'

'No, no, no. Far from it.' She spoke soothingly. 'Don't take on so. I haven't spoken to either of your appalling parents for years. My sister, your mother, decided I was persona non grata shortly after you were christened.'

So that was it! She looked and sounded like an echo of Veronica Lester.

'We've not spoken since. I live in Bath and read in the local rag about your accident. The report mentioned you'd been brought here, so I phoned the hospital. It was they who told me that you'd refused to have anything to do with your parents. They dropped a very large hint that I could be useful and I thought, if he can chuck his parents out like that, I'm interested.' She smiled at them both. 'But I don't want to play gooseberry. The staff nurse wants a chat, so I'll leave you to it.'

'It couldn't be better, Charlie,' Alison recounted to her brother, later. 'He's going to live at her house when he's well enough to leave hospital and since she lives in Bath, it means I shall be able to get to see him more easily.'

'But no more hitching lifts. Promise.' Charlie was driving them home. It was raining in earnest now, and his attention was fixed on the road in front of him. 'Imagine being stuck out in this.'

Alison shuddered. 'No, I won't, I promise. But until he leaves hospital, it's going to be very hard.'

'Steve and I'll take it in turns to give you a lift into Bath. There must be coaches that'll be cheaper than the train. Check 'em out.'

Their conversation lapsed for a while. Then Alison, who had been mulling over the changes she perceived in her brother, turned to him curiously. 'Have you any idea what you're going to do yet? Are you going to take Gran up on her offer?'

Charlie was thoughtful. 'Probably. I don't see any future for me staying on at the farm as a junior partner. But not immediately. Steve can't manage without me until things have really changed. I do have in mind a business I'd like to invest in.' Shyly, he told Alison about Linda and the pub.

'So that's why you've been spending all your spare time there. And I thought you were a hopeless old boozer, drinking all the farm's money away!'

'I certainly like the odd pint, there's no denying that.'

'Are you and Linda ... are you two going to get it together?'

Charlie laughed. 'It's early days yet. That's why I'm going to carry on with the farm. No sense in rushing things. She's been badly hurt by Stan and I'm not gonna queer my pitch by jumping in with both feet. No, it's going to be strictly business – to begin with.'

'I thought you wanted to own a motocross circuit?'

Charlie sighed. 'I thought so, too. It's something I've enjoyed dreaming of doing ever since I was a kid, but thinking about it – *really* thinking about it, it somehow doesn't seem so important any more.'

'D'ye know, Charlie, that's a little the way I feel about being a vet at the moment.'

Charlie was shocked by this revelation. 'What? But you've always wanted to be a vet. You're the brains in the family. You're not going to duck out of university, are you?'

'No,' Alison replied slowly. 'But I'm not necessarily going to train to be a vet. I've decided to have a year off before I go – a gap year. It'll give me a chance to earn some money for when I do go, and the space to decide what I really want to study.'

The journey was finished more or less in silence until they turned down the road into Summerstoke.

'Charlie, do you think Hugh Lester is going to give up trying to get Marsh Farm? I can't see it myself.'

'He's a bad loser, that's for sure. But I told him that if I so much as caught a whiff of him trying anything else on, I'd spill the story of his games to the press.'

Alison's eyes widened. 'You did? When?'

Charlie blushed. 'Thursday evening. Before Gran's meeting. When I gave him a price for the farm.'

'You didn't?! I thought you'd dropped the whole idea by then?'

'I had, but I wanted to see him squirm, knowing that I knew everything.'

Alison was impressed. 'Good. And I hope he squirmed.'

'Oh yes, he did. He tried to clock me one. Nasty little git.'

'But the press is in his pocket – they're all mates together. Why should he worry about any threat of exposure?'

'Believe me, Ali, faced with a story like this – one that is far too good to miss – friendship would take a back seat, and he knows it.'

Alison's opinion of her eldest brother went up yet another notch shortly after their return. She had just sat down to a plate of something Jenny cheerfully described as tuna and macaroni bake, when Charlie poked his head around the kitchen door and told her to join him in the yard. He led her to the bike shed.

'This is the answer to your transport problems.'

'This' turned out to be a small, rusty moped.

Alison stared at it, then at Charlie.

'It's my moped. The one Gran bought me when I was seventeen. I wanted a motorbike and I was so choked, I hardly ever used it. It's been at the back of the bike shed for years. I'll get Lenny to give it the once over – there's not much wrong with it. Get yourself a provisional licence; I'll give you a few lessons, then, hey presto – you're in business. You'll have your own wheels. What d'you say?'

For a moment Alison was overcome. Then, much to Charlie's surprise, she flung her arms around his neck, laughing and crying. 'Charlie, you are the best!'

Postscript

A couple of months later Veronica Lester picked up the local paper and read that Marsh Farm was going to be used as a location for a new TV comedy series. She was so angry that marital relations were broken off and not resumed for many weeks.